Y0-CAS-878

Theo and Ria

by Katherine Nora

THEO and RIA. © Copyright 2015 by Katherine Nora. All rights reserved. Printed in the United States of America. No part of this book may be used or reproduced in any manner whatsoever without written permission except in the case of critical articles and reviews.
For information, send mail to knora22@verizon.net.

Cover artwork: Vernon Smith: *Fall Evening* 1946

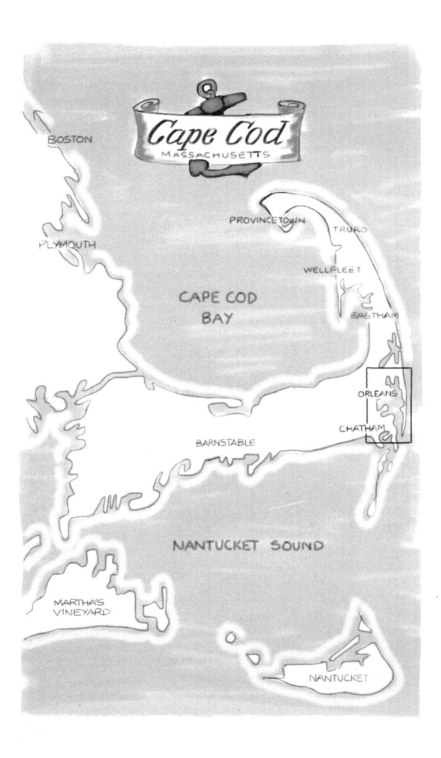

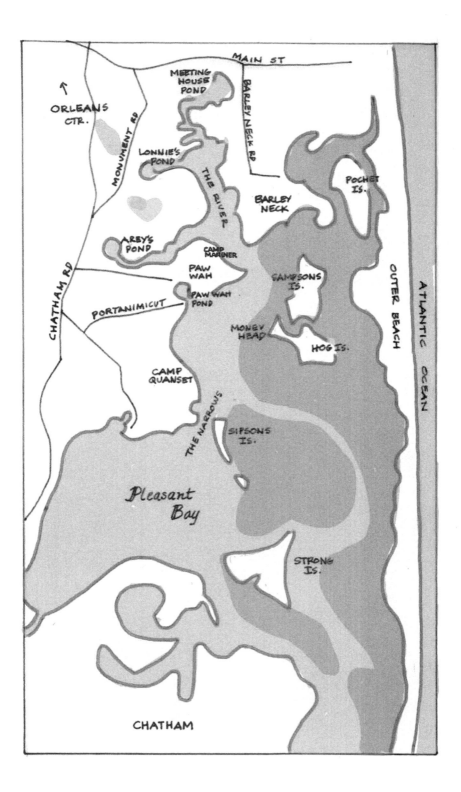

Chapter 1

I wasn't always a loner. I'm sure when people describe me, that's what they say. That's if anyone had any reason to, which they don't, and it's what I prefer. Especially right now, as I sit here at my desk in Editorial staring at the keys of my typewriter.

I'm twenty minutes past deadline but it seems we are all late today. Two of our reporters are trading notes about the seven story hotel some guy wants to put up overlooking Town Cove in Orleans. Big problem, even if it is 1968 and we are a growing town. It's rumored that the building inspector already approved the plans but I seriously doubt that. Across the room another reporter snickers over a police report about a love-in going on at the Wellfleet Cemetery. Again. We're only a small paper published twice-weekly, but we do our best to cover those minor but locally significant happenings which are important to those of us who live on the sandy arm of Cape Cod, Massachusetts.

I don't cover any stories. I file legal notices, categorize and commemorate events: theater openings, gallery shows, historical talks, nature walks, births, marriages, et cetera. Most importantly, I write the obituaries. I've lived in this little town all my life so I knew most of the people I'm called upon to memorialize. Our readers rely on my discretion when one of the town drunks falls off his barstool for the last time. They count on my diplomacy when listing the names of surviving family members. Illegitimate children are always given tactful acknowledgement, as are live-in lovers. I take great pride in the gentle compassion of my final portrayals. If you die in this town, no matter who you are, in this paper your name will be preserved with an aura of dignity.

The typing around me is petering out. Behind his glass partition the editor, Nathan, pretends calm but pulls nervously on his yellowed pipe-stem, smacking his lips as his eyes dart from desk to desk. I'll bet his right foot, crossed over the left, is jiggling spasmodically under the desk. I look over to confirm, meet his eyes for a second as they flit by. His look says *I understand Theo, but get going now. Finish.*

The others leave, mumbling their goodbyes as they walk down the hall. Nathan walks around collecting copy, scanning it briefly before dropping it into the box destined for the typesetter. He pauses at my desk.

"Look, I know this is difficult for you. Eulogizing a friend is a rough business." He relights his pipe, turns to go. "Just have it on my desk in the morning, all right?"

I roll a fresh sheet into the typer. "Ria," I whisper, "Ria Bang," I drop my head into my hands. As I gaze at the blank sheet I think about that last terrible meeting. How far we've come from the innocence of our first.

No, I wasn't always a loner. I had friends, dear friends. And Ria, who knew the secret of my soul, was my one and only love.

When I first met her in the late summer of '39, we were both fourteen years old. I was lying on my stomach in a patch of pine needles, looking out over the water of Pleasant Bay, the aptly named body of water which bathes the crooked arm of Cape Cod at its elbow. Dappled sunlight warmed my bare back. I was lying absolutely still, watching a red-backed vole burrow into the trunk of a rotting oak. The vole held a cedar berry carefully in its teeth.

My t-shirt was stuffed into a back pocket. I'd taken it off as soon as I was out of sight of any of the camp counselors. The t-shirt had the name of my summer camp printed across the front in green. It was humiliating to have to wear it, lining up with all the city kids as though we were the same, MARINER spelled out on every skinny chest. We were definitely not the same. This point, this wood, the marshes and beaches below, the bay and its creeks, rivers and ponds, its islands and barrier beach, all of it was mine. My home, my house, my whole world. None of it was theirs.

I could hear the other campers yelling to each other out on the water and the gentle thwop! of sails filling as they practiced tacking. I didn't need practice. I'd learned to sail at age ten when my father enlisted me as his personal crew. While I handled the boat he dropped fishing lines off the stern, rooted around in the muck for quahogs or had me drop him off on Hog Island for a little duck hunting. That was before he acquired a flat-bottomed dory with a 2-stroke and took off unassisted. After a summer left to my own devices it was decided that a more organized activity would be good for me, and so by arranging to trade regular deliveries of fish in return for my tuition, my parents enrolled me at Camp Mariner, just a little ways along the shore from where I now lay. I don't know what my father thought I would learn there. Most likely it was my mother's idea.

I pulled my shirt out of my pocket to swat at a deer fly and looked out over the water. My fellow campers were sailing back and forth between two orange cork markers. One of the instructors yelled at someone to sit down. The honk of a signal horn carried over the water to my little thicket: the end of today's sailing lessons. Time for me to get back. The vole was long gone, probably huddled somewhere waiting for me to leave. Standing, I shook out my shirt, stuck my head through the neck hole, then realized it was inside out. Taking it off again, I saw her.

She wore white shorts and a 'middie.' A blue scarf was rolled and tied low around her collar, like a sailor. I recognized the uniform of Quanset Sailing Camp. Girls only. She stood a few yards away, fanning herself with a stem of fern. She looked frankly at me, a mixture of curiosity and mirth in her eyes. With each puff of air from the fern her dark, short-cropped hair flopped up and down. Wide-set gray eyes were shaded by a severe swipe of dark bangs, and, as she tried not to laugh, the dimples around her mouth deepened into crooked parentheses. She was barefoot. Her legs were tanned and covered with scratches and dried blood, and when she saw me notice, she reached down to wipe at one of them. I pulled my shirt on properly. She saw the logo and smiled.

"Seems we're both escapees," she said.

Looking stupidly down at my own chest as though I never noticed the word printed there I uttered a quick-witted, "Yeah."

The double-blare of the signal horn sounded again from out on the Bay. That meant all boats were ashore and in about ten minutes everyone was to gather for the next event. None of the counselors seemed to care if I showed up for sailing lessons but I needed to put in an appearance for other activities.

She wrinkled her nose. We all knew the sound of each camp's signal horn. Dropping the fern she took a few steps toward me. "Where are you from?" she asked.

"Here," I said, trying not to squeak.

"A creature of the forest?"

"No, I mean, I'm from Orleans. Down the shore. Near the Narrows. You know?"

"Ah, the treacherous Narrows. Yes, I know. It's exactly the spot on this bay that proved me a failure as a sailor," she said, only she said it a funny way. "...a failor as a sailor," with a little lisp.

"I like the woods," was all I could come up with. I couldn't stop staring at her. I saw in her face the essence of some temperament I recognized in myself. Even though her grey eyes were laughing, they were the eyes of someone who spent a lot of time alone.

"You're far from your camp," I said. Quanset was almost a mile from where we stood. It sat on a bluff about halfway to my house if you walked north along the shore.

She sighed. "That's what I was aiming for."

"I'd better go, I said. "Do you know how to get back?"

"Yep." She didn't move.

"Want me to walk back with you?" I had never been so bold, not with anyone, especially a girl. I stood there tearing chunks of bark off the nearest pine, another thing it would never occur to me to do. Trees were as revered as the animals I studied and loved. They were personalities in my world, each one communicating an aspect of wisdom, dignity or grace. I pulled my hand away and put it in my pocket.

"Sure," she said, "but I thought..."

"They won't miss me. They'll think I just decided to go home," I lied. Probably they'd telephone my parents' house and I'd be in hot water again with my mother. But I didn't care. Right then I wanted more than anything to walk with this girl along the shore.

That anyone would see us or miss us was not part of my thinking because I wasn't thinking.

Remembering that walk now, I can say it was the smartest move I ever made in my life. We followed one of the old paths along the ridge while I babbled on about Indian trails and pointed out raccoon and badger tracks. I told Ria about the horses my neighbors kept in a makeshift corral near the water. More than once I had taken my favorite, a sweet-natured eleven year old gelding, a veteran racer from the Arlington Park track, across the Narrows to Sipson's Island for a little night grazing, hanging onto his tail as he swam through the channel. Ria made me promise to take her sometime. She said she snuck out at night on a regular basis, and wasn't afraid of anything. In fact, when we came to the inlet at Paw Wah Pond, where we had to cross a ten foot wide channel, without saying anything she ducked behind a stand of marsh grass, whipped off her shorts and waded waist-deep across.

She told me that besides sending her to a different camp every summer her parents consigned her to a private school for the winter months. Her father worked for an international bank. He was Danish, hence the name, which she explained was pronounced not like the noise -BANG! but softer, more like the deep chime of a church bell. Though the school was liberal and known as progressive, the students were as typically cruel as children can be, and she was teased for the name. In her younger years the jokes were about her hairstyle, cut sharply across her forehead. In the last couple of years she put up with a new version of the tease: the Bang-up, Bang! you're dead, Bang job, wanna Bang? Her mother had gone to camp and had hated it, so Ria thought it was doubly thoughtless that she was forced to endure it as well, but, she said, "It's been that way since I was seven. Maybe life at home is worse." She knew how to ride horseback, weave baskets, tool leather, play both tennis and the violin, and speak French. And, as I was to find out, she was also a gifted painter. I was impressed.

When we arrived at the outskirts of her camp compound, she turned to me, grinningthose dimpled parentheses, and said, "Do you want to go 'sailing' again tomorrow?" We made a plan to find each other during lessons at the channel by Paw Wah Pond.

I was indeed in trouble when I got home that evening. I checked in at camp and finished out the day with the others shooting arrows into a bull's eye, then left right before chow, as it was called. My mother sat me down in stern silence in front of a bowl of beans. I didn't particularly care. There had never been much communication in our relationship. She seemed annoyed and disapproving of nearly everything except the Bible. I'd tried often to figure out exactly what it was that made her so sad, and being an only child, of course I assumed most of the blame. But my attempts at conversation or attention-getting could do nothing to change her. It was as though she lived behind a giant pane of glass and could not hear me or touch me, nor I her. As I grew older, I longed to smash the glass and startle her into some kind of recognition of me and the rest of the world around her. By the time I was in my teens, I stopped thinking about it.

My father, Frank, was not much more forthcoming, perhaps even slightly worse in a different way. He spoke to me, but it was usually an order, a reprimand or a serving of wisdom about fishing or weather. If I struggled with a word while doing homework, he wouldn't help me. He'd take our dictionary off the bookshelf and drop it on the table in front of me. He never judged me, but he never praised me either. I was his helper, his lackey. 'My Right-hand Man,' as he called me. It was a joke he liked to repeat because I was, literally, his right hand since his entire right arm was missing. He'd lost it as a boy in a duck hunting accident. He never gave me any details. By the time I came along he was thirty-five years old and had mastered one-armed living. But there were still many things that were impossible for him, like using a hammer and nail, for example. He didn't talk about it at all, and on those occasions when he needed my mother or me to do something for him he wouldn't ask, we'd have to notice and make it happen, as if by magic. He was almost as dextrous as a two-handed person and could even rig a fishing pole or bait a hook with no trouble. He could shoot with more accuracy than almost anyone else. With the aid of a sturdy strap around his biceps, he'd swing his shotgun up under his left shoulder, taking aim and firing within seconds of spotting his target.

My father had all kinds of tricks up his empty sleeve for catching fish and attracting fowl. He could imitate any duck or goose call, and he had a large collection of decoys. When he spotted a flock of geese overhead he'd drop a decoy into the marsh, then rub the backs of two quahog shells together to get the birds' attention, then invite them down, chatting to them in their own language. It worked every time. He fished for striped bass in the Narrows, swinging a cod line around his head several times before letting it fly. When something bit, he'd reel it in by stuffing the loose line under the stub of his right arm. One thing he couldn't do was to sail the catboat we used in those days for his fishing and hunting forays, and so it was as a very small boy that I learned. Sometimes I wondered if the reason my parents had me at all was so I could be a kind of tool for my father. I even looked like a smaller version of him. We had the same physique, both tall, thin and gangly. We had the same vaguely Nordic face: long skulls, globoid nose tips and dark blue eyes. I had a thicker version of his light brown thatch on my head, and neither of us could tame the stuff into any semblance of a proper haircut. To the other fishermen on the bay we were a unit; I was merely a useful part of my father's gear. That's how it felt to me. My parents didn't seem too concerned with or interested in the rest of my daily life. My father named me Henry, and my mother gave me my middle name, Theodoros, a kind of mirror image of hers, Dorothea. Both names meant "gift of God" in Greek. She explained to me at a very early age that our names were a constant reminder not to take personal pride in our abilities or possessions, that we owe everything, even our very existence, to The Almighty One.

"For by grace are ye saved through faith, and not that of yourselves: it is the gift of God." She said it every evening at suppertime, to hammer home to my father and me that our accomplishments of the day had nothing to do with brains or brawn. She'd follow it with a prim little, "Ephesians, 2:8." and a steely look in my direction. It scared me when I was younger, but by the time I could read I had looked at her precious Bible several times and found it unintelligible, not to mention incredible. When I was six I was sent to grammar school and was called Theodoros for the first time, to distinguish me from the two other Henrys in my class. It was quickly shortened to Theo, and soon everyone forgot my original name.

On the day I met Ria, there were three weeks of summer left, and after that day we got together as often as possible, sometimes at night when we'd each walk the shore after lights-out, our rendezvous always the Paw Wah pond channel. I don't know how she managed to slip away at night, but she was always there. We could usually get away during sailing lessons, too. It was especially easy during the inter-camp races which were held every few days. If it was dark we would sit andtalk, snuggled into the marsh grass trading stories, or loll around in the warm water of a high tide. She was a natural talker. Stories, dreams, questions flowed from her easily as though we'd always known each other. I was happy to listen. The New York City she came from was as foreign to me as Paris, and the world of private girls' schools even more so. Her parents were as unconnected to her as mine were to me. She saw her father twice a year, once for a few tense days at Christmas and once for the time it took him to drive her to that year's summer camp. Her mother never went on those trips. She always said it was too hot to endure the long ride, but Ria figured out at an early age that her mother couldn't sit in the car for hours without a cocktail to go with her cigarette. When Ria was on vacation from school their housekeeper, Flora, functioned as the parent, as she had been doing since Ria was born. As I did she wondered sometimes why they'd had her in the first place, yet we never discussed this sad parallel until we were older. Then she told me of the disappointment her father had felt and made it clear to Ria and her mother, that he didn't have a son.

In school she kept to herself not out of shyness but because as she said, "They're all idiots. They're going to turn out just like my mother." She was passionate about John Steinbeck and James T. Farrell, and when she graduated she planned to run away, go to Chicago to join the "real people," as she called the scrappy Irish heros of the Studs Lonigan stories she admired. She wanted to be a Socialist, though she was a little vague about what exactly it entailed, not that I knew anything about it myself. Nowadays, sometimes I try to imagine her back then, on horseback with her classmates on the polo field, glossy hair flying, daydreaming of herself in overalls hefting a hawk full of wet cement.

As sophisticated as she was, I was surprised to find that my little world was equally interesting to her. Often she'd be in the middle of describing some aspect of school or childhood and she'd interrupt herself to say, "Oh, my insipid life." It was a long time before I learned what "insipid" meant, but I got the idea. Then she'd sigh heavily and say, "Tell me something, anything."

I wasn't very good at conversation in those days and it was a struggle to come up with my part. But I did know a great deal about the habits of animals and the routes of migratory birds. I knew what they ate and why, which animal nested where and which preyed on the other. I knew the bottom of Pleasant Bay better than the streets of my town. I rowed all over the Bay at quite an early age, studying the eelgrass, learning its direction. It undulates in long graceful clusters, letting the tide and the current direct its pointing fingers back and forth, guiding me along hidden channels in the undersea world. I could read eelgrass like a map. I never got lost in rain or fog, even when I couldn't see the shore. I simply looked at the bottom and followed the signs.

I felt perfectly secure in the natural world, because nature was perfect. Nature gave answers to questions about itself, answers that often led to more compelling questions, an almost endless labyrinth of information in which I was never lost, but always exploring. I thought all animals were magnificent creations. I was astounded by the tremendous variation in their ability to create shelter, gather food, attract a mate and reproduce. I marveled at the complex design of plants, and I believed they and all living things were interconnected, that no element was useless and their relationships endlessly fascinating. I had always thought this way. In fact, I thought of little else. So I would tell Ria about pitcher plants or bobwhites or glass eels. I would show her the entry holes of ant lions or wolf spiders, and to counteract her reaction to those two slightly creepy bugs I'd open up one of the spiny sections of a whelk egg case and dig out a miniature copy of its parents. She had a whelk shell at home on the bookshelf, and she was astonished to see the tiny snail in its living form. When I told her of the whelk's ability to stick its foot into the sand for leverage and use its shell as a hammer to crack open a clam, she gave me the first look of pure admiration I'd ever received. As I talked I felt I too was gradually being pulled out of my shell.

I tried to impress her even more with stories of shipwrecks and pirates and other Cape Cod lore. I told her the story of notorious "Black Sam" Bellamy who sailed up the coast in the spring of 1717 with a hold full of looted cargo, supposedly his final trip before retiring. Bellamy's ship ran aground off the beach in Wellfleet, only 500 feet from shore.

The old timers out on the water used to talk about the gold bars and elephant tusks and the 7,000 gallons of Madiera wine that were sure to be still lying on the bottom to be found, if only they had the means, and the exact location. I pointed out Money Head on the opposite shore from where we sat, the tapered end of Hog Island. The pirate Captain Kidd supposedly buried a cache of gold there on his way up the coast to Boston.

"Hmm, yes, let's see," she said, "....in a box, lockt and nailed, corded and sealed." They told us at camp. Have you been over to dig?"

I admitted that no, I hadn't tried. Of course I had been to Money Head many times, at first during my explorations as a lone rower and later on when I sat for hours at a time studying the bottom and waiting while my father hunted black duck. I never told her I'd learned the story just that year, too, at camp. We agreed to go over one day and give it a whirl.

One night, when we were standing in the channel up to our chests in water she said, "What about scallops?"

"What about them?"

"I adore scallops," she said with theatrical flair. Laughing, she added, "Seriously, I know they come from around here. My father took us to a restaurant at Christmas and ordered them and that's what he told me. Do you like them?"

Did I like them? Yes, when I could sneak one while my mother and I opened the seemingly endless bushels. They were the small, sweet bay scallops, a delicacy, and it was the most lucrative fishing of all for my father and the other regulars out on the water. They were shipped by train to markets in New York and Philadelphia in the late fall and winter. I had been scalloping with my father many times and wanted never to go again. It was backbreaking, freezing work. The scallop drag was heavy and unwieldy, especially for my one-armed father. He'd toss the heavy chain mail bag overboard and have me make a few passes while it scraped the bottom, ripping up eelgrass and making a mess, scallops and everything else down there tumbling into the bag's mouth. Then we'd haul the full drag back onboard and cull the scallops from the rocks, shells and seaweed. We'd get three or four bushels a day. After several hours of this my hands were wet, frozen and almost too stiff to grasp the tiller. The work didn't end when at last we went home, after dark. The little "gold nuggets" as my father called them, had to be shucked, or "peeled," as they said then. That's what really got to my hands, no matter the thickness of the gloves I wore. Inevitably I would cut myself on the edge of a shell, the freezing salt water would swell the wounds, and when my hands eventually dried the wounds would stay open and sting with every movement. Then we'd do it all again the next day. Another reason I hated shucking scallops: the circle of tiny blue eyes that they use to detect light and motion, staring up at you as you sliced the animal from its shell.

I looked down at my hands as they swished through the warm moonlit water, the same water that had caused such agony only a few months ago, and said, "Yes. My mother fries them in butter." Of course it was a lie. She would never serve anything so extravagant. There was something about the way I said it that made Ria quit the subject and stay quiet for a while.

When she did speak again she said, "You're not interested in me, I mean, *that way*, are you?"

When I didn't answer, she added, "It's OK, it's better. I'd rather be your pal than your girl."

Still I could think of nothing to say. This line of talk went beyond any I'd ever experienced. I hadn't given a thought to whether I wanted her to be my "girl." I didn't think about girls at all, in that way. I don't know why, maybe I was still too young. But to be honest things haven't changed much since then. I have never had a girlfriend, or boyfriend for that matter, in case it's what you're thinking. I have learned to be content with my life. But back then I didn't know that. I hadn't thought about it yet. My silence was becoming a little uncomfortable so I said finally, "Sometimes she adds a little parsley," and we both burst out laughing.

We didn't talk about it any more. But that night I think she understood something about me, maybe the fact that she was a stage or two ahead of me in adolescent development. Or maybe simply that we were both outsiders who had found in each other a kind of solace.

Chapter 2

Ria and I roamed all over the Bay in those last days of summer. We got bolder as the camp season wound down and the counselors were less attentive. No one ever discovered Ria's disappearances, or so she said. I simply assumed privileges because Ilived there, and took them. Maybe my parents gave permission, I don't know. At any rate, we were free for an hour or two almost every day. Simply walking along and talking would have been fine with her, but I insisted on showing her all of my favorite places. One bright afternoon as we rounded Paw Wah Point we noticed that the tide had left behind a blanket of seaweed about a foot wide and several feet long. It was a delicate, vibrant green mass of what's called Mermaid's Tresses. When Ria flipped it over with a toe we saw that the exoskeletons of dozens of tiny white Horseshoe crabs were woven into the dried weed, almost in a pattern. The crabs (I want to mention that they're technically related to the scorpion, not crab) molt many times before full maturity, and each time leave behind a ghostly pattern of themselves. "It's so beautiful," she whispered, carefully picking up the seaweed, and settling it like a shawl around her shoulders. She kept it on for most of the afternoon, and when she got back to camp she took out her watercolors and rendered it in great detail, taping sheets of paper together for the length.

One evening I took her for a row across the Narrows to Sipson's Island after dragging my father's dinghy from the yard and stealthily launching it with much giggling from Ria. She didn't ask whose boat it was, nor did she ask if that's where I lived. When we got across we climbed to the top of the hill and looked over toward the barrier beach and out to sea. Lights from an oil tanker blinked, stars twinkled. Kerosene lanterns dimly lit the windows of fishing shacks snuggled into the dunes. Small noises drifted up to us, the gurgle of warm tide filling crab holes, the cry of a night heron, the soft slapping of a halyard against a mast, the distant rumble of waves breaking. I felt all of it was mine to show off to her, to give to her. It was far more valuable than anything else I could imagine.

Another day I rowed Ria out to Money Head as promised, to look for Captain Kidd's treasure chest. We were digging half-heartedly here and there with some quahog shells when we hears voice behind us.

"'Scuse me, but do you happen to know what time low tide starts?"

Ria and I glanced at each other before turning. There stood a man in full sportfishing regalia: brand new hip boots over canvas pants, a red-checkered shirt, multi-pocketed vest. The fishing lures pinned to the side of his wide-billed hat jiggled and caught the sun. He was smoking a cigarette, holding it between thumb and forefinger and squinting through the smoke. Behind him a wooden dory had been pulled up on to the sand, a tackle box open on one of the seats. I couldn't believe we hadn't heard him approach.

I looked out over the water. The tide was halfway to low.

In an hour or two," I said.

"OK, I figured right. What are you kids digging for out here?" his eyes darted around, taking in the holes we'd made, the holes in the cliff, our boat pulling at its anchor down the beach.

"Nothing," Ria picked up a quahog shell and slid its edge back and forth along her hand.

"Ever find anything interesting?" his eyes bored into mine. I wanted him to go away.

"Like what?" Did he really believe the Captain Kidd nonsense?

"Well, I don't know, how about an arrowhead for example?"

I had in fact found several points and flakes around the area. I had a chipped clay pipe and some parts of others, and one half of a small red bowl which fit perfectly into my palm.

"Some," I said, staring at the sand.

"How about beads? Purple colored beads?" This question he posed with a slight aggressiveness, leaning into me and flipping his cigarette butt behind him into the shallows. He was talking about wampum of course. I had never found any but I had certainly studied the purple parts of quahog shells wondering at how the Indians had turned a plentiful thing into a form of currency.

"Nope," I said, backing away. I glanced at Ria, who slammed her hands onto her hips and said, "There's nothing like that here. Only birds."

He stared at Ria for a few seconds, turned abruptly and left, throwing a "Thanks" over his shoulder. We watched him push the dory into the water, jump aboard and fire up the engine. When he turned away and sped off we laughed for a bit about his tourist getup and Ria said to me, "I didn't like him."

"No kidding," I said. "You certainly got rid of him."

"Have you really found something?"

I told her about my meager collection. She asked if she could see the stuff sometime, said she was 'passionate' about native cultures. She asked me a few questions about the Indians who had lived around the bay. I mentioned the Nausets, the Monomoyicks, told her the story of Squanto. She knew it already.

"Sure, I'll show you," I said.

About a week before the end of camp I was with two other boys at the edge of the woods collecting driftwood for the evening's bonfire. Arms full, I looked up to see Ria hurrying down the beach toward us. I hadn't seen her in two days. We'd been meeting each other daily before then, either at the channel or in the woods. Once we walked along the shore in full view of the other sailing campers and counselors. They'd given up on trying to get us to join in, and as long as we participated in everything else they seemed to be all right with it. Camp was almost over, anyway.

Ria beckoned to me excitedly. I held up a finger for her to wait, ran back to camp and dumped the branches onto a pile by the firepit. When I returned she was pacing up and down in the sand. She jumped when she spotted me and ran toward me whispering excitedly.

"Theo, you won't believe what I've found. I think it's really old and I think it's really valuable, I mean, I think it's gold. I think it has Indian markings."

We walked quickly away from the others as she spoke, then took a short path up the bank and around the back of a bayberry bush where she plunked down and pulled the object from the waistband of her shorts. It was an oval disc of blackened metal about five inches long with a small hole in one end. Half of it was caked with clay and silt. She held it out to me in the flat of her hand and whispered, "Look," as she scratched the surface with a thumbnail. It was indeed a gold color.

"Now watch this," she said, spitting on it and rubbing with her finger. Slowly a line drawing revealed itself, of a hand holding an arrow. The hand looked rather like a dog's paw. I could see indentations of a decorative pattern around the edge but the rest was thoroughly blackened and crusted over with dirt. I traced the arrow with my finger.

"Where did you find it?"

She had been walking along the shore and stopped to examine the exposed roots of a cedar tree which had toppled during the hurricane.

"I saw the straight edge in all the twisty roots. It looked out of place, so I pulled it out." She turned it over. "As you can see I scraped it a little. But it's on the back so maybe it doesn't matter."

Two thin stripes of bright yellow cut diagonally across the surface.

"It looks like brass, or something. I don't think it's gold," I said. I flipped it over again. "Wipe some more off, and let's see what's there."

"I can't. I only got that much off by rubbing some vinegar on it. I swiped it from the kitchen, but I only took a little. I didn't have enough to do the rest. I colored over the spot with a charcoal stick until I could show you."

"Let's rub sand onto it," I said, grabbing a handful.

She jerked the disc away from me. "No, that'll scratch it. If it is a real artifact it has to be perfect."

"Do you want me to take it home and clean it?" I asked. My mother had a large bottle of white vinegar in the pantry.

"OK, but you have to be careful. My mother soaks her rings in vinegar and water for a while, then polishes them with a towel. She told me that if you leave it too long, the metal will dissolve."

With the disc wrapped in Ria's neckerchief in my back pocket, we split up, having made a plan to meet later that night at Paw Wah channel. When I went home for dinner I managed to pour off a measure of the vinegar into a Coca-Cola bottle. I took a pie plate from the pantry also, put them into a bag and ran back down the beach to the bonfire. It had just been lit. The salty driftwood shot flares of bright green and blue and the boys poked the fire for more action while two counselors sliced up pans of cornbread and passed them around. I found a spot and sat waiting for my chance to get away. They were all talking at once about that afternoon's game of horseshoes, during which one of them had been whacked on the forehead by a wayward toss. The doctor had been phoned; the injury required several stitches. Both the injured boy and the thrower were absent, so they were all speculating about whether anyone was in trouble.

"No one's in trouble. It was an accident," said one of the counselors, a guy named Whit who everyone liked. "I've seen much worse."

They all started talking again, the injured kid showed up with a bandage wrapped several times around his head, so I took the opportunity to slip away. Whit saw me and winked, but held up a finger which meant I had one hour before I had to be back. I ran straight to the channel but Ria wasn't there. I sat in our spot, took out the pie pan and laid it in the grass. I poured a quarter-inch of vinegar into it, took the disc out of my pocket, unwrapped it and dropped it in. I think I expected something chemically exciting to happen and sat there for a while, staring at it.

"So?" I turned to see Ria picking her way through the marsh grass.

"Nothing so far." I stirred the vinegar with a finger. Ria peered into the pan, reached in and turned the disc over. As the silt dissolved it clouded the vinegar and she swished her fingers around in it. More dirt broke away.

"Let's let it soak for a while longer." She leaned back on her hands and we compared notes on our separate getaways. She was jealous of the ease with which I was allowed to wander off.

"I faked my monthly," she said, deadpan.

I had no idea what she was talking about, so I just nodded, but she went on.

"Of course now they won't let me go swimming for a few days, but if this thing is a genuine valuable artifact, it will have been worth it."

"Yeah," I said, stupidly. "I know what you mean."

"Look, something's happening." Indeed, a faint amber colored glimmer was visible in a few patches. Ria took the disc out of its bath and rubbed it gently with her forefinger.

"Have you got any more vinegar?" Let's pour this out and give it some fresh."

After half an hour and some polishing with my t-shirt, the image began to reveal itself. Attached to the hand holding the arrow was an Indian brave wearing only a short feathery skirt and a wary expression. He looked off to one side as though embarrassed to be posing. In his other hand he held a large bow. The figure stood on a patch of grass with three flowers sprouting around his bare feet. His hair was loose, sharply parted down the middle. A border of zigzags and curvy lines enclosed the drawing. We studied it, saying nothing. The odd thing was that the figure, bare-chested, had a wide circle around each nipple, unmistakable as the outlines of breasts. There were even sort of rounding highlights etched into the circles.

"It's a woman warrior!" said Ria.

"It could be muscles."

"Look at her. She's wearing a skirt."

"That's what they wore. Grass."

"It's definitely not gold, is it?" she said, I suppose she didn't want to discuss breasts with me.

"I think it's brass. Bronze."

She turned it over. Words were etched into the surface, but we couldn't read them in the fading light. Only one word, "COUNCIL" stood by itself.

Ria pulled a length of leather thong from her pocket and poked one end through the hole in the medallion. As she worked a knot into it I bit my lip, took a breath and held it.

"I know someone who could tell us what it is." The words crept over my tongue and out between my teeth. A ripple of unease washed through me, but I couldn't help myself.

She looked up at me, lifted the medallion and spun it on the thong. "Yeah?"

"Yeah." I plunged in. "His name's Casco Swift and he's an Indian. Well, not really, only one-sixteenth or something. He lives in the woods right over there." I waved my hand at the other side of the channel, Paw Wah Point. Then I told her. I gave her the whole story, blurting out all the details, giving away Casco's secret.

Now that I think about it, it was in almost the exact spot where Ria and I were sitting, that I first encountered my elusive friend. I was twelve. It was a late-summer evening then as well, and I had spent the afternoon perched on a hillock of marsh grass watching a nest of baby diamondback terrapins hatch. All summer I'd been keeping an impatient eye on the eggs and had watched their number steadily decrease by almost a third. I assumed it was the work of a fox or raccoon until a voice behind me said, "Are they hatchin' already? Damn. I thought I'd get one last omelette before they started incubating."

I spun around, startled, and promptly fell off the grass into the mud. Standing over me was an older man wearing a dirty white shirt with the sleeves ripped off at the shoulder. A wide belt was slung low over the shirt. Purple and white lines of beads ran through the belt, a pattern of triangles. I was pretty sure it was wampum. Three small pouches hung from the belt, one of them full. Thin brown canvas pants were rolled high above his bare feet. Even more unusual was his head of pure-white hair which hung straight from a severe middle part to below his shoulders. His skin was the color of maple syrup. A sparse white stubble dusted his jawline. Deep channels of age ran down either side of a long, thin nose which bent to the left near the bottom. His brown eyes, looking down at me, were wide in surprise, but he didn't laugh. He held out a hand to me as he continued, "Without a mama or daddy in sight, they're deliverin' all by themselves. But they've got mother nature tellin' them what to do, don't they."

He pulled me up and poked a finger into the nest, smiling. "Oh, they're cute. Hey little fellas, welcome. Now you snuggle in there and get big..." He baby-talked to the turtles while I stood there gaping at his broad back.

When I thought he'd forgotten me, he turned and offered me his hand again.

"Casco Swift. Good to meet you. What's yours?"

"Uh, Theo," I mumbled.

"Theo, hunh? I've seen you often, Theo. You like to row around looking at the bottom, don't you?"

"Yes sir."

"Oh now, I am no gentleman, believe me. What's your last name?"

"Sparrow."

"You sure do have a good name." He smiled at me, a big, white-toothed grin. We were quiet for a while, watching the last of the eggs hatch. I was thinking about his omelette comment. He, not an animal, had been eating those turtle eggs.

"Are they good?" I asked.

"Oh my yes. With mushrooms and a little sea rocket, if you add it right at the end."

I wondered if he ate the adult turtles but I didn't ask.

"So, you live around here?" he said, sitting back and looking up at the sky. It would be dark in an hour. Bats swooped around, catching bugs. The faithful moon was there, in half. "I've seen you sailing too. Is that your father? That him I hear shooting ducks?"

At first I was a little wary of his directness, or maybe I was still thinking about him eating the turtles. The string of questions had answers, but I couldn't seem to put them together. Finally I said, "Yeah, that's him." Then I got up the courage to ask, "How come I've never seen you before?"

"Now, that's a good question. The answer is because I don't want to be seen. In truth, I don't want to live in this world. The modern world, I mean." He ran his hand through his hair. His hand was a black plow in a white field. "You hungry?" he asked. "Tell you what. I've got two bags of dry eelgrass over there on the shore. If you help me get them home, I'll give you some supper. You ever tried oyster stew with no milk?"

"No."

"Your parents know where you are?"

"Sort of."

"Well, what do you say? My place is right over there."

I knew for a fact there was no house anywhere near the place and said so.

"I don't live in a house. I have a wigwam. Know what that is?"

"Yes," I said, incredulous. Though I had covered most of the land around Pleasant Bay in my wanderings, I had never seen a wigwam, of all things, but I very much wanted to.

"OK," I said.

Two large burlap bags full of seaweed sat on a little wisp of beach on the other side of the channel. Casco took one and I struggled with the other up the embankment and a short way into the woods. No one ever came out to this little peninsula. Everyone knew that nothing was here except some scraggly trees. There were no deer to hunt. They knew enough not to get trapped on a dead-end stretch of land. I had explored it only a few times. But after I discovered Casco, I grew to know it well, and it became a favorite spot for small mammal watching. And as you know, it was where I met Ria the first time. I followed my strange new friend down a path I'd never noticed before. It was one of those paths you don't see until you stumble onto it, a winding track only as wide as a human foot. Suddenly Casco threw his bag down and spread his arms wide.

"Home sweet home," he said, smiling broadly again. I looked around but I could see no wigwam nor anything resembling a shelter.

"Come in," he said, bending down and disappearing into the vegetation. There, in a low thicket of maple saplings was a dark gap in the foliage. I stepped in front of the opening and saw, level with my chest and beautifully camouflaged by the surrounding branches, the spherical roof I had seen only in illustrations. I stepped gingerly into the wigwam. The floor, covered with matted marsh grass, had been dug down a couple of feet, giving the structure a low profile and the inside a cool, fragrant snugness. Casco was sitting opposite in a round room about eight feet in diameter. In the center of the wigwam a ring of wood fire smoldered. Above the coals, suspended from a lashed-together tripod of stout branches was a blackened clay pot. I hadn't noticed smoke, or smelled it outside. I was trying to work out where it went when Casco patted the floor and said, "Make yourself at home, Theo. Hungry?"

He tossed a few pine cones and a handful of twigs onto the embers, then fiddled with the burnt-out fire until flames tickled the bottom of the pot. I sat down, somewhat stupefied, and looked around at the room. Bent saplings tied together formed a crisscrossed dome. Khaki-colored canvas with white lettering stamped here and there covered the bent wood. I made out the letters USPO in a kind of all-over pattern. Small woven baskets and misshapen bowls held assorted foodstuffs. One was full of blueberries. A few articles of clothing, drying plants, sharpened sticks and other crude tools were tucked into the roof construction. A dark green wool blanket was spread over a thick bed of eelgrass.

"It's not the real thing, he said looking up. "That would've been bullrush leaves, woven. With hemp for the woof, I think." He gazed at it for a few seconds more, then added, "But I imagine they would have taken the same advantage, don't you?" He looked at me earnestly as though he needed confirmation.

I nodded, though I had no idea what he was talking about. I found out much later he'd stolen his roof of mailbags one night from the little South Orleans post office soon after he arrived here.

"The eelgrass you helped me carry? It's to add on top for the winter. Makes great insulation." He peered at me through the eddy of smoke. "You forget how to talk? Well, I suppose my humble lil' old home is quite a surprise. But you see, I'm simply living the way my ancestors did. I mean the Nausets. You know about them, don't you?"

"Yes," I said. I actually did know quite a bit about our local native people, a sub-tribe of the great Wampanoags. It was the one subject my father would talk about at any length. Though it usually took the form of a lecture, I could sense his enthusiasm when he spoke about the local native tribes. When I was only six years old he told me the first of many Indian stories, of "our Squanto," as he referred to him. I spent many an hour looking for Squanto's burial site, rumored to be somewhere on the bay, fascinated by his story and astonished by the colonists' brutish treatment of him. I couldn't believe the English could take him from his home and display him circus-like before crowds of people. Or even worse sell him into slavery in Spain. Even more baffling to me was the fact that in school the previous winter, when I brought up his name during a class discussion of the Pilgrims, our teacher didn't know who he was. I felt an acute sting of embarrassment when I realized I knew something our teacher didn't, and she didn't ask me to elaborate. I vowed never to speak up about Indians again.

Casco stirred the pot with a wooden spoon, then sampled the contents. He gave a little grunt of pleasure, and handed me another spoon. Someone had done a bad job of carving. It was more like a spatula than a spoon, but I dipped it into the pot anyway and slurped. I wouldn't call it delicious, but it was nutty and hot and it had a few oysters in it. We ate in silence until Casco said, "They used to feed babies this stuff instead of milk. Minus the oysters, of course. Ground-up acorns and corn meal boiled together. That's why I thought of it for oyster stew. It's kind of an experiment."

"It's good," I said, and so was being there with Casco. It was so comfortable I surprised myself by blurting out the story about my teacher and Squanto. "How could a teacher not know about it?" I truly wanted to know.

"You know what they say, Theo, that history is written by the victors," he shook his head slowly.

I knew what he meant, even at that age. "Your ancestors were Nausets?"

"Oh yes, right from this very area, maybe even this piece of ground right here." He patted the floor, sending up a puff of dust that joined the smoke from the fire as it disappeared through a flap in the dome. " 'Course it was many generations ago, and we've been away for a long time, but I grew up with the stories. They didn't forget, and they didn't want me to forget, either. So unlike your teacher they made sure I knew about my people and where I'm from. Part of the reason I came here to live in this stately mansion." He looked around at his construction with genuine satisfaction, grinning broadly.

I didn't understand. "Where did you come from?" I said. At this point if he'd confessed to being a visiting apparition from the past I might have believed him.

"Most accurately, from Danville, Virginia. I've been livin' here about 5 years now."

"In this?"

"Yup."

"Even in the winter?"

"Oh yeah. Sometimes that can be the best time. I like coming in from the cold and finding a fire. It's like living with a good friend. Come to think of it, you're probably the first person I've talked to in all this time, besides myself. Can you tell?" He chuckled again, then said, "C'mon outside. I'll show you something."

We ducked back out into the trees and followed the path for a few minutes. The trail was not at all obvious, winding around bushes and along fallen logs. You could cross right over it and not notice. At a small clearing Casco announced, "The north forty," nodding toward a patch of tall plants. Unbelievably, corn was growing in the middle of the woods. About two dozen fat ears were ripening nicely in the warm setting sun.

"I've got two other patches like this, over that way." He gestured off to his left. "Did you know the Nausets and all the other natives of the area used to carry a little pouch of baked-dry corn with them when they traveled? They called it nocake. All it took was a little water mixed in and they were good for a few days of travel. Come on," he said, taking off again down an invisible path. We soon came to another small clearing and more tall plants, but these were not corn. Something wispy and leggy.

"Hemp," Casco said. "Another experiment. It's very strong stuff. I need it to lash down the branch coverings on my wigwam. I've used up all the rope I brought with me. You tear the stalk into strips. I think. I brought the seeds from home though I didn't know it. Found then in the seams of my collectin' pouch." He patted the bag at his waist, then leaned against a thick oak trunk, crossed his legs and continued, "Everything else Ineed is out here. Fish. Shellfish. Berries, grapes. Ducks, though they're damned hard to catch. Plenty of fresh water. I made my cooking pot from clay I dug from the cliff on Hog Island."

I was impressed. "How do you know how to do all this stuff?"

"Books, I guess. Rowing around looking at the bottom, like someone else I know. Metaphorically, that is." He smiled at me. "Now I trust you won't go revealin' my whereabouts to anyone?"

"No sir," I said, "But can I come over again?"

"Anytime, Theo, anytime."

I left him at the doorway to his wigwam and ran home, late by an hour, but I didn't care. I was thrilled to have met such an exotic creature, a real live Nauset. That part was still a little foggy but I felt sure he was telling the truth. I sped over the rocks and shells while the moon followed along, my wondrous luck the only thought in my head.

Chapter 3

After our first meeting Casco and I spent many hours together. During the day I'd find him at home or tending his plants. It turns out the reason he was able to grow such healthy plants in less than optimal conditions was that he'd gone and helped himself to a bag of manure from my neighbors' horse pasture. "The stuff is Grade-A," he said. "You suppose those horses get cream on their oats in the mornin'?" The corn had lately been subjected to a spell of intense attention by a couple of dedicated crows, and I was recruited to stand guard for a few hours at one patch while he kept them at bay from the other. He never mentioned killing them, which is what my father would have done within minutes, letting off a stiff-armed but accurate blast from his shotgun. I asked Casco one day why he didn't, also curious about the reason I'd never seen a bow and arrow among his things. "We never will kill a crow," he said shaking his head solemnly. "A crow brought the first kernel to us in its ear. In the other ear was a bean, but so far I haven't found the raw stock for that crop."

We shared an interest in small animal behavior and while watching over the corn, we'd stay within talking distance, discussing that and many other topics, pointing out to each other movements in the underbrush and making three-way conversations with catbirds or a mockingbird if we were lucky. I helped him distribute the bags of eelgrass onto the roof and collect more for the sides of the wigwam. We leaned dead branches onto it all around, ready for the day the hemp matured and he could make rope to lash it all together.

When the sun was low enough in the sky for the bay to be clear of fishermen he took me out in his boat. The boat had no oarlocks or oars and looked like it had drifted in from some place far away. There were jagged scrape marks along the sides and a sizable piece missing from the bow, but it floated and Casco paddled it with great skill, using a whittled board which was cracked and tied together, but worked beautifully.

"I tried making a dugout canoe when I first got here," he told me. "I found a log, a big fat one washed up on the shore. Must've been a reject piling, I suspect. I rolled it, dragged it out of sight and started a fire on it, you know, the way the Indians hollow out a log, burning and scraping it down. I tended the damn thing for three days and nights. I didn't get more that a few hours' sleep. I couldn't let it go out or I'd lose my good, deep embers. About sunset on the fourth evening the wind whipped up and started to blow, and my smoldering fire suddenly turned into a wall of flames. When a couple of them jumped overboard and into the woods, I knew I was in trouble. I had no way to get enough water to put out the fire because the tide was low. So finally I turned it over, banked it with sand to make it go out. Then I ran around like a lunatic, beatin' on the flames in the bushes. It took another two days for the wind to die and when I looked again the log had a big hole burned right through the bottom. The very next day I found this one. Someone up there is watching out for me," he concluded, looking skyward.

He knew how to spot a flounder in three feet of water even though they are masters of camouflage and at dusk on top of that. He used a hook and line but I believe he could have simply reached in and plucked one out. He knew the habits, migratory and reproduction cycles of almost all of the living things on the Bay. Fish, he told me, were given direction in these matters by temperature or the salinity of the water or other minute, subtle changes in their environment but mainly they took their cue from the moon.

"If you notice a bass's eyes, they're always lookin' up. It's because they're lookin' at the sky. If you dive underwater at night and look up, you'll see the moon, the only thing in all the darkness. That's what they see, too, and the moon's cycles guide them in theirs."

I had never thought of this and still don't know if it's correct, but for the rest of my life I have looked at the eyes of every bass I've met, dead or alive, and it is true about the eyes. He also told me if you cut open the stomach of a cod fish and find pebbles, it means the fish had eaten them on purpose in preparation for a storm. The pebbles keep the fish settled on the bottom, allowing the waves to wash over them.

He knew where quahogs were easy to find, right up against the line where the bottom drops off into deeper waters. Eelgrass grows along the edge, marking it. We'd walk along at half tide or lower, feeling with our feet. The quahog shells were unmistakable, they sat solid and upright with only a piece of their hinge exposed to the water rushing past. After taking only enough for one meal he'd say, "Shall we have a dip in the pool before supper?" and we'd flop into sandy bottomed, waist-high water, clear as a tropical pool.

We used to go fishing at night, so Casco could stay hidden. My parents assumed I was alone and made me promise to stay within sight of the house, so I'd anchor my boat with a lantern fastened to the bow so they could keep an eye out for me. My father heartily approved, and told me he would buy me a surf casting rig for bass if I could get fish at night. On the way in from fishing Casco and I would tow my boat to shore and divvy up the flounder before we parted ways. My father was quite impressed with my fishing ability, telling my mother and the others out on the water that I was a "natural born."

Casco and I shared many more suppers over the next couple of years. They were mostly stews cooked in the same clay pot and contained unusual combinations of shellfish and berries, greens and roots, things I'd never eaten before, like groundnuts or sea-rocket. He kept the corn for winter use, drying and burying it into the slope of a sandy hill behind the wigwam. One evening he cooked a superb dinner consisting simply of a huge pile of two and three inch smelt, fried in a swipe of duck fat. I picked the meat off the bones but Casco tossed them whole into his mouth. He topped the meal off with a pudding made from beach plums boiled with a little home made maple syrup.

"Takes me three days to make only a cup full," he said, holding up a small clay jar. "It's worth it though. Keeps me busy just when I think I can't endure another moment of winter. I never tasted real maple syrup 'til I made it myself. The evaporation steams up the place makin' it smell like heaven, though the walls do get kind of sticky. I always think I can make it last but I never do."

When the Great Hurricane hit the Cape in September of '38 I thought I'd go out of my mind with worry about Casco. I imagined I'd find the wigwam under a pile of downed trees with him inside, flattened. That afternoon I tried to run over to see him, to warn him that a storm was coming after hearing my father shout, "Jesus H. Christ on a Crutch! The bottom's dropped out of the barometer. Theo, let's go. Pull the boats out. Now!" There really were no weather reports in those days, we didn't even use the term 'hurricane.' People watched the clouds, the birds, used their instinct. We didn't always know what was coming. When I stepped outside the bay was unnaturally calm. I had to look carefully to see any movement in the water. The sky was a sickly yellow, the birds were silent. The whole world was silent, as if poised on the brink of something momentous. We pulled the boats up on shore as far as we could then my father sent me into the house saying, "Stay put and take care of your mother. I'm going to check on Ruth." She was our nearest neighbor, a widow who lived on the hill above our house. We didn't see him until much later in the evening, well after the rain and howling winds had already passed, the tide had risen and a tremendous tidal surge had pushed a great wall of water through the Narrows that crashed over our front porch and took away the boats so swiftly they seemed to have simply disappeared. My mother crouched by the fireplace with me shoved behind her, sitting between the uprights of the andiron, the only safe place in the house, she said. We stayed that way for a few hours, until the storm had quieted somewhat and it was safe to go out. By this time I was frantic, not for our situation, but for Casco alone out there, exposed on a tree-covered bluff. I told my mother I wanted to go and look at the damage and set off. Our front porch had been ripped off the house and lay upside down fifty feet away. I dropped down into the sand and started to walk away but was stopped immediately by my father as he hurried down the hill shouting at me to get the hell into the house at once.

It wasn't until the next afternoon that I managed to get away and run down the shore to Paw Wah Point. Trees were down everywhere, great scoops of the bluff had been washed away, trees lay out in the water. Boulders loosened from the bank had rolled down to become brand new landmarks along the rocky beach. I scrambled over the fallen branches and the little hill toward Casco's wigwam. Wet leaves were plastered over every surface. The exposed roots of sturdy maples reached out to me as I snaked through the debris, scared shitless by what I might find. I pushed aside a thick branch where I thought the wigwam ought to be, watched as it toppled, collapsing into a soft tangle of pine boughs. It was then that I saw Casco thrashing toward me through the brush, perfectly fine, not even wet. We saw each other and he laughed. "I was worried about you," he said. "Looks like you made it. All okay back home?"

Stunned but immensely relieved, I stuttered, "B-but I thought-"

"Yeah, well I take it you haven't seen the wigwam. It's a mess, of course."

"But, where were you?"

"He lifted his eyebrows and smiled. "Every great estate like mine has to have a storm cellar, you know. I spent the afternoon in mine. C'mon, give me a hand with the resurrection."

He explained while we pulled the branches away from the wreckage of the wigwam. Some time previously he had found, in a clearing in the center of the peninsula, the remains of an old farmstead, a solitary chimney and abandoned root cellar. He had simply crawled in and waited out the storm.

"Don't worry. When I was a kid I spent many a summer out on Cape Hatteras," he said, "I knew what was coming. Never did see anything like this, though."

Scattered among Casco's discussions about food, his favorite topic, and living off the land in general, were pieces of the story of how he came to be here in Orleans. He began to tell me one afternoon as we walked inland to a place he knew of where a patch of cranberries were ready for picking. The berries would be dried and added to the cache of corn along with as many nuts as could be gathered. This was a couple of months after our first encounter, and our companionship was by then completely relaxed and effortless. For the first time in my life, I experienced the feeling of pride at having an adult interested in what I had to say, which encouraged me to open up to him about my life as well. As we walked through the marsh the bay was calm and the sky a saturated, purplish blue. The tips of grasses circling the shore glowed yellow-orange in the low fall sunlight. I followed Casco along another barely visible path, our legs swishing through goldenrod and fern, poison ivy leaves fluttering against the black trunks of scrub pine.

"You ever read about King Phillip's War?" he asked, pausing to pull a burr from his pant leg.

"King Phillip. Son of Massasoit," I said, trying to remember. "That one?"

"The very one, Theo, though he was called Metacom in his own language. The war was about two hundred sixty five years ago, and it's the reason I'm walkin' beside you right now in this place."

As intriguing as that statement was Casco didn't immediately elaborate. It wasn't until we'd settled ourselves into a flat, warm hollow between two sloping hills and started to hunt through the ground cover for the little red berries that he went on with the story.

"He was fed up to his eyeballs with the bad behavior of the English. I don't blame him one bit. By the way," he said, veering off-topic for one of his many nuggets of Nauset history, "did you know that the Pilgrims stopped right here at this very bay thinkin' they might make it their new home?"

"Pleasant Bay?"

"They stopped their ship right out there," he pointed toward the ocean. "At the time there was a break in the barrier beach directly opposite and they could see what a perfect spot the bay was. But they couldn't get in. They couldn't get over the bar so they sailed north to Provincetown."

I imagined the famed Mayflower anchored in the Bay, a Pilgrims' village erected on the shore, men walking the beach in their buckled shoes. Years later I learned that one of the ships carrying another wave of arrivals did founder on that shoal. The crew and passengers of the Sparrowhawk were rescued by the Nausets, who spoke to them in English, and a runner was sent to Plymouth for boat-repair supplies. These came across Cape Cod Bay and overland via a short Indian road which bisected the peninsula, leading directly to the stricken ship. The Sparrowhawk never made it further, but the road can still be found today. I discovered it only recently walking in the woods of South Orleans. It is a deep, straight channel running through the trees from west to east.

"Anyhow," Casco continued, "By the time Metacom finally lost his temper his father was dead and forty-thousand colonists were already living in the southern part of New England. There were only about a thousand Wampanoags left by then, thanks to smallpox and plague and I don't know what-all diseases that were brought by earlier traders and such. Remember what Squanto came home to find when he eventually made it back?"

"Yes. His whole tribe was dead."

"That's right. Anyhow, forty years after that, most of them had integrated well enough, mostly due to ol' Massasoit's magnanimity and the fact that by then the Indians were dependent on some of the English-made equipment."

"Like tools?"

"Yeah. Iron cooking pots. Axes. Blankets. Guns of course, and liquor, unfortunately. It was modern life for them. Making tools out of rocks or shells seemed pointless when they could simply buy a superior product. 'Course what they paid with was their land. So often some poor ol' Indian, after they'd gotten him thoroughly drunk, would make his mark on a deed, signing away rights to his own place. They were swindled even though they thought it was a good deal. Well Theo, were they ever wrong. They didn't have the same notion of property ownership that the English did. They thought they could still hunt and fish on the land. Plus the thousands of Puritans who followed the original Pilgrims were not so particular about keeping to the agreements that Massasoit made with them."

Casco looked over at me. I had just bitten a cranberry in half and my lips puckered with the sweet sourness of it. After a pause he continued, "They pushed on outward and took what they wanted. They grazed herds of cattle on Indians' planting fields and cut down trees by the thousands. The natives couldn't hunt in the migratory way they'd always done, and the English didn't need them anymore to show them how to make it in the wilderness. The Indians became a kind of problem for the Puritans because they were in the way."

Casco stopped combing through the leaves and checked the level in our berry basket. The basket was a crude execution of an original Wampanoag design, he'd told me somewhat shyly. Made from the stripped, sliced and softened bark of a maple, it looked pretty basic to me. The top edge wasn't finished off, leaving the strips sticking up all around, and it had more of a lopsided oval shape than any basket I'd ever seen, but it worked well enough. It was nearly full, so Casco emptied it into one of the burlap bags I'd helped him lug up the hill on that first day. He used those two bags for all kinds of things. They held clams along with seaweed, twigs, manure, stones and shells, and corn, naturally. I even saw him using one stuffed with grass as a pillow. He gently kicked the basket back over to me. It was October, and he was still barefoot. He had a pair of shoes but wore them only in winter, and even then as little as possible. They were in rather poor condition.

"Who knows how long they have to last me, and I'm not going to shoot a deer, am I? That would be the only way to get leather for another pair. Nor do I want to skin the poor creature even if one did happen to die in the vicinity." He gave a little shake of horror at the thought. "But someday I will be needin' footgear and I know it. Let's just say I'm workin' up to it."

It was a problem he worried about fairly often, and included more than shoes. He would automatically check the back of his pants for any tears when he stood up from the boat seat. His shirt was already torn in several places. He reattached the sleeves only in winter, he said, to save wear and tear. One day I brought him a pair of my father's socks. My mother knitted them as a Christmas present out of yellow wool, but my father had yet to wear them. He muttered to me out on the water a few days after he'd received them that he'd never wear yellow, and she ought to have known it. He didn't explain why. So I took them for Casco, who I could see liked them immediately. But he turned them down.

"Theo, you are a good and benevolent friend and I thank you, but I cannot take these. I made a vow to myself and my ancestors that I would not partake of white man's products. Now, I made an exception about my roof, but without it I wouldn't be here to uphold the remainder of my promise. I have what I came here with and I will acquire no more." I suppose the burlap bags were technically part of his original possessions since he'd brought his belongings in them.

We moved to a different area and began to comb our fingers through the leaves, palms up. The cranberries made little popping sounds as they were pulled from the plant and fell into our hands.

"So what about Metacom?" I asked when we were settled.

"Yeah. Phillip, the Christian name given to him when he was baptised. By then the English had begun to convert the natives to Christianity which they thought was necessary for some reason, even though someone else tellin' them what to believe was exactly what they'd just run away from. Even Massasoit thought it was a good idea. He asked the leaders of Plymouth Colony to give his two sons Christian names and so Metacom's brother Wamsutta became Alexander, and Metacom was named Phillip."

I had never heard anything that came close to this account. "I wonder if my father knows about that," I said idly. Casco looked at me, one eyebrow raised, and said, "Ever wonder why the Indians went for the Pilgrim preaching in the first place?"

"Why?" I thought of my mother and her stern devotion to this inflexible ideology. I couldn't imagine such a thing. It seemed a sellout by a superior race, in my twelve-year-old opinion.

"See, the Indians kept dying from one nasty pestilence after another brought across by Europeans. But the English for the most part didn't get sick. So they started to believe maybe the English God was more powerful than their own."

Casco dumped a handful of berries into the basket and snorted ironically.

"You ever heard of a Praying Indian?" I shook my head.

"Well, it's what they called those they converted. A man named John Eliot, a missionary type Englishman, came over and taught them the Bible in their own language. There were whole towns full of Christian Indians. Praying towns, they were called. We're sittin' in one right now, Portanimicut. Can you imagine, the natives dressed like Puritans, women wearing their hair all twisted up under a bonnet or some such headgear. They went to church and read the Bible. They gave up their regular ways of doin' things and followed the Christian customs. Any Indians still practicing traditional ceremonies were kicked out. Things got messy for the ones who didn'tgo along with it. Their whole tribal way of life fell apart." Casco tossed a berry into the air, leaned his head back, and caught it in his mouth.

"When Massasoit died, his son Wamsutta, or Alexander, became the sachem of the Wampanoags and married Queen Weetamoo of Pocassett. The Puritans were a little wary about this, and they didn't know what to expect. They thought Alexander was arrogant and a little too independent in his ways. So one night they invited him to a big dinner to get acquainted. I guess everything went all right, but on the way home he became sick and died the next day. The Wampanoags thought this sounded suspicious and probably they were right."

"You mean....they poisoned him? A sachem?"

"That's what I believe."

We sat in silence for a few minutes while Casco emptied the basket again. "There are council records of a certain amount of arsenic powder having been purchased that very day, and even one of them commenting that they 'had a pest to get rid of.'"

"So it's true?"

"Nobody really knows for sure, Theo, but I'm tellin' you now so it will stay alive until it's put to rest. Or not. Anyhow once Wamsutta died Metacom became sachem. The English called him King Phillip. And after a number of years he was plenty vexed over a number of issues.

The newcomers were taking over the land and wiping out his people, and he aimed to stop them. Since so many of his own clan were either dead or Christianized he began to travel around and recruit other tribes to his cause. The English weren't too worried since by then they outnumbered the Indians about two to one. Plus the Praying Indians acted as spies, going between the two sides and keeping the English informed of Phillip's progress. But pretty soon the Nipmuk and Pocumtuc were joined with Metacom and the Wampanoags, along with Penacooks and Abenakis. The rest of the Praying Indians stayed out of it, and they included the Nausets here in Pleasant Bay. They stayed loyal to the English all through the war."

I sat there in the sun, staring stupefied at Casco and trying to process all this new information, some of which I didn't understand completely. I fed another cranberry into my mouth and chewed. My stomach gave an involuntary lurch as the tart juice burst across my tongue. I spat out the pulp and dumped the rest of my handful into Casco's basket. He too, had stopped picking, and sat gazing off toward the bay, his eyelids drooping slightly as though reliving a particularly painful memory. With a somber, resigned tone, he continued.

"So. In June of sixteen seventy-five the war was sparked to life by some final straw, as they always are, and the Indians attacked first one English settlement and then another. The colonists fought back and the militia went after Metacom with a vengeance. Settlers all over New England were abandoning their villages for fear of the surprise attacks which were the Indian style of fighting. But the soldiers kept to their usual tactic of marching together in a group, which made them easy to shoot at. After several months it looked like the Indians were goin' to prevail against their uninvited guests. That is until December, when the soldiers burned down an Indian fortress in Rhode Island. Many people on both sides lost their lives in that place, but worse, it contained a large stockpile of food, which the Indians were countin' on to get them through the winter."

"Like yours."

"Yeah, only much bigger. Having no food was more than a problem, Theo. It turned the course of the war for the English. By the way, you know what happened to their buddies, the Praying Indians?"

I couldn't imagine. "They ran away?"

"I suppose they'd likely have been better off if they'd done so," he said thoughtfully.

"No, what the English did was to round them all up and dump them on Deer Island in the middle of Boston Harbor. They couldn't escape. This was in October, so the Indians threw up some hasty wigwams and then proceeded to try to live through the winter on clams and tree bark, I don't know what. Plenty of them died, of course."

"Did they take the Nausets from here?"

Casco chuckled. "Now they were lucky. The colonists figured they were so far out on the arm of Cape Cod it was almost the same as internin' them on some godforsaken island. No, they pretty much stayed out of things."

This last detail barely registered. My young brain was swimming through a soup of imagery. I saw Indians fleeing through dense forests as red-dressed soldiers aimed and reloaded muskets, houses and fields in flames. I had a vision of a Thanksgiving dinner, Pilgrims and Indians around the table. Wamsutta in conversation with his neighbor while behind him a Pilgrim in a black coat with a lacy collar tips a cupful of poison into his wine glass. I saw the prisoners of Deer Island in the snow, scrabbling for food in the frozen mud. And King Philip himself, riding up and down the East coast trailed by a loyal band of whooping warriors on horseback. I was to recall these mental pictures many times over the next year, embellishing them freely without regard to fact or how the story eventually worked itself out.

After a while we picked up and left the cranberry patch, Casco with the burlap bag slung over one shoulder, striding easily through the meadow to the woods while I trotted after, trying to keep up as he told the rest of the story.

"Meanwhile Metacom and his men traveled around New England continuing their attacks and trying to find a safe place to winter over. They likewise destroyed many a family homestead, and I'm not sayin' they weren't cruel and most likely bloodthirsty too. War is never a fair fight, never. Plenty of women and children on both sides met with unspeakably horrible deaths at the hands of those fighting. But soon enough Mother Nature took care things in her way. People have to eat, no matter what their race or circumstances, and Metacom and his band had no food in the middle of winter. Their main food supply was burned up and wild game was now scarce in the New England woods. The tribes were keeping what they did have close, because they knew they couldn't return to their land to plant the usual crops. By spring they were starting to think they might as well surrender to the English and take what they could of the life that was handed to them. But Metacom knew he would be killed immediately and so he went into hiding."

Just as Casco said that we arrived at the door to his wigwam. He turned to me, grinned, and ducked swiftly inside. The fire was smoldering as usual, a serpentine tendrill of smoke making its way slowly to the roof. Casco was Metacom at that moment, throwing himself down in a safe haven after a day of marauding. He continued to smile at me as if to say, See how grand it was back then? His nose, bent to the left, seemed to convey waywardness, his bare feet and long white hair seen through the hazy scrim of heat contributed to the image of an otherworldly being. His smile died as he tossed a pine cone onto the fire.

"They found him soon enough, but not before they captured his wife and nine-year-old son and sold them into slavery in the West Indies for a pound each. That's what they did with the natives at the time, including the Praying Indians they'd stashed on Deer Island. Some of them they sent to Virginia to pick tobacco, which is where my ancestor ended up." Casco held his hand up and said, "I promise to tell you that story, but first let me finish off King Phillip."

"After his wife and son were sold off the fight went out of him. He didn't care anymore. They found him one August day at his place in Montaup, in Rhode Island. The whites called it Mount Hope, and still do, I think. Anyhow, they attacked and he was shot. Shot, by the way, by one of the Indians on the side of the English. That guy sold Metacom's head to the authorities at Plymouth for thirty shillings, the goin' rate at the time, and they displayed it on a post in town for the next twenty-five years."

Casco threw another pine cone at the fire, this time with a flick of disgust in his wrist.

"That's about all I know of it," he said. "But I can't help thinkin' about what would've happened if they hadn't run out of food. Would we be living in a different sort of world right now?"

At the time I found it difficult to think so expansively, but I do ponder the question now and then, as I suppose so many of us do, don't we?

Chapter 4

Naturally the story of King Phillip's War came to mind when Ria first showed me the medallion that evening. I knew the metal could only have come from the colonists, and the one word we could make out, "council", was in English. I felt sure that Casco would be able to tell us something about it. I admit I was also thrilled with a legitimate opportunity to introduce my two friends to each other, secret or no. Ria wasn't as surprised as I expected to hear of an Indian living in seclusion on Paw Wah Point, but she was after all from New York City, so I supposed she was used to all kinds of unusual citizenry.

I didn't talk about King Phillip then, for all the indirect influence he had on Casco's present situation. I told her what I knew of Casco's life, starting with the stock market crash of '29. Though I had only a vague notion of the Great Depression's impact on the economy of my country and the world in general, I knew it was a major event. I grew up listening to my father and the other fishermen discuss the economy at length, though I doubt it had affected the lifestyles of most Cape Codders. But for Casco, it marked the beginning of the end of his life in Danville, Virginia. He owned a small music shop, selling sheet music and the newly available twelve inch discs to a privileged clientele. The music was mainly Victor or Columbia symphonic and operatic recordings on 78s, but he also dealt to an even smaller market in jazz music from the '20s, which was his personal interest. He told me once it was a record of King Oliver's Creole Jazz Band, featuring the young

Louis Armstrong, that was the most difficult of his possessions to leave behind.

Four years after the crash he turned fifty, and by then was homeless and destitute, having lost his business after hanging on precariously for a year or two. He had no family left to speak of, was never married nor had children, and so he decided one day to join the hordes of other homeless men and ride the rails to his ancestral home. For all of his life, his mother and grandmother had talked about his Wampanoag roots in New England, drumming his lineage into his head and passing on to him the stories and traditions of his origins. Fascinated, he spent many hours studying articles and essays about the Wampanoag, Nauset, Monomoyick, Narragansett and numerous other tribes and sub-tribes of New England, and little by little withdrawing from life in Danville.

"From the time I was a small boy I always wanted to come up here, to find the wellspring of my particular pedigree, but I also wanted to see the very landscape where my boyhood heroes had walked." So when the time came he found Cape Cod, then Pleasant Bay and Paw Wah and vowed to live there as a lone Nauset, the last of his family, quietly shunning the ways of the white man's world.

Ria listened quietly to my description until this point, then flopped onto the sand and sighed dramatically, cried out "Louis Armstrong!" then started to sing,

"Like Jack Horner
in the corner,
don't go nowhere
but what do I care."

I didn't know "Ain't Misbehavin" at the time of course. My wanderings didn't include any place where I would have been exposed to it. The nearest I came to hearing popular music was when I went to town once a month for shopping with my parents in my father's Model T. I was allowed to wander around town for the duration and always went directly to the door of the barber shop, where I sat on the stoop and drank in the radio shows of the day.

Ria looked at me as though her outburst had not happened and said, "So is he the real McCoy?"

"I don't know. I think so. He sure knows a lot about Indians, and he looks like one, too." I described Casco, the wigwam, his corn and his boat, the cooking pot and maple baskets.

"Wow. And no one knows about him?"

"No." Another pang of guilt surged through me.

"Well, I won't tell a soul." She held up a palm and looked me in the eye. "I promise. Can we go and visit him? Show him the medallion?"

"Yeah. Tomorrow?" We agreed to meet during sailing lessons.

The following day we found Casco in one of his corn patches, pulling ears off the tall stalks and dropping them gently into a burlap bag. He didn't hear us approaching, and I was about to call out to him, when he said, "Bad day for sailing is it?" Turning slowly, he glanced at Ria for a split second, then shot me a piercing look. No one said anything until I stuttered, "I - I'm sorry, Casco. I didn't think you'd mind. She's not from around here." A few more tense seconds passed, then Casco's shoulders dropped and he came toward us, smiling and holding his hand out.

"It's all right, Theo, I could do with another friend. Casco Swift," he said to Ria. "Nice to meet you."

"This is Ria Bang," I said, relieved. They shook hands as Ria said, "We found something Indians must have made. At least we think it's what it is. We thought maybe you could tell us."

From there things went smoothly, my moment of chastisement noted and passed. We helped Casco pick the rest of the ripened corn, then climbed to a higher patch and pulled off another several ears. Ria chattered away as if helping an Indian recluse harvest his corn was a perfectly ordinary event, though she shot me a couple of wide-eyed looks while Casco was bent over. By the time he led us to his wigwam, she was laughing, and Casco smiled at me saying, "I suppose there are some positive aspects to the camp experience, aren't there. Now I understand why you've been so scarce lately."

The inside of the wigwam was hung with half a dozen bundles of various plants, the beginning of preparations for winter. Casco pulled one of them down and held it out to us, large pale leaves with a velvet fuzz of white hairs. "Wonderful plant, this," he said. "If I catch a cold this winter all I have to do is smoke a little of it and my lungs will clear. Mullein, it's called. It's beautiful growin', too. 'Course I have yet to be sick so I don't really know if it works, but you've got to be prepared."

He tossed some twigs onto the ever-present fire and invited us to sit. When we'd settled, he grabbed a basket from the corner and put it in front of us. "Have some blueberries," he said, "and show me this artifact."

Ria unwrapped the medallion and handed it over. After an initial sharp intake of breath Casco put his hand over his mouth, studying the object carefully on both sides, running his fingers over the design. After a bit he said, "You ever seen a picture of the seal of the Massachusetts Bay Colony?"

Ria and I shook our heads.

"Well, it's a kind of symbol, a picture which was stamped on all the official documents of the time. King Charles granted the Colony a charter. It basically allowed them to be a recognized, bona fide colony of England. Anyhow, the picture on the seal is a lot like this one. It's also an Indian holding a bow and arrow, but the seal has a little ribbon coming out of the Indian's mouth with the words: "Come over and Help us." Now what do you suppose it meant?"

Ria and I looked at each other, mystified, and shrugged.

Casco chuckled. "It's another foolish notion the English had. It was kind of like a promotional campaign to get others to settle in the new colony. Why they have an Indian sayin' it instead of an Englishman is beyond me. They were the ones who needed help, and the natives gave it to them. Now, what it should have said was 'Come over and Help Yourself,' 'cause that's certainly what they did!" He guffawed at his own joke while Ria and I sat smiling uncertainly. Sliding the basket of blueberries closer to our side of the fire he added, "I do know what your artifact is, and it's something which touches my personal family history, that's for sure. Where ever did you find it?"

Ria described the place as he listened intently. He laid back for a few momentslooking up at the bent saplings, thinking. I reached into the big basket Casco kept full of pine cones and tossed a couple onto the fire. He winked at me and said, "Theo, do you remember me telling you about Deer Island in Boston Harbor?"

"Where they put the Praying Indians during King Phillip's war?"

"The very same, yes. It was in the spring after that awful winter that the English, desperate to find Metacom and his men, recruited about eighty of the Praying Indians from the camp and formed them into a search party. Those guys had real knowledge of the land and the skills to track. It didn't take them long to find Metacom, and we know the outcome. After the war was over and everyone went home, these Indians were taken care of and they convinced the colonists to spare their relatives from execution or from bein' sold into slavery. For this they got a medal. I believe this is one of them."

He pointed out the date etched into the back of the disc: June the 20th, 1676. "Curious. It was given before they even found King Phillip."

The blare from the signal horn out on the water startled us into the present. Ria glanced at me and said, "Merde!" which made Casco smile. "We'll have to continue this conversation at another time, I suppose," he said. "How many days do you have left, anyhow?"

The last day of camp for both of us was four days away. I was dreading it. It seemed real life had only just begun for me, with my discovery of Casco and then Ria and now the three of us together in our own secret place. Though Ria had said nothing I know she was feeling glum about it as well. Casco invited us both, if we could get away, for one more visit. "I'll make something to eat," he said, looking lovingly at the big black cooking pot. We decided on two days later, during the big inter-camp end-of-year regatta. Hopefully no one would notice our absence.

A brisk wind was blowing when I woke up that morning. A perfect day for sailing. My father was on the telephone, a rare occurrence in our house, making plans with someone to go fishing. I didn't pay much attention. My mother dished up the usual glob of oatmeal and gave me the day's biblical passage, "All flesh is grass," she said, nodding meaningfully toward my father's plate, which was draped with four slices of bacon. I bowed my head as I gulped my cereal though I had no idea what she was talking about, as usual. I guess I remember that particular quote because it struck me on the way to camp that I might at last understand what one of her quotes meant. It was scientific. If you were to take bacon, or any flesh, and trace back what that animal had eaten, it would be a plant. Even if what it had eaten was meat, the starting point in the chain of consuming would likely end in a plant of some kind. I know now it expressed no such thing, but I developed the theory further as I trudged past Quanset Camp, where Ria was probably eating breakfast. There were already people on the beach readying boats for the races. The same was true when I arrived at Mariner, where I was immediately put to work sorting life vests and coiling line. The races were to begin right after lunch, when the tide was halfway in, giving everyone plenty of room to maneuver.

"I suppose you've got other plans today, Sparrow," Whit sidled up to me as we were finishing. "I get it. A ducky little doll you've got there. But listen, it'd be easier if you didn't show at all today. That way I don't have to explain. Go on. Screw, before they spot you."

That was fine by me. I grabbed a pair of rubber boots from the boathouse, walked farther along the shore and waded into the River. The tide was dead low so I only had to swim about twenty feet across the very middle, clutching my boots in either hand. My clothing dried quickly in the August sun as I crossed Barley Neck and met the road to East Orleans. I had an idea for a gift I hoped Casco wouldn't turn down, and I thought I might find it at Bessom's store. Dave Bessom was a genial man who had only recently bought the place from old Sam Higgins and had quickly made it his own, not modernizing a thing except to mix some newer products in with those still left on the shelves. The hundred-fifty year old floorboards creaked as I entered the place. Pickle barrels were crowded in front of an old cider press, a pair of tongs for pulling them from the brine lay in an empty coal scuttle. Split peas and beans were scooped from huge canisters standing just inside the door. Kerosene lanterns hung from the ceiling along with a huge, rusty scale. Dusty bottles of ancient remedies were lined up on a long shelf behind the counter. Next to a potbellied stove the black wheel of an ancient coffee grinder, no longer in service but still fully aromatic, drew me into the nineteenth century atmosphere. Dave sat slumped on a stool reading the paper. He looked at me over the top of his glasses, then pointed with his thumb in response to my request. "In the back," he said, reading.

I sat on his porch for a while after I found the packet, nursing a Dr. Pepper and savoring the cool shade. There was a hole to the right of the door where, for as long as I could remember, swallows would enter. You could hear them chirping inside the store, but Dave paid them no mind. I watched them fly in and out, their nests within the walls. I wondered idly about the generations of swallow families that must have lived there, and tried to picture their hidden dwelling. To me it looked like an ant farm but with birds. I heard the car long before I saw it, there being virtually no traffic to speak of in this part of town, and as it came closer I made out the distinct grille and silhouette of a Studebaker Commander. I knew my models well in those days, as did every boy my age. I had never seen one outside the pages of a newspaper, and this one was slowing down to park. I tried to pretend nonchalance as I stared at the gleaming black behemoth until a man's voice said, "Hey, wasn't it you I saw out in the bay a few days back?"

Emerging from the dark interior was the man Ria and I had encountered while watching eagles out on Money Head. The one looking for arrowheads. He wore the same over-the-top hunting gear and crowded me with the same demanding energy. "Where's your girlfriend today?" he said, leering down at me. He opened the screen door and went inside, letting it go with a crack that echoed around the sleepy crossroads. I took the opportunity to inspect the car, walking all the way around it and dragging my fingers along the chrome. The metal was hot from the sun and the drive, the engine ticking slightly. In the back seat I noticed a pair of boots and a shovel. The silly hat. Soon the man burst through the door again and I walked away. He took off down Barley Neck Road. Dave came outside and we watched his wake of dust billow over to us. "Some car. Now where do you think he's going?" he said, standing beside me.

"I don't know," I answered. There wasn't much down that road but turnip fields and cows grazing. But there were a couple of good places to launch a boat, and most likely it's what he was going to do, I thought. More arrowhead hunting.

When I got back to the Bay I could see that some campers were already out on the water taking advantage of the excellent conditions to get in a few runs before the races began. I ducked into the woods so I wouldn't be seen by my fellow Mariners and found a sunny spot to dry off again while I waited for the sound of luffing sails to stop, a sign the regatta was underway. When the signal horn blared I walked over to Paw Wah Channel and found Ria sitting there, out of breath and removing her shoes. She looked up and smiled. "I brought this," she said, holding up a spiral-bound drawing pad. "I want to draw him. What do you think?"

"Sure," I shrugged. I told her about my encounter with the arrowhead hunter. I left out the girlfriend part. "He gave me the heebie-jeebies," she said, rolling her eyes.

Casco was outside his wigwam when we stepped into the little clearing. With his back to us he stood braiding his hair with practiced speed, the white strands flying back and forth between his fingers. "Welcome," he said, turning and smiling. "Go on inside. I'll join you in a minute."

The black pot was on the fire, an appetizing aroma drifting from its mouth. I could see that Casco had tidied up, maybe because of the prospect of a female presence, but surely this was an occasion for him. There were no drying plants hanging and the two burlap bags had been stuffed with grass and were arranged on either side of the fire. As he entered I saw that he had the wampum belt wrapped around his waist, and his shirt looked cleaner than I'd seen before.

He got right to the point. Rubbing his hands together he said, "Theo, if you'll forgive me. I snared a pair of bobwhites yesterday and I've made a stew. Have a seat and make yourselves comfortable. You ever heard of Filé Gumbo? It's a Creole dish from New Orleans, but the filé part comes from the Choctaw Indians. Still does. It's a kind of thickening agent for stews, and it's made from sassafras leaves which I happened to find up the road apiece." He held out a small dish of brown powder for us to inspect. "You put it in at the end, otherwise it gets stringy. I also added crabapples, corn and cranberries. Sound good?"

I nodded. Ria, enchanted by the interior of the wigwam, the woven branches and the Post Office bags, dragged her eyes back to the cooking pot and said, "It sounds delicious." Casco dumped the filé into the pot and stirred.

"You happen to bring that medal with you again? I sure would like to have another look at it," he said as he dished up the stew into three wooden bowls I'd never seen before.

"Yes, I did," said Ria. She opened her drawing pad and there it was, stuck between the pages. I glimpsed several sketches of it, rubbings of the border design and the entire back with its dedication and signature and the unfortunate scrape Ria had made when she pulled it from the roots of the tree.

"Good," said Casco, handing her a bowl. He passed one to me and we sat back. "Oh yeah, I forgot. I made some spoons. Now don't laugh,

Ria, I don't know if Theo's mentioned my vow but I don't have anything here manufactured by anyone but myself." He fished the utensils from behind his back. The rim of a small clamshell, what we call a cherrystone, had been carefully drilled and a whittled stick forced into the opening, to serve as a handle. It was elegantly simple and surprisingly strong. Ria turned hers around admiringly, then tried it.

"It's perfect," she said. "And so's the stew. Thank you."

We ate in silence for a few minutes. The stew was wonderful, a mélange of peppery meat in a sweet and tart broth. My lifelong interest in cooking was sparked all those years ago by Casco and his foraged meals, the inventiveness and flair of his ingredient combinations, the knowledge he had of plants and their uses. The pepper came from a weed I've seen growing all over town in the worst soil. "Lepidum Virginicum," he told me the first time I tasted it. He made a kind of mustard with it, which he brought out one day to top off some oysters we were enjoying. "Poor Man's Pepper is the common name," he said, "Perfect for yours truly."

"Theo told me how you came to be here," said Ria. I think it's remarkable. Powerfully dramatic." Ria was given to inflated expressions sometimes, but it went along with her confident nature. "I'd like to try living in the wild sometime."

"You would find it dramatic in the middle of January, but more along the lines of a tragedy. It's mighty cold and very quiet. The first winter I spent out here I thought I wasn't going to make it. I wasn't as informed about fishing and such. Food gathering. I had studied up a little on the flora and fauna of New England, but this here is a whole other environment. I arrived in the month of March, so there wasn't much in the way of foliage out here, or anything growing I could eat. I watched the others out on the water, saw where they went and what they got. I ate a lot of mussels that spring, lived off a small supply of fat. He patted his stomach. "The problem was the loneliness. You can probably tell I like to talk." He grinned, his teeth as white as the hair on his head. I wondered idly how he brushed them.

"Did I ever tell you, Theo, about the day I arrived in this great state?"

I shook my head. "I don't think so."

"The damndest thing you ever saw. We were just passin' over the line from Rhode Island. A guy gave me a ride on the back of his truck and I was all bundled up against the cold, rolled up in my blanket. I happened to peek out to see where we were, and saw that it was snowing. But it wasn't regular snow. It was red, red as clay. The sky was red, the ground was red, red snow was falling all around. My home was welcoming me, don't you see? The red man returns."

Ria and I exchanged looks. Casco saw and added, "Honestly. I saw it with my own eyes. It was a miracle. I knew I'd made the right decision."

We nodded in unison, believing. Years later we were to have this confirmed, as I will tell.

"By the time the second winter rolled around I was used to being alone. I do talk to myself a lot. And the birds. I have long conversations with my friend the mockingbird."

"No one has ever found you?"

"Not that I know of, miss."

Ria finished her soup and picked up the medal. "You wanted to look at this again," she said, passing it across the fire pit. "And I want to ask if you'll pose for a portrait." She held up the sketch pad. "It won't take long. I'm fast."

"Well, no one's ever asked me that before, sure. How would you like me to sit?"

"As you are, you're fine." She dug a pencil out of her shorts and inspected the tip. Casco lounged against the wall on his side. He picked up the medal, rubbed his thumb across the surface and flipped it over. He read the inscription aloud, in an attempt at an English accent.

"At a Council Held at Charlestown June the twentieth, sixteen seventy-six, in the present war with the heathen natives of this land, they giving us peace and mercy at their hands. Signed, Edward Rawson. Hmph."

He put the medal around his neck, smoothed it onto his chest and lifted his head, assuming the Noble Savage expression of the archetypal "Injun" in countless Westerns. Ria began to draw.

"Although he probably wasn't one of the men recruited from Deer Island to fight for the English, my ancestor was there at the time," Casco said after a few moments of posing. This piece of information got my attention. I had been slumped against the door pole, full of stew and drowsily thinking of going outside to relieve myself, but I sat up as he continued.

"He was born here, right here," he pointed at the floor. "His mother was a Nauset." He chuckled. "She called him 'Bad Boy,' and he was too, so I'm told. She was only sixteen and as the story goes, his father was one of the English who built themselves houses on the other side of the Bay," he gestured in the general direction of Chatham. "Although she was a Praying Indian her Christianity didn't lead her or any of the others to accept this child fully. So when he became old enough he ran away. Ran smack-dab into King Phillip's war. He then had the bad luck to be taken with a group of Praying Indians to Deer Island. You know that story."

"Did he die there?" Ria asked.

"No, he didn't. That would have been bad for me." He smiled as Ria realized her mistake and put a hand over her mouth to stop anything else from coming out. "But probably wished he had, because what happened to him is that he was sold into slavery after the war ended. They sent him to the West Indies to harvest sugarcane, but somehow or other he ended up in Virginia, working the tobacco fields. Down there were lots of African slaves as well, them bein' like the Indians no better than pack animals according to the English, Dutch, whoever was running things. Well our boy fell in love with one of them and had a baby daughter with her. Her family wasn't too happy about it, and so they killed him off."

Ria and I exchanged glances. Casco was talking to the fire, his voice a kind of monotone, reciting something he'd heard countless times. He was fiddling with the medal, running a finger along the edge so that it swung a little on his chest. I could see that Ria had drawn a good likeness of his face and was working on his shoulders and arms. The medal was not included yet.

"What they didn't know when they killed him is that because he was indentured, ah, do you all know what indentured is?"

Ria piped up and said, "Like a prison sentence, right?"

"Yeah. Kind of. He's a slave to someone for a certain number of years. Well, turns outthe daughter, because of the laws of indentureship, had to serve out his time for him. But the most remarkable turn of events is that she then meets and marries a genuine Wampanoag from Cape Cod. And from there follow eight generations of mustee and half-breed Swifts until me. I'm the last one. I've come full circle." With that, he straightened up and reassumed the noble pose he'd started with, and Ria sketched with brisk strokes to capture the moment before it changed again.

"One more thing," he held up a finger, "while I remember it. They named me Lucius because I was born at daybreak. But because of my unclear bloodline, I renamed myself Casco. That means muddy in the local Indian language. I thought it more appropriate, given my less than clear lineage. I'm tellin' you all this because in my family that's what we did. You have to know where you come from. Now you two are the ones who can tell my story, if it comes up, and I'll live beyond my time. How's your drawing comin' along?"

Ria held it up for us to see. It was an admirable likeness, and, more than, that she'd managed to reproduce the atmosphere of the smoke and the story, something in his eyes, his hand at the medal.

"Why, it's masterly," said Casco. "I'm deeply honored. It's almost like magic, isn't it, Theo, the way she did it so effortlessly." I agreed. It was wonderful.

"I want to paint it when I get back," said Ria, "add some color. Also, I'd like to give the medal to you."

Casco sat up, clasping it to his chest. He stared at Ria, then dipped his eyes to the fire.

"It's a mighty fine and generous gift. Are you sure?"

"Yes. It's part of your heritage, you should have it."

"Thank you," he said, bowing to her. I am honored." You could see he was touched by her sweet gesture. So was I. "That reminds me," I said. "I have something for you too."

"Well Merry Christmas on the Bay. What is it?" Casco laughed.

I pulled the package I'd bought at Bessom's from my pocket and handed it over. Casco looked at it and beamed at me. "So, the sparrow has brought it instead of the crow," he said, holding up the bag marked 'Pole Beans.' "Thank you, my friend. I shall make a small exception to my rule and accept this. More meals for us next summer."

We spent the rest of the afternoon talking, telling stories and laughing. Ria and Casco got onto the subject of Louis Armstrong and started singing 'All of Me' together, Casco scatting the trumpet parts while Ria drummed on her overturned bowl. I sat spellbound as she sang 'Pennies from Heaven,' which Casco had never heard. After she and I gave a giggly rendition of 'Flat Foot Floogie,' with its tongue-twisting lyrics I had go to outside to pee, I heard them singing 'Moonglow.' Casco's tender intonation blending with her sweet soprano there in the middle of the woods is something I will never forget.

We left him standing by the wigwam after he shook my hand and kissed Ria on the cheek. It had been a momentous day for all of us. Ria and I walked along in silence, lost in our own thoughts about the day. When we parted at her camp she said she was going to skip activities so she could add color to Casco's portrait while the scene was still fresh in her mind. We said our goodbyes and arranged to meet at the channel the next evening, both aware that we had only two more days together. She ran up the hill and I stood on the beach with my hands in my pockets and watched her go.

Chapter 5

The person my father had been talking to on the phone was a fishing pal of his. And when I came through the door that evening, he said to me, "Be ready to go out at five tomorrow morning, Theo. We're leaving from the harbor. We need you to drive one of the boats."

I nodded. Rock Harbor was on the other side of town, an inlet from Cape Cod Bay, the body of water which the Cape held in its curled arm. If you were to travel out of Pleasant Bay, turn north and run the length of ocean beach to Provincetown at the tip of the peninsula, then follow the shore as it coils in on itself, you would arrive in Cape Cod Bay. Its roughly six hundred square miles are home to flounder and fluke, dolphins, bluefish and everyone's favorite, striped bass. When the tide is out much of this bay is a vast patchwork of sand flats stippled with clam and wormholes and teeming with crabs, snails and shrimp.

My father didn't tell me what we were going after that day. I assumed it was bluefish because of the time of year. When they 'run,' or swarm after baitfish, churning up the water, the call goes out, and everyone jumps into their boat. When we got to the harbor my father's friends, the brothers Hank and Allan Reese, were standing in their big Elco angler, High Hat. The boat was fitted for serious fishing with a winch on the stern for hauling a net. Hank was a big, brash, aggressive fisherman. I'd been along on a couple of trips with him, and I hated the way he seemed to relish the killing part of fishing rather than the sport or the gathering of food. If he found an undesirable fish on the end of his line, he'd rip its jaw in half to get the hook out, then toss it overboard. He laughed too loud and drank rum all day. Allan was not much better, but he kept his mouth shut. They'd likely worked out the arrangement years ago. My father and I were to use a banged up rowing skiff with an outboard which sat sputtering at the end of the ramp. I could see immediately why my father needed me. The fuel tank and a knot of hose were fixed to the deck on the right side of the engine. He needed his right arm to operate the tiller. Me.

"See you out there," Hank yelled as he revved his big engine and chugged out of the harbor. His brother stood leaning against the pilot house smoking a cigarette and staring cheerlessly at the deck.

I stepped into the skiff and my father tossed down a bag of sandwiches and a pair of boots. The last thing I wanted to do was to go fishing with him and his booze-soaked fishing buddies. There were only two days left to see Ria, and I was angry about it but I didn't dare go against my father's orders. I cast off reluctantly and we were soon underway. We cruised north in silence for almost an hour. It was a beautiful day out on the water. The Bay was calm, the tide an hour past high. The sun felt good on my shoulders, and I let my mind wander as I eyed the coastline of Eastham, the next town over. Its white sand beach rose into low dunes, here and there a small shack poked a shingled roof above the beach grass. The sea smelled of summer, salty and fertile. Sunlight penetrated its depth, reflecting off the bottom sand and glittering on the surface. I wished Ria were with us, making me laugh, neutralizing the tension that was always there between my father and me.

I guessed we were going to fish off Billingsgate Island where the incoming tide rushes past, and sure enough there sat High Hat idling in the channel. Hank stood on the pilot house with a pair of binoculars looking west and waving us over. I brought the skiff alongside as Hank shouted, "I found 'em, right where they were before. Frank, you stay south, I'll take north and we'll drive 'em toward the beach, make it easy. Easy money boys. Let's go!"

As he pulled away I realized my father hadn't brought any fishing gear and opened my mouth to remind him. At the same time I saw with horror what Hank was talking about. A pair of shiny black fins broke the surface of the water about fifty feet from the bow of High Hat, then disappeared. The tip of another dashed through the water scribing a long half-circle. The sun-flecked water heaved slightly with movement. We weren't going after bluefish at all, but the small whale they call a Blackfish, actually a Pilot Whale. Large schools migrate into the Bay every summer to calve and feed. Ten to twenty feet long with shiny black skin, they have a distinctive dorsal fin and the unfortunate trait of being easily duped into schooling and stranding. I knew what was coming. My father and his friends wanted the blackfish not for meat, but for the ball of oil which each fish has in the front of its head. A company in New Bedford paid good money for this oil. The refined product was sold to watchmakers and other manufacturers of precision instruments because the oil did not congeal at low temperatures.

With dread I turned the boat toward the Eastham shore as my father said, "Now, keep your distance from High Hat, about a hundred feet, OK? I'll watch the water and direct you. If we see one heading off, we'll go around and herd it back toward the others."

I wanted no part of this scheme. I hung my head, saying nothing. I could feel him staring at me, waiting for a response. For several seconds I sat frozen, one hand on the tiller, but I knew there was nothing I could do. He couldn't operate this boat, and I had never disobeyed him. I started cruising back and forth as he directed, slowly making our way toward shore, the blackfish between us and High Hat. They were around fifty fish, the young ones sounding but staying with the pod. For a couple of hours we stayed close on either side of them, herding them like a flock of sleek black sheep until the water became so shallow they began to dart back and forth, searching for depth. But we were always there, hounding them, engines and hulls forcing them ever shoreward. Soon the water was too shallow for High Hat to come any closer to shore, and Hank shouted to me to press them toward Boat Meadow, an inlet with a narrow strip of sand at its entrance, and it was here that many of the blackfish found themselves stranded as I zigzagged back and forth along the shore while everyone shouted directions at me.

I knew once the blackfish were beached in the shallows it was the end for them. I desperately tried to think of a way to stop what was happening, the horror I was participating in, even as I turned and turned again until the last whale was lying in the sand with the others, all thrashing and pounding their massive tails onto the sand.

I fought back tears as my father leapt overboard and joined Hank and Allen who were climbing around on the giant, heaving bodies as they gasped for breath in the lowering tide. Hank pulled a large knife from a sheath tied to his leg and plunged it into the side of one of the fish. Allen picked up a pole with a blade attached to it and did the same, thrusting and jabbing as the blood spurted from the black hides, turning the beach red and billowing out into the water. My father did the same with his good arm, with a large knife I'd never seen before. Somehow I hadn't seen it on the trip out. They made their way down the beach, attacking the great beasts one by one, the heart-rending moans and cries and thunderous pounding of tails on sand drove me to bury my face in my arms and sob, not caring who saw. It took just over an hour for them to run their knives through fifty whales, but the animals' pitiful cries and tail slapping went on for much longer, even through the next phase. I sat with my fingers thrust painfully into my ears, my head between my knees. I wanted to murder my father, the murderer.

Then the harvest began. Hank and Allen started to cut the melon-sized orb of oil from the head of each animal. While Allen pulled back the flesh with a grappling hook Hank sawed carefully into the head, prised out the valuable organ and handed it to my father, who beckoned to me. I shook my head, the first act of open defiance in my life. He stared at me for a long moment, then, cradling the ball in his arm, trudged past me through the shallows over to High Hat and laid it carefully on the transom. Hank and Allen meanwhile shot me twin looks of disgust, Hank pulling on his rum bottle with a greasy, dripping red hand.

One by one they cut the booty from the heads of the blackfish. It was afternoon by the time they were done, the tide past low and already rising again. A tarp on the deck of High Hat covered the giant oozing pile. Hank and Allen stood in the shallows and shared sandwiches with my father, the three of them laughing and calculating how much they'd made for a half-day's work. My father glanced over a couple of times, and even offered me something to eat. I glared at him with hatred. The stench of blood and guts coming off them and the abomination on the beach made me gag. When they were finished with their picnic Hank and Allen headed over to High Hat, and my father waded toward me. Together we pushed the skiff over the flats into deeper water, climbed on board and started the ride home. We didn't say a single word to each other for the entire trip. I was seething with anger, tormented by the hideous sight of the slaughter of those elegant doomed creatures. My heart pounded almost out of my chest. I couldn't understand why my father had forced me out on that boat. He had other friends who would have been willing. Probably they didn't want to share the bounty with a fourth person. Maybe he wanted to give me some manly experience which would shape my future. Whatever his reason, he made a grave error. I wanted nothing more to do with him. When finally he pulled the big Ford into our driveway and killed the engine I turned to him and spat, "I never want to see you again." I jumped out and ran down to the shore, tears cooling on my face, the awful smell still clinging to my clothes, the obscenity of the day replaying over and over in my brain.

I meant what I said. I would never go home again. As I stumbled down the shore my only clear thought was to go to Casco. Stay there for a few days while I figured out what I was doing. I was in a crazy rage, but my decision, no matter how abrupt, was solid.

I thought of trying to find Ria as I passed the Camp Quanset bluff, but quickly ruled it out. I didn't want her to see me as I was, red-eyed and stinking. I decided to go straight to Casco's and then see if she showed up at Paw Wah channel later that evening. I ran over the rocks, splashed through the low tide and across the channel. It wasn't until I came to the bottom of the hill where Casco's wigwam sat that I stopped for breath. I scrubbed my hands with sand, then crossed the little strip of beach to rinse them, the image of my father's blood-covered hands still fresh in my mind. I scrubbed them over and over, trying to wash off the sight, the guilt of my participation. At some point I stopped and looked out at the Bay. There were no campers out on the water, so it was fairly quiet, only the put-put of an outboard in the late afternoon heat. As I swept my eyes over the water from one end to the other it soothed me a little, my heartbeat slowed, and I stood up. I took off my boots and started up the path to Casco's, wondering what I'd do if he didn't want me to stay with him. I didn't know any one else who wouldn't turn me over to my parents.

When I got near the wigwam, I gave my usual signal, the whistling song of a field sparrow, something I'd worked long hours perfecting. I got no response so I poked my head inside. The place was empty. Casco was probably up in his corn patch fiddling with the plants. I started up the path, whistling again, and had gone only a few yards when I tripped over something which sent me sprawling into the bushes. My fall barely made a sound in the dense foliage. Cursing my clumsiness I rolled over to get up and immediately let out a scream. There, lying beside me was Casco, his nose bleeding a line down his cheek, his eyes open and staring. I scrambled to my feet and backed away, not wanting to believe what I'd seen. Panting with shock, I backed all the way to the wigwam and leaned against it, my heart pounding so hard I thought my chest would explode. "No! No! No!" I shouted, sliding to the ground. I took several shallow, stuttering breaths, then slowly crawled over to where Casco lay and parted the bushes.

It was his foot I'd tripped over. Thrust out to the side at an unnatural angle, his leg lay perpendicular to the rest of his body, which was on its side, one arm behind his back and the other in front, a hand clutching his throat. I bent over him, looking for the rise and fall of his chest. I put my hand there, to feel for a heartbeat. His body was completely still. I rolled him slightly to check for any signs of injury, dislodging his hand. It flopped to the ground with a thud. I rose to my knees, took his pale, cold face in my hands and turned it from side to side, willing him to wake up. That's when I noticed a bruise on the back of his head that extended from the hairline above his ear. I felt the swell under his thick hair. Something had knocked him out. Panicked, I stood up, looking around for a fallen branch, a tripped-over rock, something to explain what had happened. There were no branches, nor rocks, nothing except scraggy, waist-high bushes and a few healthy saplings. A woodpecker hammered out a staccato note. A fat fly dipped in to investigate. All was eerily normal in the woods. I looked back at my friend. He stared up into the trees, into nothing.

The fly buzzed around my head and neck, drawn by the scent of blackfish oil. I swatted it away, crawled into the bushes and threw up. Then I started to sob again, my heaving sobs turning into long wails which silenced the birds and must have been heard as far away as Camp Mariner. I didn't care. I was done, finished. I wanted to die too, to lie down in the woods beside Casco and breathe my last. I don't know how long I lay there, the trauma of the day having sent me into a trance. I was in shock. When at last I came to it was with a jolt of anger more powerful than I'd ever felt before.

I jumped up and began to search the bushes around the wigwam, ran up to the corn patches and looked for a sign of something amiss. The stalks swayed peacefully in the breeze. A crow perching in the leaves of one screeched at me and I ran full-tilt at it, flailing my arms and yelling. I yanked the cornstalk out of the ground and swung it around my head, hitting the other stalks and felling a few. Somehow the act calmed me and I suddenly felt tired, so tired I closed my eyes for a minute, swaying slightly with the cornstalk still in my hand. I walked back to Casco's wigwam and ducked inside, falling onto one of the burlap bags which was still fragrant with the grass he'd stuffed it with for yesterday's luncheon. I struggled to understand what had happened to my friend. Heart attack? Some fatal condition he hadn't mentioned? What, or who had given him such a blow to the head? Was there a more sinister reason for his leaving Virginia and was he really in hiding out here, not from civilization in general but from something far more specific? I began to go through his things looking for a clue, anything to give me an explanation. Crawling around the room I carefully picked up everything he owned. His possessions triggered a fresh wave of sorrow. The misshapen baskets, the shell spoons, the little cloth bags turned inside out revealed only the wrinkled herbs he'd likely gathered that morning. Their fragrance filled the room, smelling of him. I found a little stack of quahog shells which had been carefully polished and carved with designs. His shoes, gnarled and coming apart, were wrapped carefully in the dark wool shirt he wore only in the dead of winter. I fished in the pockets and brought up a tiny photograph of a white-haired woman, her dark face woven with wrinkles. That was all. I looked around for the wampum belt but it wasn't there.

I searched a while longer, feeling between the layers of the canvas roof until it started to get dark, then I lay down on the burlap bag and fell asleep.

I slept on and off through the night and the next day, curled into a ball with my back against the canvas, Casco's wool shirt draped around my shoulders. I shivered even though it was warm, waking up to relive the events of the day, then passing back into sleep. Ria came briefly to mind several times, but I couldn't rouse myself to go down to the channel to see if she was there even though I knew it was the last day of camp. I didn't leave that spot the next night, either. I thought I might as well lie there until I died and joined Casco wherever he might be.

In the end hunger forced me to get up. It was just before dawn, the sweet smell of the forest drifting in through the open door. I knew what I had to do. After I stuffed the rest of Cascos blueberries into my mouth and swallowed mindlessly I left the wigwam, heading east through the woods. I could see the sun breaking over the outer beach, the red streaks of sunrise in a pattern I knew meant rain. The birds were quiet. Done with mating for the year, territories already long established, they slept in. I was barefoot, my boots lay outside the wigwam where I'd dropped them. Stealthily, I made my way to the cabins at Camp Mariner. There was a toolshed not far from the last cabin. Inside were an assortment of rakes, a rusty lawnmower and three shovels. I took one.

I will never be able to accurately explain why, instead of going into town and bringing back the police or some authority to see to the body of Casco and investigate his death, I buried Casco out there on the point. It would have saved me countless hours of worry and maybe I would have found out the reason for his death much sooner. But I didn't. Maybe it was my innocence which allowed me to decide that if Casco wanted to live out his life here in secret, away from those very organizations which would delve into his life and bury him in a public, anonymous cemetery, then he should be buried here, too. Anyway, I was simply not in my right mind.

Long ago, as a boy of no more than ten or so, I read about the burial rites of the Narragansett, the way they laid the body to rest and the things they put into the grave. Though Casco was a Wampanoag, I felt sure that this other New England tribe's ritual would suffice as a final salute. I would have preferred to lay Casco to rest up in his corn patch, but I knew it was impossible because I didn't have the physical strength to drag his body more than a few yards. After I cleared the bushes from an area closeby, I dug a hole about four feet deep and the same length and width. I gathered leaves and small branches and lined the bottom of the grave. I looked over at my friend, his leg askew and the blood on his face crawling with flies. Forcing a steely determination on myself I ducked into the wigwam where I scooped up some of the ashes from the firepit and smeared them over my face. I found the quahog shells he'd carved and put them into one of his little herb sacks. I took two of the drying corn husks and his shoes and returned to where Casco's body lay. Then I took a deep breath and grabbed his legs, bending them into his torso. It took considerable effort, as rigor mortis was still in the process of passing, something I knew nothing about at the time. His arms, normally so robust and muscular, now lay inert and useless at freakish angles from his body. I folded them one by one onto his chest.

For a long while I sat panting and sweating beside him, charcoal running in streaks down my face, remembering everything I could about him, reliving the times we'd fished, followed the old Indian paths through the forest and fields, or simply sat by his fire, talking. I ran my hands over my face again and again, wiping away tears and smearing the ashes of grief. I wanted to blacken my face, blacken my very existence into nothingness and go with Casco, wherever he was. Finally, with a glance skyward I swung his body around so his head would be in the south-facing end of the grave, then took a deep breath and rolled him into the hole. He landed well, legs still bent fetus-like into his belly. I rearranged his arms in the same manner and made sure his head was facing east, then I laid his belongings next to him and sat back. That's when I noticed the leather thong which had held the peace medal around Casco's neck lying beside me. I picked it up and examined it. It had been severed cleanly by something sharp. I looked all through the bushes, scrambling my hands along the thorny ground and breaking branches to get a better look. The medal was nowhere to be found. But I couldn't think about it except to add it as another question to the mystery of his death.

I covered Casco's body from his feet to his head with dirt, handful by handful. I didn't know any prayers other than Christian ones, and I refused to utter a single syllable of them. Instead I gave my sparrow whistle through my quivering lips, over and over until I couldn't anymore. "Goodbye, Casco," I said. "I hope you meet your ancestors wherever they may be." I wanted to tell him I loved him, but I didn't know how.

I filled in the grave and walked down to the channel, where I collapsed in the grass and watched the hermit crabs scampering in and out of their holes. My mind was blank. It began to rain.

Chapter 6

That was the start of the longest year of my life. It was also the most beautiful, the loneliest, coldest, the busiest when gathering food and firewood, and the laziest, lying around in the weak winter sun, trying only to stay warm. It was a year of self-analysis, reflection and a profound self-pity that crept into the wigwam at night, snuggled into bed with me and licked my mental wounds until they bled again.

At first all I could think of was food. As weeks, then months passed I began to understand Casco's preoccupation with it. I confess the night after I buried Casco I walked to Bessom's and broke into the back room. It wasn't difficult, as the door was left unlocked. I wolfed down half a loaf of bread while I looked around, then took a can of pork and beans and ran. It wasn't until I got back to the woods that I remembered I needed a can opener. I went back three nights in a row and got one, along with more canned food and a pocket knife. On the fourth night I spotted Mr. Bessom sitting out back, puffing a cigarette in the dark. I ducked behind a tree and never went back.

Then I started to get practical. It was, after all, late summer, and I knew I'd need food for the long winter if indeed I was to live there, which I had resolved to do, having no alternative. I would not go home. I checked Casco's cache of dried corn and berries. It didn't look like enough. In a hollowed-out sandy hillock were fifty-two ears of corn bundled in marsh grass, dried or drying. I found the cranberries we'd picked, dried and layered carefully in oak leaves, and a tightly woven basket of dried blueberries and beach plums. Several small lopsided clay jars contained unidentifiable powdered foods. Two kinds of roots were simply tucked into the sand alongside the corn. I knew one of Casco's important foodstuffs was the crushed meat of acorns. He'd taken me the year before to gather them from under a large oak near Arey's Pond. They wouldn't be ready until late September. Black walnuts were another treat he loved. I'd helped him stomp on the husks and clean the meat in the sea, but I didn't know where the tree was. I made a mental note to look for it.

But I did know where the shellfish were, and I had Casco's boat. I began a series of nightly fishing trips, coming home late and gorging myself on flounder and rockfish. I simply skewered them whole on a locust stick and roasted them over the fire.

I tried to smoke some bluefish, thinking ahead. After painstakingly constructing a cage of sticks to suspend over the smoke, I filled it with hunks of fish and set it over a fire of leaves and green twigs and almost asphyxiated myself in the process. I kept the arrangement going for a couple of hours but all that happened was the wigwam filled with acrid smoke and the cage fell apart. The soot and smell lasted for the next six weeks. I tried salting it, too, boiling it in seawater, then laying it on the rocks to dry, but that was an even bigger failure. All I got was a nice bloom of maggots.

Nobody ate them in those days, so mussels were plentiful. The glistening black clusters clung to rocks all along the shore. They were also easy to get at night. I steamed them open in the black pot. I went apple picking along Barley Neck Road and pulled more than a few turnips from the fields on either side. I wrapped them in marsh grass and shoved them into the sand. In true Casco style I concocted stews from these few ingredients, tossing in a handful of poor man's pepper and chopped sea lettuce for taste. I started to be happier after a few meals like that, and day by day I became more optimistic about being able to stay alive in the woods. I told myself I wouldn't touch the corn until it got too cold to go fishing. I would try to eat as much bluefish as I could for the oil my body would need later on. (More precious info gleaned from Casco.)

I cut down the six hemp plants. I wasted two of them figuring out how to make twine but got the hang of it after a while, rolling and twisting the fibers together on my thigh while holding the end between my toes. The branches on the roof needed to be secured, something Casco worried about doing before the winter winds. I finally succeeded in making a three foot length of thin, lumpy rope, then went outside and used up my five hours' work in two minutes. That night I snuck over to the horse pen at the Narrows and lifted a coil of rope from the fence.

I often worried about my parents searching for me. I was afraid I'd wake up one morning to find a police officer staring down at me and

I'd be sent off to some youth home for teenage rail-riders and other delinquents. I had no idea what to expect. One night I went back to Bessom's, creeping along the road in the dark, the fresh chill of fall nipping at my ears and foreshadowing worse weather in store. I wanted to check for any indication of a search for me, a notice, a -God forbid- poster. Something in the paper. In our town of roughly two and a half thousand I doubted that there were many who hadn't heard of my disappearance by then. On the other hand, knowing my parents, I suspected them of taking me at my word, of thinking I was old enough to be on my own if it's what I wanted. I could picture my mother, Bible open in her lap, trying to find words of justification for letting me go. And my father, what would he be thinking? Despite his detached, mechanical dealings with me, there were glimpses of affection there, the way he kept up with my fishing skills and acknowledged them, the fact that he'd found a way to send me to camp, even though I would've probably progressed much further in life if he'd simply talked and listened to me instead. Was he suffering now, regretting the trip out on the bay and what he'd forced me to do, or did he simply move on, find a way to live without me?

I found nothing at Bessom's. But here and there I did see, in the weeks after I disappeared, a man walking the shore at odd times of the day, then climbing the bluff into the woods for a while, then reappearing, calling out something I couldn't make out. I saw Lonnie Chase one day rowing up into Paw Wah Pond. I'd never seen him out this far. He fished around the rivers and in the marsh. I climbed a tree and watched. He walked the shore for fifty yards in either direction then sat on the stern of his boat and chewed tobacco for another hour. If they were looking for me they weren't making much of an effort. After a month or so I stopped worrying. I didn't see my father searching, ever. That part bothered me more than I care to admit.

Gradually my life became a routine: Gather firewood, get water, hunt for berries, grapes, acorns, anything under cover of the forest. In the evening go fishing, either by wading into the marsh for clams and mussels or by boat to drop a line and hope. It depended on the tide. Cook something. Sleep. The weeks passed and the leaves turned color, dropped off, piled into skirts around the tree trunks and blew into drifts which hid a thousand burrowed mice and the gathered berries of other small animals. The geese left, as did many of the birds. I ached to be one of them, to stretch out my arms and leap into the sky, leaving the bloodthirsty world of humans behind.

As it got colder, the fishermen dropped scallop drags and made lazy crisscrosses in front of Camp Quanset, stopping now and then to sort. I saw my father a few times, dragging the bottom with Allan Reese at the helm. The first time my stomach did a little flip and after that I just noted his presence, but felt nothing. I heard shotguns at the duck blinds over on Sampson's and Hog Islands. In those days the hunters would dig a big hole about the size of the one I made for Casco. They were back from the water a ways so when the tide came in they wouldn't fill. The soft marsh mud was fairly easy to dig. They'd pile it around the edge to lean on while taking aim. Once I found one of their decoys and threw it on the fire. It lasted all night. Knowing the prices some of them fetch these days, I might easily have burned up several thousand dollars. I slept in Casco's wool shirt and stuck my feet into a burlap bag, then rolled myself up in the green blanket. Those yellow socks came to mind often as it got colder and the wind began to howl through trees, battering the sides of the wigwam. I learned to wake up instinctively when the fire needed stoking and so was able to keep things fairly warm. One night I was out by the channel digging razor clams and cut my boot on a piece of broken bottle. Freezing water percolated up through my toes, covering my foot within seconds. I sloshed home, my foot numb and my hands lifeless, clutching half a dozen clams. After I built up the fire and thawed myself, I examined the boot. There was an inch-long gash under the toe. The thick rubber was cleanly severed, but it was a disaster as far as going out in the water to get food.

I spent a few despondent days by the fire, not moving. I considered going to my parents and asking for a new pair of boots. I even thought about stealing my fathers boots from inside the back door at night. I walked over to the now-deserted Camp Mariner and looked at the boat house. The windows were boarded up, and the doors had a two-by-four nailed across them. I tried the camp itself but all the buildings were secure except the one with smoke coming from the chimney. Devastated, miserable, I walked back. That one-inch tear had effectively eliminated my ability to get my hands on any of the abundant protein all around me. I gave up hope of being able to eat much except turnips and corn until spring. But then, two small things happened. First, as was my habit, I passed Casco's grave to say hello and there, lying exactly in the center of the cleared area, was a dead bobwhite. I picked it up. It was still warm. I peered into the trees, listening for a fox or some other predator I might have frightened in mid-hunt, but all was quiet. I looked back down at the poor bird, and suddenly it came to me that it was Casco, watching over me. I wasn't ordinarily prone to this kind of supernatural thinking, but I suppose in desperation all kinds of magical thoughts descend. Cradling the little bird in the crook of my arm I looked down to where Casco's head was buried and, choking up, uttered, "Thanks." It was the first word I'd spoken aloud in three months.

I prepared the bird as I had watched my mother do with countless chickens, but with a far greater mess. There were feathers everywhere, down drifting in the smoke from the fire. As I stoked it a pine branch snapped suddenly to life. A small flare, a glisten of oozing pitch. As I stared at the pitch, a smile slowly cracked my stony face and my spirits lifted. I had the solution to my boot problem. I put the bird into the pot and went to work. A waterproof, flexible goop that was certainly worth a try, the pitch was so near to hand I'm surprised it hadn't occurred to me before. I grabbed the branch from the fire and held the melting pitch near the flames, letting it soften even more. When it was ready I scraped it off with my knife and smeared it onto the bottom of my boot, spreadingit over the cut. I did this several times. Then, using a piece of quahog shell, I did the same to the inside and let the whole thing dry, but not before I lined both boots with the down from the bobwhite. It worked beautifully. I still have those boots, kept as a reminder of the smooth dark hides of the murdered blackfish, my time in the woods afterwards, and Casco's final gift to me.

When the first snow fell one night I pulled them on and walked out to the point. The tide was high, the water undulating sluggishly along the shore. It was so quiet I could hear the fat flakes whisper as they hit the ground and I looked up to watch them materialize out of the blackness. I stood there with my eyes closed, letting them gather on my lips, the hollows around my nose, my eyelids. As they mounded up around my feet I imagined I was in heaven on a tendril of cloud in limitless space, untethered to earth, reborn as air.

We had a lot more snow that winter, often accompanied by a steady, biting wind from the north east. I didn't have the clothes to withstand the worst of it and spent many days inside by the fire, perfectly happy but wishing I had some books, or a drawing pad like Ria's to pass the time. I tried my hand at basket weaving but failed completely. I spent two days carving designs into the bark of the saplings which held up the roof. I tried to tell Casco's story in stick figures and bogus hieroglyphics, but got bogged down when it came to illustrating the Depression. I wanted to draw it as a great Illumination, with multiple sun rays that morphed into railroad tracks, tracks that widened as they descended the poles, as though arriving in the wigwam. But they looked to me like prison bars, so I pulled the bark away, erasing them.

For long stretches of time I simply lay in the wigwam. I suppose I was depressed, barely able to perform even the most mundane functions like stoking the fire or going outside for a pee. I felt profoundly sorry for myself and ashamed to be feeling it, which exacerbated my sorrow, an unending cycle with no reprieve. I was deeply angry at my parents. I often sat up abruptly, awakened from some reverie by insistent images of the murdered blackfish or my mother's stern, disapproving face. I never wanted to see them again, and yet I wanted them to come and find me, to apologize and beg me to come home.

Thoughts of Ria haunted me. I would often sit in our spot trying to ignore the bitterly cold wind, reliving every moment I spent with her. I went to each place we visited together, trudging along on the frozen sand, pretending it was warm again and that she was beside me. I told myself to forget her, knowing that, since her parents sent her someplace new every year I had only a slim chance of seeing her again come summer. But I couldn't help myself. All I had of her was the leather thong from the Peace Medal, which I wore around my neck.

On windless days I spent much of my time outdoors following the tracks of small animals, observing their behavior and keeping an eye on the Bay. It was quiet. January is not a good fishing month because of the bitter winds which sweep across the freezing water. I'd wake up, stoke the fire and go outside. There were always fresh tracks in the snow, and I became adept at identifying the animal or bird, often following their trails for hours. I knew where all the squirrel nests were, and where much of their food was hidden. They scolded me at first, passing the info of my whereabouts on to the others as I made my way around. But after a while they got used to my roaming. I had read that wood mice keep mostly to their nests in winter, breeding or lying around sluggishly, eating from a cache of seed stashed earlier in the season. But I saw many a track running lightly over the fluff of new snowfall, crisscrossing each other in a neighborly social network. The family of crows that raided Casco's corn patch was still living up there in a big nest wedged into the crotch of a white pine. One day I watched them collecting mussels together, dodging wavelets as they ripped the clusters apart, then dropped them from the air, smashing on the rocks to get to the meat. The crows also used to steal from the ducks, waiting for them to chase small fish into the shallows, then swooping down and snatching them away before the ducks arrived.

The dunes of the outer beach were snow-covered, the few fishing and hunting camps out there shut down for the season. A pressing urge to go out and inspect the camps finally set me on my way one sunny day. I walked west around Arey's Pond to the Chatham Road, then followed it north to Monument Road with its Civil War statue, staying out of sight for most of the way. Because of the snow there were very few vehicles on the road, neither cars nor wagons, but I was still cautious. I passed behind Lonnie's and Meeting House Ponds and headed east to Pochet Neck. The ocean was straight ahead over the hill. I slid down the dune to the snow-covered beach, not another soul in sight, nor the track of any animal. The long stretch of sand, always soft and erratic in shape, had been blown into yet another profile, blinding white peaks of meringue framed by the uniform gray of sky and sea.

There was a duck hunting camp close by, down the beach. In the summer an enterprising Orleanser had guests flown in by seaplane for the sport. It was a rather grand place for a dune shack, with a screened-in porch and a garage. I untied the string which held the latch in place and entered. The windows were boarded over so it was dusky inside, I could barely see to find and light a kerosene lantern. A large, comfortable room with oak floors and a big stone fireplace opened into a long narrow kitchen painted uniformly Battleship gray. I set the lantern down and opened the cupboards one by one. There the most exciting thing I found was a stack of tinned sardines. I took them all, plus a precious can of Borden's condensed milk. Chowder! There was no other food in the large kitchen. I took a spoon, a fork, a fillet knife and a small frying pan, then made my way to the sleeping quarters. The closet was tightly packed with folds of wool blankets, I pulled one out. I almost took two, thinking I could make one into a coat but after an extended search for a needle and thread I gave up on that idea. With my loot bundled up in the blanket I lay on the bed for a while, thinking it might be a luxurious treat but I felt strangely indifferent to its softness. Likewise, when I went back to the garage to check out the tool supply I found that of all the equipment hung neatly on pegs or piled onto shelves. The only thing I took was a book for identifying birds. I didn't even need it, but I thought it would keep me in good company.

When I stepped outside, I saw that the sky was unusually dark. It looked like it was about to descend on us all at once. The ocean was perfectly still, a vast life form holding its breath in suspense. I knew what was coming, and I began to run back the same way I came, circling back around every salt water pond leeching into the bay, no matter that Paw Wah Point was close as the crow flies. I considered making my way across the frozen marsh, but I knew it was a bad idea. Every fisherman knew the dangers of misstepping in mud and water. It could easily fill your boots, anchoring you there for the tide to cover.

About a mile into my trek, I could see only a few feet in front of me. The snow fell silently in fat dollops, building up swiftly in my path. I trudged across Pochet Neck to Barley Neck Road, and by then, I knew I'd have to find shelter. At that point I was in the back pasture of Bailey's farm. They kept about a hundred head of cattle out there and sold the milk I had poured over my oatmeal every morning for most of my life. It was their turnips I'd been stealing. I vaguely knew the son, Martin, who was only a few years older than I. He went out of his way once to give me a lift in the family horse and buggy when I was walking home from school in the rain. I knew they'd call my parents if I showed up at their door, but the milking barn was warm and open, and it was there I spent the night. I crawled into a corner and dozed until I heard the first rooster, picked up my loot-filled blanket and left, plowing my way through the thigh-high snowfall. I'm sure someone saw my tracks and I worried about it all the way home. Near Arey's Pond I took a shortcut across the low-tide River, giddy with relief and thinking only of sardines, lovely sardines.

By the time spring unfurled itself on the bay I was quite used to living on my own. Food and warmth were no longer a worry but an occupation that kept me sane. By the end of March, I had tilled the soil in the corn patches, the mounds widened slightly to accommodate pole beans. They could climb onto the cornstalks, the way the Indians taught the settlers. I roamed freely over the area, assuming I'd crossed a line and achieved independence, that no one was interested any longer in finding me and taking me home. I took long walks to Nauset Beach and down the Chatham Road in broad daylight, ducking into the bushes if I heard a vehicle approaching. When the moon was full, I made several trips to the horse corral by the Narrows to collect manure for my garden. It was there I picked up a discarded Provincetown Advocate, the local paper from the tip of the Cape. I read all six pages with desperate interest, although it didn't contain much. The town hall was being washed in anticipation of the tourist season. The senior class of Provincetown High School was about to take a five-day trip to Washington, D.C. Page five had a large photo of Clark Gable embracing Vivian Leigh in an ad for 'Gone With the Wind' currently playing at the Orleans Theatre. Under it were several ads for local enterprises tying their services to the event. Heath's Pharmacy wanted us to "Top off 'Gone With the Wind' with a Scarlett O'Hara Sundae." The Ship Ahoy bar came up with "When you've 'Gone With the Wind,' let it blow you in for excellent food!" It was obviously a big event. I had no idea what all the hoopla was about, but the picture spoke to me, so It tore it out, adding it to those I'd torn from the bird book to decorate the wigwam.

Although I didn't know it at the time, reading the newspaper was a whisper of civilization that would eventually draw me toward the companionship of my fellow humans. I wasn't fully committed to living in the woods for the rest of my life, but I was comfortable enough after the long winter to not have considered anything else. I was looking forward to growing corn and beans, to fishing in the sun, to my birds and animal friends coming to life again. I clung to the hope of seeing Ria, that she would return to Camp Quanset. I was hoping she might convince her parents of her love for Pleasant Bay, if only to see me again. I worried that at fifteen she was too old for camp and she'd moved on to other more cosmopolitan pursuits.

In May I planted and in June I started working on the wigwam, repairing the damage from ice and wind, airing it by removing a couple of canvas bags to create a cross breeze. I transplanted an oak sapling on Casco's grave. I cleaned out the store of food and, with a Blue Jay egg I found on the ground, I made the last of the corn and acorns into jonnycakes with cranberries. I had no way to know when exactly July first would occur, so late in June I began to spend my evenings and into the night down at Paw Wah channel, hoping Ria would appear. After a month I gave up. If she came to the Cape and wanted to find me she, would've been there, or would have walked up the hill to find Casco. I would never see her again. At that point I sank into an unshakable melancholy I thought would undo me. I sat for days in the wigwam, sweating and stinking, lying there staring at Clark Gable and Vivian Leigh embracing among the birds. At one point, disgusted with myself, I ripped the picture down along with the others and burned them. I had decorated the wigwam in anticipation of her return as much as to please myself. Her return was what had seen me through the long, grueling winter, the steady glow of hope for some kind of happiness.

I passed the rest of the summer mechanically gathering food and storing it. I didn't feel the sun on my back or hear the crazy chatter of the mockingbird. The glitter of the moon on the water as I fished alone in the Narrows only made me sad. I'd wake up each morning and try to savor those first blank moments of awareness before my sorrow, waiting there beside the bed, invaded me for another day. I took chances coming out in the daytime to bathe in Pilgrim Lake or to walk to Bessom's store. I doubtless wanted to be caught, now that I faced another winter alone in the woods. It occurred to me to jump on the train as Casco had done, but I was nowhere near old enough. Besides, I had virtually no knowledge of the world outside the bay. I was stuck there. In September I began to dry the corn and talk to myself out loud. I commented on every activity, telling myself how capable I was, how compelling outdoor life was, how true a life I was living, a real-life native, close to the creatures I loved on the land I was born to.

I had almost convinced myself of this when, one day in October, I was outside admiring the new carpet of orange and yellow leaves and heard footsteps crunching through them. I was looking for dead branches to break into firewood. I watched as two men in overcoats tromped through the underbrush smoking cigarettes and talking in low voices. I couldn't make out what they were saying. They went nowhere near the wigwam but after that I worried every time I left it. Three days later I saw a man walk along the shore and round the point. When he came back the same way he stopped and spent a long time looking out toward Sampson's Island, smoking and flicking the butts into the shallows. A week later, around my birthday, I was on my way to pick grapes near the River and saw, fluttering in the breeze, a strip of white cloth tied to a wooden stake which had been driven into the dirt at the edge of the shore. I made my way over to it. W. Askew 1547 was written in thick black letters down the stake's length.

Someone had bought a piece of land there in my woods.

For the next month I lived in anticipation of being discovered. Now that I'd resigned myself to the life of a hermit who talks to himself, I wanted to get on with it. I was ready for winter. Then one morning I heard two men shouting and the rhythmic whine of a crosscut saw and I knew it was over.

Chapter 7

For some reason the ad for the "Ship Ahoy" Restaurant stuck in my mind all that summer. 'When you've Gone with the Wind, we're here,' it said. I couldn't shake it. It was a poem that spoke to me. I often found myself singing a little ditty with those words at the start, adding and rhyming and making up whole stanzas I can no longer remember. The point is there must have been some sixth sense at work because the Ship Ahoy is where I ended up after I walked into town. I went straight there. I knew it had a reputation as a place where respectable people did not go, but that was another draw. My parents would never think to set foot in a place like that. I had taken only two things from the wigwam, just Casco's shirt and one of his baskets. I buried everything else with all the food in the cache. It didn't amount to much. I packed the cooking pot with most of it and pushed it into the sand. I left the wigwam standing. I wouldn't be able to live there anymore, not if someone were living nearby.

An L-shaped bar took up one end of the restaurant. Out front stood a single gas pump and up a rickety staircase built into the corner of two ells was a small room which was mine for a portion of my salary. For twenty dollars a week I washed dishes, pumped gas, chopped onions, cleaned floors, lugged cases of food and drink and went to the dump. I loved it. My employer, Mister Ray Bruce, was an affable man who also lived alone upstairs in a suite of rooms in one of the ells. Over six feet tall, with a Lucky Strike smoldering perpetually between his fingers, he was seldom clean-shaven and his eyes, already a dark brown, were shaded further by two shaggy black brows. But there was nothing thuggish about him. He was about the most gentle, funny, and gregarious people I've ever met. He took me in without hesitation. As I stood there in the doorway of the empty bar in my boots and MARINER t-shirt, he waved his hand at a barstool. I sat.

"You want a glass of water? You look like you walked all the way from Provincetown." Without an answer from me he scooped up a glassful of ice, filled it with water and set it in front of me. I'm sure I looked scraggy and rough, though he was polite enough not to mention it. I hadn't had a haircut or a real bath in over a year, my clothes were filthy, the boots scratched and sunbleached, their toes cracked and repaired with more pitch.

"You a fugitive?" he said, pointing to my shirt. I looked down and covered up the word with my hand.

"No, ah, well, it's the only one I have actually. That is, at the present time. I hope to..." I couldn't finish. I shook my head. I was so unused to talking to another person, I simply clammed up.

"Need a place to stay?"

I was stunned by his intuitiveness. I sat staring vacantly at him, but I didn't want to appear more simpleminded than I already had and croaked out a "Yes, I do," then took a sip of water and blurted out, "and a job."

"Hm. What kind of skills you got?"

Two days later, I was set with a bath, a haircut, a clean shirt and a pair of borrowed shoes and was happily working in the kitchen. I told Ray I was eighteen and out of school and let him gently poke around for other pieces of my story. At first I thought to pretend I was from somewhere else, but I should have known someone would identify me. Orleans was, still is, a small town, my face part of the landscape like any other's. I was wary enough to stay in the back, but on my third day there, tossing bags of trash into the back of the Ford pickup and admiring its whitewall tires, suddenly Lonnie Chase appeared, leaning one arm along the window frame. Lonnie lived alone on one of the ponds that fed into the Bay and took care of the herring run nearby. Everyone calls it Lonnie's Pond. Casco and I used to pick grapes across from his shack until he spotted us one day and waded hip-deep into the water, chewing a cud of tobacco and glared at us until we departed.

"Well you been gone a while, Sparrow. Where you been? I even looked for you, once. Out on the bay. Your pop asked me to. You workin' here?"

"Yeah." I turned and went in.

Later that day, Ray appeared, leaning against the doorway of the kitchen as I made my way through a pile of codfish, cleaning and fileting them and cutting them into pieces for deep-frying. This was not one of my jobs, but the cook, Davey, was outside talking to a girl. She came to the back door and beckoned him. He handed me the knife and said, "Take over for a sec. Urgent business." He was grinning.

Ray stood for a while watching me. "This is good news," he said, raising his thick eyebrows enough that his eyes twinkled for a split second. "This is very good news. You know how to fix fish. Ah, listen, I don't want to poke my nose into your business, but as this is mine, I have to ask. Do your people know where you are?"

I looked up from the chopping block. "I don't know."

"Well, Lonnie just told me, and if I know him, it won't be long before they do."

"That's OK," I said.

But they never came. They never even called. A week went by, then two. By then I'd told Ray the whole story. The blackfish, the wigwam, the corn. Except the part about Casco. I told Ray I'd made the wigwam and knew how to get by out there like a native. He was impressed and I felt bad about the part that was a lie, but essentially it was the truth. What he kept from me is that he'd telephoned my parents. He had to, he told me later, what with child labor laws and all. President Roosevelt had recently signed the Fair Labor Standards Act, which limited many forms of child labor, though he wasn't sure if restaurant work fell into a category.

"What did they say?" I asked.

"Your father told me that as far as he knew, you were on your own. He didn't want to know anything else. He just put down the phone. Sorry, Theo."

By then I was sixteen, barely. I told Ray my real age.

"That'll do for me."

So I added cooking to my work at the Ship Ahoy, and Ray added another five dollars a week to my salary. I discovered I had a talent for it, and I liked Davey, who was as knowledgeable about food as he was about women, or so he boasted. Davey's father had been the cook before him but had dropped dead of a heart attack only the year before. Ray had hired Davey as swiftly as he did me. As the months went by, I heard a lot from Davey about cooking and women but it was the cooking that made me leap out of bed in the morning and stay in the kitchen until the bar closed at midnight. The restaurant served up basic man-food, meat and potatoes in various forms, canned vegetables on the side and for dessert a choice of pie and vanilla ice cream. Within two months I'd added Indian pudding, then clam chowder and corn bread, and together they made one of our most popular meals. Davey and I established a rhythm, a smooth dance between the stove, the fridge and the dishes.

Sometimes Ray would get Liza DuBois, the woman who made the pies, to help out on Saturdays if the crowd got bigger than usual. Davey loved Liza, a tough, stick-thin woman in her mid-forties who had been married to one of the guys operating the cable relay station. She'd lost her husband when he drove head-on into a truck on his way home from Hyannis one night. She'd never had the chance to have children, so although she teased Davey she mothered him too, drawing from him statements about his thoughts and feelings that I imagine were highly personal.

"I love her because she wants me to," I overheard him tell her one day when they were discussing a girl who'd just visited at the back door. Liza shook her head, looked over at me, and rolled her eyes. "Casa-nova," she said with a little sarcastic eyebrow-waggle. She knew somehow not to tease me, and I was thankful. I would probably have run away.

Orleans was a fairly typical East Coast small town then, and still is today, with a few modernizations. Main Street runs east from the harbor on Cape Cod Bay to the Atlantic Ocean at Nauset Beach, bisecting the peninsula. Route 6 runs south from Provincetown right through Orleans, then heads West all the way across the United States to Long Beach, California. The intersection of these two roads forms our town center and from there various business establishments fan and then peter out within a block or two. Town Cove tongues its way in from the Atlantic almost to the center of town, and from a little building perched on its shore America received the news from Europe for almost sixty years via an undersea telegraph cable connected to Brest, France. The operators were from the tiny French islands of Saint Pierre and Miquelon, located off the south coast of Newfoundland. To this day part of our population have French surnames, all descendants from that project. When I first moved into town there was a new movie theater with a proper marquee, a pharmacy with a soda fountain, a barber shop next door with its twirling red, white and blue pole, a hardware store, an A&P, a coffee shop, a train station, a post office and two banks. Down the street was Bill Higgins' Restaurant and Bowling Alley with its doughnut-making machine in the front window. Ray thought the doughnuts were wonderful, but I never bought them. As a child I had watched one day as Bill, a veteran tobacco chewer, tested the temperature of the oil by spitting into it.

In summer a policeman stood on a painted circle in the center and directed traffic. A small graveyard still takes up one of the four corners, The Knowles Block with its curbside corner entrance stood opposite. A Mobil station flew its red Pegasus logo on another, shaded by a row of majestic elms. On the fourth corner sat the Ship Ahoy.

The Ship Ahoy started out with an exclamation point tacked onto its name. The day he bought the place, Ray climbed up to the sign and painted it out, and that change turned out to be the only one necessary. The bar already had a reputation for decent food and lively nightlife. In the summer, Ray would pack the place playing records on an over-amplified phonograph or tune in the radio on weekends to whatever band was playing on the Lucky Strike Hit Parade. He would shove the chairs and tables to the walls and his customers would dance until midnight, the closing hour always strictly monitored by our local police sergeant. Now and then Ray would hire a little three-piece band from New Bedford or let Manny Amaro, a skinny Portuguese man who lived in one of the other rooms upstairs, play his accordion. I never saw Manny except at these concerts, and don't know where he ate or spent his time. Orleans's summer season lasted from Memorial Day to Labor Day and not a day beyond. The Ship Ahoy was a smooth operation, kept that way by the sober and even-handed management Ray brought to every aspect of the business. Drunken rowdiness was a normal part of life there, but all the regulars loved Ray and were so afraid of banishment that they kept a lid on most of it and even helped when the occasional tourist got out of hand. When Labor Day came around and they all left, an abnormal quiet descended on the town which took a few days to get used to.

We had regular deliveries of meat, potatoes and onions and huge number ten cans of vegetables from a supplier in Fall River whose driver came through on Thursdays. Our fish came from a variety of sources. Ray had an open door policy for all who came to the kitchen door with something they'd caught, if they could pass the fresh test. First a fish had to come in whole. Ray would grasp it in both hands and look into its eyes. He could tell almost to the hour when it had been caught, and didn't suffer any arguments to the contrary. Shellfish had to be alive. That was it.

The guys who delivered beer always sat for one, no matter how early in the day. They were a pair of semi-thuggish old timers from Rhode Island who had been bootleggers during prohibition and had wisely used their loot to set themselves up in legitimate business. They still referred to cases of booze as "boxfish," a tag left over from the days of snagging the goods from bays and sounds after they'd been dropped off. They brought news and stories from the various establishments along their route, days before anyone heard or read of it, and it was always delivered with their particular caustic slant. They were fond of Ray, maybe because he laughed at their hard-boiled jokes, and I'd often hear their guffaws in the evenings after the run to Provincetown which was infamous for its night life and always a font of new material. Both were unhappily married and were always on the lookout for some available female company.

"A man without a woman is like a neck without a pain," one of them would declare.

"There are only two ways to handle a woman, and nobody knows what they are!"

Their raunchy jokes deteriorated steadily beer by beer to a level of obscenity that inevitably got them ejected, or in an argument, or both.

Usually we had our gang of regulars, the guys who operated the French Cable Station coming in for soup, fishermen and laborers in after a day out in the cold, and the Huff boys, a pair of huge quahoggers who lived in a dilapidated shack up the road. They kept chickens and dogs in the house with them and raised pigs out back. They drank the cheapest beer and insisted the empties be left on the table, so they could keep count. To my knowledge neither one ever went out back or to the toilet. Another regular was Phinneas Fletcher. He had his own seat at the end of the bar and drank carefully but steadily as he held forth on a diversity of subjects from anarchism to horse breeding to e.e.cummings' poems. Sometimes Phinneas and one of the Huffs would get into loud, belligerent arguments, inevitably the result of skilled baiting on his part. About fifty, Phinneas came from a sturdy New England family somewhere north of Boston and had run away from his father's expectations and disapproval, though not from a small allowance. He lived upstairs, shared a bathroom with me, and introduced me to the blues of Robert Johnson, Blind Boy Fuller and many others we here on Cape Cod were oblivious to. He also played modern jazz recordings by Dizzy Gillespie, Charlie Parker and repeatedly, Thelonius Monk, whose recording of "Round Midnight" he played at low volume after the bar closed and we'd all gone to bed.

Every once in a while a group of military men on pass for a day or two would stop in on their way to Provincetown. About 30,000 soldiers were being amassed at the newly WPA-built Camp Edwards down in Barnstable, making ready in case we entered the war in Europe. Provincetown was a big draw with its seaside restaurants, bawdy entertainment, unconventional theater productions and modernist painters. The soldiers would come through Orleans, the halfway mark, fill up the restaurant for a couple hours and run back to the station to catch the train North. At these times Phinneas would retreat to the kitchen to get away from their aggressive fervor. They talked non-stop about the possibility of combat, the battalions of krauts they'd "blip off," and the broads they were off to meet in P-town. Phinneas was disgusted by the whole performance and made a nuisance of himself in the already crowded kitchen. Davey always got quiet at those times. He was twenty and dreading the day when he'd receive a call-up letter. He didn't want to leave his girlfriends. Inevitably one did come, a six page questionnaire he brought straight to Ray. They sat pouring over it for two hours looking for a way to defer his induction. It must have been the precise language of the form, the respectable way it asked manly questions of worthiness, that gradually changed Davey's mind. By the end of the session he walked quietly back to the kitchen with the envelope, stood staring at the stove for a few minutes then said, "I'm going over to the Post Office, Theo, maybe you should start the potatoes." Ray sat with his head in his hands, sipping a whiskey, a rarity for him. After that, for the three additional weeks Davey worked before going off to basic training, he was quiet in a kind of purposeful way, but happy, I think. Ray talked Liza into working full time in the kitchen to replace him, and the day before he left she came in with a big cherry pie which she presented to Davey.

"This is in honor of your accomplishments here in Orleans, and with hope for more of same wherever you go," she said, tearing up.

During the war years it was the custom to hang a white cloth in the window of those households with a man in the service. That white cloth is still in Davey's mother's front window. He never came back to Orleans.

I thought of Ria often in those days as I went about my work. I worried she would never find me away from the bay, if indeed she tried. From listening to Davey talk about the subject, I began to think that I loved her, truly. I cursed myself for not having kissed her, or something. Why hadn't I left her a note, a sign? I went over and over the events of those last few days of camp, but a large portion was blank. I knew I had spent a period of time in the wigwam lying in an oblivion of sorrow, but I wasn't sure anymore for how long.

This was in the bleak depths of March on Cape Cod, an especially conducive atmosphere for reflection and longing. I also thought a lot about Casco. He would have enjoyed sitting at the bar talking with Phinneas. I mentioned King Phillip's War once, in the middle of one of Phinneas' rants about the Pilgrims and religion and the dishonorable methods by which the country was settled. I could tell he was impressed when I mentioned the Praying Indians of Portanimicut.

"Very interesting, Theo," he said, "about the Praying Indians. Did you know that Harvard University and Dartmouth College were established in part to educate those very Indians?"

"No." I couldn't keep the surprise from my voice.

"Yep. They were 'committed to educating both the English and Indian youth of the country, in knowledge and Godliness,' I believe their words were. They built an Indian College at Harvard, but there weren't many who actually graduated from it. Still, it showed a certain principled paradigm, don't you think?" How I wished Casco was sitting there discussing this and much more with the gang at the bar. Instead I was his poor representative, running upstairs to look up 'paradigm' in Phinneas' dictionary.

In June I met another interesting man, and one who is still a friend, though I haven't seen him for years. One morning I was dumping trash behind the bar when he came in carrying a large square-bottomed satchel. His quiet demeanor as he trained his blue eyes on me and asked after Ray made me worry that he was a doctor and someone was ill. By the time I returned with Ray the man had moved a couple of tables together and spread a cloth over them. He was emptying the contents of the bag and arranging jars, rags and paintbrushes.

"Nolan," Ray almost shouted with glee as he enveloped the slim man in his hairy arms, pressing him to his massive chest. "Theo, this is Nolan Wright, one of the finest people I know, and a most accomplished and exceptional artist to boot."

Nolan, straightening his wire frame glasses as he recovered his stance, gave me his hand saying, "Pleased to meet you. Phinneas tells me you make an excellent chowder."

"Theo's a marvel," said Ray, going over to the bar to pour coffee. "Walked in here and perked up the whole menu. Now we can't live without him."

Nolan smiled at me, sipping coffee. "I heard you're from out on Pleasant Bay." He wasn't very specific, allowing me to answer however I chose. The issue of my parents was fading, but I never knew whose disapproval my abandonment may have prompted. I just nodded while Nolan and Ray glanced at each other. "Nolan's here to touch up the mural for the season," said Ray, changing the subject.

The sprawling scene which adorned the bar's back wall was a lively, intricate art deco-ish weaving of sea, ships and whales, rolling dunes and swirling winds, birds and fish. It was modern yet traditional, and I thought it the classiest thing about the place. Scrape marks from the backs of chairs and scuffs along the floor had damaged the mural, and the whole thing was coated in a drippy layer of nicotine. But after only an hour of Nolan's gentle washing, the true light of the scene began to emerge, in a variegated blend of natural color, with flashes of thalo blue or bright white, or a hot pink dot of beach rose. Nolan spent four days there, coming in right after breakfast and packing up his paints before the after-work crowd drifted in. We took to each other almost immediately. I spent a lot of time standing in the doorway to the kitchen, one eye on a simmering pot and the other on Nolan. He worked freely as he swept over the images with a loaded brush. Fresh lines glistened, undulating through and around each other. Another brushfull, and color filled the spaces created by those lines. Sometimes another wash was layered over all of it, then he'd flip the brush and scrape lines into the fresh paint, revealing the color underneath. It was fascinating. He listened to the radio while he painted, humming along to classical music, then standing back to light another Pall Mall and admire his work.

At noon that first day, I took him a bowl of freshly made chowder which he took to the bar to eat while we waited for the lunchtime crowd. After only one spoonful he sat up and looked at me with delight, his enthusiastic blue eyes magnified by his glasses, and said, "Well. I might need to spend a little more time on this job than I thought." After that he'd come into the kitchen several times a day to talk, or watch me cook. He asked me questions about what I was doing, something I was too shy to do when I watched him, which was infinitely more interesting. We talked often about Pleasant Bay, about the wildlife out there. He was quite knowledgeable about the nature, biology and geology of the Cape. He could draw anything, could render the compound curve of a floating dory with one stroke, the rigging of a clipper ship from memory. To me, it was a form of magic. A couple of times he asked my advice about certain details, like the placement of a dolphin's fin or the length of a swallow's tail. I suspected him of humoring me, getting me to open up, and it worked.

"Does this look right to you, Theo? You think this guy looks too grumpy?" he'd say, pointing to a whale. I shook my head.

"I was standing on Pochet Island last summer, looking out to sea," I said, "and I saw a pod of six Humpbacks on their way north. They were feeding. But it looked like they were playing too, spouting and breeching, slapping their tails and making huge splashes,."

"I've seen that too, but it turned out to be the Huff boys taking a swim." He turned and smiled at me. "Once I put my glasses on."

That afternoon I wandered over to check the progress. There, standing on a newly created bluff and looking out across the rolling waves, was a person who looked a lot like me, and in the distance a tiny group of whales frolicked in the gray-green expanse.

As the months went by I would sometimes find Nolan sitting at the end of the bar laughing and gossiping with Phinneas, Ray leaning close and adding commentary, their cigarette smoke rising overhead like a mushroom cloud. Often they would have a chess board between them, and one would explain the game to me while the other stared at the bottles behind the bar, piecing together his next move.

By June the tourist season had not yet officially started, but the town was more alive each day. People strolled around outside or sat in the sun on the benches bordering the graveyard. We began to leave the doors open and sounds of life drifted in with the fresh air. I found myself running outside more often to pump gas, or to watch as the daily train made its stop, waiting for the miracle of Ria stepping off and strolling up the street. The elms leafed out, their graceful branches danced in the breeze, making dizzy shadow patterns on the crossroads. Down the street, Dorrie's screen door slapped every few minutes, kids buying candy after school. The town felt peaceful and orderly, and I was a part of it. Though I longed to see the Bay again I was also afraid to revive the memory of what happened there. At sixteen I felt grown up, I suppose because I was surrounded by adults. By then I had earned enough money to buy new clothes and shoes, a tabletop radio and a few books. I had an idea that cigarette smoking might be a mature habit to adopt, and one day I asked Nolan for one.

"Take my advice; I don't use it anyway," he said, "Don't do it, Theo, just don't." Nolan had returned that afternoon from one of his trips to Provincetown, his black jalopy stood ticking outside the door, cooling after the long drive. He sat at the bar with Phinneas, sipping a beer and making notes in a little book.

"He's old enough, Nolan," said Phinneas, "to experience one of the great pleasures in life." He shook one out of his pack, handed it to me and struck a match. Nolan shook his head and went back to his notebook.

Phinneas watched him write. "Find anything today?"

"I think so. Come out to the car. I've got them in the back seat."

They slid off the barstools and went out the door, Phinneas winking at me as they passed. I took a puff of the cigarette and watched through the window as Nolan took a framed painting from the car and showed it to Phinneas. After a few puffs my brain felt like it was melting, dripping slowly down my throat, spiraling past my stomach directly to my bowels. I put a hand out to steady myself as one of the Huff boys said, loudly enough to be heard outside, "Oh boy. More government sponsored pictures of green men with purple heads."

I watched as Nolan and Phinneas lifted their eyes from the painting and looked at each other. Nolan shook his head again, pursing his lips. He pulled a flat block of carved wood from the car and showed it to Phinneas.

"Artists. The cream of the welfare crop," said the other Huff.

"I know, let's get a couple a brushes and some paint. We'll do each other's portraits, then stand in line for a check. A life to be truly proud of."

Nolan handed the woodblock to Phinneas and stepped smartly inside the door, staring at the Huff boys. The other customers fell silent. I was so dizzy I didn't think I'd make it to the toilet before throwing up. As I hung on to the bar waiting for it to pass Ray came in from the back and looked around.

"What's going on?" he said. Then he looked at me and added, "What the hell happened to you?"

Before I could answer Nolan walked over to the Huff boys' table and leaned on it.

"Would you like to discuss something with me?" He looked from one Huff to the other. In all the years I've known him, I'd never heard Nolan raise his voice to anyone, or speak authoritatively. He didn't swear, or spit. He showed interest and received respect.

The Huffs sat with their arms crossed high on their chests.

"I forget. What is it you do for a living?" said one in a sneering, mocking voice.

"I work for Works Progress Administration, the same program as the one that got the canal bridges widened, or the new high school built, or a hundred thousand miles of highway laid. It's a program of jobs. Being an artist is as legitimate and valuable a job as any of those."

"Oh yeah. Pictures of hobo-hemia. Precious assets for pinkos."

Nolan opened his mouth to answer, then sighed, closing it, and turned away.

"Sometimes too much drink is not enough," said Phinneas, as Nolan sat down beside him. "Don't bother. You'll never get anywhere with those two. They're morons. Take it from me, I've tried."

The Huff boys got up, fished around in their overalls for coins, dumped a few on the table and left, snickering. I went over and cleared. I had barely recovered from my introduction to smoking. Surely there was something wrong with me, I thought. This was definitely not what was supposed to happen. As I passed Phinneas and Nolan on my way to the kitchen I paused. "What was that about, anyway," I said, dumping the ashtray. Ray groaned, "Oh, don't let's talk about it. I'm sick of the subject. I'm going to the kitchen."

"Part of the New Deal," Nolan said to me. I had heard of it but I admit I didn't know that much about it, except for snippets of commentary on the radio and a single "Fireside Chat." Nolan gave me a little rundown of President Roosevelt's plan, spotlighting the WPA programs and ultimately getting to his own involvement. It turns out Nolan was the regional supervisor for Southeastern Massachusetts' Federal Art Project. He was responsible for finding qualified artists, collecting their work and taking them to Boston for distribution in public buildings such as post offices, hospitals and government offices. Each artist received a weekly check in return for his or her output. Phinneas had pulled strings to get him the job.

"There are people making beautiful work in this country, Theo, inventive and fresh, and our government recognizes its importance to a true democratic principle. We're breaking away from European traditions and making American art. We've been given the freedom to experiment, to explore, to not have to worry about catering to anyone simply to make a living."

He got up and ran back out to his car, returning with a flat case. "You see this?" he said, laying the case on the bar and opening it. He pulled out the carved block of wood I'd seen earlier. "It's a woodcut for making a print. It's by an artist named Blanche Lazzell. As far as I know, no other artist in the country is making this kind of thing. It's an old Japanese technique: white line printing. This one's called "Four Boats."

The image was of multiple carved channels orienting toward a central point and contained within a neat square. Some curved into each other, others shot straight to the edge at different angles. It was pretty, but I didn't understand why it was so exciting. Then Nolan put the print in front of me and I saw how it had been made. I saw boat hulls on a beach and even a fisherman, but it was really a kind of synchronized dance of color and line. The actual imagery was secondary. "You see?" he said, "And there are lots of artists doing just as modern and experimental stuff. I'll take you along on one of my trips, if you like. You can see for yourself."

"Okay," I said. "So the Huff boys think its a waste of money."

"Yeah. Don't pay any attention to them. They think WPA workers are lazy bums who are getting a free ride. They think all artists are Communists, and the President's one too."

I thought Roosevelt sounded wise, or at least calmly commanding. I was aware that things were happening in the world, big frightening things my isolation on the bay had prevented me from knowing. I wasn't sure I wanted to know, now that I found myself in a world populated by humans instead of animals. I didn't want to think about Communists or government sponsored programs or, most of all, war. I was very afraid of what had begun in Europe while I hid in the woods. The atmosphere in the bar that spring was one of anticipation, a certain eagerness to get on with it. A month earlier we had listened on the radio to Roosevelt as he made his announcement about weapons now being manufactured in Detroit and sent to Europe to assist the Allies. Liza said it was only a matter of time before we were either fighting over there, or here.

"New England's where they'll attack first. Think about it. We're closer to the bastards than anywhere else in the U.S."

Ray didn't talk about it. Neither did Phinneas or Nolan, but Liza was a gung-ho proponent. She wanted the US to get over there and free her fellow French from the bashing of the Germans and Italians and let them get back to what they did best: make all the fine things in the world. "Wine, cheese, clothing, art, philosophy. And of course they're the best cooks. We all know that. What a waste!" she'd lament. When she'd get on one of her day-long rants about the Axis powers and Roosevelt's wavering leadership everyone knew to stay out of the way. Nobody got involved, but it was as though she wanted someone to disagree so she could do a little fighting herself. We had to be very careful not to ignite one of her tirades. She'd pick up on the slightest reference to the war and she'd be off. Ray was the only one who seemed to be able to negotiate her mood swings. He calmed and soothed her, murmuring simpatico phrases and distracting her with jokes. Then he'd emerge from the kitchen rolling his eyes.

"Word of wisdom, Theo. Never argue with a woman when she's tired. Or rested," he'd add.

That first year the summer season came on with a bang, or so it seemed to me. The bar business picked up considerably and I found myself in the kitchen juggling an endless round of hot dog-fish fry-burger flip, washing dishes in between and keeping the garbage and deliveries organized. I'd put a row of buns on to toast and run out to pump gas while Liza dished out mashed potatoes, French fries and canned corn onto a procession of plates that didn't show signs of slowing from lunch right through the dinner rush and beyond. I hardly ever made it into the bar anymore, and fell into bed at closing, exhausted and reeking of grease. The twenty-five dollars a week I earned was a fortune to me, and a good enough wage for anyone in those days. My father mentioned that figure many times when we were out in the boat waiting for a duck to pass overhead or a fish to bite his line.

"Twennyfive bucks," he'd say, "that's all I need. Twennyfive bucks by Sunday."

In those early days I had no idea Ray's bar was so popular with tourists, or that Orleans had such a buzzing summer night life. The conversation at the bar had a new flavor to it, a different language full of slang and references to people and events I'd never heard of. Our regulars came in, but less often. Their seats were taken by out-of-towners, the usual topics of fish and weather replaced by recounts of sights seen and meals eaten, of money and property, fame.

There were other restaurants and bars in town, some more respectable than ours, such as the Southward Inn down the street. Open only in summer, it was rambling, turreted, graceful construction from an era of whaling and sea captains. The Inn featured a massive fireplace, refined dining and several elegant rooms upstairs. In the evenings one could enjoy the ambience of the 'Green Room,' so called because of cluster of potted trees lit by a trio of skylights, where jazz quartets would be imported from Boston or New York to entertain the guests. Farther along Route 6 toward Brewster, was The Four Aces, a hot spot for the younger crowd where the music was loud and girls went to dance on Saturday nights. For three months of the year the town was busy, brassy with outside life, the silken warmth of summer nights vibrant and lyrical and unbound.

Phinneas stayed the course, enjoying himself thoroughly and basking in the glow of being an insider privy to local gossip, which everyone wanted to hear, to belong to such a paradise for longer than the week or two of their vacation. They brought with them the culture and gossip of his class, which he soaked up along with the numerous rounds Ray slid down the bar to him. He held court at the end of the bar, hardly eating, staggering to the bathroom to pee bourbon. By August his eyes were clouded over and his clothes weren't receiving the fastidious attention they normally got. Ray had to gently ask him to change his shirt after a prolonged rainstorm steamed up the inside of the bar and the myriad hidden pockets of filth began to bloom with peculiar new odors. Phinneas' mortification at the request sent him into hiding for two days. I did hear Robert Johnson giving voice to his self-pity in his rooms late at night. On the third day he reappeared, clean and clear-eyed, quietly seated at the bar. Ray offered him a beer and life went back to normal.

As the seasons passed from summer to fall, and winter loomed again, the talk in the bar was most often about the war in Europe. The Huff boys monitored attacks by the Luftwaffe, British night bombardments of German targets, the surrenders, invasions and campaigns as though it were a giant board game. When first Japan joined the Axis, then were followed by Hungary and Romania, they became angry and drank even more beer. Liza was furious with Roosevelt and swore me to never speak his name in the kitchen until he had sent American troops to France. There were heated arguments in the bar two or three times a week, always broken up by Ray in his usual calm but firm manner. I didn't know what to think. Of course I hated the thought of any conflict but it seemed to me that, since we were sending arms to help the Allies, wouldn't it be quicker to get it over with by sending along men to operate them? At the time I was seventeen and wouldn't be eligible for call-up for another year, but I had registered. Ray brought me the postcard directing me to do so, with its forwarding scribble in my mother's hand. I didn't want to go, but I would if I had to. I dared not speak this to anyone, not even Phinneas, who was of the opinion, as were many Americans at the time, that we should avoid war at any cost. The atmosphere in the bar was often tense. The radio, tuned to news programs in the kitchen at Liza's insistence, was strictly monitored by Ray in the bar. News broadcasts were forbidden.

"The bar is a place to relax," he said, "and we'll goddamn well do that and not pollute the ambiance with the goddamn news."

Ray sent me on many of the bar's errands that winter, probably to get me out of the atmosphere in the kitchen, but also because he knew I loved to drive. He taught me himself, driving us out the long Beach Road after Labor Day when it was practically deserted. He'd switch places with me and talk me calmly through grinding gears and multiple stall-outs. It didn't take long though, and soon I was driving to the dump, to the harbor, past Bessom's store to Mayo's duck farm out by Nauset Beach for eggs and chicken, sometimes giving Liza a ride home to Brewster late at night. I drove the length of Barley Neck Road a couple of times, just to sit and look out over the water. I could have gotten out and walked around the corner to see my old haunts but I didn't. Once I drove the hilly, deeply shaded Chatham Road for a few miles until the bay came up to run alongside, then I stopped to gaze out over the water to the barrier beach and the Atlantic beyond. From there I could look north through the peephole of the Narrows to Hog Island, Money Head, the marsh. It made me sad. I didn't do it again for a long time. Instead I drove Route 6 north, through Eastham to Wellfleet and out to the pier, where I'd park and watch the fishing boats, the gulls, and the sparkle of sun on water. It was good to get away from the bar.

One February day Ray called me outside. He was putting chains around the tires of the truck, even though the snow on the roads was practically melted.

"I need you to run a little errand for me, if you don't mind," he said. "Up in Eastham. My mother's pump broke. I want you to go and unhook it, take it over to Kurt at the welding shop. Okay?"

"Sure," I said, stunned to learn that Ray had a mother nearby. He'd never once mentioned it.

"Now, I can't do it because the tank truck'll be here any minute to fill. Reason for the chains is, she's out by the beach. Hardly anyone drives that road in winter. You might run into drifts." He gave me directions and said he'd call the welder. I should wait for the weld, take it back and hook it up again. "Think you can do it?"

I had often made small repairs to the temperamental pump at the bar, so Ray thought I was an expert. I was glad for the opportunity to take a ride.

As Ray suspected I did run into quite a pileup of snow on the little dirt track through the woods. Even with the chains I had to dig under the tires three times on the mile-long road. Eventually I came to the house, a little cottage nestled under a stand of listing locust. A thread of smoke rose straight from the chimney. A small garage sat to one side, its roof partially caved in. As I came to a stop, the side door opened and a tiny white-haired woman stepped out onto the landing in her slippers. Covered by a blue shawl which draped to her feet, she turned and gave me a feeble wave, gesturing for me to come in.

"Thank God you've come, you noble boy," she said, smiling up at me. I saw immediately where Ray's eyebrows had originated. Although now white, hers were possibly even thicker than her son's. They lay across her forehead like a giant furry caterpillar. The eyes beneath were dark, glittering and kind.

"Ray told me you were the best there is when it comes to pumps. He's useless when it comes to machinery. Don't ever mention I said that, will you? I'm so glad you could come. Here, give me your coat and I'll direct you to the cellar."

She led me through a dining room and over to the stairs. The room was cluttered with belongings. Leaning towers of books and laundry perched on barely visible furniture. A large table held stacks of dishes, bowls, two soup tureens, gravy boats, mountains of silverware, toppling piles of napkins, and a candelabra. Chairs stood stacked one on the other up against the walls. It was as though she were awaiting a large contingent of dinner guests. We threaded our way through and down a steep set of stairs as she chatted, things toppling in her wake.

"I heard a loud crack and the pump started, well, the only word I can think of is wheezing. It did that for a few minutes and wound down. In due course it stopped. Then water started spraying out. Luckily all I had to do was turn the faucet handle and it stopped. Now, tell me I did the right thing." We stood in front of the broken machine,which was sitting in a little brick-lined depression full of water, a long thin crack easily visible on one side of the housing.

I had the pump unbolted and in the bed of the truck soon enough, promising I'd be back by afternoon. As I drove away I could see her standing on the stoop, shawl wrapped around her shoulders, and I thought of my own mother. What would she do if anything ever happened to my one-armed father? Could I go back there and take care of her? Surely it would be the only thing to do. Ray's mother had called me noble. What would she think if she knew I had abandoned my parents? I made a vow then, driving along the wintry road, chains clanking and gray, leafless trees silhouetted against gray sky an illustration of my thoughts: I would go back if my father died and stay with my mother, So Help Me God.

After I hauled the pump into the welding shop and set it on the table, I sat waiting by a huge fireplace, sipping coffee and watching Kurt work, the torch moving slowly back and forth along the crack in the pump housing. It didn't take more than a few minutes once he started, and I regretted having to leave the heat of the fire to go back out in the cold. As we were carrying it to the truck Kurt stopped suddenly saying, "Wait. This is not right." He held up one of the wires to the plug. It was stripped and frayed, the copper bright. It had happened somewhere on the trip.

"Let's take it inside again. I'll solder this, then you can be on your way,"

I had just settled again by the fire when he said, "Damn."

"What?"

"Hate to tell you this, but my roll of solder is on the truck, which is over at Central Garage getting a new water pump." He laughed softly. "Look, I know Ray's mama needs to have this thing back today. It's a simple repair. Why don't you take the pump back to Orleans, to Smith's, and Louie can solder it."

So off I went with the pump, on one of those machine repair quests where the line from problem to solution is never, ever direct.

Smith Bros. Hardware was next door to the Southward Inn. From the rickety front porch they had a nice view of Town Cove. I wrestled the pump up the steps and stood looking out over the water. Salt ice slopped against the pilings of the boat launch, breaking into pieces and tumbling back on itself. Canada geese stood huddled together near the shore, pecking in the mud. I stepped inside, the door scraping across the floorboards. Like Bessom's, the dim atmosphere was of another era, smelling of kerosene and liniment, leather and mildew. Sagging shelves, loaded with decaying cardboard boxes bisected the tilting emporium, their contents spilling into the aisles. Nail barrels were lined up against the far wall, a wood stove bled smoke just inside the door. Rope, lanterns, wire, chain, copper piping, rolls of screen hung from the ceiling or were shoved into the rafters. Buckets of plumbing parts stood here and there in no particular order, jumbled lengths of pipe stood in the corners along with rolls of canvas, broom handles, rakes and hoes. A toppled pile of toilet plungers shrouded in cobwebs, open canisters of lime, fertilizer and rabbit feed led the way to the sloping counter. A large, open bucket of spit tobacco juice stood proudly on one end, and behind it stood one of the bearded, taciturn brothers, who merely pointed to the ceiling with his thumb when I held up the broken wire. Upstairs, Louie Rutledge would now and then set the place on fire with his soldering and welding business, but was considered to be a genius of sheet metal manipulation. Eventually the store did burn down, but Louie was long gone before that happened. I lugged the pump up the creaking steps to find Louie standing as always behind a vast table littered with scraps of metal, wire and other detritus of his business. Several small triangular pieces of tin were clamped to the table and he was drilling a hole through them, bearing down as the metal screeched. He looked up briefly, then shut the drill off.

"Whatcha got?" he said, looking the pump up and down.

I held up the wire again and he said, "Oh. Okay. Hang on a sec. This'll only take a minute."

I relived the next few moments of that visit many times over the following months, trying to understand how I could have been standing in exactly that spot at that moment. I can still replay the loop of mental film which shows Louis plunging the drill into the hole, squeezing the trigger switch and the sudden searing pain in my left eye. I fell backward and hit my head. I remember bits and pieces after that, the feel of Louis cradling my head, the smell of Smith Bros. tobacco spit, the sound of the ambulance, the long trip down the stairs. I guess I was given some kind of sedative because I woke up in the hospital with the left side of my head wrapped in a thick bandage and Phinneas reading in the chair next to me.

As soon as I moved he was sitting on the bed saying, "Jesus Christ, Sparrow. That was close. A little too close." He chuckled to himself and added, "Ray asked me to stay here while he talks to Louis. I'd like to witness that conversation."

Apparently what happened was that when Louis started up the drill again, somehow he dislodged the clamp which held the tin triangles to the table. They went spinning all over the room, and one passed right across the front of my eyeball, slicing a neat line through the retina.

"So, am I blind in this eye now?"

"The doc doesn't know yet. It has to heal first. Does it hurt?"

"No, not at all."

"We called your parents, Theo. The hospital wouldn't give you treatment without their permission. So I met your father. He just signed the papers, looked at you and left."

After week I graduated to an eyepatch, and by early spring I was able to keep my eye open naturally, but I couldn't see more than a blurry version of what was in front of me. I was given glasses with one very thick lens which didn't help much and steamed up so often in the kitchen that I stopped wearing them altogether. I'm quite used now to seeing things two-dimensionally, though driving is always a little scary, so I try not do it at night.

That winter the festering boil of war talk in the bar finally burst. After December seventh, when Roosevelt declared war on Japan, and Hitler in turn declared war on the US, I expected all hell to break loose, that the Huffs would take their shotguns out and blast the town in celebration, that Liza would board the next train to the recruitment center in Boston. But if anything, the bar was more peaceful than ever. Now that the decision had been made and the course of our lives had a direction, the discussions came to an abrupt halt. The usual contingent of soldiers on weekend pass came through, their fervor somehow calmed. It was now with sober intent that they went to Provincetown for what could be a last fling. Due to gas rationing and other conservation measures that summer, fewer tourists visited, and the town began to experience an economic downswing that would hold until the end of the war. We bought fewer cases of beer and turned away fishermen at the kitchen door. In the middle of June one could easily find us all at our various stations, but none of us working. Ray read the paper, silently turning the pages and murmuring comments to Phinneas. Liza and I sat in the kitchen, she fiddling with her fingernails and listening to the radio while I read Dime Detective Magazine, which Ray bought me every month. At first I wasn't sure why he thought I might like such a publication, but I quickly grew to love it, and looked forward to every issue. I studied the cover illustrations of desperate criminals, curvy women whose shoulder straps never seemed to stay up, and steel-jawed detectives who grasped a lapel or a pistol with equal intensity. I savored every word of stories like "Cover the Corpse's Eyes,' or 'The 10:30 to Sing-Sing.' I loved T.T. Flynn and Raymond Chandler, and practiced talking the way their characters did, saying to Liza, "What's it to ya?" and "You blankety-blankety blank!" until I was asked to stop.

It was right before the Labor Day weekend that a man I recognized began sitting with Phinneas in the evenings. Without the hat and Abercrombie & Fitch getup he didn't immediately register, but by the time they were on a third round and talking about Indian artifacts, I knew. He was the man Ria and I had encountered on Money Head. I wedged the kitchen door open and eavesdropped. He was bragging to Phinneas about another person who he referred to as 'the collector.'

"He'll buy practically anything I can find, if it's Indian. There's a lot of stuff lying around, once you know where to look," he said, taking a self-satisfied swig of beer.

"Interesting," said Phinneas. "And where is that exactly?"

"Let's just say in the area. I've done my research. The collector's the one made me curious about the Cape. Nice town you got here. I plan to put down some roots."

After he left, I asked Phinneas about him. "I don't really know much, except that his name is Walter something and he bought a piece of land over on Pleasant Bay. Building a house. I suppose we'll have to put up with him."

An image of fluttering white cloth tied to a stake driven into the ground came to me. What was the name written on that stake? Thinking about it brought on a parade of other thoughts. They marched through my mind while I reviewed them, one by one. I spent the remainder of the day brooding about my father's stony-hearted doggedness, my mother's thorny indifference, the Bible, the blackfish, the wigwam, Casco, the medal. Ria Bang. Some thread linked them all, but I couldn't find it. I wanted an explanation for the seemingly random events which had catapulted me into this other life. I liked my new life well enough, but I wanted somehow to connect it to my old one.

All at once I wanted to go back to the bay, to walk along the shore, hear the familiar sounds of crows arguing, sails luffing, the murmur and swish of incoming tide. I began to plan a visit. I would stay away from Paw Wah Point and the Narrows, the camps. I traced a mental map of my old stomping ground. Realistically, I couldn't walk in very many places without running into some memory or person I wanted to avoid. But I could go out on the water, if I had a boat. I could row around, stay away from shore. The idea didn't leave me alone but nagged, lurking around the outskirts of my thoughts and interrupting my attention to 'Fibber McGee and Molly' and the other radio shows that got me through my evenings. I turned off the news the minute Liza left for the day. I couldn't listen to reports of the internment of thousands of innocent citizens of Japanese descent. It reminded me of the Indians out on Deer Island. Finally, a week after the season ended and the town was quiet I asked Ray for a day off.

"Jesus, Theo, of course," he said, slapping himself on the forehead. "Take as many as you want. I forgot, sorry."

Liza's husband had owned a boat that still lay overturned in the weeds at Arey's Pond. I was welcome to use it, if it still floated. "Black hull with a red stripe," she said rather wistfully. It was there, miraculously intact. Though there wasn't much black or red left on it, but I identified it by the name 'Belle Fille' carved into the transom. A pair of oars were wedged behind the seats. I flipped the boat over and pushed it into the river. It splatted into the mud of low tide, but I got in anyway, glad of the impossibility of going anywhere yet. I still wasn't sure if I wanted to go out on the water, to break the spell of my disconnect and take my reinvented self back to the past. I watched a fiddler crab scurry around, one small and one outsized claw probing the marsh grass for tidbits. Soon others emerged claw first from holes in the mud to run circles around and over each other, clacking and scrambling with the activity of food gathering. I stayed in the boat, the sun strong on my back, hypnotized and half asleep until it began to rock gently and I knew the tide was in enough to shove off.

After some initial leaking, the wood absorbed enough water and the boat moved quite robustly down the river. I was surprised to find that my rowing muscles were still strong after almost two years away, and I pulled hard at the oars, slicing through roiling currents of incoming water with boyish glee. When I passed the site where the wigwam of John Simpson, the last of the Nauset sachems, had stood, I raised the oars in salute. A blue heron, startled out of the concentration of stalking fish, flapped noisily past me squawking expletives. A herring gull laughed. A muskrat slid into the water and swam alongside. I could smell the salt marsh, ripe in the summer heat, hear the dull roar of tumbling breakers in the Atlantic beyond. I was back. All the bottled-up heartache of the past couple of years flooded my chest with such a wallop of longing that I dropped the oars. I sat with my head hanging, shoulders collapsed, taking gulps of the soft, warm, salty air. The boat drifted, turning lazily in the current. I lifted my face and took in the panorama of my former home, the blue-gray waters, the blooming marsh grass waving a thousand white flames against electric green, swallows making figure eights, trailing their young. Everything was as it had always been. The gentle power of the bay had absorbed the fact of Casco's death and my own abandonment, turned its back and moved on.

Tears welled up in my eyes, blurring blue into green, sparkling birdsong all around me merged with the sound of trickling water. The Bay was host to a cycle of life and death and transformation that I was not part of anymore. I was back but I no longer belonged. The Bay had let me go as the swallows would let their offspring go, the grasses let their seed be taken by the wind. Strangely, this thought gave me a measure of comfort. I had found solace in the world of the Ship Ahoy and all the men and women there who, like the Bay had for my entire childhood, given me what my parents could not. I took up the oars again and headed out.

When I reached the mouth of the River, instead of turning south and into the greater body of the Bay I pulled hard with my right arm and coasted north toward Barley Neck, away from Paw Wah Point, the islands and a possible run-in with my father or the other fishermen. It was enough for me just to be out there, to trace my old routes in the upper reaches of the rivers and ponds. I rowed around for an hour or two, gradually feeling better, content to simply glide through steadily rising waters. I rowed around the elbow of land north of Arey's pond called 'Weesquamscot' by the Nausets. Casco told me it meant 'Neck of land which has a pond with an island in it." That would be the fresh water we now call Pilgrim Lake, which lies between Arey's and Lonnie's ponds, both salt. I pulled smoothly up the estuary into Lonnie's and found it completely still except for a small boy making engine noises and plowing a piece of wood through the water near the landing. At Meetinghouse Pond, I paused for only a few minutes, making a quick circuit and then shooting back past the old packet landing, reveling in the power of my strokes and freedom of weightlessness. Soon enough I was back at the mouth of the River, about to turn in and call it a day, when, heartened by the tour, I decided to go a little farther and coast out toward the point. I had to see it. Sitting backwards, I wasn't looking as I approached, and wished I'd never turned around to get my bearings. As I neared the shore where Camp Mariner's boathouse sat I saw with horror that the tree line beyond, about where Casco's corn patches had been, was no longer there. A great gap in the growth at the top of the hill, a stark denuding changed completely the contour of the point. Someone had cleared that land.

My cheeks flushed with anger, I wrenched the boat around and started to row back as fast as I could, giving myself a clear view of the disfigurement. Cursing my stupidity, I forced myself to look away as I went back around to the river and up into Arey's Pond, not slowing until the boat's bow smashed through the marsh grass and thrust itself up onto land. I sat on the overturned hull, breathing heavily and willing my mind to erase what I'd seen and what I couldn't stop visualizing further, a cellar dug, a house being built, Casco's grave opened up. I got up and trudged down the road into town, the giant elms and oaks along the way creating a dark and comforting tunnel for my brooding. So lost in thought I saw only the road surface, I didn't immediately hear the car slow behind me until a voice called out.

"Just the person I was looking for."

I turned to see Nolan smiling at me from behind the wheel. "C'mon, get in. I'll give you a lift." I flopped into the seat. "Thanks," I said, trying to sound cheerful, but staring at the floor.

We cruised down the shady road for a bit before Nolan said, "You all right?"

"Yeah. I'm fine. I was out on the bay."

"Ray told me." He glanced at me, frowning. "Good to get out of the bar, eh?"

"Yeah."

We drove in silence. Then I remembered. "You were looking for me?"

"Yeah. I was in Provincetown today. I had to go over to the Hofmann studio to pick up some paperwork, see some friends. They were all going out after a class to get something to eat, so they invited me. There were a few new students with us, and I got to talking to this pretty girl. She was there for an interview, to enroll. I noticed her because of her drawing. It was excellent. Anyhow, when I told her I lived in Orleans she immediately asked if I knew someone by the name of Theodoros Sparrow. That's you, right?"

I stared at him with my mouth hanging open.

He grinned at me. "Her name's Ria, Ria Bang. You know her?"

Chapter 8

Nolan had not only stumbled upon my long lost friend, but had been sent by her to fetch me. "She begged me," he said, incredulous. "What did you do to her, Theo, and why haven't we met her before?"

"She's just someone I know from camp," I said, but I couldn't keep a straight face and Nolan started to laugh.

I could hardly believe this startling piece of luck, this miracle coming so soon on the heels of what had happened out on the bay. The image of my denuded former home flashed garishly in my mind, but I scrambled to stash it in some mental cupboard for the time being. I needed to gather my thoughts, to hear what Nolan was telling me.

"Okay, Theo, you don't have to give away your secrets, but you'd better act on this. I made a promise, and I can tell by the look on your face you're not unhappy about it."

"How can I find her?"

That they had met was hard to believe. But even more remarkable was what he told me next, that the lunch in Provincetown had been a good-bye meal, that she was leaving to go back to school that very afternoon. She'd arranged with Nolan to have me stand at the station and wait for the train. It stopped in Orleans for exactly six minutes, and in that time we could see each other before she went on to New York.

"The train will be here in half an hour," Nolan said, looking at his watch as we pulled up outside the Ship Ahoy. "I suggest you put on some shoes," he added, grinning, "In my experience it makes a better impression."

I looked down at my patched-up boots, then my eyes traveled up past my muddy pants to the undershirt I'd grabbed that morning, the one covered in overlapping grease stains. Bolting up the stairs I yelled, "Thanks, Nolan, thanks for everything!"

I was standing at the station, out of breath, trying to arrange my still-wet and uncooperative hair into a facade of orderliness when I heard the train's whistle. Several people waited with me. One couple had a pile of trunks and two toddlers. The children took turns taunting a small, yapping dog in a cage, sticking their fingers through the bars so the dog could lick them. I hoped they might stall things with such a load. I took deep breaths to calm my heartbeat. I tried again to picture what Ria would look like two years on. I didn't want to waste a second of the six minutes searching for her among the other passengers. How many times had I stood in the doorway of the bar when this very train came through, visualizing the image of Ria stepping onto the platform, looking around and walking up the street toward me?

That's not exactly what happened, but close. I spotted her bangs first, blowing in the cracked-open window, her hands grasping its edge, her eyes already grazing the length of the platform as the train slowed to a halt. When she found me she leapt back, her mouth open in mid-shout, and disappeared. She reemerged in the doorway, jumped the steps and ran to me, yelling, "Theo, my God I don't believe it!" She had changed. She was taller and curvier and she wore lipstick, but she still had the same haircut, the same gray eyes dancing around my face, the parentheses on either side of her mouth deepened now into full-blown dimples. She gave me a little hug, suddenly shy, or as shy as it was possible for her to be, then said quickly, "We only have a few minutes. I want you, no, I need you to tell me what happened. I looked for you for hours that last day. I even tried to find your house. My parents were furious with me. Did I say something wrong? Was Casco angry with me? I went to his place but no one was there. Why didn't you wait at the channel? Theo, what happened to your eye?" I started to answer all of her questions but she fired them at me so fast I couldn't get a single word in. Finally I took her hand and squeezed.

"Ow!" She reared back, eyes wide. "What was that for?"

"I want to tell you. You won't believe how much I have to tell you. Do you have to go?"

"Yes, unfortunately. Look, tell me at least why you didn't come to the channel on the last day."

What could I say? I was lying in a stupor of grief and shock in the bottom of the wigwam, Casco's body nearby, cold and stiff with rigor mortis. As I searched for an easy answer she stared into my eyes, zipping from one to the other with hers. The train whistle blew and we both looked over at the open door, the passengers watching us.

"Give me your address," I said. "I promise I'll write everything to you. I can't tell it here."

She pulled a piece of paper from her pocket, her ticket, as I discovered later, fished around in her handbag for a pencil and scribbled quickly.

"I have vacation at Thanksgiving. Shall I come? Oh, we have a cottage in Eastham now, by the way. I can get my mother to come up. She'll do anything to get away."

"Yuh, ah, yes, of course. Come, please. Please come," I sputtered as the train began to roll and someone shouted at us, "Get on!"

"All right, I'll come. Please, please write to me, Theo. Will you?"

"I promise," I said, as she hugged me again. Her thick hair fluttered across my face and I touched it. I wanted to hold on to it, to keep her. She turned and ran toward the train and I said, "Casco."

"What?" she jumped onto the steps.

"I have to tell you something." I ran alongside as she hung on to the railing.

"What? Tell me, quick," she yelled, already too far away.

I stopped and waved, waved with my whole body, my feet lifting off the ground, as she held on and waved back, shouting something that was lost in the sound of the wheels on the track. Then she was gone. I stood watching as the other cars rushed by and out of sight, still waving, my other hand clutching the paper with her address.

September 16, 1942

My Dearest, Theo,

I waited anxiously the three days it took your letter to get here and you cannot imagine my heartache upon reading it. It was so wonderful to see you again, to know where you are. But my God, the stories you told! I can hardly believe all that's happened. How did you possibly manage to live through it?

It was Casco, wasn't it, that's what you were trying to tell me as the damn train was leaving. Why couldn't I manage to stay and let you tell me in person? I'm cursing myself! I have so many questions. Do you mean to say you buried Casco there in the woods? It's not enough to simply write, 'I found Casco dead next to the wigwam, and so I buried him,' etc. You must provide me with some details. What happened? This letter is turning out to be merely a series of questions, isn't it? I cannot write you a proper letter until I know more

about what happened to you. That's why I'm going to find the
number for the Ship Ahoy and telephone you in three days' time,
on Saturday, when I'll be home from school for the weekend.
I hope you're not too busy at 2pm.
Yours, Truly!
Ria

September 19th, 1942

My Dearest Theo,
It was wonderful to hear your voice. Too bad we were
cut off! I'm so glad you found a place in town with people
who care about you and don't bother telling you how you
ought to live your life. I can't stop thinking about everything
you told me. I'm sitting here in the library, lonely and blue,
picturing you in the wigwam, freezing and starving & you,
all alone, digging a hole for your friend's grave. I can hardly
believe I just wrote those words! How can it be that I was
standing there at Casco's wigwam and didn't have the nerve
to call out, I thought I might disturb his sleep! Goddamn!
I can't tell you how many times I thought about that
last day, about the wigwam and Casco's world. Theo, what
could possibly have happened to him? You never really said.
You say he had a bruise on his head, but from what? Did
a tree fall on him?Could he have stumbled and hit his
head on a rock? I don't understand. You must tell me more,
if you have any ideas about it. I'm so sorry for you, my friend.
Why didn't your parents look for you?
My father and I fought bitterly over my wanting to go
back the following summer. He said I was too old for camp.
I said I'd work as a counsellor, and so that's what I did. I
was driven to Camp Mee-ne-wa, Lake George New York!!
I won't tell you any more about it, except to say that I came
to call it Hell-on-Earth. But there I was, teaching archery and
listening to silly girls gabble on about Gary Cooper while you
were foraging for food and talking to no one but yourself.
It makes me nuts just thinking about it.
My father is in serious trouble. He doesn't tell us very
much, but it seems he can't communicate with his associates in
Denmark, now that the Germans have occupied. I'm not sure
what it means for his business, but we haven't seen him for

almost six months. My mother stays in her room, mostly. Flora waits on her. I see lots of little glasses of sherry going up the stairs, and most of the food Flora lovingly cooks coming down, untouched. I am almost happy to be away at school.

I've been accepted to the Art Student's League next year, if my parents will take the time to notice I'm alive and have graduated. Next summer my mother and I will again be in Eastham. I can't wait to show you the charming cottage we bought right on the water! My mother says I have to get a summer job somewhere, but I want to start attending classes at the Hofmann School in Provincetown. Mr. Hofmann is a marvelous teacher. He let me sit in a few times even though I wasn't enrolled. Listening to him talk about the way color must move through a painting makes me believe I've got more than rocks in my head, that I could be a good, even great painter. Maybe.

I must go. My mother has instructed Flora to take me out and buy me a winter coat.

Write to me!

Ria

In November she came to the Cape as promised, but only for a day. Her mother had serious reservations about anyone spending Thanksgiving in an unheated cottage by the sea, but to her credit she let Flora accompany Ria on the train. Flora spent all day and one night stoking the fireplace and shivering so Ria could visit me. Ria told her mother she had to come up for a job interview, of all things. A preposterous excuse, but it worked.

"A month from now I'll just tell her I didn't get the job. She won't remember, anyway."

We sat at a table under Nolan's mural. Ray had given me the entire day off and promised that neither he nor Phinneas would stare at us if we accepted his offer of a free lunch. But from the moment Ria stepped inside the bar we were all so mesmerized by her that nothing we'd agreed on came to pass as planned. I watched from the kitchen as she strode directly to the bar and, slinging an arm around Nolan's shoulders, ordered herself a Coca-Cola. She was wearing a burnt-orange wool coat with a fox collar, her dark hair weaving itself in and out of the fur with each delightful move of her head. I hesitated, nervous and embarrassed by the situation, then walked over and sat beside her. She eyed me in silence while we all waited, and my face turned bright red.

"Hello," I managed.

She threw herself at me, hugged me to her and said, "Oh my God, Theo, at last!" Nolan and Phinneas looked at each other, Phinneas' eyebrows slowly rising. I made introductions, hoping it would calm my nerves.

"A great pleasure," said Phinneas smoothly, taking her hand.

She gave Ray a radiant smile and thanked him for taking me in and giving me a job. "Theo is part of the family," he said, winking at me.

Eventually Ray steered us to a table which I noticed had been set with a vase of paper flowers. Ria took off her coat and tossed it over a chair while she scrutinized Nolan's mural. "Good painting," she said, fishing in her pocketbook for a pack of cigarettes. "Want one?" she said, placing one delicately between her lips. I hadn't smoked since that first dizzy-making Lucky Strike.

"No thanks."

"A habit I picked up at school," she said, her mouth curving into a smile, "Everybody does it." She was staring at me, her eyes glittering. Then the dimples deflated. It almost looked like she was about to cry. She launched right in, as I should've known she would.

"Theo, what happened? I don't want facts, I want to know everything. Tell me from the beginning."

As we made our way through oysters on the half shell, which made her eyes light up, then chowder ("Theo's recipe," Ray announced proudly), followed by baked cod and cole slaw, I told her the story from beginning to end. Well, I didn't tell her about the picture of Clark Gable and Vivien Leigh, but everything else. She cringed when I talked about the Pilot whale killing, covering her face with her hands.

"That is truly monstrous. I would have done the same thing," she said, staring at the flowers. "Surely he must know how wrong it was to take you along on that trip."

"He doesn't know how wrong it was to kill the Pilot whales in the first place," I said.

She led me through a long, whispered interrogation about the discovery of Casco's body, questioning me again about what might have happened. She decided he'd had a heart attack and hit his head on a tree trunk when he fell over.

"It's the only explanation," she said, staring at her chowder.

"I know. But he seemed fine the day before."

"To think of what you had to do, Theo. I can't bear it. But you made a ceremony. That was beautiful. We can never tell anyone about it, you know."

"I know."

"What if he wasn't telling the truth about having no family down South. What if someone comes here looking for him, asking around?"

It was a question which had only worrisome answers. We sat in silence for a while, dreading the possibilities, weighing risks. She brought up the police: shouldn't I have notified them? Then answered her own question. I had not been in my right mind.

"Did you put the Peace medal in with the body?" she said suddenly.

I told her about finding the leather thong, sliced clean, about searching all through the underbrush for it, and for his wampum belt.

"Maybe he knew, and did something -I don't know- ritualistic with his things before he..."

She trailed off. We sat again in silence, mentally visualizing possible scenarios, until Ray harumphed from behind the bar, thinking I might need a little jump start. It was enough to get me to continue with my account, and I told her about night fishing, rope making, Casco's gift of the bobwhite. She was fascinated by my stories about food gathering and storage and the meals I made. She got a big kick out of my fish-smoking attempt, though she tried not to laugh too hard. I made little of the loneliness and despair I so often felt in those months. I didn't want to recollect the hours I spent curled into a self-pitying ball on the dirt floor. I led her right to the door of the Ship Ahoy with my tale, and a little beyond. She looked over at Ray, Phinneas and Nolan sitting with their heads together talking, and said, "You landed well, Theo. Now, what happened to your eye?"

After lunch I thought it would be nice to go for a walk around town. But as Ria was putting on her coat and saying goodbye, Ray pulled me aside and said, "Listen. We pooled our ration coupons and bought a few gallons of gas. Nolan says to take his car and drive her out to the beach, take a walk. You know, romantic." He said that last word in kind of an oily mumble, and I pretended I didn't hear.

The rest of the day went by too fast. Ria loved the beach. She took off her shoes and ran into the freezing surf in her stockings, chasing the bubbling wake of outgoing waves, then dodging the next incoming curl just before it crashed. She said very little about school, only that she wanted to get through the final year so she could be back on the Cape taking classes in Provincetown.

"What about you, Theo? You'll be drafted, won't you. Tell me you haven't been already. I couldn't bear it."

I hadn't yet received my notice, but since I'd turned eighteen I expected it with every delivery of the mail. I remembered Davey and Ray pouring over the forms, Ray sitting and sipping whiskey when it was done.

"I guess I'll do whatever it takes." It felt heroic, saying those words, but I wasn't sure I meant them. I had little choice in the matter, either way. Generally, I tried to not think about it, but of course it was the biggest topic of discussion in the bar, the kitchen, the dump and anywhere else my daily routine took me. "You'll be going over soon," people would say to me, smiling and excited. Old men whacked me on the back, shook my hand. Everyone was in it together, happy to pitch in and conserve, collect scrap metal and paper, knit socks, patrol the beach. Ria said nothing more about it, only, "You'd better take me back. It's getting dark." We got up and brushed the sand off our clothes. Ria was shivering, so I took my socks off and gave them to her. She laughed but pulled them on and squeezed into her shoes. The car had no heater, so she sat huddled against me for the ride up to Eastham, which was a largely silent one. The moon, sliced cleanly in half, followed along flickering through the treeline. We had so much to talk about, but for some reason we didn't. It was dark by the time I pulled off the main road and down a narrow path toward the Bay. There were no other houses along the way, only the black branches of windblown scrub pine which scratched against the wheel wells, making little clicking sounds. I had to drive very slowly because of my poor eyesight, but also because Nolan's headlights were taped over, part of the blackout effort. The sandy track reflected just enough light to see by. Ria sat up and watched the road until we pulled into a little clearing. A dark wedge of long, sloping roof covered a small house with a generous porch facing the water. A low dune separated it from the beach.

"Come in and meet Flora, then you can go," said Ria, opening the car door. She sat with one leg outside, then turned and added, "Theo, you can't imagine how happy I am to have found you again." She gazed steadily me as if to memorize my features, waiting for me to say something. For the length of the drive, I had been debating whether to kiss her at this point, but I honestly didn't know how. I wasn't sure she wanted me to, or how any of it was supposed to work. So I just sat there and said, "Me, too," like an idiot. Someone else would've known that, especially since there was a war on and we might not see each other for another long stretch of time. This was not nearly enough to say to someone you loved at a time of parting. I struggled to put together a sentence which would express all my longing, the tenuous threads of hope that this very moment would happen someday. Here I was in the middle of it, and I was frozen, incapable of speech or movement. I opened my mouth to say something, but as I turned to her she was already out of the car, closing the door and saying, "C'mon. It's freezing out here."

We parted, promising to write to each other with news of anything remarkable that happened to us over the next six months. Ria and her mother would be back on the Cape in early June if all was well in the Bang household, and as soon as she had secured a job and registered for classes in Provincetown, Ria would take the train to Orleans. We stood shivering on the porch making these sketchy plans, unable to take steps away while the waves made shushing noises crumbling against the shore. I wrenched my hands from my pockets and clamped them around her shoulders. "I don't want you to go," was all I could manage, but I suppose that said it all.

"Theo, let's know each other for our whole lives, all right?" She hugged me around my waist, her face smashed against my chest.

"All right," I said. I leaned over and kissed her frozen lips, just once, for only a second. Then I turned and walked to the car.

On the drive home, I mumbled prayers to God, to the sky, the ocean, the moon and stars that when she returned, I would be waiting at the depot in Orleans, and not stranded in an Army uniform somewhere on the other side of the Atlantic.

In March the packet of enlistment papers came in the mail. This time it was delivered to the Ship Ahoy in person by my father. He simply walked in, tossed it on the bar and left. As he walked away Ray realized who it was by the pinned-up right sleeve of his coat. He handed the envelope to me in the kitchen as I was finishing the cleanup after lunch, which wasn't much work. We had to make do with shortages of shortening, sugar, many of the canned goods we relied on, and coffee. Every scrap of tin foil had to be either reused or saved. Liza and I adjusted as needed, but realistically we needn't have worried. We'd served a total of two meals that day, one to Phinneas, and that was average for the week. One contributing factor to the loss of business was the Officer's Club at Camp Wellfleet. The previous year the US Army had constructed a training base there on the ocean side which, among other activities, was used as an anti-aircraft firing range. They would send a radio-controlled drone out a couple of miles over the water and shoot at a piece of cloth that it towed. I can remember the sound of their practice, hair-raising reports that echoed down the length of the Cape. The Officer's Club was a lively scene which attracted young women and some of the girls from Orleans would head up there on the weekends for a change of scenery.

I wondered if Ray felt the pinch of keeping both Liza and me employed through these lean months, though we had cut back on our hours together already. So when I saw the draft board's return address on the envelope it was with a sense of relief that I filled out the forms. I had given the matter considerable thought. I would serve my country and at the same time allay the guilt I felt having Ray keep me on. I was to mail the forms back and wait for them to tell me when to report.

Around that time I saw glimpses of a disturbing matter developing in the bar, though no one else was aware of it at the time, or was affected by it as I was. Walter, the man who had boasted to Phinneas about finding artifacts around Pleasant Bay, and who Ria and I had encountered years before, began to come into the bar several times a week. At first he was simply boring, as Phinneas and Ray noted almost from the beginning. Walter blabbed away, trying too hard to belong, wearing his expensive country gear and dropping local names. After a couple of weeks he stopped sitting at the end of the bar and took up residence across the room, under the mural. To my annoyance he practically claimed as his own the table where Ria and I had shared our lunch. He seemed to have a steady supply of cash, and would buy a drink for anyone who sat with him, always at his adamant invitation. After he snared a victim he'd proceed to blather on about himself, his New York life, his various professions which all sounded a bit shady, and about the property he'd bought on the Bay. He had a certain flair, his wit was sharp and he knew how to tell a story. I would often hear raucous laughter coming from his table, shouted orders for another round. I was sure it was he who had cleared the land out on Casco's point. In fact, I overheard him asking the Huff boys about quahogging in the marshes around Barley Neck and Sampson's Island, which were just across the river. That's why I began an obsession with him that was probably unhealthy, but couldn't help myself. I wanted to hear about what he'd found out there, if anything. I started to spend more time hanging around the bar, sweeping the floor of the dining area, clearing tables, ferrying drinks. Ray didn't seem to notice. Maybe he thought I needed something to do. Walter had a kind of charm, was always ready with a smarmy joke or a lengthy story about a business deal gone wrong from which he inevitably seemed to emerge the wise victor. He was like a kind of appetizing poison. He talked with his mouth full, spraying tidbits far and wide as he entertained his guests, clanking the silverware and taking mighty gulps of whatever libation was that night's choice. I was often given the task of waiting on his table. He asked my name early on, and decided to call me "Birdman," a nickname I secretly liked.

I wanted to see the site, or house, if one had been built. The worry I'd be sent overseas and Walter would somehow find Casco's grave nagged constantly at me. Not that I could do anything about it even if I were to stay here, but I needed to reassure myself that the house was nowhere near the body. I had Sundays off then, and each time the day rolled around I told myself to go out and have a look, but somehow I couldn't bring myself to go. Walter never came in on Sundays, because the Huff boys spent the better part of the day parked at their usual table. On a few occasions, the two camps had already come to near blows over some jingoistic remark or commentary by Walter on the local hicks, and without discussion they'd worked out a loose schedule that allowed them all to drink in relative peace. So Walter could likely be out there on a Sunday. But every time he stepped over the threshold into the bar it sent a pang of dread through my gut. Each time I would promise myself that I would go and have a look. I knew that if I were still here in a month when the season hit, there would be no opportunity for me to get away from the bar in daylight hours. The knowledge of Casco's body out there and my interment of it slowly drove me a little crazy as I waited day by day for the letter ordering me to report to the nearest recruitment center.

In early April, two men from the lumberyard came into the Ship Ahoy. They were in high spirits and bought the bar a round (that would be Phinneas and Ray), then ordered hamburgers for themselves. They had spent the day loading up lumber and other materials needed for a good-sized house, and delivering it to the landing at Paw Wah. Flush for the first time in months, they wanted to celebrate, as there had been almost no building going on in town for several years except for WPA projects. The lumberyard, previously a solid and solvent enterprise, had been reduced to getting by building doghouses for the Welsh Terriers the military imported to patrol the beach, on the lookout for submarines.

"Soon as the ground thaws the backhoe's ready," said one of the men, clinking glasses with Ray.

This was good news, a sign that things might be picking up and tourism would hold steady, God willing. But for me the news meant only one thing. It was time to go out and see the site for myself and finally put an end to my anxiety.

Two days later Nolan appeared early in the morning, coming into the kitchen through the back door. I was sitting on the counter drinking coffee and listening to the radio.

"I wonder if I could enlist your help for a couple of hours," he said.

"Sure, anything." I pointed to the coffeepot.

As he fixed himself a cup he explained that he had been given a small shed to add on to his studio if he would take it down and move it.

"Ray's okay with it," he added.

We got in his car and drove toward the beach. It was still cold, though the faintest dusting of green could be seen here and there at the edges of the road. Nolan was chatting away about his studio, a long low tin-roofed outbuilding inset with a row of mismatched windows lighting a stretch of workbench. I had been there on a few occasions, and always liked the atmosphere of paint fumes, curls of shaved-off wood and dusty, half finished projects. Nolan's two little towheaded daughters wandered in and out or climbed into his lap for a quick doze. He planned to add the new shed as an el for storing canvasses. "If I ever get around to painting again," he said.

When he took the left for the boatyard at Arey's Pond, and I saw how close we'd be to Walter's building site, I knew I had to take advantage of the situation. As we bumped along a little track skirting the South side of the pond I said to Nolan, "Would it be all right if I took the car on a small detour before we begin?"

"Of course. Where are you going?"

I told him I wanted to go out to the point, see my old stomping grounds.

"Great. I'll go with you. I haven't been out there in ages. Where to?"

"Paw Wah," I said, trying to keep the dread out of my voice.

Nolan turned the car around and we headed back out. Along the way he talked about his nights of late. He'd been assigned to patrol against submarines on the Outer Beach, armed with a government issue .45. Not only did the North wind pound its frozen fist on his back, but the dark, the danger, the gun completely panicked him.

"I don't know if I'll be able to shoot the thing should anyone come ashore," he said. "They really need to get someone else." As it happened they did, only a few weeks later, when it was decided that his talents were better used drafting plans for proposed temporary government buildings, and he was let go.

As the car crested the hill and faced the point, the obscene gap in the tree line looked even more startling than from the water. Nolan glanced at me as I leaned forward and grasped the dashboard. Then he saw it too.

"What the hell? When did that happen?" he mumbled. He pulled the car to a stop at the landing, and we got out.

"This is where you were," Nolan said gently as we stood gazing across the channel. "Isn't it." Ray must have filled him in.

"Yeah." I wanted to blurt out the whole story then and there, to have Nolan take charge; tell me what to do. Take on my burden of guilt and fear. I turned to him and opened my mouth to do so, his kind eyes willing me to unload whatever was troubling me about this place. But I couldn't do it, couldn't risk his disapproval or the chance that he might think some authority needed to be informed. I just reached down and upended a thick plank which was lying at my feet, and let it fall with a splat into the mud of the channel. The tide was low enough so we could make it across without getting too wet. It was obviously used for that very purpose. We trudged along the shore in silence until we came to Casco's path, still visible in the barren, frozen woods, and climbed the short hill. My stomach flipped over a few times along the way, my forehead beaded with cold sweat. Sure enough, the area around where Casco's wigwam had stood was cleared of trees. The pulled stumps now lay in a pile of tangled roots. The rounded hollow of the wigwam's floor looked like a portal to an underground world, its entry point the black bull's eye where the fire had burned steadily for years. The six bent-over saplings which had formed the roof had been yanked out, leaving ragged, caved-in spots along the rim where leaves had caught and rotted, and now bloomed with blood-red mold. Even though I heard birdsong and the chatter of squirrels in the trees as we walked up the path, a lifeless quiet hung about the house site. It was a void, a vacuum in the midst of the life going on all around us. Nolan must have felt it too. We stood staring down into the bowl where Casco and I had both lived. A wave of sorrow passed over me. I looked up at the clouds to shake it off, then forced myself to drag my eyes to the spot where the body was buried. No trace of the grave was visible, except for the chunk of granite I had placed there before I left. But fifteen feet behind it was another of the stakes, a strip of white cloth hanging limp against the name written down its length. Nolan walked over and read it.

"Askew." He turned to me. "That's Walter, isn't it? This is the place he's been blabbing about?"

I nodded, completely distracted now, trying to ascertain where the future cellar hole might be located, and whether Casco's bones would be scooped up into the backhoe's shovel in the process of creating it. There was nothing I could do about it. Not now, not ever. I had to put it from my mind, let what would be, be. Nolan walked the perimeter of the clearing, eyeing me while he paced off the dimensions. "Big," was all he said.

"Let's go. All right?" I said. "I've seen enough." Suddenly I wanted to run the hell away from that place, to never have had anything to do with it. It was cursed, even the birds could tell. Walter could have it. I turned and strode down the path.

Nolan brought me back to town as it was getting dark. The shed had come down easily and was strapped in pieces to the roof of his jalopy. Then we reassembled it onto a block foundation he'd cobbled together the day before. His girls were around, laughing and chattering, teasing us and helping with small tasks. The gloom of earlier lifted and was all but forgotten in the sunny, calm atmosphere of Nolan's household. So when I stepped inside the bar and Ray handed me my call-up papers I felt unhampered and fully committed to joining my fellow Americans in something far weightier than my own predicament. I was to report to Camp Edwards in two days' time. Ray said he'd drive me over, and gently suggested I might want to go and say goodbye to my parents. He was right of course, though my first reaction was to turn away and head into the kitchen to start chopping onions. I had made my way through about half a dozen when I glanced up to see Ray leaning in the doorway, arms folded on his chest, a cigarette glowing against his dark, wool shirt.

"I'll go with you if you like, but I'm serious Theo, man to man. You need to do this."

I stared at the pile of onions and said nothing, but nodded slowly. I knew he was right, that as cold as they were, as cruel as my father had been, my parents were owed a last look at their only son, if indeed it turned out that way.

"And stop wasting onions, if you don't mind. They just went up two cents a pound yesterday."

I looked at him and we both burst out laughing. I nodded, resigned to the task, and said, "Okay, yeah. I know. I'll go tomorrow, after the dump."

"Don't worry. You'll thank me later."

I felt surprisingly nonchalant on the drive over to the house. I hadn't given my impending visit more than a moment's thought either during the night or the next morning as I assembled the dump run and packed it into the truck. My mind was full of Army, Navy, Air Corps. To which division would I be assigned? I spent several hours in the middle of the night willing myself to remain calm, to stay with those thoughts only, to take it one step at a time and not fast-forward to the moment I'd be called on to actually kill someone. I tried to remember all the reasons Liza had for wanting me to go, but I couldn't come up with a single one that didn't involve her being French.

When I turned into the driveway though, it was a different story. My father happened to be standing about ten feet in, straddling the strip of grass that ran down its center. He was holding his shotgun and staring straight at me. I had obviously startled him in mid-hunt, probably some innocent raccoon who'd had the bad idea to look for spring buds on his property.

"Theo," he said, dropping the shotgun to his side.

I rested my elbow on the window frame and let the engine idle. "I came to say goodbye. I've been called up. I go for my physical tomorrow."

A flicker of pain crossed his face, his shoulders sank.

"Well. I guess you'd better come in and see your mother," he said.

I drove on past him rather awkwardly as he hefted the gun to his shoulder and followed. My mother was surprised, of course, and very nervous. She invited me in for coffee, which felt strange, but I accepted and sat down in my old spot at the kitchen table. She bustled about with the kettle while I repeated my reason for the visit. She didn't turn around at the news, but there was a second or two of hesitation while she steadied herself against the countertop. My father came in and sat down.

"So," he said after a few moments of silence.

"So," I said.

"You enlist?"

"No."

"Got the draft notice?"

"Yep."

My mother still hadn't turned from the stove. With her back to me she said, "Can you see out of that eye? It looks painful."

"No, not very well."

"They won't take you."

I didn't understand at first. I thought she was saying that Ray wouldn't give me a ride to the recruitment center. "What?" I said, confused.

"The army. They'll reject you with that eye." She turned to us, a cup in each hand, and set them down.

Involuntarily, I raised my hand and covered my eye. Could it be true? Why had no one said so?

"Now, you don't know that, Dorothy," my father piped up.

"You'll see," she said with her own brand of finality, and a rather odd choice of words. That was the end of it, but the thought distracted me throughout the rest of that uncomfortable visit. Somehow we got through the coffee and a stilted conversation about the winter's fishing. My mother sat staring at the table cloth and twisting her fingers together

"Everything is fine at the Ship Ahoy," I said. "I have some money saved up, and after I get back I plan to go to college." This was a lie, I'd never considered it. But Ray had suggested I say it to mitigate any doubts they had about what kind of lifestyle I was leading working in a bar and living above it.

"That's great, Theo," my father brightened briefly. My mother said nothing.

"Well, I guess I'd better go. I have to get the truck back." I wanted badly to get away.

My father stood up as I rose and stuck out his hand. We shook, left-handed, then he walked to the door and opened it. I looked at my mother. She had picked up her Bible. The last thing I wanted was a quote from it to send me off to war, but she was flipping through it.

"Goodbye, Mom." I edged toward the door.

She looked up, thumb lodged between the pages. Lifting the corners of her mouth she said, "Goodbye Theo, may God be with you."

I hesitated a moment or two, in case she wanted to kiss me, but she just stared straight ahead. So I walked out.

On the porch, my father waited for me. I nodded to him as I passed, and he reached out and grabbed my shoulders with his one arm, squeezing hard. His breathing was heavy, he was looking wildly around at the porch roof, the steps, the yard.

"I love you." he said, then turned and walked inside, shutting the door. The latch made a soft click.

Stunned, I got in the truck, backed around and drove up the track, my hands and feet moving automatically. He had never once said those words to me.

Of course my mother was right. I didn't even make it through the physical. They took one look at my eye, tested it, and rejected me on the spot. I put up a mild protest, insisting they give me a desk job, a job humping crates, cooking. "Sorry. Got all we need of those. Come back in two years and we'll see," was the only response. Ray didn't seem surprised when I showed him the papers with the IV-F stamp. I suppose he also knew I'd never be taken, and now I'm amazed it hadn't occurred to me. It took some time to come to it, but I will be forever thankful that I did not go, that my brief dalliance with the duty of taking up arms against my fellow human beings was cut short. I do believe that particular war had to be fought, that brutal, despotic regimes should be demolished, as was accomplished. But as for the war we are involved in now, in Vietnam, I suspect we are committing atrocities which may be comparable to those carried out by the Nazis. So, for me it's best to stay in the woods with the chipmunks and chickadees and not engage in theory or analysis, simply keep out of the way of the mighty machine as they try to do.

We arrived back at the Ship Ahoy to find a banner hanging over the bar with colorful dancing letters saying, 'Good Luck Pvt. Sparrow'. Liza had obviously been busy planning a party for later on. A huge vanilla cake sat cooling in layers in the kitchen, despite the rationing of sugar. Phinneas took one look at my face and reached up to unpin the end of the banner that hung over his head, while Ray got the other.

"Sorry, son," he said, mustering a somber tone. He studied my face for signs of anger and despair, but as soon as my eyes met his we started to laugh, and then Ray joined in and poured us all a beer. We clanked the bottles together lightly so as not to alert Liza, and secretly toasted the happy fact that we would not be separated.

Life went back to normal for about a month. Nolan came in to touch up the mural as he did every June, and we celebrated the beginning of summer by hosting a War Bond rally with a goal of two thousand dollars, which netted three, much to everyone's surprise. Walter's house was underway with no mention of any bones having been unearthed. The builders often came in for lunch, so I knew that the cellar had been dug and poured, the framing begun. Walter was away for weeks at a time, then suddenly he'd be in the bar almost every night, holding court at the table under the mural. But he didn't bother me any more. Somehow the trip up to the point had erased my obsession with him and his connection to Casco's and my private domain. It was as though I had joined Casco in his otherworldly realm, the wigwam and the woods now relocated there, where I could freely reminisce without the intrusion of reality.

Ria was due to move into the cottage in Eastham with her mother and Flora. I still have the postcard she sent that year, a picture of the Flatiron Building with the message, "Goodbye, New York! Flora and I will arrive on the 21st with the car, Mother taking the train to meet us the following day. Can't wait to see you! Wait by the 'phone in the pm. XO, Ria.

I saved the card specifically because it had been mailed on the 20th, the day before I discovered the first clue to the mystery of what happened to Casco.

It was a Friday night and the bar was almost full. It was unseasonably warm that night, all the doors stood open and people were milling around outside, coming in for a shot and sipping on the doorstep. We operated by the light of a single lantern to comply with the blackout regulations. The guys from the lumber company were in, their overalls covered with splashes of concrete. The Huff boys sat solidly at their table, arms folded, beer bottles stacked to one side the way they liked it. Phinneas was in his usual place, leaning against the back wall with the latest issue of the Provincetown Advocate open on the bar. He and Ray had been having a long discussion about Victory gardens. Phinneas wanted to plant one "out back," which was really just a strip of scruffy grass between the parking lot and the road to Town Cove. The newspaper contained an editorial about the soil in parts of that town.

"Listen to this," said Phinneas, reading. "'...the ancient mariners who left this port for the distant and curious corners of the world brought back chunks of land from those places to make them forever Provincetown! There is no doubt at all...'" he went on, holding up a finger to stop Ray from delivering a beer to one of the tables, "'...but that soil from India was brought here, and doubtless there is soil from the Azores, and from South American countries, and probably from China, now all mingled and congenial. George Rogers swears that Rear Admiral 'Fighting Bob' Evans had his men unload a great many bags of rich Cuban soil here, when the fleet was in, to surface the athletic field for the recreation of the sailors.'"

"Wasn't it also used as ballast?" said Ray, setting down the drink.

"Yes, and with it they brought back trees and plants from all over the world. It says here that the cedar trees in the old Winthrop Street cemetery are from Libya. Good God!"

"Baloney," said one of the Huffs.

Walter was there, fresh from one of his trips. He'd ordered a steak and had sawed his way through it, washing it down with great gulps of beer. Two men from out of town sat with him, one of them wearing a beautiful linen suit in the "Hollywood" style, kind of like a gentleman's safari jacket. "Taupe," he said, with a prissy little popping sound, when someone asked him about the color. Walter had been boasting about the pile of gas ration stamps he had in the glove compartment of his car. "Enough to go anywhere I want," he said. He waited for someone to ask how he had acquired them, but no one did and he moved on to other topics. After a while a woman came in and sat with her arm threaded through that of the man in the taupe suit. She was wearing a colorful beaded necklace in a pseudo Indian style which sort of zigzagged across her chest. Walter reached out to finger it and Taupe Suit swatted his hand away to peals of laughter from the woman. They ordered another round. She wanted some complicated thing, a Pink Lady maybe. I remember Ray had to ask Phinneas for help with the recipe. The other three were drinking Manhattans.

I went into the kitchen to fry piles of clams and chop more cabbage for cole slaw. We never seemed to make enough. Liza was upset because one of her cakes had burned, and she was scraping at it with a knife trying to make it edible. The orders kept coming at a pace we could barely keep up with, and the kitchen was hot, even with the back door open. I kept going to the bar for ice, or to refill Liza's ever-present Coca-Cola, and on one of those trips I overheard Walter pontificating about Indian artifacts. I looked over at his table, where the four of them were obviously drunk and heading toward sloppy. Walter had the woman's necklace in his hand and was leaning over it, holding it up to his eye.

"This is a piece of crap," he said.

The woman grabbed it out of his hand and stuffed it into her purse. Walter leaned back and started in on a rambling discourse about Northeastern wampum beadwork while the woman, listing in her chair with her chin in her hand, tried to focus.

"Everyone thinks the stuff was used as currency by the Indians, but it's not true," he said, slurring his words. "It was more of a communication, a marker of events, a deal-sealer. Plus it kept a kind of visual history, if you know how to read it. The Europeans were the ones who started using it as money. You can imagine what happened to the quahog population!" He roared with laughter. The others snickered politely.

"Now, for example," Walter was saying, a belt might have white designs on a purple background, but if it is surrounded by a white border it indicates a relationship that was once hostile is now peaceful. Or say," he turned to one of the men, "you wanted this dilly here to be your bride," he flicked his thumb at the woman, "you'd give a friend, a go-between, a little string of wampum to take to her. That meant you were interested."

"What if she's not?" said the woman, coyly sucking on a straw.

"She'd give it back." He rolled his eyes at the other men. "Now, these wampum items are quite rare and valuable, and as a matter of fact, I found a nice belt right in this area not too many years ago. White triangles on a purple background."

I was heading into the kitchen with a load of dirty dishes but stopped cold when I heard this. Casco's belt had white triangles on a purple background, with inch-wide strips of white beads top and bottom. Stunned, I fumbled the stack of dishes and almost lost my grip. They rattled loudly as I tried to catch the rest of Walter's conversation.

"How valuable did you say?" one of the men piped up.

"I didn't say. Don't get any ideas. It's not like they're just lying around. You have to know where to look." Walter slung his arms up behind his head and crossed them. He tipped his chair back as a gloating, preening, fluttery-eyed look spread itself across his face "I put in years of research."

"So who buys this stuff?"

"I've got a guy."

I pushed the kitchen door open with my foot and staggered over to the sink. I knew. My arms lowered automatically and the dishes dropped into the soapy water with a muffled clatter. I knew what Walter had done to get that belt, and I was certain it was Casco's belt he was referring to. Not only the belt, I was sure he had stolen the Peace medal as well. I pictured the leather thong Ria had fed through its hole, cleanly sliced and discarded in the bushes near Casco's body. Of course! My face flushed with anger as I swatted my forehead. How could I have been so dense? Heaving with outrage I stood immobilized by my revelation, the vision of him, the killer, the thief, sitting out there with his self-satisfied smirk.

I began to pace in front of the dishwashing station, trying to figure out what to do. I wanted to run out and confront him, or knock him down with a well-placed punch. Of course I could do neither, and I knew it. But what could I do? I had to take some action. He killed a person! My friend! For a couple of Indian artifacts! He needed to be arrested and sent to prison! I continued to march furiously back and forth, sputtering my disgust, lost in different versions of the same mental scenario - Walter cowering, confessing, while I stood over him accusing, wringing the truth from those flabby lips, the police on the way, siren blaring, the restaurant in an uproar.

"Girlfriend trouble?" Liza put her hand on my shoulder.

I stared blankly at her for a few seconds, then mumbled something and shook my head.

"Okay, so you don't want to talk about it. Boy do I know the feeling." She held up her Coca-Cola glass and rattled the ice in the bottom. "Get me a little refill?"

"Sure," I said. I grabbed the glass and pushed through the door. Walter and his party were as before, the woman now leaning against

Taupe Suit, snoring into his sleeve. I glared at Walter, who gave a little wave, then described a circle with his finger to order another round.

"I'll bring that over," I told Ray when I returned after delivering Liza's Coca-Cola. I took the tray of Manhattans and walked slowly toward Walter's table. My hands were shaking and the glasses clinked ominously as I crossed the room, like the threatening soundtrack to a horror movie. I didn't know what I was going to say or do. My mind worked furiously to come up with a savvy line that would put Walter in his place, let him know that I knew, scare the shit out of him.

"Thanks, Birdman," he said as I distributed the drinks. "Busy tonight."

"Yes we are. Busy, that is," I stammered. I stood there with the tray clamped under my arm, staring at Walter.

"So?" he laughed nervously.

"I heard you talking about wampum.".

"Why, yes. We were. You interested?"

"Know where we can find some?" Taupe suit piped up, and they all laughed. The woman's head, lolling on his shoulder, jumped a little with each guffaw.

I said nothing. I kept on boring my eyes into Walter's.

"Something on your mind, kid?"

"No, nothing at all." I turned and walked away. I needed more time to work out what to do. It was neither the time nor the place for a confrontation of any sort. In the back of my mind I saw myself rolling Casco's stiff body into the grave. Who knows what laws I'd broken? I could easily be ruled as complicit in a murder. I would at least have some elaborate explaining to do if I were wrong and Walter's belt was just a coincidental find.

"Don't tell me that grandstander is a friend of yours," Liza said as I sidled back over to the sink.

"No. But he was talking about something I'm interested in. He seems to know a lot about it."

"Let me tell you something, honey, about guys like that," she said. "Knowledge is knowing a tomato is a fruit. Wisdom is not putting it in a fruit salad. That guy is about as unwise as they come. Be careful."

I looked over at her and she winked, then went back to frying onions. There was something prophetic about that statement, though I had heard her say it before. I took it as a confirmation to retreat, to think about this matter thoroughly before doing anything. To be wise. As I slid the big pots into the water and added more soap I remembered that Ria was coming the next day. I would tell her everything. Maybe she would know what to do.

Chapter 9

Ria and Flora arrived at their cottage in Eastham the following night in a heavy rainstorm. The winter winds had blown the shingles off a section of the roof and driven water into the cracks and seams underneath. Ria's mother's bedroom, specifically the bed, was awash in oily brown water. They had the roof repaired the next day, with only a few hours to spare before rushing to the station to pick her up, after which she was installed on a dry bed with a dry sherry and Flora in attendance.

Ria managed to secure a weekend job at The Clam Shack, a tourist eatery within walking distance of the cottage. She had also enrolled in the Hans Hofmann School of Fine Arts in Provincetown. It took almost a full week for us to get together, though Ria called the bar almost daily.

"Okay," she said breathlessly when I picked up the phone. "I'm free, and I'm coming to Orleans on the 6:50. You busy?"

"Just come," I said. I was bursting with my discovery of Walter's probable guilt and couldn't hold out much longer. I couldn't risk talking about it during our daily phone calls, even though the bar was one of the few in town that didn't have a party line. Orleans had real, live operators who could easily listen in on any conversation, and I knew a few of them. Added to that, I had seen one of them having dinner with Walter in the bar on more than one occasion. I tried giving Ria hints that something was amiss, but without being able to mention Walter, or Casco, or Indian artifacts, or Paw Wah Point, there wasn't much for her to go on.

"I know," I said abruptly during one of her rushed reports.

"What?"

"I know." I tried saying it in a deeper voice for emphasis.

"What do you know?"

"Something."

"Okay," she said after a pause. "What?"

I couldn't go on with the ridiculous cloak-and-dagger tactic. "I'll tell you later," I said, sounding even more screwy. Ria remembered though, and brought it up as soon as she stepped off the train. It was almost dark, the moon just coming up and turning the tracks silver. I spotted her as she marched toward me, already talking.

"What happened? Did you find something?" she said, firing a slew of questions at me. But I couldn't answer. I was trying hard to fully accept that she was standing in front of me again. It had been seven months since we'd seen each other, for one afternoon. That direct gaze of hers was alive with what I can only describe as luminescence in the true, moonlit sense of the word. I felt shy meeting her eyes. The intense gray I knew so well was now a shimmering reflection of every light around us. She was wearing a white dress with a sailor's collar which had a double row of blue piping running along the edge. I wanted to follow that blue with my fingers up her neckline, around the back under her glossy, dancing hair and down the front of her dress. She was simply so beautiful I couldn't speak for a long time and stood there gaping. She must have had an inkling of the effect she had on me, because she stopped talking, put her hands on her hips and smiled. In that moment I fell in love with her again. The feeling overtook me with a force I will remember for the rest of my life. But I didn't say so, instead I blurted out, "That creep Walter. He did it. He killed Casco for a lousy couple of artifacts."

"What?" her eyes danced between mine.

"I overheard him in the bar talking about it. He was talking about this wampum belt he found. Ria, it was Casco's belt he was describing. And now he owns the land where Casco's buried and--"

"What?"

"Yeah. He bought most of the point. He's building a house on it. Right next to Casco's grave." I hadn't told Ria this in any of the letters I'd written. I didn't want to risk anyone else having a look at them. Maybe I didn't want to believe it myself, wanted to be done with the entire matter. After that day out there with Nolan, I thought I was.

"Theo, let's go some place where you can tell me this from the beginning. Do you have to work?" We were walking toward the bar. The blacked-out town was quiet, and no one was about.

"No," I said. Ray had given me the rest of the night off when I said I was going to meet Ria's train.

"Where's your room?"

I looked at her, not sure if this was proper. Liza had an entire set of rules about what was and wasn't, and I could never keep track of them. I brushed them aside.

"Around the corner, up some steps," I said, mentally reviewing the state of my bed, my cast-off clothes, the deep-fry smell which permeated the second floor.

As soon as we entered Ria briefly took in her surroundings, then threw herself into a dilapidated easy chair I'd dragged in from the hallway. She kicked off her shoes, tucking her legs up onto the seat.

"Okay," she said, extracting a pack of cigarettes from a pocket hidden somewhere in the folds of her dress. I stood there, speechless again, gazing at her hair, her legs, her lips as they closed around the tip of the cigarette.

"This all right?" She held it out to me.

"Yes, yes of course," I stammered, pushing an old coffee cup toward her.

"Theo, please. Go on. Who is this Walter?"

"Do you remember that day out on Money Head? The guy who was asking about arrowheads?"

"Yes of course, Theo. I remember everything."

"He's sitting downstairs in the bar right now," I said, pointing to the floor and lowering my voice almost to a whisper. I began to pace to keep my head clear, so I could talk without being distracted by her beauty. I told her everything, describing every event I had suffered, from the day I'd seen the sickening hole in the tree line to the day the boys from the lumberyard came in and announced the house project. I recounted Walter's appearance at the bar, the way heclaimed as his own the table where we'd had our lunch together. She waited patiently for me to get to the point, smoking one cigarette after another, listening.

"Now he comes in here all the time. He's a dealer, a hunter of some kind. He has this person, this collector he sells stuff to. Indian stuff, I don't know what-all."

Finally I recounted the discussion of wampum at Walter's table and his description of Casco's belt. She made me repeat what he'd said several times. She too remembered the pattern on Casco's belt, the distinct triangles, the white border.

"My God, Theo, could it be?" she pulled pensively on her cigarette. I didn't answer.

"Why would he come back here, buy that land, if he killed someone there?" Her eyebrows gathered, momentarily rearranging that perfect swath of bangs. It was a good question, one I had asked myself numerous times already. One answer was that he wanted to cover up something.

She asked me to go over the details of what I'd found when I went to Casco's the day of the blackfish killing, the exact position of his body, the bruise, the blood, the bushes. I did, to the best of my ability.

"Do you think he knows you lived out there for a year?" she added.

I shrugged.

"Well, how does he behave toward you? Does he give you any looks, does he talk to you?"

"No, just normal bar stuff."

"Let's go downstairs. I want to see this guy."

I stopped pacing and leaned heavily against the door. I didn't want to go down to the bar at all. Telling Ria about Walter had calmed me for the first time in days. As I paced and talked the tension had drained out of me. I felt like lying down on the bed. I wanted to stay up there in my room with Ria sprawled barefoot in the chair, and listen to her talk, simply talk, about anything except Walter. Suddenly none of it seemed to matter anymore, the only important thing was that Ria and I were reunited and we had an entire summer ahead of us. She drummed her fingers on the arm of the chair and looked at me with the same candid, affectionate regard I remembered from our days roaming the shores of Pleasant Bay.

"Or maybe not," she said. "It's nice up here. I can always get a look at him. Anyhow, I remember his face." She paused and lit up another cigarette. "I don't think you need to worry about him, Theo. If he had something to say to you, wouldn't he have brought it up by now?"

A soft knock on the door startled us both. "You in there?" It was Phinneas.

I opened up to find him standing in the hall fiddling with the buttons on his vest. He peered past me at Ria who put her hand up and said, "Hey Phinneas. How are you?"

"Hello," he replied with a little nod and a smile. "Theo, I've been sent up by Liza. She needs help. The restaurant is all of a sudden full."

"Okay," I said. I glanced at Ria and cursed silently.

"I'll help," she said, stubbing out her cigarette and pushing her feet into her shoes.

Liza gratefully positioned her at the sink in front of a mound of dirty plates, which she launched into with surprising gusto. I doubt Ria had ever done a sink full of dishes in her life, but that night she not only kept up, but kept us all entertained, singing along to the songs on the radio, flicking soapsuds at me and laughing at Liza's commentary. Phinneas manned the bar while Ray ferried plates in and out of the kitchen and I tended the deep fryer, lowering chopped potatoes, batter-dipped clams and cod filets into the bubbling oil and feeling happier than I had in months.

A couple of hours later, I walked Ria through the darkened streets to the station, in time to make the last train. We strolled down the sidewalk, both quiet after the din of the kitchen, and halfway there she put her hand through the crook of my arm, flashed her eyes at me and grinned. I can still see her at that instant, the exuberance of her spirit enveloping us, separating us from the rest of the drab, war-torn world into a sparkling sphere of our own. Neither one of us brought up the subject of Walter. As we wound down our time in the kitchen I'd asked if she still wanted to see him. I knew he was in the restaurant, had heard him droning on whenever the door between the bar and the kitchen opened, but somehow the opportunity never came for us to spy on him.

"No, not tonight." she'd said. "I don't want to ruin the evening."

We stood on the dark platform for a few moments. I could hear the low rumble of the train as it made its way north. "I have Sundays off," said Ria. "Do you think we could..."

"Yes," I said. I would have Sundays off if I had to quit my job.

We said our goodbyes and she jumped onboard. I watched the train move away, a shadowy behemoth crawling slowly up the spine of the peninsula, and walked back to the Ship Ahoy. I stood outside the entrance for a while, reviewing the evening and watching the light inside the bar dance through a little tear in the blackout curtains. I was in heaven.

As June melted into July, the heat of the kitchen intensified and the tourists, what there were of them in those war years, brought with them a much-needed influx of cash. Ray paid off all the debts from the winter and, in a lighthearted mood one night, hired a band to play Friday and Saturday nights. It was a little jazz trio. They divided their time between us and the Southward Inn's Green Room where they played during the week. Phinneas had been in college with the piano player, a man by the name of "Red" Beaulieu, who'd grown up in New Orleans and had been hanging around New Haven since he dropped out of school. "To pursue a much nobler purpose in life: music," he told me when we met. Indeed, the sound the trio generated for a steady four hours each night was rich, stylish and featured Red's creamy vocal interpretations of jazz standards. He'd reach down beside the bench to pluck an alto saxophone from its velvet-lined case, wet his lips and start to blow. The sound he produced gushed through the room like a flow of molten lava. Listening to Red play made me fully understand what Phinneas loved so much about jazz: the way it circles around a melody, dipping into and expanding it, running away with it and then sending it home, straight into your gut.

If you've heard the song I probably don't have to explain why "You Don't Know What Love Is" had the power to collapse my legs whenever Red sang it that summer. I was more than a little preoccupied with thoughts of Ria, and as these things go, since passion had been kindled in me I tended toward the dramatic when it came to music. I was still a teenager, after all. Red had a way of almost crying when he sang the words "...love that cannot live yet never dies," which utterly undid me. I wanted to ask him about it, tell him about mine. Of course I never did. But toward the end of summer I had to ask him to stop playing the song.

"Sure, kid," he said, with a sympathetic nod.

The first of our Sundays came only a few days after Ria had helped us out in the kitchen. Her job at the Clam Shack was a step or two up from dish washing, but nothing very engaging. On Fridays and Saturdays she chopped onions and potatoes, pulled steamed-open clams from their shells, refilled the ketchup bottles and bussed the picnic tables outside. She gathered up the greasy leavings in paper tablecloths and threw them into a foul-smelling can behind the place. She laughed about her job, calling it 'research.' She was still somewhat of a budding socialist and had gone after the job not because her parents required it, but to ally herself with the class of people she considered morally superior to her own.

Her father was still away from home most of the time. Although he took care of his wife and daughter, it was from a distance and financially managed by a lawyer. The lawyer had even arranged the purchase of the summer cottage in Eastham, where Ria's father was never to set foot. Decisions about Ria's future were made through the lawyer, and the only contact she had with her father was through a series of letters which were written in his hand, but had such a false tone of warmth to them, that she had taken to skimming them for pertinent information and discarding them. She told me this that day when, for a change, we were off the subject of Walter.

I'd driven her to Nauset beach in Ray's truck, which she loved, and we walked the beach for miles that day, the ocean as still as it can be and flickering blue after a winter's worth of steel-colored chop. She had an orange scarf wound around her head and wore white linen trousers rolled above her knees. I watched our bare feet trudge together across the wet sand in perfect unison as they had on the shore of the bay when we were escaped campers. I was so excited that first Sunday, to see her, to have her to myself for the entire day, that at first I found it difficult to hold up my end of the conversation. I mumbled distracted replies to her questions about Walter, his house, his friends. She probably figured I was tired of this subject and she was right, but it was not the reason for my lack of response. I was trying to muster the courage to hold her hand in mine, to put my arm around her waist, to touch her somehow. I kept glancing at her as we walked, to gauge whether she was feeling the same things. When she started to talk about her parents, about her mother's emotional absence, her father's physical desertion, the texture of her voice became rougher, a hesitant little hiccup punctuated her sentences, changing her usual singsong cadence into a jagged, forced delivery of information. A look of pain formed on her face and she shook her head to get rid of it. Then she laughed and kicked at a line of foam left behind by a retreating wave.

"It's better this way, when you think about it. I'm almost completely free. I'm going to art school full time, which is all I want, and they don't bother me about it. Flora's a good friend, and between the two of us we keep mother happy. Well, as happy as she can be, I guess. Father probably has someone else, I may as well admit it." She stopped and aimed a candid look at me. "Is it all so terrible?"

I was the last person she should ask for an opinion about the ethos of a family unit, but I said, "It seems to me that you're okay. Aren't you?"

"Yeah. I really am." She put her hand on my shoulder. "As you seem to be, my friend."

Just as she had before, the evening she asked me about scallops and wondered if I thought about her that way, she was now telling me once again her view of our relationship, and I should have taken the gentle hint for what it was, but I persisted in fantasizing that she felt something more for me. Otherwise, why would she be walking beside me, confessing her hopes and fears, describing intimate details of her life, or making plans for future Sundays with me?

I took her back to the bay the following week and we rowed around in Liza's boat. We cruised out the River and past Camp Mariner, rounding the point of Paw Wah without comment and into Little Pleasant Bay. We crossed over to Money Head to have a look at Camp Quanset from a distance.

"Yuck," was all she said about her former summer home.

I rowed us through the Narrows to the larger part of the bay where the campers were busy with sailing lessons. I stopped and let the boat drift while we lounged on the seats eating fried clams from a greasy bag Ria had brought from work. We were laughing, singing snatches of camp songs, basking in the sun and kicking little sprays of water at each other. I was insanely happy. The intensity of my passion weakened somewhat after I admitted the probable truth to myself about Ria's affections. But simply being with her was almost enough. Most of the time.

Ria put the last of the clams in her mouth, sat up suddenly, grabbed the oars and said with wicked glee, "Let's row across their sailing course and mess things up." She pulled the boat around with such force I almost fell into the water and headed off toward the far shore, setting a course which I saw would shortly intersect with the nearest sailboat. The two girls at its helm began immediately to yell at us to get out of the way as they scrambled to maneuver. Ria pretended she couldn't hear and winked at me, laughing as the two hulls passed within inches of each other. The sailing instructor shook his fist at us. Ria lit up a cigarette and laughed again.

"Oh, that felt good," she sighed.

"Jesus, Ria," I was a little shocked, but laughed anyway.

The sailing teams took up positions again, and went on with the lesson while Ria rowed with great, long strokes around the perimeter of the Bay and toward the Narrows again, all the while with the cigarette burning between her lips. This was a side of her I hadn't seen. She was quite strong, and shook her head when I offered to row. The current shot us through the Narrows with the incoming tide, and when we were at last alongside a marshy area Ria shipped the oars and let out another sigh.

"Remember the day I found the medal?"

"Sure."

"The reason I was out walking in the first place is because of an incident at camp that day."

"What happened?"

"Three of the girls were teasing a couple of others. One of these girls was the daughter of, I don't remember his name, a guy who worked for Henry Ford." She ran her finger along one of the oars. "Did you know Ford was an anti-Semite?"

I had only recently become aware of the term, and found it difficult to understand.

I was a fisherman's son from a small town. I didn't interact with city kids. It wasn't a subject that had ever come up at school. I remember once finding a postcard lying in the road, an advertisement for a hotel in Chatham, the grandest in our area. I took it home and asked my mother what "Strictly Gentile Clientele" meant. I don't remember what she told me, likely because knowing her, she wouldn't have missed an opportunity to quote something mysterious from the Bible, which I would have dismissed.Overheard discussions between Ray and Phinneas, or political arguments between them and the Huff boys were my only source of information about the world's problems and preoccupations at the time. I made a mental note to ask them about it.

"This Henry Ford?" I steered an imaginary car.

"Yeah. Anyhow, a trio of girls just like those little blue-eyed sailors back there made life very difficult for others there, with their comments, their teasing. What did they understand? Nothing. It happened in every camp I went to, not only that one." She jerked her thumb in the direction of Camp Quanset. "That day I slapped one of them, the captain of the sailing team, who refused to sit in a boat with certain other girls. I was sent on a walk to cool off. That's when I found the medal."

I nodded my head. I didn't fully understand the intricacies of upper-class interaction and I wasn't sure why she was telling me about it, except to explain her behavior. I guess Ria put something to rest that day, because it was the last I ever heard about it.

But the incident did serve to remind me that Ria was part of a world which would be forever foreign to me. She lived in a realm of experience and interaction I couldn't even imagine. Whatever she felt for me would always exist within the confines of Sundays on Cape Cod. This flash of insight was added to the growing pile I'd had about the chances of Ria and me as a couple. My throat closed a little as a wave of self-pity washed over me. I suppressed any display of emotion by looking into the water at the eelgrass undulating in the current. Its long strands were pulled by the rushing water into a graceful, intertwining dance, each finger of green pointing again and again toward the point and the land beyond. As it always had, the eelgrass was showing me the way. Stay here, it seemed to say, This is where you belong.

Ria picked up an oar and poked me with it. "Your turn," she said. "My arms are killing me."

I sat up and took the oars. Ria was smiling, radiant in the orange scarf, oblivious to my ruminations.

"Where to?" I said.

She made me row back toward the point, saying she wanted to have a closer look. I didn't think we'd run into Walter. He hadn't been in the bar for over a week, so I assumed he was away. She studied the hillside. Strands of yellow Scotch Broom swayed in the breeze. Her eyes traced the shore, the interrupted tree line. She looked over at me. I was swishing the oars back and forth, trying to stay in one place and not look too much at my former home. Thankfully, she made no suggestion of going ashore and hiking around, only shook her head and sighed again.

"What do you think?" I said,

"I want you to come up to Provincetown," she said, a non sequitur which clearly ended any talk of Walter or Casco before it could begin. "I want you to see the school. I don't know if you'll be able to meet Mr. Hofmann, but you've got see the place where I spend my time. It's so inspiring, Theo. I've never been so stimulated in my life."

"All right," I said. It went without saying that I would do anything she asked.

Chapter 10

In those days I thought of Provincetown as a rowdy place of honky-tonks where the night life was much more exciting than here in Orleans. What cultural knowledge I had of the place was mainly due to overhearing Nolan and Phinneas discuss various artists and read aloud to each other from the Provincetown Advocate. When I was a little boy my mother and I often went along with her friend Doris, who brought milk from Bailey's farm to the new pasteurization plant there every day. They wedged me into the back seat of her big black Roadster with four or five huge metal cans that clanked as we drove, drowning out their conversation. As the car crested the hill at Truro I would stand up and hold onto the swaying, sloshing cans to look across the water, waiting for the first sight of Provincetown. Its panorama of roofs and wharves laid out along the waterfront was like a giant banquet table, the long candle of the Pilgrim Monument rising from its center. I was only a kid then, but I have heard many people since describe the same thrill of that hilltop view at the end of a long trip, the sun setting, illuminating each bit of white trim, transforming the village into an Oz of inspired ideas, of dreams about to come true.

Of course in school we'd learned about the landing of the first settlers that long past November, that the Pilgrims signed the Mayflower Compact while the ship was at anchor in Provincetown Harbor, the bare bones of our democracy pieced together by the frozen hands of exhausted travelers. The same teacher who didn't know about Squanto told us that when the Pilgrims first landed they saw the waters off Provincetown teeming with pods of frolicking whales.

We were taught of its importance as a whaling port during the heyday of giant ships that roamed the world in search of bright-burning oil. As a child, whenever I thought of Provincetown, a picture came to mind from a series of engravings that were passed around our classroom. It was an image of the rendering process, though I didn't know what it was at the time. It showed a clipper ship at sea with its sails luffing. A sperm whale was attached with ropes along the ship's length, with several tiny men crawling over it. The beast's thick flesh had been cleanly cut in a line from head to tail, skewered onto a giant hook and hoisted aloft. The skin was still attached at the waterline, and the men were peeling it off by rolling the body and slicing. As soon as I saw the image I slammed the book shut. The teacher gave us a prideful speech about our forefathers as great providers of light to the rest of the world, but that picture may have headed me down the opposite, naturalist, path even earlier than my rowing turns around the Bay.

From spending time in Nolan's company, I knew there were many artists living and working in Provincetown. He spoke reverently about the place as though it were a Mecca of some kind and not just a disheveled fishing village where booze flowed easily and the dregs of history remained mostly forgotten, which is the way my father and his friends spoke about it. They referred to the town as the Oddball's Oasis. But Provincetown's story is so much more than the wild ride steered by rumrunners, mooncussers and pirates, adventure stories brought in from all corners of the world. Ria was the one who made me aware of a different aspect of the town's history. She taught me about the influence this little village had on the scope of American art, and she was a good teacher. When she and I first started walking around Provincetown, I gradually began to see the place from a completely different point of view.

Physically it is somewhat typical of a New England fishing village. Commercial street runs along the harbor front, gray-shingled shops lined up on either side. Between them stand modest two-story houses, a silent audience watching the action on the wharves and waters beyond. Widow's walks top many roofs. A warren of intimate neighborhoods rises from Commercial Street to the monument at the top of the hill, tiny lanes running through them. The town's population was made up of Portuguese descendants from the whaling days, families of the fishermen who have inhabited the place since the beginning, and those of us who have followed their instincts and moved there after falling in love with Provincetown's humble, yet magnificent, offerings.

"It's the light," Ria explained. "It has a particular quality here. Even on cloudy or drizzling days it has this purple-hued luminosity. It makes surfaces glow, shadows deeper, colors more vivid. Can you see it?" She pointed out examples. I could see, sort of.

"Have you ever heard of Charles Hawthorne?" I hadn't.

"He probably wasn't the first painter to notice, but he loved the light and of course all the other picturesque stuff around: The shingled cottages, the endless stretches of white sand. He moved here and started an art school because of it."

"Oh yeah?" I looked around, trying to make my eyes see like a painter. "When was that?"

"Right around the turn of the century."

We were walking along the street with ice cream cones. Ria made me buy Rum Raisin, a flavor that was forbidden by my mother, and I loved it. Ria described Hawthorne's class standing in the sand with easels clustered around a model. He had innovative theories about the interaction of light and color and brought these ideas to the artists, who came in droves by steamer and train to spend the summer in the company of the master.

"Other teachers came too and started their own schools. It's kind of what got the tourist thing really going here. Most of the tourists were art students, like me."

By 1916, when Hawthorne had been teaching there for fifteen years, six different art schools were operating in town, with over three hundred students. In August of that year The Boston Globe ran a front page headline, 'Biggest Art Colony in the World in Provincetown.' I saw it tacked up in Hofmann's barn when I went to visit Ria there.

In the years after the first World War many of the expatriate Americans studying in France returned home to New York. Of course they found their way to Provincetown. It was by then famous, or infamous. They were drawn not only by the light, the sea and the scenic fishing village, but by the bohemian community of painters, playwrights, poets and journalists they knew from back home. If I were to list the names of distinguished American painters and writers who have lived in Provincetown over the past fifty years, it would be a fairly comprehensive picture of the avant-garde and modernist movements that partly shaped American culture.

For Provincetown's attraction has one consistent thread woven through it, from the very day the first Europeans sailed into the cupped hand of the harbor and spotted the wealth of fresh lumber, pulled in the first fish, and rested from the long trip. It is the atmosphere of freedom that prevails even today. Freedom to express oneself, to live without a cloak of judgement, are part of the reason for the explosion of creativity which emanated from this tiny town in the thirties and forties, a force that swept across the country and changed forever the way we think about art.

Over the course of that summer I was to learn a lot more about the place, mainly from Ria's weekly reports and from trips I made to see her at school. I even briefly met the illustrious Hofmann himself. At the time Ria attended his school, he was burning on high, cultivating his theories of abstract art. Hofmann is still thought of as one of the most important figures of the American art scene, and its finest teacher. Ria came to our Sunday meetings bursting with stories about his manner, his ability, his way of speaking to his students as though they were colleagues, all involved together in the work of solving the problems of space, light and color. Ria was the youngest of Hofmann's students that year, and, due to the war, one of only fourteen. He immediately recognized in her initial drawings something of the artist she would become. The school was held at that time in a barn on Miller Hill, Hawthorne's old Cape Cod School of Art. The barn is still there, a large shingled gable-ended edifice, just an unfinished open space with a huge window set high into one wall. It was always full of light. Hofmann, a large man, would stroll in wearing a loose lab coat and sandals, his gray hair combed straight back from a wide forehead and alert eyes.His manner was relaxed and gregarious as he walked from easel to easel, looking, commenting, often telling humorous stories. To Ria and the others, he had a noble, elegant air, perhaps because of his supreme confidence in his ability, his extensive knowledge of the art of painting.

The day I met him I was on the porch, leaning against the wall outside the door waiting for Ria's class to end. I could hear Hofmann talking to the students in his thick Teutonic accent, though I couldn't make out what he was saying. The students would have been drawing from a model or a still life, concentrating in silence on the seriousness of their work. Ria told me that for the first several days she attended, she drew with a stick of charcoal on an opened newspaper, a chamois cloth in her other hand for erasing. She said that every once in a while Hofmann would clarify a statement by grabbing a piece of charcoal and drawing a diagram, illustrating his ideas directly onto someone's work, or making a miniature sketch in the corner of a painting. Sometimes he would tear the work in half and reposition it upside down to make a point.

It was during a quiet moment in the class, when I was completely absorbed in watching a chipmunk climb a stalk of hollyhock, that suddenly he appeared by my side.

"And who are you, if you please?" he said with a smile. His eyes were twinkling but I felt the force of his character, the energy emanating from every limb.

Startled, I began my stammered explanation, but he cut me off, saying, "Why don't you wait down there, with your friend," and pointed to the exact flower I had been studying. That was it, but at least I can say I met him.

Nolan laughed when I told him later on.

"Consider yourself lucky," he said excitedly. "You have met an important artist. Try to imagine, Theo. This man is busy joining the...the structure of Cubism with the exuberance of Fauvism! He managed to ignite an entirely new movement!" Nolan jumped off his stool and began pacing, waving his arms around in the dingy light of the bar.

"Artists are freeing themselves from the bonds of representational art and launching themselves into the realm of the unconscious," he went on. "They're explorers, Theo. None of them sure which brush stroke is the truth, but you're seeing the search for it. It's extraordinary."

I had only the barest understanding of that statement, but I nodded sagely. Phinneas sat at his usual spot, lazily stirring a cup of coffee, a rare thing for him. He didn't comment.

"Ria is fortunate to be attending there. Very fortunate." Nolan couldn't contain his enthusiasm, but there was a wistful note in his voice. He rubbed his chin with a thumb and forefinger, something he did when lost in thought, then turned and looked over at the mural, letting his eyes travel around his own brushstrokes.

"You a little jealous?" said Phinneas.

Nolan looked over at me, assessing. I was sweeping the floor by the kitchen. "No," he said. "I'm happy with my life. I only wish sometimes that I was eighteen again. Don't you?"

Phinneas didn't answer, just went on stirring his coffee. I tried to imagine sitting down with a few globs of paint and a brush and opening a door to my mind, letting what's inside flow down through my arm to animate my fingers. The closest I could come to an awareness of unconscious feeling was on those nights in the bar when Red would pull out his saxophone, play a tune through and then close his eyes and go off into something unrecognizable with notes all over the place, the others keeping the beat, waiting. I loved this new style of music, Red's unconscious expression. It made me better able to understand what Nolan was saying, but I still couldn't imagine how one would actually do it.

That summer and the one following Ria and I spent several Sundays in Provincetown. Like those rowing on the bay, they were some of the most magical, sublime hours I have ever in my life experienced. Though we did very little but simply walk around, the rough form of our platonic relationship was molded in those days into aharmonious combination of affection and self-effacing humor, the bond of two somewhat lost souls. In the beginning we often talked about Casco and Walter, the Peace medal and what to do about my discovery, but since there weren't many options for action, by the second summer the discussion had petered out. We returned to our old conversations, talking about our different worlds. She would tell long stories about life in school, her friends, her teachers, the struggles and self-probing necessary to put marks on canvas. Her dedication was impressive. Sometimes we'd be in the company of her fellow students. They all liked to spend their day off wandering down Commercial Street and gawking at the tourists, or sitting on the pier sketching each other. I never felt entirely comfortable in those cliques, and I resented having to share Ria with anyone else on my one precious day a week with her. I would sit at the edge of the group and watch the crabs scuttle around in the shade under the pier while I listened to their conversation. In the beginning, I didn't understand much of what was said when they discussed various aspects of the sessions with Hofmann, but I listened carefully, often bringing their comments back to the bar for translation by Phinneas or Nolan. I was desperate to grasp the concept of abstract art so I could impress Ria, or at least be able to participate in the conversations around me. But I never really did, not then. It took years of sitting in Ria's studio, seeing the day-to-day progress of a piece and listening to her talk, sometimes with great brush-throwing frustration and displeasure, about her work.

I never ceased to wonder what she saw in me or my prosaic lifestyle, but she greeted me each week with as much enthusiasm as she had the Sunday before. Perhaps in those days I represented a relief from the constant searching and introspection she engaged in with her other friends.

One of those friends was someone she worked with at the Clam Shack, a skinny redhead named Rusty. He was a lively, fast-talking kid who washed dishes and mopped the floors after closing. The main thing I knew about Rusty was that he was a Woody Guthrie fanatic. He knew all the songs from Woody's recently released "Dust Bowl Ballads." Ria told me he'd stand at the sink and sing them in the order they appeared on the record in a kind of whiny, nasal drawl which was supposed to suggest an Okie background, like one of the Oklahoma refugees Woody sang about. He let his curly, carrot-colored hair grow a little longer and wore brown button-down shirts rolled up at the sleeves. He always had a cigarette hanging out of the corner of his mouth, just like Woody on the album cover. Because of this, within a few days of meeting him, Ria started calling him "Dusty" and they became fast friends. He had a droll, ironic sense of humor which he would aim mostly at himself and his adopted persona, so I forgave him when I found out the truth about his background.

"He's not at all from Oklahoma, or anywhere near," Ria told me, not long after our first meeting. He came from somewhere up near the Great Lakes, a small town where his father sold insurance and all of sixty kids attended the high school. His parents had named their only child Russell long before they noticed the pinkish fuzz sprouting from his brand new head and so he was doubly destined for the nickname. Not only was Rusty the single redhead but the only Jew as well in a student body of Norwegian and Czech immigrant offspring. He bided his time all through school, keeping his head down and spending most days playing guitar in his room, thus avoiding any trouble while he waited to grow up and get out. His only friend was the school's Social Studies teacher, a man who, among other things, had introduced him to the music and politics of Woody Guthrie. When Rusty received a IV-F classification by the draft board halfway through his senior year, this teacher persuaded him to apply to Columbia University. His dishwashing job was just for the summer. He'd be going back in September. I can't say I was ever glad I met Dusty, but I grew to like him, despite his place in Ria's life, not only here on the Cape but in winter, when they both went back to New York.

Sometimes it occurs to me that we are all manipulated by the hand of some all-knowing god who amuses himself with a giant human board game. Dusty, in his earnest role as jester and minstrel, unwittingly made a move in that game which eventually led us back to Casco.

The day I met him was one of Ria's and my Provincetown Sundays. We stepped off the train and headed for Commercial Street. It was one of those brilliantly sunny July days when the weather is hot, but not oppressive yet. Our bodies were still soaking it up after months of fending off the cold. The town smelled wonderfully of fried dough, fried clams, and the hot-sugar scent of salt water taffy. Ria was dressed in a white skirt and peach-colored sweater over a white blouse. She had belted the sweater with the orange scarf she'd worn on the beach the day of our reunion. It was twisted and tied into delicate square knot. She was beautiful, animated and full of energy. The town was packed with Coast Guardsmen on liberty and Commercial Street was a sea of white canvas caps bobbing along between slow-moving cars. The men strolled in twos and threes, resplendent in blue and proud to be serving, drawing on cigarettes and winking at girls, Ria included. She laughed, delighted with all of it. Other people were gathered in dark pockets of shade under the town's huge overhanging elms or sat on benches watching the summer tourist shuffle. We passed a man sitting on the porch of a smoke shop, a sketchpad braced on his thighs, sketching away. He waved lightly at us. In between the clapboarded shops and houses glimpses of the sea twinkled. Behind picket fences flower gardens had been converted to vegetable patches for the war effort. We saw neat rows of lettuces, kale and onions. Bean vines climbed tripod poles, the sharp, earthy smell of oregano wafted from one plot to the next. Up on the hill the Provincetown Monument loomed above it all, watching over the activity. We were both in high spirits that day. Everyone was, it seemed.

"Let's get something to eat and sit on the pier," Ria said, pulling me into a bakery, a display of breads and pies lined up in a glass case.

"Two meat pies and two Coca Colas, please," said Ria immediately. She turned to me. "They are the most delicious things, Theo, believe me. I have a friend who brings them to me at work."

"Don't tell the boss but I'm sick to death of fried clams," said a voice behind us. I turned to look. A young man with orange hair stood grinning at Ria. A big brown guitar was slung across his back, taking up most of the available space in the tiny shop. He stuck his hand out to me as Ria exclaimed, "Oh, Dusty! Hello. We were just..."

"Yeah, I know. The pies. Me too. Who's this?"

Ria introduced us and immediately invited him to join us. "You can be the entertainment," she said, tapping his guitar. "Come on." She sailed out the door with him while I paid for the pies. I was less than happy about him eating lunch with us, but I smiled at him when I stepped outside.

"So, you work with Ria," I said.

"Yeah, I'm a dishwasher. You too, I hear."

"Actually I'm a cook." I did my share of dishes, but it was none of his business.

"Theo and I were at summer camp together," said Ria. The three of us walked awkwardly toward the harbor trying to stay abreast but getting knocked off stride by the passing crowds. The neck of Dusty's guitar stuck out at a threatening angle, forcing people off the sidewalk. He managed to stay at Ria's side, oblivious.

"Theo is a gen-u-ine Cape Codder," Ria added. "His father is a fisherman."

Why Ria, who had always been so considerately silent on the subject of my parents chose to add this was beyond me. It felt like a tiny betrayal.

"Where are you from?" I said, fending off any questions.

"I'm from Oklahomee, home of the dustbowl. I was a sharecropper before I came up here, 'cept the crops is a-blown away," he said. The cigarette hanging out of the corner of his mouth made him squint, pulling his mouth into a sort of one-sided grimace.

I didn't know what to say to this. I had no idea what a dustbowl was, and could only guess about the sharecropper part. We had just stepped from the pavement onto the beach. In those days it wasn't the inviting stretch of sand it is now. It was still used as a catch-all for spare fishing equipment and all kinds of trash. Crushed-up lobster pots, empty bottles, newspaper and torn fishing nets littered its length. An entire staircase, broken chairs, barrel staves, engine parts lay damp and rotting. The broken pilings of derelict wharves limped two by two into the sea, scraps of grey planks still clinging to them, vestiges of the whaling days when dozens of them stretched like fingers into the harbor. As we trudged along Dusty chatted about the goings-on at the Clam Shack. He had fed the boss a story about a playing gig in town so he could have the day off.

"Of course he bought it, hook, line and sinker," he said. "The guy loves me." He swung the guitar around to his front and with a flourish strummed a chord that sent a flock of seagulls flapping rapidly away. They relocated to the pilings and squawked at us.

We sat on the edge of MacMillan Wharf with our feet in the sand. A big wooden spool stood on its side nearby with a few yards of thick wire still wound around its spindle. We tipped it over, and Ria laid out our lunch. I looked out across the harbor, counting boats. I wondered how the town's fishermen were getting by with the small amount of gasoline allowed them. As I had that thought I heard the familiar sound of a two-stroke engine. A small dory with three Coast Guardsmen was making its way toward us. With a burst of speed the boat was beached and the three jumped out and walked along the shore, nodding as they passed us. Ria gave a little salute.

Dusty kept up a light strumming on his guitar, lulling us into a sun-soaked stupor as we ate. He puffed thoughtfully on his cigarette, studying the three sailors as they settled themselves nearby. I watched out of the corner of my eye as the cigarette's glowing tip dumped ashes down his shirt where they tumbled further to the sand and were blown away. Even when the butt was down to half an inch and coming dangerously close to scorching his lips, he seemed oblivious to it. I was fascinated by his smoking abilities. I never once saw him burn himself, even though I admit I wished for it at times.

The sailors settled themselves nearby and passed around a bag-covered bottle.They talked quietly, occasionally erupting into laughter. I had to look away when they decided to make a game out of trying to hit fiddler crabs with lit cigarette butts when they emerged from their holes under the pilings.

"How about a song?" Dusty said and started playing his rhythmic three-chord refrain louder, adding individual notes with his thumb, and when he started singing the sailors stopped the game to listen.

"There is a house in this old town
And that's where my true love lays around
He takes other women right down on his knee
And tells them tales he won't tell me."

Dusty smiled as Ria sat resting her chin in her palms, gazing rapturously at him through several verses of false-heartedness, sorrow and hard times. The sailors snickered, murmuring comments to each other. Dusty exaggerated his dustbowl drawl even further as he belted out the final chorus.

"It's a-hard and it's hard, ain't it hard
To love one that never did love you
It's a-hard and it's hard ain't it hard great God
To love someone who never will be true?"

"You said it, sir," said one of the men as we all clapped politely. Dusty took a lingering swig from his Coca-cola and lit another cigarette.

"You familiar with Woody?" he asked me.

"Dusty, no one is as familiar with Woody as you are," Ria said. She turned to me.

"He's talking about Woody Guthrie. Don't get him started by asking questions, please. I've been hearing about him all summer and I'm getting sick of it."

"I heard him sing it in the subway, in New York," Dusty said, shifting the cigarette to the other side of his mouth and squinting at the harbor as though picturing the scene out there in the chop. "That was the first I ever saw or knew of him, and it hit me so hard I followed him around for the rest of the day," he added.

"Here we go. Thanks Theo," Ria said, laughing. She gave me a little shove.

"Went right out and bought a recording. I like his politics. Woody and I sing hard-hittin' songs for a hard-hit people." Dusty dragged on his cigarette and thumbed another reverberating chord.

"That's what 'Woody sez'," Ria nudged me with her foot.

"Back in nineteen an' a-twenty seven, I had a little farm and I called it heaven."

I was about to politely ask where when I realized he was singing another song. Except he was talking. Ria shot me a helpless look along with a barely perceptible shrug.

"Well, the prices went up and the rain come down, so I hauled my crops all into town."

It was a sort of two-chord chanted poem, a no-frills recitation that sounded as though he were telling his own story, but of course Dusty would have been about two years old in nineteen twenty-seven.

"Rain quit and the wind got high and a black 'ol dust storm filled the sky. I swapped my farm for a Ford machine an' I poured it full o' this gas-i-line," he drawled. We all listened to the story of the wild Ford trip to the West coast, "scattering wives and childrens," and arriving there broke.

"So dad-gum hungry I thought I'd croak an' I bummed up a spud or two, an' my wife fixed up a tater stew."

At this point he gave Ria and me pointed looks, and playing at top volume, delivered this last spoken verse:

"We poured the kids full of it, mighty thin stew though
You could read a magazine through it.
Always had figured that if it'd been a bit thinner,
Soma a these here pol-i-ticians coulda seen through it."

He ended with a such vigorous twanging I thought the strings
might break. Ria and I looked at each other. I didn't know what to say.
Ria giggled and said, "Oh, Dusty. Well done!"

"What the hell is that supposed to mean?" yelled one of the Coast
Guardsmen.

Dusty said nothing, just smiled and raised his eyebrows.

"What are you, some kinda draft dodger?"

Dusty sat staring out across the harbor. He didn't answer except to
mutter, "That sir, is none of your business."

"Look, it's going to rain," said Ria. She pointed to the sky behind
the monument. An enormous wall of gray cloud, its top edge roiling
against the blue, was coming toward us. I watched as rooftops were
swiftly smothered in fog and sleet and a slap of rain washed across
Commercial Street. A great crash of thunder made us leap to our feet
and start running. Ria held the bakery bag over her head and led the
way toward the nearest building, a restaurant called the Lobster Pot. We
pushed through the door straight into a crowd of people. Like us, they
sought shelter from the rain, most of them Coast Guardsmen packed
together in the tiny foyer. The place was like a steam bath. Everyone
was soaking wet. They all shifted to accommodate us, and when Dusty
burst through the door a few seconds later there was little space even to
close the door against the splash of the pummeling downpour.

Someone yelled, "Hey, enough already! There's no more room,
buddy. We're already a tin of sardines here." Everyone laughed. Dusty
shoved in anyway. "Watch the guitar," he said, ignoring glowering
looks as he made his way over to us. Ria and I were smashed against a
low half-wall which separated the prep part of the kitchen from the
entryway. I peered over it, studying the restaurant's setup. Next to a
wide, gently smoking griddle a giant cauldron simmered on a four-
burner stove, the lid hopping and clattering. On the radio Johnny
Mercer was singing "The G I Jive."

"If you're a P-V-T, your duty
is to salute the L-I-E-U-T.
But if you brush the L-I-E-U-T
The M-P makes you K-P on the Q-T."

Someone yelled "Clams, large!" and a sweaty young man sidled
over to the pot and lifted the lid. He withdrew a basket of steamers

which he upended into a bucket sitting on the counter and with a shove sent it down the line. Then he poured most of a bottle of beer into the pot and dumped another bucket full of clams into the steaming broth. He finished off the beer in one gulp, tossed the bottle into a trash can, and winked at me, singing along with Johnny Mercer. It was then that three things happened at once, three small intersecting events that cancelled my Sundays with Ria for the rest of the summer.

Dusty had made it halfway across the foyer and stood at the bottom of a flight of steps. A sign posted there had an arrow pointing up with "Cocktails" written along its length. A man appeared at the top of the steps and began to make his way down. He carried a black walking stick by its silver head. A thick black beard matched his head of hair, both curly and touched with white at the edges. He smiled broadly when he saw the crowd, a perfect row of teeth flashing white in their shadowy nest. He wore a dark green shirt under a black vest, along with a pair of beige linen trousers. A bright red triangle of handkerchief peeked out from the vest's pocket. I was so engaged in watching his descent that I didn't notice the increasing clatter of the clam cauldron's lid until it was thrown off and sent rolling and crashing along the length of the countertop, to sudden yelps and much swearing from within. A hissing, bubbling froth boiled over the sides of the pot and into the fire below, sending fragrant billows of steam out into the crowd. We all turned to look, including Dusty who whirled around in the same instant the gentleman coming down the steps tripped, putting his elbow through the back of Dusty's guitar with a resonating rip of veneer.

"Oh shit," Ria said, and pushed her way over to them. The man pulled his elbow out of the splintered wood and cradled it in his other hand. "My deepest apologies," he said. Dusty lifted the guitar's strap over his head and turned it over. "It's ruined," he wailed. Ria ran her hand along the guitar's neck and said, "Dusty, I'm sure it can be fixed."

"If not, I'll buy you a new one. It's my fault, and I'm terribly sorry. Look, can we step outside?" The man in the suit took Dusty's arm and turned him toward the door. Dusty, still in distress, let himself be led through the crowd. Ria and I followed.

"My name's Achilles," the man said when we got outside. "Achilles Overton." He held out his hand, but Dusty just hugged the guitar to his chest and stared at him. The rain had tapered off somewhat, but we were all still getting wet. Achilles talked us into walking a short distance to his place, a two-story cottage on the beach. We ran fifty yards down the empty street and onto a generous porch that wrapped around the house to the waterfront. He invited us inside and we stood there dripping on his carpet while he disappeared for a few minutes, then returned with a towel for each of us and a further invitation to stay for lunch. "Sure, why not?" said Dusty.

Achilles was the age of our parents, but as we settled onto two generous sofas which faced each other over a coffee table he seemed as excited about meeting us as he would be over a trio of his contemporaries. He lit a fire in the grate while we dried ourselves, calling over his shoulder to someone in another room, "Cal, bring food. In here." He asked us our names, where we were from, what we were doing in Provincetown. He spoke very quickly in a soft, cultured, slightly-accented voice that flowed over and around us, making each of us feel that our presence was not an accident, but an event. He was particularly interested that Ria attended Hans Hofmann's school and stopped what he was doing to stare at her and ask several questions about the classes, finally saying, "Bravo Ria, you will never forget the experience. I would like to see what you're doing one day, if I may."

"Sure," said Ria, not looking sure at all.

Dusty had left the ruined guitar by the door and when the fire was going Achilles brought it in and laid it out on the coffee table to be examined.

"I am truly sorry," he said, standing over it. "It doesn't look like a repair will be sufficient to bring it back to its former glory, does it?" He looked at Dusty and smiled. Achilles' eyes were the color of some kind of semiprecious stone, one that, when held up to the light, would glow a rich greenish brown. They sparkled constantly, the way Santa Claus's did in children's books. When they were aimed at me I felt at the same time comforted and somewhat intimidated. The guitar was nothing special. It was a rough five-and-dime purchase by the look of it. It had no varnish, no inlays; it was only a basic music box. We sat in silence, staring mournfully at it.

"I have an idea," said Achilles, then left the room. He returned holding another guitar, this one of blond, lacquered wood, with a neck of something reddish like cherry, and ivory carving around its sound hole, bridge and head. This he held out to Dusty saying, "Will you play for us?"

Dusty took the guitar, ran his fingers gently over the finish, then played a single chord. A rich, multilayered sound spilled over us. The last note hung in the air for several long moments. Dusty, listening, his head back and blowing smoke at the ceiling,launched into a song. Naturally it was something from "Dustbowl Ballads."

A tray of food appeared, brought in by a tall, thin man in a shorts and a shirt with the sleeves cut raggedly off at the elbows. He set it down in front of us. A stack of sandwiches and four bottles of beer surrounded a large glass ashtray, which was placed directly in front of Dusty with a flourish.

"Thank you, Cal," said Achilles, gesturing for us to eat while taking a beer for himself. Dusty droned on through some fairly dense lyrics about the billowing black cloud, the blinding, choking dirt which blew over the farms and buried everyone's livelihood. Achilles listened with rapt attention, tapping his foot and lifting his eyebrows to smile at Ria every now and then, soulful, eye-twinkling grins that made her blush. I had never seen Ria blush, even in the bar when she overheard some of the Huff brothers' treasury of closing-time one-liners. I looked around the room while Dusty plucked the opening notes of another Guthrie song.

An entire wall was lined with books. There were books stacked on the floor, pyramids of books on tables and under them, books in piles up the staircase, even a book lying open on the bathroom sink, which I could glimpse from where I sat. I went in, shut the door and picked it up. It was the first issue I'd ever seen of The Partisan Review. I flipped through the slim volume, stopping to read here and there. I know now that I held a famous volume of the journal in my hands, but I stopped only briefly at Clement Greenberg's essay on modern art. When I saw the title, "Avant Garde and Kitsch," I thought I might gain a quick bit of knowledge with which to impress Ria, but I found it bewildering so I put it back, pulled the chain on the toilet and rejoined the others. Dusty had stopped playing and sat eating a sandwich. He was talking to Achilles, who lounged elegantly in a wing chair, drawing thoughtfully on a cigarette. He was like a mythical animal, his long hair curling around his collar and blending into his black beard. The green shirt was silk. It oozed along his arms, rippling slightly with every movement. He wore a wide silver bracelet on one wrist, the first time I'd ever seen a man with jewelry. The silver-topped cane was propped against the chair. He leaned forward, plucked a bottle of beer off the tray and handed it to me as I sat down.

"What do you think happened to it, Mr. Overton?" said Dusty.

"Call me Achilles, please," he smiled.

"All right, Achilles. I've asked everyone, and no one seems to know. It was only ten years ago. Seems like someone ought to remember."

"Well, I think most of it ended up in the south of Texas. Maybe some in the Gulf of Mexico. It blew all the way to the East Coast."

Ria smiled at me across the coffee table. "The dustbowl dust. Where it ended up. That's what they're talking about."

"Of course," I said, rolling my eyes inwardly.

"I remember reading a news article about the dust turning the snow red in this area. Do you remember that, Theo?" Achilles aimed his luminous eyes at me.

Red snow? On that last day, hadn't Casco told us that he arrived in Massachusetts in a snowstorm, and that the snow was red? Because I had no memory of it I thought it was some kind of Indian metaphor of his, the sky welcoming him back to his homeland with this symbolic color. But it was real. I looked at Achilles' silver bracelet gleaming in the firelight and shook my head. "No," I said. "I must have been too young. Those inland storms don't usually reach us out here."

I widened my eyes at Ria. Did she remember that detail about Casco? She was watching Achilles, smiling at him as she said, "I don't remember it either, and I was in New York."

"Where in the city do you live?" Achilles asked her.

There followed a discussion of various neighborhoods of New York while Dusty fired up another tune, blessedly not another Guthrie. He got up and wandered through the rooms as he played. I was stunned by my realization, not paying attention to the conversation, only coming to when Cal brought in another tray of beer. I couldn't believe Ria had seemingly passed over the detail about the red snow. She'd been right there when Casco told us his story. She hadn't even looked at me. She was leaning forward, laughing at everything Achilles said, smoothing her bangs away from her eyes and talking about New York. The Village. Dusty wandered in and out, grabbing a fresh beer, another cigarette, playing "You Are My Sunshine" and "John Henry" before going back to Guthrie's songs about the caravans of starving Americans living like animals to pick fruit for pennies. He sang almost to himself, rushing through the lyrics in a monotone, memorizing more than singing. I sat there, listening but not hearing, reading titles on the spines of books, titles which made no sense to me at all. The steady purr of Achilles' voice lulled me into a semi-stupor, and I lost track of things for a while, until at a certain point someone noticed that the rain had stopped and Ria jumped up, smoothed her skirt and said, "Let's go outside and look at the water. C'mon Theo."

We left soon after that, Dusty reverently cradling the blond guitar which Achilles had given to him, as Ria, slightly tipsy and holding onto my arm, shook Achilles' hand and thanked him over and over for a memorable afternoon. I wasn't surprised when Ria called the following Saturday night and begged off from our usual Sunday date. Not hiding the excitement in her voice, she told me Achilles had invited her to go for a sail on his boat. He wanted her to bring her portfolio. I hung up the phone, leaned on the bar and stared at the hole in the blackout curtain, imagining myself slipping through it onto the dark pavement and slithering down the streets, across the field and all the way to the Bay, plopping into the black water where I would remain forever. I told myself it was good for Ria's career, that Achilles was a substitute father, that they were city people and could therefore discuss a number of topics about which I was ignorant. I told myself it was just one Sunday. Then I turned to Phinneas and said, "Have you ever heard of The Partisan Review?"

Chapter 11

I hadn't seen Walter for more than a year when he began to spend time in the bar again that fall. He ate dinner in the restaurant several times a week, often alone at the table under the mural with his nose buried in the paper, or sitting at the bar. Ray was polite, offering up a simple rejoinder if necessary along with a fresh Manhattan, but Phinneas ignored him. Nobody liked Walter very much, but he didn't seem to notice.

I kept an eye on him. He must have been living in his house by then, and I wanted to hear anything he had to say about it, but he was surprisingly reserved about full-time life among us townies, not his usual boastful self. He had acquired a boat, a wooden dory which he fitted with an engine. And though he didn't mention it, we heard stories about his endless moseying around the bay, burning up gasoline that the other fishermen doled out in drops. He wasn't even fishing, they said. He'd anchor the boat or pull it into the shallows and tie it to a rock, then disappear into the woods for hours. They thought he was a naturalist of some kind. I knew he was hunting for artifacts. He asked Ray about every island and point of land out there, who owned what, how many acres, etc. Ray kept telling him he had no idea, that it wasn't a big topic of conversation in the bar, that he ought to go down to the town hall and see for himself, it was a matter of public record. After a few weeks he dropped the subject, and according to one of our regulars whose wife worked in the town hall, he never checked.

One bright October day he stuck his head into the kitchen where I was feeding hunks of beef into the grinder. Meat rationing had been lifted that spring and we were selling more hamburgers than fish of any kind. At the same time the allotment for red points to purchase butter, milk and cheese was cut in half, so chowder, our most popular meal, was more expensive to make. But the burger sales more than offset the difference. I was lost in calculations and didn't hear the door.

"Hey, Birdman," he said.

I stopped grinding . "Hey, Walter. Ray's not out there?"

"He is. I wanted to talk to you. Guess who I saw yesterday?"

I didn't say anything, just stared at him.

"Your father. You never told me we were neighbors. I guessed he was your father because you look exactly like him. Anyone ever told you? So I asked, and you know what he said?"

I waited.

"He said, 'Tell him happy birthday for me, will you?' So I am. When was it?"

"It was yesterday."

"All right then." He backed out the door. I stood there for a long time, thinking about the message. Not about the birthday or my age but about my father. I hadn't seen him since the day I went to say goodbye, thinking I was off to war. He told me then that he loved me, and now he was wishing me a happy birthday. Scraps, I know, of a real relationship, but for those of us who have never experienced the real thing, a doled-out morsel like that can feel like a full blown meal. A desire to see him fluttered through me and I let it. Maybe I would visit one of these days, I thought, then went back to grinding.

A postcard from Ria the day before. She had drawn a birthday cake with lit candles but no other message. It was the first time I'd heard from her in over a month, since the last Sunday before she went back to New York. We had spent the day together at the beach, and she'd been full of excitement about returning, which was surprising. She didn't mention Achilles all day until I asked if she'd seen him, and by the way her eyes lit up at the mention of his name, I knew that what was between them was more than a mentor-father-daughter relationship, though she said nothing of the sort. She was carefully casual in a way Ria is not. Perhaps she thought I'd be shocked. She told me much later about all the people in her life who were. That and more. But I wasn't, I was just sad, and I think she understood. I shoved the postcard into my back pocket and left it there.

Nolan was still busy drawing plans for the military, so his visits were few and far between. I missed him. He had become an important part of my life, not only for his easygoing manner and gentle humor, but for the way he taught me, without actually telling me, many of life's little truths. Through the years I spent in his company I came to believe that the image I had of myself, the Theo who roamed the bay watching the natural world in silence, was not an outsider, but a person as vital to society as Ria and her artist friends. Not that I spent much time dwelling on this sort of thing, but when he was gone I reverted to my old ways, spending as much time alone as I used to when I was out on the water or roaming through the woods. I stayed in the kitchen, chopping, scrubbing, sweeping, frying. I suppose the combination of losing Ria and Nolan at the same time was so depressing, it was all I could handle. Ray and Phinneas tried to get me to sit with them when business was slow, but I preferred the predictability of the kitchen routine.

It was in November, the first hint of winter's bite whipping through the leafless trees and snapping at anything moving, that Walter came back to the kitchen again. He opened the door and put his head through.

"Birdman," he said, "I've got a question for you."

"What," I said. I remember I was shucking scallops, my old torture. I was thinking about standing waist-deep in the Bay with Ria that first summer, when she told me she 'adored' scallops. She pronounced the word like 'gallop,' which makes me cringe whenever I hear a tourist say it. I was clearly annoyed with her. I spent a lot of time reviewing in those days, trying to understand what went wrong between us.

"You ever do any work outside? I need a little help with a project at the house. Ray suggested I ask you."

I hated the sound of his voice, and the way he stuck his head into the private refuge of my kitchen. But I confess it was an intriguing request. I briefly weighed the awful prospect of spending time with him in that place against being able to check out Casco's gravesite again.

"What kind of project?"

"I need some help with some brush clearing, maybe burn the dead stuff, that sort of thing. Interested? It would just be a couple days. It needs to be done now, while the leaves are off. Before it's too cold."

My obsession with Walter and Paw Wah Point had cooled somewhat by then, but I couldn't pass up a chance to go there, to be able to see for myself the house I'd heard so much about. Though I didn't relish the thought of working alongside Walter, I thought I might be able to detect a whisper of guilt, if I observed him in that setting.

"All right," I said. I was sure Ray could spare me. The bar's business had slowed to its usual winter pace. Phinneas was often our only customer for dinner.

"Great," said Walter, with a little bounce. "I'll pick you up tomorrow morning."

The day was perfect: a fresh, bright fall morning. We drove around behind Paw Wah Pond and onto a brand new dirt road. The bushes had been roughly cleared on either side leaving another gash in the trees, a slice up the center of the point. I said very little on the ride over. I was more than anxious about seeing the house. I felt like a traitor to Casco, sitting there beside his probable killer, on my way to clear a piece of his beloved woods. I didn't think about that part. I stared out the windshield and steeled myself for what was ahead.

The first thing I saw was a white stone chimney against blue sky. The house was not exactly modest, but I'll have to admit it wasn't as bad as I expected. Three crisply outlined dormers poked out of a shingled roof which ran down from its peak to a thick dark beam running the length of the house. The first floor was coated in some kind of white-painted stucco. Black trim delineated doors and windows, other sections of the structure. The whole pile rested on several rounds of red brick. It was not something any Cape Codder had ever built on these shores, but a sort of Mock Tudor by way of New Jersey. A generous veranda faced east. Through the trees and bushes I could see across the bay to the Narrows and the Atlantic beyond.

"You see my project," said Walter, grinding the car to a halt in the gravel driveway and jumping out. I was too shocked by the sight of a building on the point to comprehend his gesticulating or hear what he was saying. I climbed slowly out of the car and stood next to a redwood fence which opened onto the front yard. There was Walter, now quiet. He looked up at the roofline, puffed his chest with pride and said, "Quite something, isn't it? Come on out front. I'll show you what I want." He set off at a good clip, striding across the lawn, talking all the while. "Now, as you can see the only thing missing here is an actual view. Of course this time of year with the leaves off the trees it's not a problem, but what I want is an unobstructed year-round panorama. If we take out these, and these here," he swept his arms across a fifty foot swath of windswept pine and scrub oak. "And then those over there," indicating another stand of trees and some tall bushes I knew to be blueberry.

"I bought a felling saw and all kinds of pruners, clippers. We can burn the whole pile over there." He pointed to a gravel-covered patch by the driveway. "It might take more than a couple of days, now that I really see it, but you can clear it with Ray, can't you? Or come back and we'll finish next week."

He babbled on, trying to herd me over to a tool shed at the edge of the driveway. But I wasn't listening. Something else had my complete attention. There, sitting in one of the blueberry bushes, was a good-sized crow. It sat very still and stared at me. As improbable as it sounds, I thought for a moment I recognized the bird as one of the family that used to plague Casco in his corn patch. It squawked at me again and then launched itself flapping into the sky. I watched as it flew in a wide circle around the house, cawing to the beat of its wings. I glanced over to see if Walter was watching, but he had disappeared into the shed. The crow continued circling for three more leisurely rounds and then, only twenty feet away, where I knew Casco's grave to be, it settled on a rock, the piece of granite I'd laid there as a marker.

I took a few slow steps toward the crow, but it didn't move. I took a few more, and it only danced a little on the granite, still watching me, unblinking. With sudden certainty I was convinced the crow was the embodiment of Casco, the way it gazed at me as though trying to speak with those dark, sparkling eyes. I looked closer and imagined that its beak even made a little dip to the left, like Casco's nose. For several moments I stood in a kind of trance, the back of my neck tingling.

The moment I opened my mouth to say hello to my old friend the crack! of a stone hitting the granite marker sent the crow screeching away into the trees. I whirled around to see Walter standing spread-legged, taking aim with a large slingshot. He was grinning. The sight made me flush with outrage.

"Stop!" I yelled, running toward him.

"You want to have a go? The damn thing's been plaguing me since I moved in." He held out the slingshot.

"Leave that crow alone. Don't kill anything else out here." I was so angry I almost slugged him. I glanced up to see the crow sitting quietly in one of the oaks, watching. I had to get out of there. I was ashamed to be seen together with Walter even by a bird.

"I'm leaving," I said. "Cut down your own trees. Or better yet, don't. You've done enough damage." I turned and started down the driveway. The sight of the crow had reignited my desire for revenge, but I had no idea what to do except run.

"What the hell are you talking about?" He came toward me. "Why did you bother to waste my time coming out here?" At the gate he stopped and fiddled with the slingshot, fitting another stone, an indignant look on his face. His incongruous, ugly house loomed up over his shoulder. The image filled me with another surge of rage and I stopped abruptly.

"What did you do with Casco's wigwam?" I blurted out. I spat the question at him and saw him flinch. I wanted to wipe the house and Walter off the face of the earth, cut him down with his own axe, clobber him the way he had Casco. I was panting, almost drooling with anger. I said again. "Tell me, Walter, did you rip it apart? Did you fill it in? Was it all because of a couple of artifacts?"

At that he ducked his head, choking a little. He stared at me, shock freezing his face in mid-cough. He dropped his arm. The stone he was holding rolled away across the grass.

"What are you doing here, anyway?" I said. "What do you want?"

Walter backed slowly away to a safe distance. He didn't say a word, only stared at me as I crossed my arms over my chest in an effort to calm my heartbeat. My face flushed again, so hot I began to sweat. Neither of us moved. My heart pounded away as the reality of what I'd said bloomed in the air around us. Walter began to pace, four steps one way, four back, glancing at me every now and then. I could see him weighing his options. It was too late for him to feign ignorance. For that he should have immediately asked, "Casco who?" or some such question. But he didn't, and it gained me measure of confidence so I calmed down a little. I had him. Finally he stopped, ran his fingers along the rubber of the slingshot, picked up another stone and laid it carefully in the middle, balancing it there as he said, "So, he's a friend of yours."

I said nothing. The woods around the house were absolutely still. Walter was going to do this alone, I told myself, with no prompts from me. I waited.

"I knew he lived here. We're old friends," he spoke carefully. "I bought the land intending to give him a parcel. But when I got here it was obvious he was gone, so I tore down the wigwam. I had the guys fill in the hole. Do you want to see it?"

"No, I don't need to see it. And yes, Casco was a friend of mine."

"Was?"

"That's right. But you know all about it, don't you?"

Walter spat, licked his lips and in a measured, almost venomous tone said, "I don't know anything about your relationship with him. Why should I?"

"You won't get away with it."

"What the hell are you talking about?"

"I know. I know everything."

Walter raised the slingshot, leveled it at me, pulled back the rubber. "Get out of here. Leave my property now." With that he shot the stone. I ducked as it whizzed past my head. I could hear the hiss of wind as it nearly grazed my right ear. Suddenly I was very afraid. It was clear that I was dealing with some kind of psychopath. I turned and ran, but Walter chased me down, grabbed the back of my jacket, flung me to the ground and pushed my face into the gravel. He was quite strong. I flipped over and tried to shove him off but he dug his knee into my stomach and leaned into my shoulders, putting his face close to mine. We were only a few feet from where Casco lay buried.

"What are you saying kid? Where is he?" We were both out of breath. I tasted blood, felt around with my tongue and located a split in my lip.

"He's right here," I said, gesturing with my head.

"What the hell are you talking about?" he said again.

I knew I shouldn't have said anything more. I needed time to gather my wits. I had already blurted out too much, and there I was with a murderer sitting on my chest. But all the torment of the past three years was there too, and revenge was what I wanted then. Confession, penance and revenge.

"You took his wampum belt. I saw you out here, and I heard you describing it to those people in the bar. You didn't just find it, did you? You knocked him out and took it. That and the Peace medal." I couldn't help myself, I spat the word "Peace" right in his face, then tried to heave him off me, but he held fast and slammed his knee back into my stomach.

"The belt was mine to begin with, not that it's any of your business."

"It didn't give you the right to kill him." I said it very softly.

Walter stood up, backed away a few steps. He pointed a finger at me. It was shaking.

"Kill him? Who said anything about killing? What the hell are you saying? That's a powerful accusation, Birdman. I'd even say a dangerous one." His voice became more menacing with each sentence.

I was afraid, but I sat up, looked him in the eyes and said, "I found him as you left him. Dead. He's buried under that rock." I gestured with my chin.

Walter looked over at the lump of granite, then back at me. "What the.....?" he kept looking back and forth. Me, the rock, me.

"How do you know this?" he asked quietly.

"Because I put him there." I gritted my teeth.

Walter sat down heavily, thrust his head into his hands and rocked back and forth a few times. "I don't understand," he said after a few moments.

I waited. I wanted to run, but something about Walter's behavior, his grieving posture made me sit still. The birds began their twittering again. An outboard engine whined in the distance. Walter shifted, shook his head, looked at me.

"Tell me what you found," he said levelly.

This was so different from the confrontational scene I'd imagined hundreds of times that for a moment I couldn't think, couldn't remember what the truth was. It was all backwards. It should have been me questioning him and not the other way around. A shiver of panic ran through me. What if I was wrong to bury Casco? What if, in my dazed state after the blackfish killing, I had missed some essential clue to the truth? I conjured up a mental image of Casco lying dead in the bushes, the bruise above his ear, his leg at a crazy angle to his body. Then I remembered that Walter had just claimed the belt was his.

"Why don't you tell me first," I said. "Did you come here? Did you hit him? Did you take the belt and the medal?"

Walter sighed, looked over at his house, then back at me.

"Yes," he said. "I was here. I got the belt. As I said, it was mine. We had other business. We argued. But I did not hit him. I left him standing next to the wigwam. He had the medal around his neck." Walter narrowed his eyes and looked away, reviewing the scene. "That's about it. Now, what about you?"

I briefly described finding Casco, burying him.

"You didn't tell anyone?"

"No one knew he was here." I didn't feel I needed to tell Walter about my state of mind that day. It was none of his business. "It was what he wanted."

"Yes, I can imagine." This he said softly, I might even say wistfully. I was utterly confused. Could it be that Walter was telling the truth, that he hadn't killed Casco, he hadn't even hit him?

"Look," he said, shrugging. "We were friends, colleagues. Both interested in Indian stuff. Artifacts yes, but mainly transcribed oral history, documents. We were both searching for the same thing. Oh, Christ. I can't believe he's dead." He put his head in his hands again, raked his fingers through the stubble on his face. "Would you like a beer?"

I shook my head. I did not want to drink a beer with Walter. My lip stung, but that wasn't the reason. I still didn't trust him. He got up and went into the house. I suppose I could've gone at that point, but I wanted to hear more, even if it was from my enemy. I looked over at the blueberry bushes. The crow was sidestepping back and forth along a branch, watching me again.

When Walter returned he was carrying a little tray with two beers, two glasses and a wad of cotton, which he handed to me.

"Sorry about your lip," he said and sat down on the gravel beside me. "Tell me again about the bruise above his ear. Was there any blood? Could he have fallen? Hit his head on a rock?" He glanced at the grave marker.

I studied his face for signs of duplicity but it was open, inquiring, concerned. There was even sadness in his eyes. Still I said nothing. I had given away my secret, confessed what amounted to a crime. I couldn't speculate with him about the circumstances surrounding Casco's death, I was still too caught up in the idea that he'd killed him, though I was beginning to doubt it.

"I saw him the day before, and he was fine. We had lunch together."

"I swear to you Theo, I did not kill our friend. As a matter of fact I returned a few days later to see if I could discuss the matter peacefully with him. For some reason I changed my mind and left, decided on another tack. But I saw smoke coming from the wigwam, so he was there."

136

"That was me," I mumbled.

"You?"

"I lived there for over a year after he died."

Walter took a long pull at his beer and leaned back on one elbow, picked up a few bits of gravel and shook them like a pair of dice.

"By yourself?"

"Yes."

He didn't ask why, or how. After a few silent minutes he said, "Casco ever tell you his Indian stories? The war? His family?"

"Some. He told me about Metacom and Wamsutta, and about the Praying Indians out on Deer Island." I would have said more, but the crow let out a long cackling screech followed by a series of caws that mimicked the rhythm of my sentence.

"Metacom, Wamsutta. King Phillip and his brother, Alexander. Yeah. I met Casco in the library at the University of Virginia. They've got a substantial collection of documents there, reams of info to slog through if you're so inclined. He was researching his family." He rattled the handful of pebbles again, reflecting. He finished off his beer and started in on the other one.

"Listen," he said, peering at me intently. "Did he ever show you a diary?" Was it among his things in the wigwam?"

"A diary?"

"Yeah. A small leather-covered book about yea big." He held his hands apart.

Was this what Walter, or whoever killed Casco was after? I had never seen it, if indeed he had it there somewhere.

"Why?" I said cautiously.

"Why?" He repeated. "We were both looking for it in Virginia. I just wondered if he was the lucky one who found it."

I doubted his sincerity. I reminded myself about his boasting in the bar, his "collector."

"What's so important about it?" I asked.

"Nothing really. Belonged to a distant relative of his, I think."

I wanted the conversation to stop. I didn't feel comfortable sitting around discussing Casco with Walter. I had so much to think about, and the longer I sat there the more confused I became. If Walter was telling me the truth, then someone else had killed Casco. Or he'd fallen and hit his head against a rock after Walter had left. But I had thoroughly searched the area not once, but many times, and the trees too, looking for signs of an accident. There were none. Someone hit Casco so hard it caused his death. Of that I was sure. And that someone had cut the medal from Casco's neck. But I was no longer sure it was Walter. I had also confessed a crime to Walter. My head swam with confusing detail, random memories of Casco, my winter in the wigwam, Walter in the bar. What exactly had he said? I needed to leave there, to walk away down the road and think. I got up, pressed the cotton to my lip.

"I have to go," I said.

"OK kid. I understand. I'll take you." He got up.

"No," I said. "I'll walk. I feel like it." The brush clearing was not mentioned. I turned and started down the driveway, the crunching of my shoes in the gravel was the only sound. Soon I hit the dirt road, stepped up my pace until I was almost running, so badly did I want to get out of there. When I was halfway to the main road I heard the caw of the crow overhead and looked up. It sat high in the branches of a tree looking down at me. I gave my old sparrow call, a little rusty now. The crow sat still for a moment, then it hopped into the air and circled around, flying back in the direction of Paw Wah Point. Just an ordinary curious crow. I watched until it was gone, then started off. My foot crushed something hard into the sand and I picked it up. It was the shell of a black walnut. Casco had said there was a tree nearby, but I had never found it in all my hungry months in the wigwam.

Chapter 12

It was a long time before I saw Walter again. For the first few days, I worried constantly that he'd turn me in for burying his old friend and not reporting it. Different versions of the same scenario plagued me night after night, depriving me of sleep. Cops banging on my door, the exhumation of Casco's body, me in handcuffs watching, Walter providing information. The artifacts, the wigwam, the Peace medal, all pointing to foul play with me at the center.

When nothing happened, and he didn't come into the bar for a month or so, I began to relax. At first Ray joked about it, saying I'd done them all a favor and pushed him off the bluff, and then, when he hadn't been in for over three months, implied, jokingly, that I was to blame for the lack of much needed winter revenue.

"What the hell happened out there, kid?" The question became increasingly serious until one day Phinneas suggested someone go out and have a look. I wondered myself. Did Walter have an attack of conscience and shoot himself in the head? Even though after much deliberation and a couple of telephone conversations with Ria, I had come to the conclusion that Walter had not killed Casco. Still, I couldn't be sure.

The matter of Walter's disappearance was put partially to rest one day when one of the guys who had helped to build his house mentioned that he'd been hired to keep an eye on the place "indefinitely." Then I began to speculate about what I had said that would force him to leave his newly established home. The most likely explanation was that he didn't feel comfortable alone out there with whatever ghosts now plagued him, the body of his old-friend lying in the dirt outside his door. I spent a lot of time at the sink taking apart and re-forming the phrases we'd said to each other, making mental lists of facts, reviewing Walter's actions and skill with the slingshot.

I wondered about the diary. Casco had never mentioned his research at the University of Virginia. I thought he knew that his family's history had been passed down, an oral tradition kept up by generations.

As soon as I knew that Walter was simply away and not dead or hiding like a deranged hermit, I made a plan to go out there and do a little snooping. I kept putting it off, though, telling myself it was too cold. It could wait.

That winter Ria phoned several times but she seemed distracted, going through the motions, asking after Walter, feigning interest in my life at the bar and talking about life at school. She said she hated the "drudgery" of learning perspective and anatomy but enjoyed working from a model and often would stay up late at night reworking her drawings, translating what she'd seen and felt into the parlance of her individual style. It was during these sessions that she'd phone, always joking that she hoped the call cost "a mint" and that it would get her father's attention. I could hear her smoking, the scratch of charcoal, the jiggle in her voice as she rubbed at some detail. The most animated conversations we had were about my encounter with Walter. The rest were just vague recitations of our different schedules. But hers had giant gaps, which I suspected were filled with Achilles. Though I asked her every now and then about him, she didn't tell me very much. I knew something exciting was going on besides manipulating paint and smoking cigarettes. She was not a gossipy, girly kind of person. Those things didn't interest her. But she did make many references to events, people and places I guessed were not part of a normal college girl's activities, though I wasn't exactly sure what those might be. There was simply and unquestionably something in her life that pleased her, made her almost purr with contentment. I knew what, or rather who, it was.

We were both nineteen that winter. Ria would turn twenty in April. In Europe, hope for Allied victory was turning toward actuality after D-Day and the liberation of Paris. Liza was beside herself with excitement, and, since August, she had taken to singing French songs in the kitchen and baking Madeleines for us to eat after the bar closed. She baked them in scrubbed scallop shells to get the distinctive shape, and Phinneas almost fell off his barstool after sampling the first one. Swooning with ecstasy he said she'd transported him back to his glory days: Paris in the twenties. Then he took her in his arms and kissed her while she swatted at him, laughing. It was the first spark of genuine joy we'd felt in a long time, the beginning of a certain wary giddiness that it might be over soon. That winter Ray let her listen to the news in the kitchen again and she took full advantage of it whenever she appeared, and I stopped caring.

Nolan came back in April, done with drawing plans for the military, back in his studio and now beginning to experiment with woodcarving. He brought a few pieces into the bar to show us. Like the water painted in the mural, incised lines undulated into and through each other, crisscrossed thicknesses in the surface, or were simply allowed to follow the grain. There were fewer identifiable images, only suggestions of things which echoed and repeated in the overall design. They were quite beautiful, and he was more animated than I'd ever seen him when talking about his process. Nolan asked several times about Ria and I told him what I knew. But it was difficult for me to talk about the business of art with him. I repeated her description of her late-night interpretations of the day's Life Drawing classes, but I was clearly inept on the subject of art. I told him she'd be back soon enough, and he could see her progress for himself, though I wasn't sure it would ever happen. I knew she'd return, but I suspected I wouldn't be spending much time in her company.

What happened next, I suppose I could say, was perfectly timed to take up the slack of ennui that had settled over my life then. But that insight took a while to dawn on me. I did what had to be done without thinking about it.

I was peeling potatoes one afternoon and listening to the radio, an episode of "Duffy's Tavern," a show I ordinarily skipped. I guess it was a little too close to home. Ray came into the kitchen and stood for a few seconds, watching me. Then he turned the radio off and said, "Theo, there's someone out there who wants to talk to you." He paused while I wiped off my hands. Of course I thought the day had at last arrived when I'd get questioned about Casco's burial.

"Look," he continued, "It's a cop. But don't worry. I mean it's not good, but you didn't do anything wrong."

Still, I was terrified. "What then?"

"Ah, dammit, kid," Ray said. He laid a hand on my shoulder. "I hate to tell you, but it's about your mother. She had an accident. She's...." He paused again.

"It's okay Ray," I said. "Is she alive?" I felt quite calm.

"No son, she's not. She drowned. I'm sorry. Listen, they want to take you out there. I said I'd drive you and that's all right with them, but this guy wants to see you first."

I had to sign a form confirming my identity and then Ray and I drove to the Bay. On the way he told me that he didn't know any details, only that someone had pulled both her and my father out of five feet of water about a hundred feet in front of our house. The tide was on its way in and had enveloped them during some activity, he didn't know what.

Ray and I entered my house to find my father sitting at the kitchen table wrapped in a blanket, his feet in a bucket of hot water. Our neighbor Ruth was making coffee.

He looked up at me, nodded hello to Ray then said, "I don't know. I don't know what she was doing out there, she.....Listen, sit down, will you? Ray please, sit down. I'm sorry. I can't...Ruth, make them some coffee, okay? Do you want some coffee?"

Ruth stepped over to him and cradled his head against her side, stroked his hair.

"It's all right Frank," she murmured. "Theo, Ray, sit. Here." She went back to the stove and poured two mugs from our battered coffee pot while Ray and I settled at the table.

"I'm so sorry, Theo," said my father. He shook his head as if to clear it, looked at me steadily and went on. "I saw her out in the water. It was about up to her waist. She was doing something, waving her arms. I could see she had that goddamned Bible in one hand. The pages were flapping like a bird. That's why I noticed. I thought she was holding a seagull or a tern; couldn't understand it. Then I saw her fall backwards. She went under and I waited. But she didn't come up. So I ran out. Oh, god." A shudder ran through him and he slumped forward, broken breaths jerking his shoulders. Ray coughed. We sipped our coffee and waited uncomfortably for him to continue. He finished his account with his head in his hands.

"When I got to her, she was lying there, face up. Her eyes were open, staring into the sky. Her mouth was open too. I swear Theo, I thought she was smiling at me, playing some kind of joke. I don't know. I pulled her up, and she...I couldn't hold on to her. She just slid off my arm and back into the water. I tried again but I couldn't hold her. So I grabbed her by the collar of her dress, and..." He looked up at me. "Did you know she couldn't swim?"

I didn't answer, I couldn't speak.

"I saw them out there. I helped your father bring her in. We tried everything but she was gone." Ruth leaned against the counter and fiddled with the lace on her apron. I recognized it as one of my mother's.

"I'm very sorry, Frank. What do you suppose she was doing out there?" said Ray after a few moments of silence.

"I don't know." He moved his head slowly from side to side. "I don't know."

A week later, I was sitting out on the porch with a beer after checking on our supper when a clue to the mystery appeared. I had stayed on to take care of my father.The man I remembered from only a few years before, the strong, fully capable fisherman of my boyhood was like a helpless child. My mother's death had undone him so thoroughly he could barely function. I soon found out that he was incapable of making even a cup of coffee or frying an egg. My mother had prepared every single thing he ate. After we'd put him to bed the first night, Ruth offered to stay on and help, but the sight of her wearing my mother's apron made me refuse the offer straightaway. I don't know why I felt so strongly about it. After all, I hadn't been living there for years and had practically no relationship with either of my parents. But somehow, in that instant, I decided to stay. Ray had parked by the front porch overlooking the water and as I walked him out I told him I didn't know when I'd be back to the bar.

"Don't worry about it, kid. I understand. Take your time," he said. He got into the car and lit a cigarette. It was a beautiful night, clear and still. In the silence we could hear small bubbling sounds of the tide was going out again. In those blackout war years, I had become used to seeing the star-filled sky unobscured by streetlights. But I'd forgotten how heartbreakingly beautiful the sight is out by the water. Ray and I looked up for a few moments while he smoked. The shallow water was so still it reflected every star, almost surrounding us. It felt as if we were suspended in space with only the car to hang on to. We didn't talk. I wasn't sad. Nothing touched my heart that night but the humble magnificence of the natural world, even though it had just taken my mother. When Ray drove off, I watched the truck's tail lights fade into the darkness, then turned and went inside. In the kitchen I emptied my father's foot-soaking water, and then without a second's thought, stepped to the wall where an oak-framed portrait of Jesus had hung over our lives, eyeing our dinners and judging our conversation. His blue eyes looked heavenward for inspiration but I always thought he looked tormented, that he was stretching toward the sky to escape the oppression of that room. I took the picture off its hook and went out onto the porch with it, intending to fling it like a giant discus as far as I could into the water, but remembered the tide was out and there was now only an inch of mud to receive it. I leaned it against the wall, and it was still there a week later when I was sipping my beer and my mother's Bible washed up ten feet to the right of the house.

I fished it out of the shallows and hefted it. The sodden pages were stuck together byglobs of algae. I splayed the pages and left the booksitting in the setting sun while I went in to coax my father to the table for supper. He was beginning to come to life and had made a couple of forays outdoors to gaze at the water and idly kick at the side of his boat. The second time he was out a couple of buffleheads flew right over the house and he glanced up. It was something. A funeral was arranged, largely by Ruth. My father and I stood in the drizzle with her and listened to the pastor read something from his Bible. It was over in an hour.

We didn't have much conversation, but he thanked me when I put his plate in front of him at mealtimes. I felt comfortable there, useful and purposeful, but if I was going to stay any longer, I needed to go to town the next morning for some supplies. More clothes, for one thing. Food. The chickens had escaped from the pen, and I could find no wire for mending it. As I was searching for the wire, I had a look around the place and noticed there were several areas of the house which needed immediate repair. It seemed my father hadn't been keeping up, even before my mother's death.

"If I go to town tomorrow, will you be all right here?" I said as we tucked into the mashed potatoes.

He looked up at me, chewing. "You coming back?"

"Yeah, Dad. I am." I wasn't sure for how long, so I didn't say.

He smiled then, possibly the first time I'd seen him smile since I pulled an eleven pound bass from Cape Cod Bay on a fishing trip with him and my uncle. It felt good, and it marked the end of whatever mourning was taking place in our house. I came home from the trip to town the next afternoon to find him on the porch, music playing on the radio in the kitchen, some big-band stuff cranked up high. He was tapping his foot and looking through the Bible. All the seaweed had been removed and he was busy unsticking the pages. The Jesus portrait was gone.

"Look at this Theo," he said, not looking up. "You won't believe it."

I sat beside him as he opened the book to a random page. All down the margins on either side was my mother's tiny, cramped script. It was almost unreadable from the water damage but several words and phrases were clear.

"Mysteries become unravelled," said one entry. On another page: "Giving yourself to God the Creator, if a person is Baptized, other Christians will not be attacked or suffer harm." The words 'baptized' and 'suffer harm' had been heavily underlined. I took the book from him and flipped to another page. The entire surface had been blotted out by two scribbled-over, rubbed-at words: 'NOAH'S FLOOD.' I glanced at my father.

"Huh?"

"Yeah. Look here," he opened it to a page toward the back. Written in red crayon over and over like an exercise was the phrase, 'Unless one is Born Again.'

"She was trying to baptize herself." My father closed the book and tossed it onto the floor. "She talked about it, wanted me to help her, but

I wouldn't. What a screwball, crackpot business Theo, No? What kind of..."

His words drifted into a mumble that I couldn't hear over the radio. I was not surprised, to tell the truth. She'd always seemed vaguely unhinged to me. Why not a baptism? Though I could not imagine why she felt the need to be cleansed of sin, I also had so little knowledge or understanding of her religion, all I could do was say goodbye and hope that she achieved a better life on some other plane. I think my father reached the same conclusion because from that day on the mood around the house was downright pleasant. My father began to talk to me, to ask me questions about my life in town. I stayed another two weeks. We fixed the chicken pen, shingled the north side of the house, replaced broken windows and did some painting. When we caught fish for supper he wanted me to show him how to cook them.

"I'm going to need some basic life skills for when you're not here," he'd say as we battered fillets and dropped them into hot fat. But I had no desire to leave yet. I enjoyed being with him, admired anew the modest dignity with which he performed tasks one-armed. He spoke to me as a person with a measure of experience and wisdom under my belt, though I was only nineteen. It felt so good to be back on the bay, especially in early summer. Everything growing was a brand-new color, a tentative, bright almost-green. The variety of budding bushes, trees with baby leaves pushing out into the sun was seemingly endless. Fingers of fern uncurled in speckled sunlight by runnels of fresh water seeping into the bay. Salamanders stirred under last fall's dead leaves. And the bay itself, sanguine, imperturbable, running on schedule as always, giving birth to a summer's worth of living creatures. The sun rose in our porch windows and threw out a glittering, enticing carpet for every fisherman to launch his boat and follow to its end.

One day in mid-June, I drove into town and walked over to the bar. The door was wide open, the blackout curtains gone, music drifted outside and I could see Ray standing in his usual spot at the end of the bar beside Phinneas. They broke out in wide grins when I stepped in and Ray came out from behind the bar to envelop me in his massive arms.

"Hey Theo. Boy is it good to see you!" Phinneas shook my hand, then put it next to his mouth for an aside. "We've got a situation in the kitchen." He lowered his voice to a whisper. "I love Liza but she cannot cook fish. She boils the damn things. And this one is afraid of her." He jerked his thumb at Ray.

"Phinneas, come on. He only just got here. How are things out on the Bay Theo?"

"Boils them?" I laughed.

"Yes. You know they're done when the eyes pop out. She told me." He shuddered.

"All right Phinneas," Ray said, "I'm working on it. Theo, what about a beer? Can you sit for a while?"

I spent the entire afternoon drinking beer with them, something I'd never done in all the years I worked there. I suppose it marked the beginning of my status as a customer and not an employee, because during the course of that afternoon I decided to move back home permanently. The solace the bar and its inhabitants had given me had saved my life but I no longer needed it. I didn't have to hide anymore. The weeks spent with my father had given me a feeling of serenity, of purpose. More importantly, I didn't want to leave the Bay again. I was back in its domain, and it welcomed me, swaddled me in green marshes and whispered in my ear a siren's song of steady breeze.

Ray knew, of course. He knew the moment I said I'd stay out there that night. I had unfinished business, and it was clearly time to start in on it. For the week it took Ray to find a replacement for me, I drove into town to work the dinner shift and managed to talk Liza into giving up the boiled fish recipe she'd brought from the Old World. She introduced Phinneas to Bouillabaisse, and both were happy. Ray hired a kid to take over the gas pumping, dishes and dump runs, and Liza was hired full time.

Back at home, I moved into my old bedroom and installed a record player in the living room. Remarkably, my father liked the music I'd collected. He especially liked a record by Woody Guthrie recorded while he was serving in the Merchant Marine. Dusty had given it to me, but I admit I only listened to it once. My father played it several times a day. It made me think of Dusty, which naturally made me think of Ria, but I couldn't ask him not to play the record, since it made him so happy.

We spent June and July lazily fishing, talking, fixing the house. One day we were out by the inlet dropping lines to catch striped bass. They liked to hover swimming against the current and were easy to spot. We sat still for over an hour, holding our lines. Out of nowhere my father said, "Theo, I can never forgive myself for what I did to you that day. The blackfish. Oh, Christ." He peered at the horizon, shaking his head. "I was crazy for the money. I know it's a poor excuse. I didn't know it would be so bad. And I admit I thought it would be a lesson in manhood: give you the sense of what it's about, supporting a family." He turned and looked me in the eye, his chin quivering slightly. "I was wrong. I wanted to find you, bring you home, but she wouldn't let me. I didn't stand up to her and that was another mistake. I loved her. It doesn't make any sense to me now."

He went back to pulling on his dropline, making the hooked grub dance. I didn't know what to say. The memory made my stomach lurch, but I didn't want to talk about it. It would sully our new harmonious way of life with bitter words of reproach. The episode was way behind me, and what I remembered more was the year I spent living in the woods as a result, and although the experience had its sadness, it also gave me a certain strength. Strength enough to forgive.

"It was a long time ago, Dad," I said finally.

"I'm sorry, son."

"I know." It would have been a good moment for a fish to grab one of our lines but it didn't, and we spent the rest of the day trolling around my father's sweet spots, coming up empty-handed.

That evening I drove into town and sat at the bar for an hour or two talking to Ray and Phinneas, joking with Liza and listening to the tourist conversation.

"You ever see that marvelous girl of yours, Theo?" said Phinneas at one point. I hadn't heard from her. She didn't even know that my mother had died. The thought was troubling but I tried not to dwell on it. I assumed she stayed in New York for the summer, otherwise she'd surely have contacted me. It was almost August, she had school in a month. I suppose I could have driven up to Eastham and knocked on the door of the family cottage, but I did not. I sent her a postcard in April for her birthday, but I hadn't heard back, so I took it as a sign that she'd moved on. More disturbing was the possibility of her being here on the Cape. I could picture her on Achilles' sofa, feet drawn up under her skirt, smoking elegantly, as he read aloud to her from the Partisan Review. I saw myself entering that little scene, standing in the doorway in my rubber boots, a fish in my hand. Or something like that. No, I would wait for Ria to contact me.

A few days later, she did. I was cooking dinner. My father answered the telephone assuming it was Ruth, who had a habit of checking in most evenings. He spoke for a few minutes, then came and leaned in the doorway.

"It was a friend of yours, Ria. She wants to drive out, so I gave her directions. All right?"

I was stunned. I stood gaping at him until he took the spatula from my hand and said, "Maybe you'd better get cleaned up. She's coming right away."

I glanced around the kitchen at our bachelor's sprawl, the dirty dishes, the dismantled fishing reel in the center of the table, our drying underwear slung over the porch railing. I went outside and gathered it up, tossed it into a chair, washed my face and tried to scrape at the black paint which had spotted my fingernails for over a month. It was useless. I changed my shirt and sat at the kitchen table, fidgeting. My father turned to look at me, barely stifling a laugh.

"Interesting," he said, as he flipped a slice of bacon.

A few minutes later headlights swept across the yard and I went to the door. Ria stepped out of a shiny black Nash convertible, smiled at me and closed the car door with a graceful flick of her wrist, then ran over and flung herself into my arms.

"Theo," she laughed. "Hi."

She was even more beautiful than the previous summer. Luscious was the word that came to me. She hadn't changed her hairstyle, the signature bangs still defined the shape of her face, but her eyes were outlined, glittering and made larger with brown shadow. Her lips were painted a dark red and so were her nails. She wore a simple white sleeveless dress and sandals. She kissed me on the cheek. I was speechless.

"So, I found you. How are you? Oh Theo. I'm so sorry. Nolan told me about your mother. I saw him in Provincetown, and I came right away. Why didn't you 'phone me? Yes, I know I've been bad not calling you, but I've been so busy. I..." She lifted her hands in a helpless gesture and said, "Is your father home? Can I meet him?"

We went inside. I hadn't said a word until I introduced the two of them. My father was gracious, Ria said words of condolence.

"Let's sit out on the porch." I plucked two bottles of beer from the fridge. My father switched on the radio, politely giving us some privacy, then went back to cooking.

I have to admit the view from our porch is quite impressive. The Bay stretches all the way to the barrier beach, and that night the moonlight glimmered on the ocean beyond. Ria sat gazing out into the night.

"No matter what I say,
All that I really love
Is the rain that flattens on the bay,
And the eel-grass in the cove..." She turned to me. "Do you know that one? Edna St. Vincent Millay?"

I said nothing. I suppose it went without saying that I didn't.

"Oh, Theo. I have so much to tell you. And I guess you have news too. You've moved back here?"

"It seems so," I said, as though I wasn't definite about it. I still had a residue of pique left in me from all the months of non-communication.

"Are you annoyed with me? I hope not. Was it awful? Your mother's death I mean. Are you all right?"

"Yes, I'm fine," I said. "And no, I'm not annoyed. You're here, aren't you? I'm glad. I missed you." I forced myself to say it. It was surprisingly easy. "She drowned," I added.

"What?"

"She was trying to baptize herself. We don't know why."

"Jesus."

"Yeah, him."

Ria smiled. "I like your house. I want to live in a house like this. I don't want to be in the city anymore."

We talked for a while about city versus country, a conversation we'd had many times. I told her about life with my father. She didn't say whether she'd been in Provincetown since June and I was dying to ask her. I thought if I just let her talk I might find out, but there were large gaps in her narrative. She talked about her mother, who had withdrawn further into her own world.

"She has no idea where I am half the time. Flora keeps track though. But neither one of them seems to object to my activities."

"Are you still at the Hofmann school?"

She launched into a long explanation of what they were working on that summer, the focus on color and space, rather than the freeform gestural drawing they were so used to. She talked about Hofmann's push-pull theory, the creation of form by light, creation of light by color. I understand it now, but back then it was a mysterious world that, no matter how hard I tried, I couldn't enter. But I loved listening to her talk about it. She was telling me a story about Hofmann, how one day he arranged a still life consisting of an eggbeater, an electric fan and a rubber glove, and left them there all summer for the students to draw repeatedly. Suddenly my father appeared, strolling around the corner of the porch.

"That's some automobile you drove here, Miss Bang," he said. "Is it a Nash?" He knew full well what kind of car it was. Everybody did.

"Yes, I believe so," said Ria.

"It's not yours, is it?"

"No. I borrowed it from a friend."

"It's a beauty. Be careful when you drive out. You wouldn't want the bushes to scratch the finish."

He bid us goodnight and left the same way he'd come. He also left the radio on.

"I've got a feeling that's Achilles' car," I said after a silence. "He's the only person I know of who could afford something like that."

"Well, you're right. It is his."

"So," I said. "You two are good friends now? I remember that day. Dusty and his silly guitar."

"I'm completely in love with him, if you want to know the truth."

I was glad of the semidarkness which hid my blushing cheeks. The declaration was not unexpected, but I didn't think it would be so brutally honest.

"Well," I began, but I couldn't continue. Ria turned to me and beamed a bright smile.

"Oh, Theo. You must meet him again. He's wonderful, he's so...cultivated, so stimulating. And funny as hell." She chuckled at some private joke and lit another cigarette. "He loves me."

"Well," I said again, counting adjectives. "I'm happy for you."

"I want you to come up to Provincetown and have dinner with us sometime. Would you?"

"Sure," I said. But I would bring no fish.

"Good. I have to tell you something else. And then I want to hear about Walter."

"Not much to tell," I said. "I haven't seen him since that day. What else do you want to tell me?"

"He's not here?"

We both laughed. "Okay, I'll go first. No, he hasn't been seen since the day I went to his house." We both glanced in the direction of Paw Wah Point. "But he has someone looking after the place. I'm going over there one of these days. There's something I want to see.

"Strange," said Ria. "Wonder what made him leave?"

"Believe me, I do not know. But it's been nice not having him around."

We ran through the details of that day. Ria asked me again to describe Walter's reaction to the confession that I'd buried Casco, what, exactly, we had said to each other, his body language, anything distinctive.

"Strange," she said again. "I don't think he killed him. It sounds like they were friends."

"I know."

"Yeah, so how -?"

"Yeah. That's the question." I still wasn't convinced of Walter's innocence, and we discussed it for a bit. That, and rocks, trees, heart attacks and brain hemorrhages, all the possibilities. Though we got nowhere it felt good to be able to discuss our secret, to dissect facts, go over the whole thing out loud all over again. We fell into a companionable silence.

"Got another beer?" Ria held up her empty bottle.

When I got back, she said, "All right, I have to tell you something. Everyone thinks I'm nuts, but I'm doing it anyway. I'm going to Europe with Achilles for the winter. He's been asked to consult on some of the Nazi-looted art. He wants me to come along." She looked straight ahead and sipped her beer, waiting for my response. Of course I was surprised. Wasn't she due for another semester at the Art Students League?

"What about school?" I said.

"I'm not going."

"Oh." I was not in a position to judge.

"Theo, please don't worry. I know what I'm doing. I do. It's not what you think, what everyone thinks."

"All right. Sorry. When are you going?"

"A couple of months from now."

She left shortly after saying that she had to get the car back. She made me write down my phone number so she could invite me to Achilles' house for dinner, but I doubted anything would come of it.

The very next day I walked over to Paw Wah. Ria had rekindled my curiosity with her questions, and I knew I could no longer ignore it. wanted to see the house, the gravesite, and the filled-in wigwam hollow. But the main reason I wanted to go was the nagging, tantalizing idea that the diary Walter had asked about, the item he and Casco were both searching for, might still be out there on the point. I thought I knew where I might find it.

As I walked along the shore I watched some campers out on the water tacking little sailboats, navigating the Narrows. It seemed so silly, a privileged pastime in this postwar summer. I wondered if all the camps were still operating. My father told me the number of kids out on the bay had greatly diminished and indeed there were only a handful out there that day. They looked so young, barely grown. Were Ria and I possibly so young when we met? She seemed so mature, so womanly now, going off to live in some foreign place with a man twice her age. She had thrown me off-balance with her visit, lessened the measure of self-confidence I'd acquired since my mother's death. I was determined to get it back. I didn't know if a visit to Paw Wah Point was such a good idea in that frame of mind but I had to do something decisive.

A buzzing stillness hovered over the little spit of land, a quiet that seemed busy, as though there were covert activities happening right under the surface, just out of earshot. I felt the life in the undergrowth watching me, as I used to watch it. But the buzz I heard was certainly my own uneasiness covering the normal sounds of animal life on a summer's day in the woods. I walked in the direction of Walter's house, paused in the trees and listened, then went and stood on his front lawn, which had gone to seed. Long and weedy, brown in the heat, with Bear Briar sprouting up in several places. The yard looked terrible. The briars crept up to the porch and had attached to the screens. That would be difficult to remove, I thought. I walked around the house, up the front steps and peered in the window. Sheet-covered furniture, shades pulled. It was clear no one had been there in a long time. A heavy chain had been strung across the driveway with a large padlock dangling from one end, as if it could stop someone from simply stepping over. It didn't make sense.

I stood next to Casco's grave for a few minutes, glancing up into the trees for any trace of the crow I'd fantasized was his reincarnation. I gave a halfhearted sparrow whistle, then sat down on the chunk of granite. The visit from Ria bothered me. What was wrong with me? Why had I not seized the moments when we were together? A trace of her perfume was still on the collar of my shirt, and I shucked out of it.

It smelled of baitfish and frying oil, but in there something of her lived. I buried my face in the shirt and cursed myself for not calling her, pursuing her. I sniffed my shirt until all of her scent was gone, then put it back on. A chipmunk ducked out from the leaf cover and eyed me, panting in the heat. A line of ants climbed a strip of poison ivy twisted around a scrub pine, following its shiny green path like a circular staircase. Sparrows twittered above me, contentedly tending nests. I could hear the gentle slap of windblown ripples on the shore below and the distant rumble of waves farther out. Gradually the life of the point made itself heard and my own murmur of disquiet faded.

I lay there for a long time thinking about nothing, drinking in the sound of the natural world, my old home. I might have dozed off for a minute, because I remember being brought to life again by the sound of crows cawing. A hawk or a fox, something making them uneasy. I looked for them, but couldn't see anything in the leaf cover. Finally I hauled myself up and walked over to where the wigwam used to be. I identified the spot by the trees surrounding the area, but there was nothing to see. Waist-high Huckleberry bushes obliterated any trace of the site. I turned north and made my way to the middle of the Point, the highest spot, the place where Casco had said a small farm had been, and had used its root cellar as a hiding place during the Hurricane of '38.

It took a while to find the little hump in the land among all the bushes and briars, but when I scraped the foliage away from one end I saw a small wooden door, rotted but still intact. I shoved it inward. Two wooden steps descended into a black hole. I stuck my head in, let my eyes adjust to the dark. It smelled wonderfully of clean stone with a hint of pine, the fragrance of dirt. The space was only a few feet square. I climbed down and felt around. The dirt walls were cool and dry, roots seeking moisture had knitted themselves into a kind of soft nest at the bottom. I could see it was a perfect hiding place, a comfortable shelter. I sat down and tried to imagine a howling wind slamming trees down right outside. I could hear nothing but a kind of non-sound, the neutrality of cool earth. I wanted to stay there, imagining myself in kinship with Casco underground, the stillness of nonexistence. Then I thought of my mother in her grave and sat up with a start.

I felt around the interior for a break in the surface, a shelf or something wooden, manmade. The roof was constructed of rough logs and wedged in behind one of them was a small metal box. When I yanked at the handful of roots sheathing it, a rain of dirt fell into my eyes, but the box dropped down too.

I crawled out of the root cellar and sprawled on the ground, breathing heavily, unbelieving. It was too easy. Why hadn't I done this months ago? The box, once scraped of orange dirt, was rusty but intact. A fat leather thong had been wrapped around it several times. I didn't want to break the seal with no tools so I reached into the hole, pulled the door closed, rearranged the briar in front, grabbed the box and left.

Chapter 13

When I got back to the house, my father was gone, but there was a note on the kitchen table held down with a casting sinker. "Gone out to Sipson's. Back with supper. Miss Bang called. You're invited to Ptown on Friday night. I told her you'd be there. Hope that's OK."

I didn't want to be elated, but I was. Friday was two days away, plenty of time to work on my appearance. Meanwhile, I took down my father's filleting knife and sat at the table, the box in front of me. I slid the blade between two strands of thong, then thought better of it and looked at the knot. I pried at it with the tip of the knife until a loop appeared, then pulled gently with my fingers. I have often experienced an instant connection to someone in this very circumstance, untying someone else's knot. As a child I used to use one hand, trying to untie knots my father had made to see how it felt being one-handed. Later they were Casco's knots on the roof of the wigwam. Or those made by Liza on my frying apron, even the anonymous knots made by packers of foodstuffs delivered to the restaurant. I can feel the other person, almost see the other fingers knitting what I unravel. As I pulled apart the loops of Casco's knot, my fingers were his for a second or two, a trace of our secret bond.

The leather came away easily and the box opened with a rusty creak. Inside was a small package loosely wrapped in white cloth. I unwound the fabric. It was a book, bound primitively in brown leather. The cover was scratched and stained with greasy smears. The page edges were black from thumbing. I put it aside and picked up the other item, a folded piece of paper. 'Theodoros Sparrow' was written in capital letters in dark brown ink. The paper had been sealed with a generous blob of pine pitch. I'd never seen Casco's handwriting. It was elegant, old-fashioned. I picked up the sinker and tapped the brittle pitch, which crumbled. I opened the paper. In a graceful cursive it read:

"My Friend,

I hope it is you reading this and not some other people I know. You must be very careful with this diary. Tell no one you have it or even know of it. Those people would give their eye teeth to get ahold of it. When I finally found it, I thought the answers to all my problems would be there between the pages. And I suppose they were. With the information it contains I could've sold it and bought back the shop and a place to live as well. But then I fell in love with Paw Wah, and my ambitions seemed imbecilic by comparison.

It's the diary of my ancestor, Bad Boy, the one I told you about. You remember he was converted to Christianity, taught to write. He kept this diary for a year or two. It has some remarkable entries about Metacom and his brother, some factual accounts of the events of that time. There's one item in particular. They sent him out to Deer Island along with the others, but he gave the diary to John Eliot, who promised to return it here to my family along with the belt you've seen me wearing. Eliot gave it to a person who did, but who first copied parts of it. I've seen those copies. That's how I know.

Take it to Gustav Heye in New York, at his Museum of the American Indian. Tell him my story.

I'll assume I finally froze to death out here. I know I didn't starve. But don't grieve for me, please. It's how I wanted it. I'm proud to have known you, Theo. You are a fine person."

The letter was signed with a pictograph. Three horizontal wavy parallel lines bisected by a diagonal slash, a dot at each intersection. I wondered idly what instrument he'd devised to write with. I expect the ink was made from boiled walnut shells. I had no idea about the paper.

I sat back and tried to make sense of his words. Surely Walter was one of 'Those people.' Casco imagined he might freeze to death. An image of the yellow socks flashed through my mind. They were in the bureau drawer of my room.

When I picked up the diary, it opened naturally to the middle. The paper was thick and soft with a line of tiny stitches binding it. Spread across the facing pages was a drawing, a map. Certain locations were marked, but in a language I didn't understand. It looked like two converging rivers which formed a bay with a couple of islands in it. A key labeled A through E ran down the edge of the page but the only word I could make out was 'bridge.' There wasn't anything resembling a bridge in the drawing. I could find only one corresponding letter, E, but couldn't make out what E was in the key. Then I saw a word I knew, 'Sakonet,' written along a wavy double line. A river? Rhode Island's Sakonnet River runs from Mount Hope Bay and out into the ocean. Mount Hope is where Metacom held his tribal meetings. The rock where they met is a well known site. Casco had told me all of this. He called it 'Montaup.' I made a mental note to compare it to the map in our atlas.

I turned to the first page. A stylized drawing of a wolf's head and the words "Bad Boy" were visible through a smudged print of four fingers in reddish ink. I recalled Casco telling Ria and me about his distant relative. He'd pointed to the floor of the wigwam and said that Bad Boy been born "right here."

The next page was all script, half of it recognizable words like 'him' and 'went.' A fragment of a sentence said "for myn eyes never seen yt place befor." This followed by "last dayik pakodjteauunach wame, asquam wayont," and more of the same back-and-forth language: "He remained ther all yt nigh in saftie neit nahen meetseen."

I flipped to another page where a drawing of a raccoon faced one of an owl on the opposite page. The word "Ausupp" was written across the racoon's back and snaked across the page to join the word "Wewes" that flowed down the owl's wings. Between the two were several pictograms like the one with which Casco had signed his letter to me. Little symbols, an arrow, a pair of crossed, forked twigs, a capital P with two dots in front of it.

I turned several pages of writing with the strange half-English, half-something else with its looped capitals and descenders, little wavy marks above certain letters or words. On another page was a crude but detailed drawing of a musket. The words 'one, two, three, four, five' ran down the side of a page with the words 'aquit, nees, nis yoaw, and abbona lined up beside them. I noticed the name Eliot here and there with mentions of a Winthrop, Captain Church and Sasamon several times. I recognized other words from Casco's teachings. His name, which I remembered meant 'muddy,' written along a wavering line in another tiny map drawing which ended at a place labeled 'maskpoag.' Small parallel lines surrounded the 'maskpoag' and were labeled 'sasco' The whole thing was titled 'mattawamkeag.' Many of the pages had the same capital P with two dots hovering in front of it interspersed throughout the text.

I pulled our atlas off the shelf and turned to a map of Rhode Island. The drawing in the center of the diary, if held sideways, was a fairly exact map of Narragansett Bay. Mount Hope Bay was easily identifiable, as was the Sakkonet River. I peered at the drawing. On the island of Bristol, overlooking Mount Hope Bay was a circle of small lines marked 'monomonak.' Nearby was another marker, the word 'saugus.'

I rubbed my eyes. How I wished for Casco's presence at that moment. I picked up the letter again. *You must be very careful with this diary*, he'd written. He had instructed me to take it to New York, to some Indian museum. How was I to do that? *Tell no one you have it or even know of it.* Needless to say, I was dying to tell Ria, I had to tell her. But I couldn't.

Of course I did, but not when I went to dinner Friday night in Provincetown, though it was my primary reason for going. We never had even a minute alone. The fact was I had such a wonderful time with the two of them that I decidid to wait, tell Ria at another time. Achilles opened the door when I knocked promptly at six o'clock, a tinkling cocktail in his hand. He was wearing another beautiful shirt, dark blue linen embroidered in a darker shade across the shoulders.

"Theo," he said. "Come in, come in." He shook my hand and gave me a warm smile, opening the door wider and ushering me through the small foyer. When I entered the living room Ria stood up from the sofa, gave me a quick, fierce hug and said, "I'm so glad you're here. Now we can all be together."

I sat next to the sofa on a rattan chair, sinking into a thick cushion covered in brown velvet. Ria chatted nervously about the last time we'd been there, as I nodded my head and smiled. A cool breeze swept through from the porch, smelling of sea and bringing with it faint sounds of laughter from the beach. I looked around. The same piles of books covered almost every surface. In the other half of the room a generous dining table held a huge bouquet of rose hips and beach peas. I could see that someone, likely Ria, had been sitting at the table painting. Large pieces of paper were scattered over it and a coffee can holding a dozen brushes of varying sizes sat in a nest of rags. Around the room her work had been tacked up between framed drawings, photographs and tapestries.

Ria noticed me looking at them. "What do you think, Theo? I told you I've been busy."

Of course my lack of knowledge about abstract art left me unable to say, but I looked around while Ria and Achilles discussed some detail of the meal. The paintings seemed to be variations on the same theme: a kind of loose grid of drooping squares made with bold strokes in two or three shades ofblue, some filled in, some just outlined. They crashed into each other or stood separately or slopped across dividing lines. A single square or outline might be of contrasting color, which gave the whole a sense of them floating in space, more three dimensional than flat plane. They danced with the action of Ria's gestures. I liked them quite a lot, and said so.

"How do you know when it's finished?" I asked, and Achilles laughed.

"That is the question, isn't it? One of them, at any rate," he said.

"Something almost magical happens to me when I paint," said Ria, leaning forward excitedly. "I slam away at the thing, trying to realize a vision. Usually nature in some form or other. You can see I've been looking at water and sky."

Well, they were mostly shades of blue and white. "Yes," I said.

"At some point, and it's why I paint really, the painting begins to tell me what it wants, what it needs. I become an instrument, a tool the painting uses to create itself. I simply, automatically know where to put marks, color, my hand does it all while I stand by, watching. I don't know how to explain it any better." She looked at Achilles and smiled. "Although sometimes that doesn't happen..."

"Often," Achilles interjected, laughing.

"...and so I keep doing it, moving, trying to see beyond the surface and reveal what's already suspended there. I suppose to answer your question, I know the painting is finished when it stops needing me." She started to laugh too, so I joined in but the truth is I understood what she was saying. I looked again around the room with a new curiosity and appreciation.

"Ria is very talented," Achilles said, now serious. "And she has the courage to go beyond what she has been taught. Who knows where it will lead."

"All right, enough about it, thank you. Theo has already been forced to listen to me talk about my work more than he wants."

"I like it," I said.

Achilles cleared his throat. "Listen Theo, Ria told me about your mother. I'm sorry." He sat across from me in another of the rattan chairs, the silver-topped cane I remembered from the last visit leaning against the arm.

"Thank you," I said. "It's all right. The good thing is it brought my father and me together."

"Yes, she told me. What's interesting to me is that you immediately rose to the occasion. Quit your job. Moved back home."

Ria said, "I hope you don't mind, Theo. I told him the entire story."

Had she told him about Casco? I looked at her and widened my eyes with the question. She closed her eyes and shook her head once. "About the blackfish," she said.

"A regrettable business," said Achilles

At that moment his cook, Cal, came in and said, "It's ready. Anytime you are."

We went outside to the porch where a small table had been set. The harbor glittered with reflected light from the restaurants lined up along the waterfront. To see such a change, after all the dark years of the war, was exhilarating, but in a peaceful way, as though everything would be all right from then on. A party was taking place on a large boat not far from Achilles' house. Paper lanterns had been strung in the rigging and I could hear snatches of conversation, a woman's laugh, in the quiet evening. I felt genuinely happy.

"Do you want some wine?" Ria held up a bottle and pushed a plate closer to me. On it were thin slices of salami and cucumber, some black wrinkled olives and a small block of something pure white which crumbled a bit at the cut edge. She poured some red into my glass.

"Sure," I said, fingering an olive, then putting it on my tongue.

"My mother died when I was nineteen, the same as you," said Achilles, continuing the conversation he'd started in the living room. "And she drowned, like yours."

The double revelation of that statement and the salty, sharp flavor of the olive took me by complete surprise. My mouth was so dry I was unable to respond for a few seconds. I took a sip of wine which added another facet to the sensations of the moment. I never drank wine, especially after tasting the stuff we sold at the Ship Ahoy, but this was a different drink entirely. It melted across my tongue and fanned out, arousing areas of my mouth I never knew existed. It blended with the olive and washed into my throat. I coughed lightly, trying not to let my eyes water, and said, "She drowned?"

Achilles smiled. "Yes. I was there. A cruel age to lose one's mother, isn't it? Though, at any age, I suppose it's unacceptable." He looked at Ria and winked, then took her hand.

"What happened?" I said. I wasn't as interested in his story as I was in seeing Ria's hand disappear into his. I asked him the question only to say something.

"I grew up in Smyrna, in Anatolia. That's Izmir, Turkey in today's nomenclature. I don't know if you're familiar with what happened in that part of the world in the years just before you and Ria were born, and there is no reason for you to be." He cut off a piece of the white block and laid it carefully on a slice of cucumber, which he picked up and poised in front of his mouth. "My father was a paleographer, a dealer of icons and manuscripts." He put the cucumber slice into his mouth and chewed. "He was also a brilliant forger, and got himself into trouble with a couple of other dealers, Russian, I think. I don't know exactly. At any rate he disappeared about a year before the Great Fire. I grew up in a house stuffed with antique things, carpets, embroideries, old carvings and such. My father collected everything. My mother was always annoyed with the dust those things collected, so there was usually a battle going on between them. He would leave us for weeks at a time, and my mother would take the rugs outside and beat them, polish carved icons with lemon oil and wipe dust off ancient calligraphic masterpieces with a dishtowel." He laughed quietly, sipped his wine and continued.

"Anyway, he was also good at faking things. He knew how to make paper in the old way, vellum and parchment, and to cover it with illuminated calligraphy. Our kitchen was often given over entirely to this activity. He'd roll these documents carefully and take them away. He told me once that several of his forgeries were in the British Museum." He stopped talking to make himself another of the cucumber slices.

"Have you ever tasted feta?" he said, pointing with the knife at the crumbling white block.

"Try it," said Ria, extracting her hand from his and cutting off a little cube, which she passed to me. I put it in my mouth and again experienced a salty, sharp flavor, but creamy too. It dissolved on my tongue. "Very good," I said, and reached for another.

"Cheese from sheep. From Greece. Well, made in New York..." said Ria.

"By a friend of mine from the old country, another refugee of the Great Fire," Achilles finished for her. "That's where my mother died. In the harbor, trying to escape. He gazed out at the boat with the lanterns. "My stepfather, Henry Overton, was an American freelance journalist, among other things. At the time my mother and I met him, he wrote a literary column for the New York Times. He was a Hellenophile, and a collector of books, so he had traveled extensively in Greece and western Turkey, sending back to America a sort of literary travelogue from that area. One day he knocked on our door wanting to speak to my father, whom we hadn't seen in over six months. I let the man in anyway because he was so exotic, so foreign, and he spoke perfect Greek. He was looking for a certain book which he thought might be valuable for more than literary reasons. My mother invited him to tea, and he fell in love with her on the spot. Well, she was a great beauty, even at the age of forty. By the time he left two hours later he had forgotten all about the book and asked if he might visit us again. Henry spent a lot of time at our house, and I grew to love him, too. This was in a time of great conflict, the last months of the Greek-Turkish war. And before that the years of deportations, labor camps, massacres." He shook his head. "A strange time in my city. Many Europeans, businessmen, speculators were there as well in the years after the first World War. Who would control the former Ottoman Empire? Smyrna was such a splendid city. Cosmopolitan, international, yet interbred. Lord, it was complicated. The blame for the Great Fire remains a bitter debate, but I believe it was genocide."

He paused for a moment, fixed me with a meaningful look, as if to confirm that I would listen to what he was about to say. He took a deep breath and went on. "In September of twenty-two, when the Turkish army swept into Smyrna and retook the city from the control of the Greeks they set entire Christian neighborhoods on fire. Greek men were shot at almost randomly. Worse things happened to the women." He glanced at Ria and sipped his wine. She put her hand over his and fiddled with his silver bracelet, twisting it around and around.

"At any rate, Henry secured papers for our passage out, a place for my mother and me with him on one of the boats. He knew someone at the American Consul. We hurried to the harbor, having had time only to gather up a few things. This was my father's." He picked up the silver-capped cane. "I grabbed it and my good shoes, that's all. The house, the whole street was on fire, and we ran."

Engrossed in the story, I barely noticed when Cal came out to the porch with a platter and set it in the middle of the table. Achilles paused to thank him, pulled a box of matches from his pocket and lit one of two thick white candles. He passed the match to Ria and she lit the other.

"Please," he nodded to the platter. "Help yourself."

It was a chicken, stuffed with lemons and surrounded by onions, potatoes and long cylinders of leek, another food I had never seen nor tasted. Cal returned with a large wooden bowl which he set on a side table. Ria poured more wine, and Achilles continued with his story.

"The harbor was overflowing with people wanting to get out, Turkish troops trying to control things, dozens of boats of all sizes bobbing side by side. People threw bundles of belongings down and leapt aboard. Mostly women and children. The smoke from the fire blinded us, but Henry led us to a good-sized ferry and shoved me ahead of him onto the boat ramp while he handed over our papers. We were the last to board, the crew had already cast off the lines. Apparently one of the Turkish soldiers herding people onto the boats got a little impatient and prodded my mother with the butt of his rifle, and she tripped and fell into the water. Neither Henry nor I saw it happen. Our ferry had been loosely tethered to another, and my mother fell between them, hitting her head on the gunwale of the other boat on the way down. Those who saw it began to yell. Henry saw what had happened, jumped overboard and grabbed my mother, but the blow to her head had killed her. It was obvious. I tried to help, but he ordered me to stay on board. The boat was leaving. Henry kissed my mother once, let her go, and grabbed a rope dangling from the stern. He held on as the boat gathered speed, bobbing in and out of the water while I screamed at him. He wouldn't let us pull him aboard until we were well away. Then he and I collapsed on the deck and cried. We stayed that way the entire night as we watched our city burn, people still crowded on the quay under a rain of sparks and cinders. Awful. As we sailed away, we saw the horizon become a solid wall of fire two miles wide."

I sat leaning on one elbow in stunned silence, my hand over my mouth. I didn't know what to say. Ria had tears streaming down her face.

"Ela agapi, don't cry," Achilles said to her. "You already know the story." He turned to me and added, "Long time ago. Sorry. Come, let's eat."

We ate in silence for several moments. The chicken was delicious, moist and lemony. Ria made it many times for me over the years, but it was never as rich and flavorful as that night. "I'm very sorry," I said finally.

Achilles nodded, his mouth full. Ria said, "Sometimes I'm ashamed to belong to the human race."

"Yes, I know what you mean," said Achilles. "But please, let's change the subject. I never meant to go on about it like that."

"What happened to you after? Where did you go?" I asked him. I wanted to understand how the nineteen year old Greek from Smyrna became the man sitting there in the beautiful shirt on the back porch of a beautiful house in this beautiful American town on a beautiful night with a beautiful woman. I knew nothing of the events he'd described. I didn't know anything about Smyrna, or Izmir, except that it was in Turkey. So he told us more of his story, about Henry bringing him to America and adopting him, about the schools he attended, the death of Henry a few years later, and the twenty-two gold coins from the treasury of King Darius of Persia which Henry left him in his will.

"That was the beginning of my career as a trader of antiquities, like my father before me. Except that I don't manufacture any of them myself." He grinned.

By then we'd finished dinner and Cal brought out a tray with a bottle of cognac and three little glasses.

"Here's to motherless boys," said Ria, as we swirled and sniffed.

We talked further into the night, about Cape Cod and tourism, and fishing. Achilles made me promise to take him out in our boat one day. I did eventually, but not until years later, and he was completely inept at even the simplest task. But it didn't matter, he kept my father and me entertained with stories, jokes and a thermos of gin and tonic.

I left that night with a feeling of heady expansion, as though I had traveled to a foreign country for the evening and spoken a different language for several hours. I was still jealous of Achilles' affair with

Ria, but I could understand why she wanted to be with him. In the years following, even though they spent increasingly less time together, I came to appreciate their deep connection and need for each other. She for his education and worldliness, his understanding of art, and yes, maybe for the father she never really had. He in turn delighted in her determination, her individuality, and the playful, unaffected way she looked at life. As I drove the long road back to Orleans I mentally reviewed mine since leaving Paw Wah Point and the wigwam, pictured the boy I had been. I knew very little about life outside the world of the Bay until I met Casco, and he could almost be considered one of the species inhabiting those waters and woods. But, from that time on, my entry into civilization had been a series of fortunate encounters with fascinating people. Ria, Nolan, Phinneas and Achilles all had something in common, something I did not have. They'd all been educated formally, they all shared the experience of the larger world. What did I know? The Bay and how to make a pot of clam chowder, the social structure of a wasp nest, where to drop a lobster pot. Tides, wind, stars. Not much. And yet, these people seemed interested in me. Why? My father's old car ticked along the empty road as I thought about it, the headlights making two holes in the darkness.

Chapter 14

That fall of 1945 Ria and Achilles left for Europe. Paris, to be exact. I saw them once before they went, when they came to Provincetown to pack up the house and collect some books for the trip. Ria phoned me to say they were there and asked if could I drive up to see her. I admit my initial feeling was that I did not want to make the long trip just to say goodbye to her and her lover and so I suggested we meet somewhere in Orleans when they were on the way back to the city. I pictured myself turning on my stool at the Ship Ahoy bar as they entered, feigning interest, saying a quick farewell. But of course she talked me into taking the train up the next afternoon and driving back down with them. I would always do whatever Ria wanted. And of course I had another wonderful time. We parted with promises to write regularly, which we did. I received a package a month later containing smoked oysters, dried figs and dates, candied ginger and other exotic treats I'd never heard of before. My father was in ecstasy over the oysters and immediately set about trying to duplicate them. He constructed a smoker in the back yard and experimented, usually with clams, to get it right. I think it must have been his very first attempt at making food, and he succeeded for the most part. It led him to begin smoking bluefish and scallops and over the next few years he developed a little business selling it to the fish market in town.

A long letter from Ria was also enclosed. She was very excited to be in Paris, she said, and although the city had been mostly spared much of Europe's destruction, the general post-war state of the city was 'heartbreaking.' She had attended a ceremony held when the Mona Lisa was rehung in the Louvre, she was 'in love' with Django Reinhart, and had stood outside Picasso's studio. 'His actual door!' Achilles was working as part of a team in a makeshift warehouse sorting hundreds of paintings and sculptures, entire collections stolen from the Jews. Ria spent her time painting and wandering around the city and was 'deliriously happy.'

When I read her letter, I sat down at once and wrote a long, disjointed reply about what was happening out on the bay (not much), the Ship Ahoy (ditto), and some amusing anecdotal stories about Provincetown culled from the gossip that came to Orleans with the beer deliveries. I had made a habit of spending Saturday evenings at the bar with my friends, sitting with Phinneas and Nolan and Ray for a bowl of chowder and a few beers before driving back to the Bay and my father.

I mailed off the reply and only then remembered I had yet to tell Ria about the diary. I had intended, on that second visit to Provincetown, to ask her if she knew about the Museum of the American Indian, and to tell her, if somehow we could find a private moment, that I'd found what Walter was looking for. But again Achilles dazzled me with his charm, his excellent food, and a Greek drink called ouzo which, after a couple of glasses made me forget about everything except my immediate company. But even before the ouzo took effect I had thought better of bringing up the tired old subject of Walter with Ria. She had clearly moved on from what suddenly, by comparison with Achilles' world, seemed almost childish, another camp legend like Captain Kidd's treasure. A story from one of my old detective novels. I decided I would let her ask if there were any news, and she didn't. So after a month, I wrote another letter, not only for me to set down my thoughts on paper, but to give Ria an update without having to witness any disinterest she may have developed in our time apart.

"I forgot to tell you before you left," I wrote. "I found the diary Walter was looking for. Casco hid it out on the point in an old cold cellar." I paraphrased Casco's note to me and gave a brief description of the diary. "I cannot understand most of what is written in it," I said, "because it's Wompanoag or something." I asked her if she'd ever heard of the museum and told her I intended, as soon as I could, to take the diary there. I know Casco's note warned me strongly against telling anyone about the diary, but I figured Ria knew everything else, so why not tell her this as well? I suppose I thought I could keep some sort of hold on her with it. Maybe that part was in my subconscious. I had no plans to go to New York to find Gustav Heye and his museum. The thought of going there made me distinctly uneasy. Maybe when Ria came back we could go together if she was still interested.

Ten days after I mailed the letter, I received a telegram from Ria. One of the guys at the cable station brought it into the bar. Ray drove it out to the house and sat, clearly more than curious, while I read it.

In true Ria style it read: CANNOT BELIEVE YOU DID NOT TELL ME STOP WRITE ALL STOP LEAVE NOTHING OUT STOP RIA.

Ray was looking out at the water, but his eyebrows jumped up and down.

"It's nothing," I said. "Just Ria saying hello."

So I wrote her a more detailed letter, described the appearance of the little book, copied out Casco's note word for word and duplicated his pictograph signature. I told her about the first page with the wolf drawing and Bad Boy. I described the map and my matching it up with Narragansett Bay and copied some of the strange sentences for her. I wrote down all the English names from the diary. I asked her if she would go with me to find Gustav Heye. I told her about my father smoking fish. I asked when she planned to return.

"Thank you for your letter Theo," she wrote back. "Don't ever leave me out again, all right? We are in this together. After all, I found the Peace Medal that started all the trouble, and we cannot give up on solving the mystery of Casco's death. Of course I'll go with you to New York. As soon as I get back. I don't know when that will be though, Achilles is knee deep in paintings and provenance and comes home each evening looking grimmer than the night before. The appalling details of Nazi barbarity are revealing themselves day by awful day. But he is dedicated to seeing the worst of the job through to its end. There are many people involved but even so the task is immense. Each piece of artwork has a story, and every story ends in disaster.

Anyway, I'm still painting like mad, even though paint is hard to come by. We'll be together again soon, my friend, I promise. Meanwhile write to me often and tell your father to try smoking snails, they are delicious!"

She signed off with a flourish accompanied by a tiny heart at the end.

Ria and Achilles stayed in Paris for a year, then Munich for one more. They returned in the spring of '48, drove straight to Cape Cod and bought another house. Ria told me she insisted they have a place on Pleasant Bay and simply pointed on a map to a spot she thought would be nice. As luck had it, there was an old hunting shack sitting on a bluff at the end of Barley Neck which had a spectacular view south through the Narrows and east across the barrier beach to the ocean. She said it wasn't difficult to persuade the owner to sell. Paw Wah Point lay in between our two places, so she also had a view of Walter's roof, but she didn't mind. The best part about it was that Ria and I could see each other's lights at night. She and Achilles set about updating the house, adding a large kitchen, a substantial fireplace and another bedroom for the daughter who had been born to them six months before.

They named her Eugenia after Achilles' mother but called her Ginny. It was at first very strange to see Ria taking care of a baby, and she did so almost entirely by herself, since Achilles was not around much after the first summer. Ginny was a placid baby who happily stuck to the schedule Ria imposed on their little household, sleeping or crawling around or sitting on Ria's lap, according to the clock. She had a head of glossy dark hair and Achilles' green eyes, which she trained on me with a kind of inquisitive delight. The first time I went over, two men were busy shingling a sidewall on the baby's bedroom so Ria put Ginny to sleep in a carriage and wheeled her outside to the front yard where we sat drinking tea.

"The next time you visit me you can come by boat if you want," she said, pointing downhill at a brand new dock that I hadn't noticed. Achilles bought a ten foot dory with a motor, and I showed Ria how to use it. She became quite adept at cruising around the Bay, the baby on her lap and a clam digger in the bow. I took her around to the sweet spots Casco had known about, and she often left Ginny and me sitting in the boat to wade around scratching for supper in the shallows. It reminded me of the days when I used to wait in the sailboat while my father went ashore in search of ducks. Ginny would sit peacefully watching her mother or pointing out birds or smacking her feet in the water while I dangled her over the side. Ria loved that boat. She was a natural helmsman and could navigate as skillfully as the old-timers in open water or snake through the marsh grass at half tide. She was much better at docking than I and had the enviable ability to lightly kiss the end piling with the bow, then let the boats length drift alongside without ever making the slightest mark on the paint. Achilles never used the boat except when Ria insisted they go out on the water, and then she was always at the helm.

We spent almost every weekend together that first summer. Achilles came up for all of August except for a couple of forays back to New York. He still had the house in Provincetown and the little family went there for a few days when he first arrived. But Ria wanted to live in the house on the Bay and so he drove back and forth. Cal stayed in Provincetown while Achilles was on the Cape. I got the distinct impression Cal and Ria did not get along.

Achilles loved to cook, and he was able to concoct fairly exotic dishes with what he could find around town or bring from New York.

As soon as he got to Orleans that August, he spent an entire afternoon hauling a couple dozen good-sized rocks from down on the shore and piling them into a waist-high plinth with a pit for a fire and a metal rack for grilling. There was even a little hollow he used to roast eggplant and peppers and the other vegetables which figured heavily in his middle eastern cuisine. I had never seen an eggplant, but I certainly ate many then and in the years to follow, as Ria adopted Achilles' taste for those dishes. We ate kebabs of all kinds, eggplant stuffed with lamb and rice and raisins, grilled tomatoes, baba ganoush, potato latkes and tsadziki. Imam Bayildi. I have sorely missed those dishes. I never had the knack for cooking them anyway, but I have lost the desire as well.

My memories of those relaxed, spontaneous, spice scented dinners that first summer at Ria's house merge into one long orange-tinted twilight. We were always in the front yard overlooking the bay, Achilles at his grill and Ria in a cotton dress, lounging on a canvas sling chair, the hauraches she wore all summer kicked off. Ginny crawled around in the dry grass at their feet. I would often lie on my stomach at the edge of the lawn to gaze at the eddying water currents below, or track hawks circling effortlessly in the still air as I listened to their conversation. Ginny loved sitting on my back while I watched the bay, humming softly to herself as she twisted the skin of my earlobe between her tiny fingers. With Ria's binoculars, I kept an eye on my father's movements from there, and often felt a little guilty about leaving him alone, but at that time he was fixated on his fish smoking and wasn't much company himself. I would watch his miniature figure moving from porch to back yard to stand in front of his cooking contraption for hours, curls of white smoke disappearing into the sky. Achilles and Ria would gossip and laugh about the people and events of their life together, Ria often interrupting her laughter long enough to make sure I understood at least a smidgen of what they were discussing. They both loved to listen to music, and so one or the other would get up to change a record or fiddle with the dial on the radio, though hardly any signal reached all the way to the end of Barley Neck. They often sang along to something while Ginny did a kind of bouncing dance and giggled at them, clapping her hands with delight. I quickly saw the deep connection between them, the similarity of spirit, a relaxed, jocular sort of indifference to the rules of convention and those who uphold them. They were like a pair of foreigners who enjoyed that state of being, taking only what they desired from their adopted country and choosing not to belong to the rest.

One of the most beautiful of Ria and Achilles' home improvements was a generous studio for her, still partially under construction at that point. I had never seen anything like it. It was separate from the house, a short walk through a stand of wind-whipped cedar and mounted on a platform to compensate for the slope of the land. It was like a shingled box, but had a roof which shot sharply from its nearly two-story peak almost to the ground and featured four large north-facing skylights which leaked from the beginning and which I would re-caulk regularly. At the end of August, when the carpenters finally pronounced it done, Ria furnished the room with a long work table, an easel and two fat armchairs with a low table between them. The chairs faced the Bay beyond a stand of cedars, but unlike Walter, Ria left them alone, so the view was not as spectacular as from the front yard. But still it became, over the years, the place we spent most of our time together. And I loved the view of the trees. It reminded me of living in the wigwam. A few days after the studio was finished, Ria invited me for dinner. "Just the two of us. I'll put the baby to bed and we can talk. I want you to bring over the diary, Theo. Okay? I know I've been preoccupied, but I still want to see it, you know." I' had, for the time being, put the diary out of my mind, to tell the truth. I hadn't taken it out since I copied parts of it for Ria when she was in Paris. But of course she would want to see it and Casco's letter.

We settled into her studio with a pitcher of vodka and grapefruit juice and I looked around. The day before Achilles and Cal had arrived with a truck full of more studio gear and several completed canvases which were stacked face to the wall, so I couldn't see what she'd been working on, and she didn't offer to show me. Ginny was asleep in her basket and there was a pot of bean soup on the stove in the house. I sat marveling at the simple, elegant design of the space and looking at the clouds through the skylights. I took a slow sip of my cocktail, enjoying myself thoroughly. But Ria started tapping her fingers on the arm of her chair. Of course she got right to the point. "Unwrap the damn thing will you? I've been wanting to have a look at it for two years," she said, handing it to me. It was still in its box, wrapped in the same white cloth and the leather thong with Casco's knot. I took it out. First she read Casco's letter, her eyebrows knitted in concentration.

"Hm. 'One item in particular,' he says. I wonder what it could be. Did you look for it?"

"I tried. You'll see. It's unreadable."

She picked up the little book and carefully opened it to the first page with Bad Boy's name and the wolf's head drawing. "Bad Boy. Clear as day," she said, shooting me a look of amazement. She turned the pages carefully, studying them in turn, murmuring the few English words and names, trying out the other language.

"Kah seip wutchilaw. I wonder what it means?"

"Look at the map," I said, opening it to the middle.

"Oh yes. It is Narragansett Bay, isn't it?" She showed me, tracing with a finger, the route the train took from New York tthrough Rhode Island. "I see clearly where Newport is on this map. I've sailed right by it." Probably with Achilles, I thought, though she didn't say.

We looked through the rest of the diary, pausing on names and the few other words we could make out. Ria noticed the word 'amen' after two long passages of illegible language.

"Maybe Bad Boy was converted, after all," she said. We paged through the diary again more thoroughly, but to be honest, it was an eye-crossing job, with sentences made from words like nutaquontamanounonog following one after the other. Finally we wrapped it back up in its cloth and tied it with Casco's thong. Then Ria brought some of the soup out to the studio and we sat eating in silence.

After a while she said, "We must take it to the Museum, as Casco wanted. When can you go?" That was a good question. Of course I did not want to go to New York City, and certainly not on my own. I was not made to be in a place like that, or what I imagined it to be, a noisy, hyperactive, dirty snarl of concrete and steel. So far I'd managed to avoid it, simply because Ria had been away. And now I had an even better excuse. I couldn't possibly go. I had a job.

I started working here at the newspaper in the months before Ria and Achilles returned. Quite by accident, I happened to be sitting in the Ship Ahoy one afternoon during the week, not my usual Saturday. It was only because my father had pulled in a three foot cod earlier that day and, it being far too large for the two of us to eat, I took it in to the bar to sell to Ray. It was a gorgeous day at the end of June, and the restaurant was nearly empty. When Ray opened the door to the kitchen I saw only one man sitting at the bar reading the Advocate.

Ray picked up the huge, slippery fish, held it up to his face and peered into its eyes.

"This morning. Good. You catch this monster?" he tossed it onto the table.

"My father," I said.

Ray smiled at me and said, distracted, "That's good. Very good Theo." He stared at me for a few seconds and said, "Yes. Of course. Why didn't I think of it before?" Baffled, I just stood there and waited.

"Listen, you want a little job? It would be a few days, not here, down the street. You can paint a room, can't you? Sure you can."

"OK," I said, "I think so." I needed a job. My father and I were only scraping by.

"Come out to the bar. I'll pay you for the cod, and you can meet Jack." Ray pushed through the door and I followed. Ray put a beer on the bar for me and opened the till.

"Jack, this is Theo," he said to the man at the bar, who put down the Advocate and turned to look at me. His face was thin, his protruding cheekbones made a perfect triangle with a pointy adam's apple that struggled to escape his collar. He stuck out his hand, and I shook it, as

Ray said, "Theo could paint your office, Jack. He's good at everything." He handed me some bills and added, "Jack is the editor over at The Cape Codder. Have you seen a copy?" I had. My father had every issue of the year-old Orleans publication. He was proud of it, and pored over each page as though it contained information more profound than 'A large white male cat was found, hit by a car Tuesday night and slightly injured. Call Orleans 109M evenings, except on weekends.' Or that a whale's eardrum was found in a barn in East Orleans, the box labeled 'Found in Durban, South Africa.' It gave the average take per day of quahogs from Rock Harbor (350-400 bushels), informed us of a sixty-three foot finback whale washed ashore in Wellfleet, the fourth in a two-month period. Jack Johnson's editorials were short, sharp and thought-provoking, and the advertising was sparse, but informative. "There's nothing like a new dress to lift the spirit," we were advised by Newman's Clothing. "Bowl The Playroom," our local alley's ad said, "Wood or Plastic Pins. Take Your Pick!"

It was a wonderful newspaper. Still is.

We all walked down the street to the office, just one room with four large desks, one at the front facing the door and the rest at right angles to each other in a z formation. On each desk was a typewriter squatting in a nest of paper. One of the desks was piled high with books, magazines and twelve volumes of the Oxford English dictionary. A woman sat talking on the phone at the front desk and waved vaguely at us as we passed. Behind her, a man sat typing furiously on a big black Underwood. A cigarette burned in an ashtray at his elbow. He didn't look up.

"As you can see it's a bit shabby. Thought we could use a spruce-up," Jack said to me. I looked around. The walls were indeed a filthy green with sizable cracks criss-crossing behind dozens of photos, posters, notes and other papers taped to the walls which fluttered every time the door opened. "As a matter of fact the windows outside could use some reglazing too, if you know how to do that. C'mon," Jack flew back out the door, stirring several pieces of paper into a mini whirlwind. I watched them glide through the smoke-filled air to join others on the floor. We looked at the outside trim which was in pretty bad shape, then went inside again and through another flurry of paper to a back room, where an immense, hulking iron machine took up most of the available space. About twice the size of an upright piano, it was a mishmash of belts and levers and wheels, steel arms and a huge frame supporting a giant upright tray. In a little console area to one side of the contraption, a chair was pulled up to a wide keyboard divided into three sections. The room smelled of heated metal and stale cigar smoke. A cigar smoldered in an ashtray next to the chair.

"Needs it in here too, I suppose," Jack jammed his hands deep into his pockets and looked around, sighing. I couldn't take my eyes off the machine.

"What is it?" I said.

"Oh. That's a linotype. Y'know, sets the type for the printer."

I didn't know. I had no idea. But I would become quite intimate with it over the next several years and come to think of it as almost human.

I took the job of painting the offices and started the very next day. I finished two weeks later and drove home with a generous wad of cash in my pocket, feeling quite pleased with myself. I stopped off at the A&P for a steak to cook for my father and me and, by the time I arrived home, Jack had already telephoned with another little job for me. Things went on like this all summer until one day he offered me a permanent position, as a sort of 'anything' person. Three days a week. I swept the floors and made order of the vast sea of paper, drove to Yarmouth to the printer or ran to the market for cigarettes. I put up a shelf for the OED. I answered the telephone when Jack's wife, Laura, who ran the front desk, had to run over to the school to pick up one of their children. I often took their kids to the beach when things were busy. Over the years I taught all three of them to sail. But I spent most of my time dusting and wiping and oiling the linotype machine while the typesetter, Tony, a refined, serious, Italian gentleman, clacked away on it as though he were part of the mechanism. I never tired of watching the process. A linotype is a piece of mechanical genius. It has extraordinary spirit and character, more than any other automated equipment ever invented, in my opinion. I would stand mesmerized, listening to the tick, tick, tick of the keys falling and the matrices dropping back into the magazine. Little by little I understood how it worked, the slug of characters (a line o' type) composed, smooshing into a squirt of molten metal, then dropping into place beside the other lines in the galley. A graceful arm swung down to pick up the used letters and distribute them into their proper slots for reuse. It was so much more than brilliant mechanics, it was a dance, the keyboard a castanet accompaniment to a steel on steel pasodoble. I was in love with it.

Tony was never one for spending time talking when he could be typing. He didn't waste a single movement unless you count puffing on his cigar, but that too was part of the dance. Nevertheless, he managed to teach me without saying much. Tony also came in three days a week, two to work the linotype and the other he spent hand setting the larger lettering -headlines, advertisements and such. I learned how to do all of it eventually. Tony was quite tolerant of me and my endless questions, and Jack encouraged me to ask anyone at the paper anything, except of course when we were working against a deadline. Then it was best to keep quiet and stay out of the way.

One lovely day in June, the third summer of my employment at The Cape Codder, I was sailing out on the Bay with Jack and Laura's two boys. The tide was low and we had almost no wind, so we drifted. The kids were pleasantly quiet, watching horseshoe crabs crawl over the bottom and waiting for them to do something interesting, like attackeach other. We stayed in the small part of the Bay at the mouth of the River because the boys weren't skilled enough yet to brave the Narrows and the larger bay. It was my first time out sailing that year, and I was hoping for a gust of wind that would send us past Barley Neck so I could get a glance at Ria's house. I knew they were due at any time, and I lay in the boat idly daydreaming about summer evenings on the bluff with Ria, Achilles and Ginny. Ria's and my correspondence had been fairly steady throughout the fall and winter, but I hadn't heard anything since March, when I got a postcard from Achilles letting me know they were coming soon and would I please ask my father to set aside a large portion of smoked mussels for him. A catbird off in the distance called now and then, and as I thought about how much more a catbird's call is like a baby rather than a cat in the same moment I heard my name called from the shore. There stood Ria, having walked around the point with Ginny following surefooted across the stones. The crying was coming from the bundle Ria held.

"Theo!" she called again, waving me over. I scrambled to my knees and grabbed an oar. The kids kicked their legs off the stern and we arrived soon enough to where Ria had waded out.

"Hello Theo," she laughed. "What a lovely surprise. I stopped at the paper. Laura told me you were out here and I came to see if I could spot you. Not too difficult, you know. You're the only sailboat on the water. Ginny, look who's here honey, your uncle Theo." Ginny waded closer, grabbed my pant leg and tried to climb into my arms. I picked her up, and she stuck her knee in my face, presenting a halfway healed scrape. "It's called a scab," she said gravely. "Don't touch it." I had missed her. Ria looked lovely, softer. Her hair was its usual glossy chestnut color, but instead of the severe line across her forehead, her bangs had a slight curl. She told me years later it happened with her second pregnancy. "Some kind of hormonal thing, I guess," she said. She had shadowy circles under her eyes and wore no lipstick, but she was if anything more attractive. She chattered away to the boys while helping to pull the boat closer, ordering everyone around until she was satisfied. The kids ran down the beach and plunked themselves in the sand. Ria unwrapped her bundle. There, now perfectly still, lay a tiny baby, its head a mass of black curls, it's dark little eyes staring up at me.

"Meet Lottie. Her full name is Charlotte. She's only two months old. Sorry I didn't tell you. I didn't know what you'd think, me having two kids now." She looked at me intently in her special, disarming way.

"I think it's wonderful, I said. Ginny's arms were wrapped around my neck, choking me somewhat as she bounced exuberantly, her bare feet almost knocking the wind out of me. I couldn't speak, but shot Ria a broad smile.

"Come up to the house. I'll make us some coffee." I put Ginny in the boat and pulled it around the point to the dock, wading in the shallow water, while Ria walked along the shore. We caught up on the events of the past months.

"Achilles is in Provincetown. He won't be here 'til the weekend," she said. "I haven't seen much of him all winter. He went back to Paris for a month and then he and Cal had a big project in Philadelphia, selling off some wealthy old lady's belongings, I don't know exactly. He tried to tell me, but I've been a bit distracted," she laughed, as both Ginny and Lottie started to wail at the same instant.

I called Jack's kids, and we all climbed the stairs to the house, where Ria put Lottie to bed in a basket on the kitchen table then made sandwiches for everyone.

"I did manage to get some work done this winter," she said. We sat on the porch steps watching the kids fool around. "I want you to see." I hadn't been to her studio at all the previous summer. She claimed there was nothing to look at in there. She had had her hands full with Ginny and the running of the house. "I worked at night this winter. Napped with Ginny in the afternoons. C'mon, I'll show you."

Ria picked up the basket with Lottie and we walked through the cedars, kids trailing behind. She kicked at the bottom of the door, handed me the baby and shoved it open. I expected to see it as it was the last time I'd been there, when it was brand new, but there were so many paintings hanging, I could only see tiny bits of wall. Her work table was covered too, and one giant painting lay on the floor half unrolled against the chairs. Done on large, slightly curling squares of unprimed canvas, Ria's work was a hurricane of motion and gesticulation. Most of the paintings were thick gray curvilinear swipes pushed into a ground of white, one over the other, repeated into an overall rhythm. Dollops of ochre and pale green peeked through, as though swept up in the brushstroke as it passed. There were several paintings in bold colors, warm contrasting with cool tones, horizontal tangles of black, drawing the colors close. It was more than a little overwhelming standing there, especially when Ria marched into the middle of the room and threw her arms wide. The kids were silent. Still holding Lottie, who gurgled melodically, I took in a deep breath, trying to come up with a comment that sounded halfway knowledgeable. But all I could say was 'Wow."

"I know," she said, laughing. "I had one hell of a winter, didn't I?"

The paintings seemed to pull me toward them; the white left around the edges barely contained their wild energy and spirit. It provided a calm, unifying presence in the face of all that movement. I thought about the bottom of the Bay, sand under swirling water, the cedars outside being blown around against the sky.

"Looks like a tree I know of, over on Lonnie's Pond." I pointed to a large green and white canvas with fluttery brushstrokes. For all its action, a certain treelike dignity and stance was there, one I was quite familiar with.

"It is a tree, you got it. Well, it's the way I thought a tree might feel, if you know what I mean." Ria took the basket from me and set it down on a chair, the only thing in the room not covered by her work. She lit a cigarette and stared at the painting. "It's the way I feel thinking about the tree." She smiled at me and said, "Anyway, I'm finally getting somewhere. I so want to do this, but I'll probably have to wait for this one to get a little bigger before I have the time." She tapped the side of the basket. I wondered how she had accomplished so much. I had two years of babysitting part-time for adolescents to compare to her full time motherhood. I had an idea how much attention it took.

"What does Achilles think of your work?" I asked.

"Oh, he's quite impressed, or so he says. He wants to hire us a nanny so I can spend more time in my studio. Of course it would be wonderful but..." She looked at Ginny, who at that moment was crawling into the rolled-up part of the large canvas on the floor.

"All right, let's go outside," she said, extracting her daughter and herding everyone out. "Stay for dinner, will you?"

The boys and I sailed back into Arey's pond where I'd parked the car and drove over to the newspaper. Everyone but Tony was gone, the door wide open to catch the afternoon breeze. I left a note on the front desk saying we'd be back later that evening, bought a bottle of wine and stopped at Howard Johnson's for a quart of vanilla ice cream. It was quite an evening. I cooked spaghetti for the kids, while Ria fed Lottie in the bedroom. The boys, at ages eight and ten, were uncommonly tolerant of Ginny and let her climb all over them. And Ria was wonderfully unfazed by the spaghetti mess they created at the table, while she and I sat on the porch drinking vodka and grapefruit juice. She told me more about the past winter in New York, about Achilles' business trips and her almost constant isolation. But she spoke of it with joy instead of resentment. She was so happy with what she'd produced.

"I wouldn't have been able to do so much if he were at home, so it worked. We missed him, but it was OK," she said emphatically. She looked at the door as if expecting him to walk through it. I could picture her in their apartment, waiting but making the most of it. Just like the way she grew up, I thought.

That was the first of many dinners Ria and I had with the children. Jack and Laura were delighted with the routine, as the paper was growing and it was the season. I spent far more time that summer being a babysitter to their three kids than oiling the linotype. The oldest was a sweet and capable girl of twelve who loved babies and wanted to spend as much time as possible holding, feeding and changing Lottie. The boys were allowed to run along the shore and into the shallows, as long as they checked in every now and then. Ria rang a bell when dinner was ready and we all sat in the front yard, the children eating off paper plates balanced on their thighs. They thought it was exciting, a kind of free-for-all with not very many rules. Ria was fun and easygoing with the kids and more often than not it was she who took charge of them while I organized dinner. We were invited "every night, as far as I'm concerned," Ria told me. I brought the kids over three or four times a week.

The first time Achilles rounded the corner and saw the seven of us sprawled on the lawn eating supper, it stopped him in his tracks. Ginny, in a drooping diaper and with a mouth full of food, waved her spoon around as she danced. The boys were singing at the top of their lungs,

"Old and rough and dirty and tough,
I never can get drunk enough.
I drink my whiskey when I can,
I drink it from an old tin can.
I'm Barnacle Bill the Sailor!"

I must say here that the boys did not know what whiskey was nor did they know what drunk meant, but they insisted on singing this ditty several times a day for weeks. I refused to enlighten them for fear of what their parents might think of my babysitting skills. Besides, I had heard far, far worse versions of this old bar favorite, and this was innocent, comparatively. I simply told them not to sing it in front of their parents, so we had a deal for the duration.

Achilles stood slack-jawed, taking in the scene for several seconds before Ginny spotted him and yelled, "Papa!" He walked over to Ria and kissed her, picked up Ginny and smiled at me. I suppose he wondered what had happened to the peaceful retreat he was looking forward to after a long drive. But he was fine, relaxed and happy and said he was glad to see me and the kids there. He always brought food from the city, feta and dried fruit, eggplant and other staples of his cookery, ouzo, wine and espresso coffee which we drank from tiny cups. He also brought stories and jokes and his special blend of charm and sophistication. Jack and Laura's kids liked him, and Achilles never seemed to mind the brood we'd assemble for dinner. He simply cooked more, throwing hot dogs onto the grill along with our kebabs. Ria was happier when he was around, I noticed. I never saw her daydreaming the way I did sometimes when she didn't know I was watching. Achilles came and went that summer. Ria never knew if he was in Provincetown or New York but she didn't seem bothered by it.

The lines didn't yet stretch to the end of Barley neck, so they didn't have a telephone. But Ria said she preferred it that way. I worried about her alone out there at night and said so, but she waved it off. "I'm fine," she said. "I like it this way." Often, when I'd get up in the night to pee, I would look across the Bay and see her studio skylights, just dancing specs of light through the trees, but it would make me feel less worried. She managed to paint several more canvases that summer. She was happy, lively and talkative most of the time, and Achilles was as well. They were obviously still very much in love.

One day Achilles arrived fresh from a trip to New York. He called the newspaper and asked if I'd take him out to the house when he arrived on the train. His beautiful Nash was in Provincetown.

On the way out he talked about his work, unusual for him. From what I understood his profession was as a kind of antiques middle-man; he was hired to appraise collections or specific items of any kind and recommend them for sale to certain individual buyers, auction houses or museums. Or, he would buy something outright and resell it. Although Ria told me he dealt primarily in artwork, he also came across furniture, rugs, jewelry, books and manuscripts, even clothing, with varying degrees of expertise in their value.

On this day he started talking about a document he'd found among the belongings of a widow from Boston. Her husband had a family pedigree that stretched all the way back to the Mayflower and beyond, with a connection to the Earl of Sandwich, I think. Anyway, he told me he had saved this paper because it was phonetically written in what he believed was an Indian dialect.

"The reason I kept it for further perusal," he said, "is because I spotted a familiar looking place name." He turned in the seat, facing me as I drove. "I hope I'm saying this correctly, but I think it says something about Portanimicut. It was written by one of John Eliot's students in sixteen hundred and something. I forget exactly. I think the dialect is Narragansett, but I'm not sure." I didn't know what to say. Was this unusual? I had no idea. All I knew was what Casco had told me about John Eliot converting certain members of the tribe, the Praying towns and the Harvard Indians, but beyond that I knew almost nothing.

"Now, Portanimicut, or Potenumaquut," (he pronounced it slowly), "as it is written clearly on this document, is right across the water from our cottage, is it not?" Achilles spread his hands in amazement.

"Yes, it is," I said. It was the very area around Paw Wah, where Casco and I had lived, where I had met Ria, and where Walter's house now stood. I felt an old wariness come over me, a protective feeling.

"Well, I thought maybe while I'm here, you could take me over there, show me around. Are there any Indian relics or landmarks or anything to see?"

"Not really. But I don't know much about it," I said.

At that point we pulled into the driveway and all talk of Portanimicut ended as Ria, holding Ginny and Lottie, came running out to greet us.

A couple of days later, Achilles and I drove up and down Portanimicut Road. There isn't much to see, just farmland, a handful of old farmhouses and cottages. A field with cows. No sign at all of the Indians who made the land their home for who knows how many centuries. At the end of the road there is a dock landing with a small parking lot and boat ramp. If you put a boat in there, you can go to the left up a small channel into Paw Wah Pond, or turn right and be in the Bay. Directly in front of you is Paw Wah Point. I deliberately said nothing about it, though we sat there in the car facing it, talking.

Achilles pointed to it. "So, behind that land there," he said, "is more water and then Barley Neck, right?"

"Right."

"Isn't this the channel you and Ria used to cross to meet when you were at camp?"

"Yes." I was surprised to hear he knew.

"And that is where you lived for a year?" He nodded at Paw Wah.

I didn't know Ria had told him that part. How much had she told him? My heart began to pound.

"Ria told you." I said softly.

"Yes. She told me that after your father made you go on the blackfish expedition you ran away, found an old dwelling and stayed in it. Quite brave."

"Mm," was all I could manage.

"Is there a way across? Can we go and have a look? I'd like to see our house from the other side."

It was high tide, so we crossed the channel in one of the many dinghys tied up to the dock and took a long walk along the shore, rounding the point. Ria's house was clearly visible from there, and we sat in the sand looking at it and the little dock below with Ria's dory tied to it.

"I want you to know how thankful I am that you are taking such good care of my family when I am away," Achilles said, staring off across the glittering water.

"I'm happy to do it."

"I know. But I wanted to say it anyway. It means something to me."

Achilles swept his hand across the sand, making a flat rectangle. He held his hand poised above it for a moment, then began to draw. First he made a frame, then filled it with a pattern of lines and curlicues. He deftly repeated the drawing next to the first, a mirror image. It looked like an ornamental iron gate.

"What do you think," he said slowly, "about having my car?"

Dumbfounded, I didn't understand at first, but he went on to say, "I was thinking. You and Ria and all the kids. You need something better than your father's old jalopy. And he might need it. You know Ria's car. Well, it's not big enough for everyone." Ria had an old Ford she'd taken from her father's garage in the city. It hadn't been touched in years and ran fine, and we all fit in there all right, but I didn't say so.

"Your Nash?" I couldn't believe it. I had lusted after that car, and my father and I had spent more than a few evenings out on the porch discussing its merits.

"Yes. I want to get a new car. I can't keep driving back and forth in that old thing." It was about four years old, by my estimation. "What do you say?"

"Of course," I said. "If you're sure, I mean...."

He slapped his hand on the sand drawing, ruining it. "Good. I will go and get it from Provincetown. Now, let's walk through this place of yours, shall we? I want to see where you spent one of your formative years."

With that, he got up, brushed the sand off his pants and charged directly uphill into the trees, completely missing the path which was only a few feet away. I followed, still in a kind of daze about the Nash, and we traipsed through the underbrush until we got to the clearing where the old farm had been. I did not point out the root cellar where I'd found the diary, though I could see it had collapsed some. We walked through the trees toward the clearing where Walter's house sat. As usual it was quiet there among the trees. The birds were still now that mates had been found, nests completed, eggs laid. A lazy buzzing was the only sound besides our crunching through the underbrush.

"That house was built only a few years ago, but it's very close to where I stayed," I said as we came up Walter's driveway. Ropes of poison ivy and bear briar covered the entry way, snaked through the shutters and wound around the porch supports. Many of the windows were broken, the vines had crawled inside and reappeared higher up. No one was taking care of the place anymore. Ray told me the guy who had been doing it had not been paid in two years. He'd also heard that an estate lawyer had sent inquiries to the town hall requesting paperwork. So Walter was either dead or writing a will. When I heard that I breathed a sigh of relief and knew we'd seen the last of him. Still, Achilles' interest made me nervous, and just standing there I felt the old fear creeping back into my shoulders.

"Looks like no one has been here for a while," said Achilles.

"Yeah. The guy died not long after he built the place," I said it to end further inquiry, though I wasn't sure. Achilles looked around. "Hard to imagine it with only a shack and nothing else," he said. I didn't tell him it was a wigwam. I just let it go.

"He cut down a lot of trees." We stood there for a few minutes more, then I said, "There's a path down to the landing, right over here." I started walking toward it, wanting badly to go. Achilles followed slowly, distracted by the blueberry bushes which had reestablished themselves. He picked handfuls, shoving them into his mouth with glee. "Imagine that!" he kept saying between bites. I didn't know if he was talking about the blueberries or the abandoned house or my year alone out there. Eventually we left, crossed the channel, got back into my father's car and headed home. It was a thrilling trip for me. I spent the entire ride pretending I was already driving the beautiful black Nash convertible.

The first week of September, two days before Achilles and Ria were to leave for New York, we were all sitting in their living room waiting out a rainstorm. It was chilly, so Achilles lit some pine logs in the fireplace. They crackled and sputtered, sending sparks across the living room floor to the delight of the boys. They were playing poker, another secret thing I let them do. I know for a fact that both boys turned out well, so I don't feel guilty. But at the time I was often worried that someone would discover what a bad job I was doing taking care of them. School started the next day, and they were miserable about it, though I'd promised to chauffeur them there in the Nash, so they were excited to show off. I'd been driving them around in it for almost a month, and none of us could quite believe our good fortune. Driving in summer with the top down is a distinct pleasure I think no one ever gets used to. Achilles bought himself a brand new Mercury convertible with red leather seats. It was even more magnificent than the Nash.

Ria and the girls were in the kitchen making molasses cookies. Achillies and Ria had spent the day packing up her paintings, sorting clothes and papers and emptying the cupboards. I had already ferried several full grocery bags across to our house. My father came back with me on the return trip to say goodbye and bring Achilles another package of smoked quahogs. I didn't think quahogs were good candidates for smoking because even the small ones, the cherrystones and littlenecks, had dense adductor muscles which hold the two halves of the shell together. They were fine in any other form but smoked they tended to show up as rubbery lumps in an otherwise tender bite. But Achilles loved them and wanted as many as my father could produce. He made espresso in the little pot on a special grate fashioned for the fireplace. I could barely contain my laughter watching as my father accepted his tiny cup, puzzled over it, then sipped daintily. The three of us sat watching the boys make penny bets as we drank in silence. The fire felt wonderful; the kind of warmth that makes you look forward to winter. Achilles knocked the used coffee grounds against the hearth, swept them into the fire with his hand, and set up another pot. He turned to me and said, "Do you remember that paper I told you about, the one with 'Potenumaquut' in the text?" Again, he said the word slowly, one syllable at a time. I did remember, I said, and asked him what had happened to it.

"Oh, I still have it. Want to see it? I have to bring it back with me, so now is your only chance." He left the room and returned with a neat roll of brown paper tied in a ribbon. He took a pair of cotton gloves out of his pocket, put them on, and then unrolled the parchment. It was a thick, fibrous piece of paper about eighteen inches long and covered in writing. Kept within strict wide margins, the writing was cramped, but also full of flourishes and little hieroglyphs. Ornate capitals and flowery descenders decorated an even, rounded hand. The characters were Roman, but the language was indecipherable, just like the diary.

"It's obviously written phonetically," said Achilles. "Look here," he pointed halfway down the page and there was the Potenamaquut word. The capital P had a little hat thing on its top. "And there, and there," he pointed again to other words. One was Natik, another Mohegan. "That's why I thought it might be Narragansett, as those are places in Rhode Island. But I honestly don't know much about it. Luckily though, I found someone who does, and I will have it translated. Who knows? I'm sure it's worth something."

At this point, Ria came in with a huge plate of molasses cookies, and the boys sprang up from the floor as she set it down next to the document. Achilles quickly plucked the paper off the table and rolled it gently. He laid it down out of the way, took off his gloves and reached for a cookie.

"What do you think, Theo?" said Ria. She was looking intently at me, her eyes sparkling. Naturally she was reminded of the diary, as was I, and which neither of us had done anything about, nor had we discussed it since I showed it to her two years before. "Isn't that quite something?"

"Yes, quite," I said. I took a cookie off the plate and shoved half of it into my mouth. I did not want to think about going to New York, which was where recalling the diary instantly led me.

"Achilles tells me he'll most likely take it to the Indian Museum in New York. The director, Mr. Heye, buys artifacts from all over the country." She eyed me pointedly again.

"Yes, well, I find it's always best to know what it is and therefore the value before showing it to a museum," Achilles said. "So I will have it translated, if possible, and verified."

Lottie let out a wail from the bedroom, and Ria turned toward the sound, beckoning me with a sidelong glance to come along.

"Let me help you," I said, following her.

She picked up Lottie, cradling her against her chest as she whispered, "Theo, did you you hear that?"

"Yes. Mr. Heye. Translation. I know what you're thinking."

"Well? This could be a perfect opportunity. Achilles knows what he's doing."

Casco's words flitted through my mind. *You must be very careful with this diary. Tell no one you have it or even know of it.*

"But Casco..." I began.

"Yes, I know," said Ria, cutting me off. "But you're not going to bring it to New York, are you?"

"Probably not," I admitted. "But you could."

"I thought of that, and of course I could," she said quietly. "But then what if the diary truly is valuable and Achilles finds out I went secretly to Gustav Heye and didn't even mention it to him?"

"We could tell Achilles the truth."

"Which one?"

I pondered that while Ria changed Lottie. I could hear my father and Achilles in the next room talking with the boys. I couldn't tell Achilles about Casco, it would only lead to places I did not want to go. What if I simply said that I had found the diary somewhere. In an old cellar or one of the camps. In reality I had found it in an old cellar, hadn't I? In the living room the boys were asking Achilles about the Nash. How fast could it go? How much had he paid for it? Achilles was laughing, exaggerating the speed and the price. I could hear them gasp in amazement. I pictured the car, driving it with Ria and the kids. Achilles had thanked me, trusted me. Given me his car. Now it was my time to trust him.

"I suppose it would be better to have it translated and evaluated, wouldn't it?" I said to Ria.

"Yes. I think so. Then you can give it, or sell it even, to the museum. Wouldn't it be nice to get a little money for it?"

I didn't know about that part. It wasn't part of my thinking. But I had made up my mind.

"OK," I said to Ria. "Let's do it. I'll tell him I found it and where. But I won't mention Casco. All right?"

"Right," said Ria, "No talk of Casco."

Achilles was quite interested in my story and description of the diary. His entire demeanor changed, he became the professional he was, he sat up straight and eyed me keenly as he asked several pointed questions. When I told him where I'd found it, he pulled a little notebook from his pocket and wrote everything down. He remembered the old farmstead we walked through on Paw Wah Point, asked me to describe the root cellar in detail. Of course he wanted to see it, to compare it to what he had. I offered to bring it the next day but he suggested driving over to our house right away.

"I think your father wants to go home, anyhow," he said. My father shrugged, one of the few gestures that involved his missing arm, and smiled. "I am tired," he said.

So we drove over in Achilles' new car, much to my father's joy. I took the box from the shelf in my room, unwrapped it, removed Casco's letter and tied it up again. I rode back with Achilles, who said very little on the way. He asked after my father's health and said that they would miss us. When we got to their house, I herded the boys into the Nash to take them home, promising to be back the next day to talk about the repairs to the skylights and a few other things. I said goodnight to Ria, who winked at me, then shook Achilles' hand.

"Do not worry about your treasure," he said. "I will take good care of it. I will let you know as soon as I do what it is and what it says. This will be fun."

I drove down Barley Neck Road, following its twists and turns through woods and farmland and onto Main Street, then all the way around again to Arey's Pond Road, where Jack and Laura lived. As the crow flew, it was only about a mile, but it took us a good fifteen minutes to go around all the inlets, ponds and estuaries which fed the bay. For all of those minutes I was telling myself I'd done the right thing.

Chapter 15

That fall I turned twenty-five. They threw me a little party at The Cape Codder offices just before closing. It was a Wednesday, I remember, because it was deadline day. Wednesdays were always fraught with nervous energy, quick decisions, some yelling, and steady concentration at the linotype. At that point I was capable of taking over for Tony if he needed a break, or went over to the Ship Ahoy for lunch. I had become a fairly good typist, though I only used three fingers, and still do. I don't even use my thumb for the space bar on a modern typewriter, much to the amusement of those around me, but I'm fast, so they leave me alone. I started typing the obituaries that year, and the want ads too, things Tony groaned at the thought of. Tony started his career typing the New York City telephone directory. "It's the work of three men," he'd say, "Larry, Moe and Curly." He was superstitious about typing obituaries. "One of these days, I'll be typing my own," he said often. And the want ads required many lines because they were only a column wide. So there were many more slugs of hot metal to keep track of. It was the first thing he taught me to do, and I've been doing it ever since, because one of the great perks of typing the want ads is that you are the first to see them, so you are the first to call. I have acquired many wonderful things that way, including every car I've ever owned since the Nash.

After we drank the birthday punch we all went over to the Ship Ahoy for a few more, and I slid onto a stool beside Phinneas, who was looking through the Advocate, as usual. When he saw Jack he quickly folded it and laid it aside, but Jack picked it up and took it over to a table to read.

Phinneas said, "Happy Birthday, Theo. Here." He handed me a paper bag-wrapped present tied with a green satin ribbon. It was a copy of Stan Getz's "Quartet."

"It's my current favorite," said Phinneas. "Shall we hear it?" He took it from me, went behind the bar and stuck it on the new Hi-Fi turntable Ray had installed back there. Phinneas sat down and started nodding his head to the smooth saxophone. I liked it immediately. Different from the nervous energy of Phinneas' usual bebop, it was more relaxing, pretty almost. It reminded me of the days when Red blew his sax in the bar, back when I was a lovesick teenager.

"What's this crap?" said one of the Huffs.

"Quiet," said Ray, coming out of the kitchen and slapping me on the back. "Happy Birthday, kid," he said. "Drinks on the house in honor of Theo's... which is it, Theo?" I told him. "...twenty fifth year of life on this marvelous planet." He took several bottles of beer out of the cooler, lined them up on the bar and said, "What'll it be, Theo?"

I ordered a vodka and grapefruit juice. Phinneas got another bourbon.

After the third song the Huffs got up and left, each with a single overall buckle bouncing against his back and trailing the scent of fish gurry. Jack slapped the Advocate shut and joined us at the bar. We sat there talking for another hour or more. Phinneas, Ray and Jack discussed the merits of the Advocate versus those of The Cape Codder. It was not a conversation I felt I could participate in. I confess I didn't read the papers much in those days, mostly because my father read ours from cover to cover every week and told me everything that was going on in town. It was also slightly awkward for me because I knew Phinneas far preferred the editorials in the Advocate and said so whenever Jack was not in the bar. Finally, Ray managed to get the subject changed just at the moment my father walked in, hugged me, and said "Happy Birthday." He handed me an envelope, then sat down next to Jack and asked him about last week's fishing report.

Ray put a beer in front of him, while I opened the oversized envelope. It was addressed to me in Ria's handwriting. Inside were two cards, one with a painting on the front obviously done by Ria. The card was thick with paint, cracked off in places, and brightly colored. Green streaks snaked through a lighter green, with flecks of electric blue here and there. White streaks echoed the green. Eelgrass, of course. I opened it to another drawing, this one by Ginny: a stick figure with at least twelve lines emerging from the end of each arm or leg. I knew that was the way she drew fingers and toes. I had watched her practice laboriously all summer. Ria had drawn a champagne glass in one of the hands with the words, "Here's to the best pal ever! Love from all of us."

The other card was a print of the painting 'El Jaleo' by John Singer Sargent, a gypsy woman dancing The Flamenco in a long white skirt in front of a seated row of musicians. Inside was a note which read:

> Dear Theo,
> Happy Birthday, my friend. I have good news for you.
> Your manuscript is authentic, and is creating quite a stir
> here in the world of antiquities. It is almost completely
> translated and contains some information which will no
> doubt change a few lines in the history books!
> More soon.
> Achilles

His signature had a zigzag under it, like Zorro's. I read the note several times, then slid it back into the envelope. I took a long sip from my glass, contemplating this news. Around me, the others were getting louder. My father was telling an elaborate joke which I'd missed the first part of, and they all exploded in laughter. The sight of my father sitting there so relaxed and such a part of us made me suddenly flush with pride and warmth for the old man, so I went over to sit beside him.

Our life together had a satisfying rhythm. These days he fished more for our suppers and his smoking enterprise than for anything commercial. I supplied the money for other necessities, so he didn't have to worry about the weather or the competition or the fact of his getting old. He'd turned sixty that year, and I could tell the little aches and pains of a life on the water were beginning to slow him down. I looked at his hand. It was swollen with arthritis, curling closed where it lay on the bar. He often hid it from view now, kept it in his pocket in front of strangers. Many times I'd seen him straightening it by laying the tips of his fingers on the bricks of the smoker and slowly unbending them against its warmth. In June, I found a handkerchief with fresh blood on the boat and thought he'd cut himself, but he had no injuries. So I started watching him with the binoculars while he was out fishing and realized that the frequent throat-clearing he'd begun that summer and which he tried to hide from me had become full-blown hacking when he was alone. His already thin frame was smaller, too, I noticed. Ray was the one to say, a few days after the party, that he thought maybe my father ought to get a checkup. Ray's mother had died the year before and he was still far from over it. So I thought he was transferring those feelings to my father. But I knew he was right, and so I talked to my father about it.

"I've already been," he said, "and I'm fine. Don't worry, it's just a little cough. Probably caught it from that damn smoker." He grinned at me and changed the subject. I didn't think much more about it, but in January he was suddenly worse. He started coughing almost steadily without trying to hide it, and one afternoon went to bed. From that day on he didn't get up again. I phoned the doctor and he came out to the house, went into the bedroom and closed the door behind him. I heard him arguing with my father and when he came out he was shaking his head.

"Why didn't he come to see me months ago?" he said, sitting heavily in one of the kitchen chairs.

"He told me he had, and that you'd pronounced him fine."

"Well, he didn't, and he's not, Theo. My guess is he has TB."

It took a few seconds for me to work out what that was, but the doc was already talking about treatment. "His pulse is weak. He'll have to be taken to the hospital for thorough tests, injections, they'll want to keep him there. It's best at this point..."

I wasn't listening, only nodding my head stupidly as a mantle of dread spread itself heavily across my shoulders and my throat dried so that I could not speak. The doctor wrote out a prescription. "That's for the cough, but you'd best act fast Theo. He needs antibiotic treatment. Streptomycin. Take him to the hospital. I know he doesn't want to go, but don't listen to him."

Of course my father would hear nothing of it, even when I told him the doctor's diagnosis. "I don't have goddamn tuberculosis," he yelled, then was overcome by a fit of coughing. "Where the hell does he think I picked up something like that, out there?" he said, jerking his thumb at the ocean. I told him I didn't know, went into the kitchen and put the kettle on to boil. My head was pounding and my hands shook badly but I managed to make him a cup of tea. When I took it to him he glared at me and said, "For Chrissake leave me alone now. I'll be over this in a few days. I just need some sleep." It was eleven o'clock in the morning. My father had never been in bed at that hour. I did as he asked, pacing the kitchen floor with the doctor's words repeating in my head. For the first time in years my father had spoken to me in the old way, and I have to admit it frightened me. I wanted badly to phone Ray but my father's room was next to the kitchen. He would overhear every word.

I got in the Nash and drove toward town, hoping Ray would help me talk my father into going to the hospital. It had snowed two days before, but only a few inches, but then it rained, so although the roads were plowed they were covered in slush. I hadn't put chains on the tires yet so the car slid all over the place on the way. As I tried to stay on course I thought about the doctor, wondered how he'd arrived so quickly in spite of the road conditions, I thought about how I could pry my father out of bed, about the prescription I'd stupidly left lying on the kitchen table. I cursed myself as I slowed the car to turn back, but when I pressed the brake pedal nothing happened. The car did not slow down, it actually sped up since I was at the crest of one of the few hills in town. As it slid downhill the rear of the car began to swing around until it was skimming sideways and picking up speed. I fought the wheel but it was whipped out of my hands as the car turned a full circle once, twice, then slammed its rear end into one of the giant elms lining the road. The impact caused my right arm to fly up and hit the metal armature of the canvas top with such force it broke my hand in several places. My head slammed against the window, but didn't break it. In a daze and holding my hand against my chest, I started the engine and pressed the gas, but the wheels just spun. The car wouldn't budge. Slowly, painfully, I got out and looked. The trunk of the car was crushed against the tree, the back wheels three inches off the ground. I started walking toward town, hoping someone would come along, but no one passed for the entire trip. It was less than three miles to the bar but by the time I stepped inside I was so numb with cold and barely coherent as I tried to tell Ray what had happened.

Ray was not successful in talking my father into coming to the hospital with us. I sat in his car outside our house, almost delirious with pain, while they argued. I could hear my father shouting and breaking off to cough violently. Finally, Ray came out and we drove to the hospital in silence. Ray concentrated on the icy road and cursed under his breath, looking sidelong at me every time we slid. I sat holding my hand and praying. It took ages for the people at the hospital to examine and evaluate my hand. I was barely aware of it since they doped me straightaway. But, Ray told me later, he sat there while I had several x-rays and they debated whether to send me up to Boston given the road conditions. In the end, I woke up in a hospital bed with a giant cast up to my elbow and a bag of something dripping into my other arm. Nolan was sitting beside me. I was so happy to see him I forgot what had happened and started babbling away until I remembered. "My father, what about...?"

"Ray went over there, don't worry. He's going to find your neighbor, ask if she can help out." He told me about my hand. It would probably be months before I could use it again, he said. "But the nurse told me the doc is happy with the way it went back together. No nerve damage." He sat with me for another hour, then got up to leave. "I'll be back tomorrow to bring you home."

I lay there worrying about my father, worrying about my job, which of course required the use of my hand; worrying about the Nash crushed up against the elm. I was utterly undone, overwhelmed by a mixture of helplessness and self-loathing. I had failed my father. My one attempt at doing something for him involved asking Ray for help. I couldn't even manage a simple task like filling a prescription at the pharmacy, and now I lay like an idiot in bed with my hand in a giant lump of plaster. I would probably lose my job, I thought. I spent a miserable few hours berating myself for all the weeks I'd ignored my father's condition and a couple more lying there trying to figure out what to do about it until a nurse came in and gave me another shot of morphine.

In the morning, Nolan drove me home. We arrived to find Ruth at the stove stirring a pot of something which smelled wonderful. "Chicken broth," she said. "Go in and see him, he's grumpy but awake." My father's bedroom door was closed but I inched it open with my foot, Nolan behind me with a hand on my back. My father looked terrible. Propped up against several pillows, he held a handkerchief to his mouth. I could see it was spotted with blood. The circles under his eyes had darkened considerably and he was clearly gasping for breath."Hey Frank," said Nolan. "How are you feeling?"

My father didn't answer. He lay there staring at my arm in its cast, bound with gauze against my chest. Pointing to it, he started to laugh, which made him cough violently, but he was laughing at the same time. Tears spilled out of the corners of his eyes. I sat down beside him, shoving his legs to one side and somehow that made him laugh even harder. Then Nolan started chuckling too, which didn't help things. I waited it out while they wound down, but I couldn't for the life of me figure out what was so funny. Finally my father took a deep, wheezing breath and said, "Well, if we work together, we might be able to get our shoes tied." Silence, then they both burst out laughing again, my father descending into a long phlegmy croak, Nolan trying desperately to keep a straight face and not look at me. I just sat there with my head hanging like a horse waiting out a rainstorm.

Ruth came in with some soup for him, so I got up to make room. She set him up with a little table, a board across two pillows. I made a mental note to build him a proper tray table and remembered I couldn't. I glanced woefully at Nolan, who was chatting away with my father about that fall's scallop season. I would have to rely on him and Ray and Ruthfor a few weeks, if my father's condition didn't improve. I could probably drive as soon as it warmed up a little and the ice melted. I wondered what had happened to the Nash. I should arrange for it to be towed, I thought, and for the doctor to come out again to give us some idea about what to do for my father, as he clearly wasn't going to the hospital. I was in a considerable amount of pain, which made thoughts spin into knots as I tried to organize them. I looked down at my hand strapped to my chest. I could almost see it throbbing.

"Come out to the kitchen and have some of this soup, you two," said Ruth. Nolan's eyes lit up at the suggestion and we went and sat down at the kitchen table. Ruth dished out some soup for us, then went back to tend to my father.

"So," said Nolan, "About your car. We pulled it off the tree, and it's all right. Runs fine. But the trunk's dented." He and Ray had driven it to the Mobil station across from the bar where the owner, a multi-skilled car fanatic, had almost wept with joy at the chance to restore such a vehicle to its former glory.

Nolan offered to run back to town and fill both my father's prescription and one they gave me at the hospital, something which would allow me to sleep, and to pick up any supplies we might need in the next few days. He left soon after, promising to be back that evening. As soon as he did I went and sat on the sofa, leaned back into the cushions. I could hear my father and Ruth talking softly. His coughing had calmed somewhat, the awful bark from earlier now a sort of low growl. I lay down, telling myself it was only for a few minutes, then I would see to all the things that needed to be done. Ruth put the dishes in the sink and left, saying she'd be back in an hour. We lay there, my father and I, with just a pine board wall between us. I heard him chuckle, then laugh again, and suddenly it was funny to me, too, and I started to giggle. "Two grown men, and narry a right arm between them," he said, and I laughed out loud. We lay there laughing and coughing, my hand throbbing, but now that, too, was funny, and I laughed even harder.

Pretty soon the mood quieted and we must have both fallen asleep, because the next thing I remember was Ruth standing over me saying, "Theo, there's a telephone call for you. He said it was too important to wait." I got up and walked painfully into the kitchen, picked up the receiver. It was Achilles.

"Theo, hello," he said. "How are things?"

"Fine," I said, which was all I could muster. With a snort, Ruth left the room.

"I'm calling because I have great news. Did you get the birthday card?"

"Yes, thank you."

"You will be happy to know the translation is done on the diary. Not only that, but the information it reveals is quite a bombshell. What Bad Boy wrote proves the English settlers poisoned Wamsutta! I will tell you more about it in a letter."

"Oh." So Casco was right, I thought.

"I took it to the Indian museum Ria mentioned. You remember?"

"The American Indian museum." Oh yes, I remembered. "Gustav Heye."

"Yes, exactly. He wants to buy it." Achilles named an amount that was more than what I had earned working at The Cape Codder for a year. "What do you think?"

"It's a lot of money," I said. I had no idea what to think, or even how, at that moment. The whole thing was some abstract notion I wasn't even sure was real. I needed to lie down again. I needed an aspirin, a handful of them. I needed to check on my father. I couldn't remember what I was supposed to do or not do about the diary. I stood there in the kitchen looking out at the water, trying to come up with something to say. Ruth went out the back door, letting it slam. A heron flapped into the sky, disturbed. I watched Ruth start down the path that led to her house.

"Theo?"

"I'm here," I said. I had an almost overwhelming desire to hang up the phone. Achilles was delivering some very exciting news. I had to say something. "It's too much," I blurted out.

"Yes, I know." He paused. I could hear him take a sip of something, a tinkle of ice cubes. "You probably need to think about it, *neh*?"

"Yes. That's a good idea. I will," I said lamely.

"What about I phone you again tomorrow? They are very excited at the museum."

"All right, that's a good idea," I said again. I was already taking the telephone away from my ear.

"Tomorrow then. Same time, ok?

"Yes," I said, barely able to speak. "Thanks, Achilles." I hung up the phone and dove back onto the sofa. Then I got up again and had a look at my father. He was asleep, wheezing laboriously. Nolan arrived not long after, carrying a large paper bag, which he unpacked in the kitchen, then brought me a glass of water and two pills. "Every six hours, if needed for pain," he said. He laid a copy of The Cape Codder beside me.

"I told Jack what happened. He'll be over to see you himself tomorrow. He said not to worry, just get well."

For the next five weeks, my father and I recuperated together, though my father became only marginally better. He got out of bed only to use the bathroom and even then he needed help. He would sit up in bed with me next to him, my arm around his waist. As he swung his legs over the side he'd start to giggle. "Darling," he'd say, "take me now to the chamber." I would lift him and we'd stagger to the bathroom, where I would deposit him clumsily onto the toilet, then leave for a while, until I heard his call. "Yoo Hoo," he'd say in a high-pitched voice, "I'm ready." At least he maintained his sense of humor. I don't know if I was as successful in those days.

Even though he was lying in bed and quite ill, my father often pulled me out of the doldrums with his jokes and the irreverent attitude he had toward his condition. I was able to cook basic foods for us if the meals didn't require too much chopping, so Ruth came less often. We ate potatoes and eggs, fried fish, canned soup. I began to understand what life had been like for my father for all those years, and gained another measure of respect for him not only for being able to work and take care of a family, but for performing one-handed the hundreds of insignificant tasks two-handed people never think about. In the evenings, when he was feeling well enough, I would bring him out to the living room and we'd sit playing cards, listening to the radio. Even gnarled with arthritis he held his cards beautifully splayed and could lay a single one down with just a slight dip of his fingers, or reorder them in his hand with smooth, deft movements. I started by asking him to show me how, and gradually he taught me all kinds of small things one could accomplish with only one arm. Simple, everyday actions. Lighting a match to get our coffee going in the morning. Buttoning my shirt. Cracking an egg, buttering toast. Pulling up a zipper. Chopping kindling. But he was the one who tied my shoes every day.

After a couple of weeks, I was steady enough to drive his car into town for supplies or visit the guys at the bar, stop in to see Tony at the linotype. I missed that machine more than any person, and would stand there listening to the soothing sounds it made, smelling the hot metal, watching the words and sentences pile up. I would walk around with the duster and clean or drip oil into its innards. I craved the certainty of its perfect mechanism. Its rhythmic precision made me feel as if nothing could ever go wrong in the world while it did its steady, elegant dance. I suppose it comforted me in the same way the Bay did when I was a boy, the unfaltering predictability of its tides, its seasons.

Jack assured me my job would be waiting for me whenever I was ready. The kids were in school and it was the middle of winter so not much was going on anyway. I had a lot of time on my hands. The Nash sat across the street at the Mobil station waiting for a new trunk lid to arrive from the factory in Wisconsin, and sometimes I'd go over and sit in it, to think.

Achilles called me back as promised. I explained to him right away what had been the state of affairs in the house the day before. He was shocked at the news, and wanted to know every detail of our situation. I could hear Ria in the background saying, "What, Achilles? What's going on?" She didn't let up until he handed her the telephone and I had to tell the story all over again. It took me quite a long time to convince the two of them, one at a time, that my father would refuse to be taken or sent anywhere, no matter the quality of the sanatorium or whatever they had in mind. I had to go over the details of the injuries to my hand, what medicines my father had been prescribed, what we were eating, who was cooking, the prognosis for each of us, the condition of the Nash and numerous other questions that kept us on the telephone for over an hour. Finally Achilles asked me, "Have you had a moment to think about our conversation of yesterday?" Truthfully, I had not. I had been in a drug-induced stupor for most of the twenty-four hours between telephone calls, but I said that yes, I had, and I thought what he had proposed sounded quite exciting and that I couldn't wait to hear more about all the revelations the diary contained.

"Do you want to sell it to the museum?" Achilles asked.

"Yes, all right," I said. I decided in that moment to do it. The combination of sleeping pills and Ria's and Achilles' comforting voices had lulled me into a warm, hopeful state of mind. I wanted at that point to turn over all my affairs to the two of them: Achilles, the fatherly counsel and Ria, my closest friend. I wanted to be done with all the doubts and fears attached to the thought of Casco, to retain only the beautiful memories of my time with him. The diary brought to the surface all the uncertainty I felt and I wanted to be rid of it. "Sell it," I said. "and thank you for everything you've done."

"Good," said Achilles. I will send you a copy of the translation. It is quite interesting. Mr. Heye wants to include the diary in an exhibition next summer to be held at Harvard University. I think it will be the star of the show."

I received a typed translation of the diary ten days later. Achilles had underlined certain parts, mainly anything to do with Bad Boy's home at Potenamaquut. Not surprisingly, the diary recounted certain events before and during King Phillip's war. It seems that when he ran away from his home, he landed smack in the middle of Metacom's gang. He mentioned John Eliot several times. The writing contained much detail about daily life not only in the English settlement but with Metacom in his various camps. But by far the most extraordinary piece of information was the passage which recounted the events surrounding the dinner party Casco had told me about, the night the new sachem Wamsutta had been invited by the Puritan settlers. Bad Boy knew one of the women who had cooked the food. She told him she'd seen them doctoring Wamsutta's plate with the powder. "She drew her blanket about her in mourning her words Our sachem will be dead this night I ran to him and it was so."

I read it only once before putting it back in the envelope and burying it under my clothes in a drawer. The translation had arrived with a check from Achilles clipped to it. I took it directly to the bank and opened an account. At the time, I doubted I'd ever use any of that money, but as things went, I had to dip into it soon after to pay for my father's funeral.

He died in his sleep on April first, having beat me at a game of cribbage only hours before. We had a little memorial luncheon for him at the house after he was buried in the town cemetery a few days later. It was a surprisingly un-sober affair, and the first time I got to see any of the fishermen he'd worked with for all those years dressed in suit jackets. I think that might have been a reason why the event had begun with an air of suppressed humor to it which finally gave way to actual laughing and story telling. I heard some things about my father that I never would have guessed could be true. And his friends spoke about him with genuine admiration. I wrote my first obituary for him which Nolan made more eloquent with a skilled edit. And then I was alone.

By that time I had a minimal amount of use of my hand, and the strongest part of it was the two fingers I used to type, so a couple of weeks later, I asked Jack if I could come back and sit in for Tony again at the linotype, one day a week. There were other things I could do perfectly well too, like drive around doing the usual errands. I knew that the office floor was covered in a layer of unfiled paper again and I was itching to get to it. So, as spring turned into summer the one day turned back into three again and the kids were out of school and Ria and Achilles were due at any time.

Chapter 16

Ria came with the kids on the train at the beginning of July. On the fourth, to be exact. She phoned me the night before. The boys and I were on the porch decorating their bicycles with red, white and blue crepe paper, so they could ride them in the parade the next day. We had run out of daylight halfway through the project and were making do with a couple of kerosene lanterns I had resurrected from the shed. When the phone rang, I was sitting on the floor holding several pieces of paper together while glue dried, and arguing with the older boy about the number of stripes on an American flag. He guessed twelve. "Everyone knows there are thirteen," I said, for the original thirteen states.

"Maybe so," said the little monster. "But did you know that the red represents the blood shed for our freedom?" I did not, but I said, "Of course."

"All right, then I have a question about the white," he said, feeding crepe paper strips through the spokes of his bicycle wheels. "It's supposed to stand for courage, but isn't white the color of surrender in a battle?"

"Yeah, or ceasefire," I said. "Maybe that's the courageous part." Blessedly, the telephone rang.

"Theo, it's me. How are you?" I was still pinching the paper together, and had the glue bottle wedged in my armpit, forgotten. "I'm fine. When are you coming?" I couldn't wait to see her again after my miserable winter.

They were due in the early afternoon. Ria wanted me to pick them up at the station, but I had agreed to lend the Nash to Ray for the parade. He would chauffeur our three selectmen and advertise the Ship Ahoy at the same time. Knowing I would soon see Ria filled me with such joy, I constructed a giant red, white and blue flower and taped it to the spare tire on the back of the Nash. I took the boys home, their gaudy bikes in the back seat. I had a drink with Ray and switched cars with him, driving home in his clunky old truck. I was still not used to arriving home to a dark house. That night the moon rose high over the Bay and lit the ocean beyond. So I sat on the porch letting the mesmerizing twinkle calm me. I missed my father. I spent many evenings out on the porch thinking about him, about us, and the way I'd grown up around him. I still didn't understand how my mother wielded such power over him, especially now that I'd seen his unreserved side. It disturbed me to think that, in a marriage, one could stifle one's real personality simply for the sake of being together. It certainly wasn't like that with Ria and Achilles.

When Ria and the girls stepped off the train, I was there with the Nash, which I'd only minutes before driven away from the post-parade festivities. It was still trailing several colored banners and curls of streamers were tied to the mirrors. A large painted poster with a reproduction of the Ship Ahoy's sign hung from the trunk under my flower. Ria saw me, waved, and went back inside the train to collect luggage, but the girls ran over and pulled at the decorations. Lottie had grown quite a bit and even said, "Hi Theo," to me. I had no idea a two-year-old could remember me or my name. It was a tiny miracle that made me pick her up and kiss her. I herded the girls into the back seat and went to help Ria with the luggage. She gave me a long, smothering hug, kissed both my cheeks and said, "God, Theo. How are you? Let me see your hand. I'm so sorry about your father. How are you getting along out there by yourself?" As we transferred the luggage, I just let her chatter on as she usually did, asking about everyone and everything. Had the skylights leaked? Had the dory made it through the storms we'd had that winter? Was I able to type with my hand and could she go and lay some flowers on my father's grave?

"Where is it, anyway," she said, as we drove away.

"I'll show you," I said, then asked her about Achilles.

"Oh, he's fine. Busy, as always." He was due a week later. "Plans are going forward with the Harvard show and the diary. He's excited about that, but I have much bigger news," she grabbed my arm. Lottie, who already had a handful of my sleeve, was sitting on Ria's lap. Ginny was standing on the back seat and leaning over the front. At four and a half she was a natural talker, and, in my other ear, was filling me in about the time we'd been apart.

"You hafta go on the elevator to our floor but the first floor is called the ground floor and we live on the second floor," she explained. "That's number two."

I turned to Ria. "So, what's your big news?" Ria opened her mouth but Ginny screeched in my ear, "I want a Popsicle! Mom you said when we got to Cape Cod we could have red Popsicles and we're here." She said 'Pothicle.'

"I did say that, yes," said Ria. "Theo, do you mind?"

We sat outside Bessom's while the girls dribbled red juice down their fronts. I asked Ria again, "So, your news?"

"Oh yes. I've been invited to show this fall with over fifty of the best abstract painters working today. Can you imagine, DeKooning! And not only that. Hofmann too, my old teacher. Apparently it was at his suggestion that they phoned me. I'm one of seven women showing. Isn't it wonderful?"

"That's great, Ria." I knew about DeKooning, Pollock, Hofmann and some others. Ria had talked about them for years, shown me the spread in Life magazine of Pollock's drip paintings. "That's some company."

"Yeah. Hofmann suggested I show a painting I did absolutely ages ago. It's not anything like what I'm doing now, but I don't care. But to show with those guys. Can you imagine?" The kids had finished their Popsicles and were busy tearing the streamers from the car's mirror and throwing them up in the air.

"So, what is this painting?" I said.

"You'll be able to see it. It's in Provincetown. I have to go up and get it, see if it needs sprucing up before I send it back with Achilles to the framer."

Four days later, I drove her to Provincetown to pick up the painting. We had all five children with us, since Ginny had informed the boys of the plan and a trip to Provincetown means the purchase of salt water taffy and foot-long hotdogs and other marvels found nowhere else on Cape Cod. I couldn't refuse. Jack's daughter held Lottie in her lap on the seat between Ria and me. The boys and Ginny sat in back. It was one hell of a noisy trip up there with all of them talking, arguing and singing at once. The boys had tired of "Barnacle Bill" but had a new one, not as risque, which they sang at least five times on the way. It was a version of 'On Top of Old Smokey,' with different lyrics:

On top of Old Smokey
All covered in sand (?)
I shot my math teacher
With an old rubber band

I shot her with pleasure
I shot her with pride
I sure couldn't miss her
She was forty feet wide.

Something like that. Ria giggled, Ginny was fascinated, and Jack's daughter said, "I'm telling." The boys ignored her and kept it up. When we crested the hill overlooking the whole town they stopped singing, entranced by the view. I have already described the impact this approach has on a person, and I was gratified to know that it affected the kids as well.

"Do you ever see Dusty?" I hadn't heard mention of him for years. The sight of Provincetown made me remember the day we met Achilles.

"Not much," she waved her hand dismissively. "The last time I saw him, he was sitting on a bench in Washington Square with the guitar that Achilles gave him, playing those same songs. He had a little audience, which was nice. He looked right at me and I waved, but it was though he didn't recognize me. There was no response from him. He just looked away. I don't know..."

"That's strange," I said. "I thought you two were close friends."

"We were, until I married Achilles."

I'm sure there were others who disapproved. But I was surprised to hear it about Dusty. Probably, like me, he was in love with her and wasn't able to accept that she belonged to some old man. I fantasized for a few minutes about running into him in town, Ria and me with five children in tow. That would give him something to sing about.

We went directly to Achilles' house. When we pulled into the driveway, the older kids jumped out and ran to the beach. Ria knocked on the door, calling to Cal, but he didn't answer, so she took out a key and opened up. I had not been there since before Ria and Achilles went to Paris, but the place looked almost exactly the same. The kids burst through the door wanting money for taffy from the shop across the street. Ria doled out dimes, and they took off. She handed Lottie, who was almost asleep, to me saying, "I'll just be a minute. The painting is in here. She headed for a back room, but stopped when she saw a package leaning up against a leg of the dining room table. "Oh, it's here," she said. "Cal must have wrapped it up for me. Nice of him." She picked it up and brought it over to me. "Want to see it?" she said, untying the string.

"Yes, very much," I said. "How old is it?"

"Oh, about five or six years. I honestly don't know why Hofmann remembered it." She pulled off the paper and gasped. It was an oil painting of an ochre marsh with some leafless trees leaning into the scene. The sky was filled in loosely with broad strokes of blue and pale green.

"Very nice," I said. It was a lovely painting.

"Yes, very," she said, wrapping it up hastily. "But this isn't it." She retied the string and set the painting back where she'd found it, then walked swiftly into the back room. I shifted the sleeping Lottie to my other shoulder and waited, admiring the casual sumptuousness of the living room with its heavy rattan chairs, its fat silk sofa cushions and the beautiful Turkish carpet. Ria emerged with another painting, unwrapped. She showed it to me. There were the familiar Ria marks in rich blues, squares within squares, floating in and out of each other.

"Let's go," she said, grabbing a throw from the sofa and quickly wrapping the painting. We walked across the street to collect the kids, who were still dashing around, peering into display boxes, picking out one flavor at a time of the waxed paper-covered candy, filing little bags and counting.

"Time to leave," said Ria. She stood by the door tapping her foot. Her face was red, and she was drumming her fingers against her lips, teeth clenched. I had never seen her do that. Clearly something had upset her. The kids paid for their taffy and started talking about hot dogs. Ria said, "No, not now guys, we have to go back." Four little shocked faces looked at her and then all started yelling, "But you promised!" "You said we could!" Ria looked at me and said, "Theo, if you don't mind, I think I'll wait in the car with Lottie. Will you take them?"

"Sure," I said. I had the feeling I'd missed something when we were in the house, but I had no idea what. I handed over Lottie and led the kids down the street to the hot dog stand. Ginny insisted on having a foot-long, even though she was barely able to hang on to it. I got one, too. I admit I was as disappointed as the kids were at the thought of not having one. I suggested we walk down the street while we ate. I thought Ria might need a little time to herself. The town was crowded as usual. I kept the kids in front of me and slowly we continued to the pier, where they spent a good deal of time chewing taffy and spitting into the water, trying to top one another for biggest globule of strawberry-colored saliva. I sat there trying to figure out what had upset Ria so much. Something about the wrapped painting. Perhaps she was annoyed with Cal for putting out the wrong one.

On the way home, she was silent. The kids picked up on it so they talked quietly in the back seat. I'm sure they were on the downslope of a sugar rush. Except for Lottie, who woke up and started to sing, "The Itsy Bitsy Spider." She didn't know any of the other words, so she simply sang those four over and over. I sat there thinking about the itsy bitsy spider that had invaded our tranquil outing, and finally I said to Ria, "What happened back there?"

"Oh, Theo." She didn't say anything else.

"Something to do with the painting?"

"Yes." She let out a long groan. "It's not mine. I recognized it. It's something Achilles ran across in Paris when we were there. He talked about it for days. The painting was stolen from a man named Herzog, if I remember correctly. A Hungarian. His was one of the collections Achilles was in charge of. What I don't understand, and cannot bear to think about, is why that painting is now in our house in Provincetown."

"Who is the painter?"

"Cezanne."

"Why does he have it? Maybe he bought it."

"He didn't buy it, Theo."

"Maybe Herzog gave it to him."

"No, that's not possible." She put her head in her hands. Lottie pried them open a crack and said, "Peek-a-boo, Mommy."

Ria sat quietly stroking Lottie's curls and staring at the road. We were driving through Wellfleet. One of the prettiest towns on Cape Cod, it has an even more spectacular ocean beach than the one in Orleans. I suggested we stop and let the kids have a run around. I thought it would be good to sit on the beach with Ria. Maybe it would change her mood. "Sure, why not?" she said, and I turned on to the beach road.

We plunked ourselves in the warm sand and watched the kids run down to the water. They knew enough not to fool around with the ocean waves, so they chased plovers and threw rocks for a while, then started on the construction of a channel to catch an incoming wave. Ria sat there still not speaking, running her fingers through the sand.

"What is it," I said. "Tell me. If it's not too personal, that is."

She turned and looked into my eyes for several moments, trying to decide if she should. I had never seen her like that. Her normal self-assured poise had disappeared, her lip trembled slightly and she said slowly, "Maybe you think Achilles is wealthy, and yes he does have some money, but..." She stopped, looked over at the kids, then took a deep breath, and went on. "He bought me a necklace for Christmas. It's quite beautiful, rubies and pearls, gold."

"Sounds nice."

"Yeah, it is. The thing is, it's much more valuable than he can afford. I'm sure of it, Theo. I took it to a jeweler and had it appraised."

"So, what are you saying?"

"I'm not sure. But when I saw that Cezanne I..." She didn't say anything more. I didn't want her to, either. There must be an explanation for it, I thought. Achilles moved in circles none of us could relate to. International dealers of objets d'art, collectors and traders, museum directors. I had always assumed Achilles was wealthy. I said as much to her, but she shook her head.

"No, not like that. Not at that level." She shrugged. "But, to be honest, I don't exactly know. He goes away on his buying and selling trips, often with Cal, but I'm rarely sure of where he is or what he's doing."

"I'm sure there's an explanation for the painting," I said. About the necklace I had no idea. I would have given Ria something like that, too, if I could've.

"Can I ask you something?" she said lightly.

"Sure."

"How much did he pay you for the diary?"

I told her. She looked out at the water and nodded slowly. "OK," was all she said. I thought about it. I assumed the fee had been shared, and it was more than enough, but for me it was still tainted, even though the diary had ended up with Gustav Heye where Casco wanted it. So I hadn't given much thought to what the thing was worth. I had no idea, anyway.

"I think I'll ask him about all of it when he gets here," Ria said, flashing her eyes at me in the old way. "Yes, I think I will have to. You're right, Theo. Of course there's an explanation and probably a great story behind it." After another hour we gathered up the kids and left the beach, Ria's mood having lightened enough that she ran down to the water's edge and helped to excavate a large amphitheater. The waves hit on one end and thrillingly swept around to the other before washing out again. The children were completely soaked, but happy. when we arrived at Ria's house the back seat of the Nash looked as if one of those waves had crashed against it, leaving behind a couple of buckets' worth of sand, pebbles and scraps of seaweed.

Achilles was due the following day, so we left Ria to get on with whatever preparations she needed to make, and I drove Jack and Laura's kids home. On the way the younger of the boys said, "Theo."

"Hm?"

"Is Ria really your wife?"

"Shut up, dummy," said Jack's daughter.

"No, she isn't," I said.

"How come?"

I thought about it, about all the years I had longed for it and how little I had done about it before Achilles came along and captivated her. But I was happy with the way our lives were now. I knew deep down that I would never be enough for her, and I liked Achilles. There were things I could give her, nothing like a ruby necklace, but I felt in some way I had given her the Bay and my part in it, and it was enough.

"Because she's already married." I said, and then we were there.

The weeks of July passed quickly. A few days after our trip to Provincetown the linotype broke down. All the copy for the next issue had to be carted to a printery thirty miles away to be set, which made us miss our publishing date. Jack was beside himself. Tony and I spent two whole days fiddling with the machine, covered in grease with our fingertips painfully burned from handling the hot slugs and being occasionally splashed with molten lead. When finally we had it repaired, an electrical fire in the shop next to the office caused our power to fail as well, so they had to chop a giant hole in the wall between us to get at the problem. The whole place was covered in plaster dust, the worst possible substance to have anywhere near a linotype. We couldn't plug in a vacuum cleaner because of the power loss, so we had tarps hanging all over forming a maze-like tunnel into the back room. Tony and I took turns typing and soaking our fingers in a bowl of ice. In addition to that, all three of Jack's kids came down with Chicken Pox and were bedridden for three weeks, so we lost Laura. All this at the height of summer. But we managed.

I went often to Ria and Achilles' house for dinner after my marathon sessions at the paper, happy to be pampered by them and to simply sit looking out over the water with a cocktail in my sore and bandaged fingers and only one child on my lap. I don't know if Ria ever asked Achilles about the Cezanne or the money he'd received for the diary but her anxiety seemed to have vanished. She didn't mention it to me again either, so I assumed the question had been either resolved or dropped. They behaved more affectionately toward each other than before, often sitting together holding hands or touching in some way. Ginny and Lottie climbed all over Achilles or pulled at his pant leg wanting him to join in a game or to look at something they'd made. He often took them on long walks along the shore, leaving Ria and me to sit in her studio. She showed me that year's work and talked about the upcoming show with the Abstract Expressionists in the fall. She glowed with self-satisfaction as she pulled out canvas after canvas to show me, proud of her latest work. Much more colorful than the previous year's, her brushstrokes seemed to be edging back to the days when she painted squares. The gestures were slower, the paint thicker. "They're more like your old style," I said, like the painting Hofmann wants you to put in the show."

"I know. I keep going back to it. It makes me feel more in control."

Out of the blue one day she told me that Achilles had been recently talking about trying for another baby. "For a boy, no doubt," she said, but it was not said with sarcasm. In fact she looked wistful when she told me, as though it had already been decided somewhere in her mind. Three days later she confessed that she was already pregnant.

"That's wonderful," I said. I meant it. I could never understand why Ria had been so shy about announcing any of her pregnancies to me, and said so. At this point in our relationship, we were telling each other all kinds of things during our long, vodka-fueled studio visits. I had admitted my feelings for her when we were fourteen. I reminded her of the evening we stood chest-deep in warm water talking about scallops, told her it had been the first tickle of desire I'd ever experienced. I described the longing I'd felt whenever I heard the train's arriving whistle from the kitchen at the Ship Ahoy. I told her about how all the days and nights the thought of her return had kept me sane in the wigwam. She never laughed, except when I said something about wanting to kiss her at age sixteen and not knowing how, or that I'd been jealous of Dusty.

"It's because I don't want you to think I'll only be some kind of brood mare, and not an artist. I want you to be proud of me."

I knew what she meant by that. I suppose I was one of the people she held herself up to for judgement, and I know why. To her I represented something pure and unsullied, a creature from the bottom of the Bay, still connected to what was genuine in the world. I wasn't so sure I agreed, but I got it.

Achilles talked often about the upcoming show of Indian artifacts at Harvard. It was to be a display of newly unearthed items from all over New England. He was quite worked up, proud to be taking part in it. He went on about trade beads, weapons and cooking utensils, arrowheads. Apparently there was to be an entire Pequot Village recreated in a vast hall somewhere nearby.

"Your diary is creating a lot of excitement. I'm sure it will be the centerpiece of the exhibit. Of course the university has many things which haven't been seen in nearly three hundred years, so that will be fascinating as well." I could imagine the little book presented under glass on a pedestal, splayed open to the pertinent page, people gathered around it. I wondered how the translation would be attached, perhaps produced in a similar booklet for sale nearby.

"I've decided to lend something from my own collection to add to the exhibit. I think you'll be interested. From Massachusetts as well." Achilles raised his eyebrows like a bountiful Santa, eyes glistening.

"We must go together, the three of us," said Ria. The opening was scheduled for a Saturday in the middle of August. We made plans to drive to Boston, see the show and have dinner there. The girls would be left with a sitter.

Three days before the show, I was sitting at the linotype when Laura came in and tapped me on the shoulder. "Someone here to see you," she said. "Says his name is Walter something."

I sat there for a few moments with my hands frozen on the keyboard. Walter? Slowly I stepped to the door and peered around the frame. There stood Walter Askew, the very man I'd hated and worried over and was relieved to think of as dead. He was standing by the front desk, reading a copy of the paper and tapping his foot. He looked much older. His clothes were the same crisply ironed pseudo-safari attire he often wore. But he didn't fill them the way he used to, with his blustery bravado and seam-straining beer belly. His skin had a gray tint to it, an unnatural sight in the middle of summer. He looked up and caught me watching him. I gave him a stupid little wave and walked toward him.

"Birdman," he said, extending his hand. I took it and we shook weakly. "Ray told me I'd find you here. What do you do?"

"Everything but write," said Laura.

We all chuckled companionably. Then I led Walter outside. We stood on the sidewalk and he lit a cigarette. "I need to talk to you about something important," he said. I was still trying to comprehend his presence. "OK," I said. "I thought you were dead," I blurted out.

"I know. Couldn't be helped," he said. "When can we meet? I need to show you something."

"Right now," I said. "I'll meet you across the street." My heart was pounding. I wasn't sure why, but I knew it wasn't with excitement over seeing an old friend. I sensed trouble, and it was the last thing I needed, just when things were getting back to normal. I checked the linotype and told Laura I'd be back in half an hour. As I walked over to the Ship Ahoy, I wondered what he could possibly want with me. I told myself he simply wanted the vines cleared from his house, because his old caretaker was fed up with non-payment. Nothing to do with Casco, I prayed. He was sitting at the table under Nolan's mural with a beer in front of him when I stepped in. Ray winked at me, poured a cup of coffee, and pushed it across the bar. "Hey, kid," he said. "Let me know if you need anything else."

I sat down opposite Walter and took a sip of coffee. I wanted to be ready, prepared for whatever was coming my way, but instead I started blabbering. "What happened to you? Why did you disappear so suddenly. Your house is a wreck, you know."

"I know. It's all right. I've seen it. Can be fixed. Sure doesn't take long for Mother Nature to take over, does it? You wouldn't believe how many squirrel nests I found inside. The little bastards eat wood when they have nothing else, I guess. My window sash is completely gone, both floors." He shook his head wistfully, took a long sip of his beer. I didn't say anything.

"I'll tell you why I left but let me tell you something first, okay?" I nodded and he leaned in closer. "I'm pretty sure I know who killed Casco and why," he said, almost whispering. I felt blood rush to my cheeks, but I was determined to stay calm. I had been through enough calamity in the past several months. I was not going to let any more bad things enter my life. I grabbed my thighs under the table, bracing.

"I have to tell you a little story, then I'll get to the point." He looked out the window at the sky, took a deep breath, then began. "A few years ago, I was working for a guy. The Collector, I called him. He was interested in Indian stuff from around here. Particularly in a certain diary." I forced myself not to look at him at this point. I took another sip of coffee. I placed the cup carefully back in the saucer and said, "Uh huh."

"He wanted the diary more than anything. You know, the one I asked you about that day. Remember?"

"Yes."

"I told him I knew who probably had it." He looked at me, nodded, and said, "I know. But let me tell the rest. See, I wanted something from him, too. The belt, which I told you we both knew was rightfully mine. I bought it. So we went to Paw Wah together, The Collector, his man, and me. I went into the woods first to try to strike a deal with Casco. We did have a friendship at one point, after all. The Collector was offering a good price for the diary, and I knew Casco had financial problems. I found him, and we talked. He gave me the belt almost right away, but when I tried to talk to him about the diary, he got angry, told me to get the hell out. Said he didn't have it. Said he wanted to be left alone out there. Forever."

Walter paused to take another sip of beer. "Jesus," he mumbled to himself. He looked at me and went on. "So I left. I walked away thinking I could buy a piece of the point, offer it to him in a trade, if that's what he wanted. I told The Collector there was no deal. We drove back into town, and he dropped me off."

"Okay," I said.

"But later on, I think they went back. Well, I know they did. That's how Casco ended up the way he did. And that's why I left. After you told me about what you had found, I knew. I couldn't stand what I'd done by leading them to him. And now I have proof."

Walter pulled a folded magazine from inside his jacket. He showed me the cover. An engraving of an Indian sitting with crossed arms was centered under the title, Native American Indian Art & Artifacts Exhibition. The Indian wore an expression of disdain, the whites of his eyes the only light spots on the cover besides the white beads in the belt he wore around his waist. Under the picture it said, Fogg Museum, Harvard University, August 15-October 31. The show at Harvard. The diary.

"This is the catalog for a show of Indian stuff that's starting day after tomorrow."

He flipped through the pages until he came to one, then turned the others back. "Look at this," he said, pushing the catalog across the table and laying it in front of me. There was a photo of the diary, opened to the middle pages with the map of Narragansett Bay.

Under that, two smaller photos showing the back and front of the Peace Medal. I gasped involuntarily, then read the caption. Peace Medal, 1676. From the private collection of Achilles Overton, it read. I looked up at Walter, my mouth hanging open. I couldn't take it in.

Walter slapped a finger on the photo. "That's The Collector," he said. "Achilles Overton. He and his man went back and killed Casco for the diary and the Peace Medal."

I looked closely at the photos of the Peace Medal. There, on the back, clearly defined, was the long scratch that Ria had made pulling the disc from the roots of the cedar tree. I read the caption again, and then the one under the diary, trying to make sense of what I was seeing. Personal diary of Bad Boy, a Massachusetts Praying Indian, it said. Heye Museum of the American Indian.

"Overton sold it to Heye." said Walter. "I'm positive. When I suggested Heye ought to check further into the provenance of those things Overton had brought to him, he removed them from the show, and has started a legal investigation."

I was shocked, speechless. I needed time to think. An image of Achilles flashed through my mind, that of his self-satisfied grin as he informed us of his benevolent donation to the show. What if he had said then and there what it was?

"I have to go over to the office. Tell them I'll be away a little longer. Stay here, OK?" I said, getting up. Walter nodded, spreading his hands. "Not going anywhere," he said.

I walked on shaky legs back to the office. Should I tell Ria? Of course I had to tell her. Her husband was an accomplice to a murder if not the actual perpetrator. And a thief. And a liar. And my friend. I thought of Ginny and Lottie as I leaned against the wall outside the office. "Oh, Christ," I mumbled. The first ripple of anger passed through me, and I shoved through the door. "Something's come up," I said to Laura. "I need the rest of the day off." She looked at me levelly. "Everything all right?"

"Just an old friend from out of town. Of my father's," I lied.

"Go ahead, hon." she said. "We're fine here." I looked over at Jack, who was on the phone. He gestured with his head toward the door. Go on. Tomorrow was deadline day, but I knew we were ahead. I went back across the street. Walter was sitting tipped back in his chair, his head against the mural, exactly under the spot where Nolan had painted the boy who looked like me standing on a bluff watching the Humpback whales frolic in the swells. It looked like I was standing on his head. I sat down opposite and said, "He didn't steal the diary."

"Oh, yeah? How do you know?"

"Because I gave it to him."

"What?"

I told Walter about finding the diary, about Casco's note. He wanted to know where it had been hidden, so I told him.

"You mean it was there all the time?"

"Yeah. Casco found it there and put it back." Walter asked if he could see the note.

"It specifically said not to show you the diary," I said. "At least I thought he was referring to you. Now I'm not so sure."

"Listen, this guy Overton, he'll do almost anything to get his hands on what he wants. Believe me, I know him well." Walter gestured to Ray for another beer.

"And you worked for him," I said.

"Well, yeah. I did." Walter hung his head. Ray arrived with two beers. He raised his eyebrows at me, wondering if I was OK. I nodded to him, Don't worry.

"I know Overton too," I said. "Only I call him Achilles."

Walter peered at me, trying to put Achilles and me together. "Did he come in here?"

I told him about Ria, about our friendship. I gave a quick rundown of the day Ria found the Peace Medal, how Casco had identified it, that Ria had given it to him. Then I told him about Ria being Achilles' wife.

"Holy shit." That's all he said for about five minutes. I was deep in thought myself, already leaping ahead to my meeting with Ria and Achilles. I would have to go over there and find a reason to speak with Ria in the studio. Maybe I could take her for a drive to the beach. Make an excuse for needing her at my house, anything to have a private hour in which to deliver the unspeakable news.

"Sorry, Birdman. I had to tell you. Figured I owed you. I never dreamed it could be even worse."

"It's all right," I said. "Thanks."

I wanted to get away from him then, to be alone with my dilemma. I felt I had already said too much. I had to remind myself that I didn't need to be wary of Walter anymore. Still, he knew something about me which I didn't want anyone to know, except Ria. Now Walter and I both knew that Achilles and I were tied together in more than friendship: Achilles had caused Casco's death, and I had secretly buried him. I stood up, put my hand out to shake. Walter took it and I said, "May I borrow that catalog for a few days?"

"Sure, Theo," he said, using my real name for the first time. "Come and find me, will you? I'll be at the house."

I left, intending to go directly to Ria's place, but instead I ended up at the landing at the end of Portanimicut Road. I sat in the Nash, looking across to Paw Wah, remembering the day Achilles asked me to show him where I'd lived, the day he gave me the car. He had pretended innocence, but in reality he had wanted to see if there were any trace left of Casco. Maybe he wanted to go back, dig around some other day. Maybe he wanted to make sure for himself that Walter's place was truly abandoned. Maybe it was Achilles sending the request to the town hall for Walter's property information, and not an estate lawyer. My brain was spinning with speculation, the rooting out of lies, duplicitous behavior. Achilles' false bonhomie. I couldn't stand it. I started the engine and drove over to their house. When I pulled in, only Ria's car was in the driveway.

"Theo," she shouted, spilling through the screen door with Lottie in her arms. "What a surprise. You're just in time for lunch. Peanut butter and jelly."

"Yay!" said Lottie.

"Great," I said, faking a smile for her benefit. "Where's Achilles?"

"Oh, he's up in P'town fooling around with his stuff. I think."

I followed her into the kitchen, where Ginny sat at the table taking a bite out of a sandwich. Grape jelly covered her mouth, and she had a purple glob on the end of her nose. "Hi Theo," she said, mouth full. Ria sat Lottie down and put a sandwich in front of her. It had been cut diagonally twice, the way I knew Lottie insisted every sandwich be cut. Lottie picked up a piece and handed it to me. I bit into it, trying to suppress the tears I felt welling up at the sight of the little family simply eating an ordinary lunch. I knew I would soon be dropping a bomb into the center of it.

"I thought you were working today," Ria smiled at me. "Want some coffee?" She kept looking at me, and I saw her face change as she realized something was wrong.

"If you put peanut butter in a dog's mouth it will be glued shut forever," said Ginny.

"Really." I said.

"Yeah," she looked at me earnestly, then added, "They can't lick it off with their tongues because their tongues are stuck too."

"Okay," I said.

"So never do it."

"All right." I nodded gravely. "I won't."

"What's going on?" Ria turned from the counter where she was spooning coffee into the pot. She looked worried.

"I have to talk to you," I said, nodding my head toward the porch. Ria opened the fridge and poured the girls each a hefty cup of milk, saying, "If you guys finish all this you can have Popsicles after."

The girls uttered muffled sounds of joy through mouthfuls of sandwich. Ria turned down the flame under the coffeepot and beckoned me out onto the porch. There was a rocking chair out there which she used to sit in to feed the girls when they were babies. She sat slowly down in it and said, "OK Theo, what is it? I can tell it's bad."

"It is," I said. "I'm sorry." I told her about Walter's visit to the paper, our meeting under the mural, his reason for leaving and then for coming back. I used the name 'The Collector,' like Walter had.

"Wow. So now we know who killed Casco," she said. "And it wasn't Walter. But that's good, isn't it?"

"Hold on," I said. "I'll be right back. I have to show you something."

When I got back from the car with the catalog Ria was unwrapping popsicles for the girls. She came out to the porch and, as Walter had done with me, I showed her first the cover and then folded the catalog back to show the page with the damning information. I watched with dread as she grasped the significance of what she saw. A tear splatted on the picture of the diary, then another. Then she threw the catalog on the floor, covered her face with her hands and began to sob.

"Mommy?" Ginny said tentatively. I got up and went inside. The girls were sitting quietly, popsicles melting, dribbling juice down their little fists and dripping on to the table.

"What flavor is that?" I asked, sitting down.

"Red," said Lottie, but Ginny was still looking out the porch door at her mother. Ria got up and walked down the porch steps, heading for her studio.

"She just needs to find something for me," I said. Ginny took a few licks of her popsicle and said, "Red is cherry flavor, green is lime and blue is not a real flavor. Mommy said so. But it's good."

I waited for them to finish, making small talk and then took them into the bathroom for a cleanup. Their mother's tears seemed to be forgotten as soon as I turned on the tap. They were both mesmerized by the water and spent a long time holding their hands under it, experimenting with flow and dribble, the life cycle of a soap bubble. I figured I'd better keep them busy until Ria recovered, so I suggested we read a book. I knew they would do anything to be read to. Ginny brought me a pile of four or five books, and we sat together on the sofa reading about Frog and Toad, Bambi, and Babar's Cousin and That Rascal, Arthur. Lottie fell asleep during the first book. It took Ginny another halfhour, but she dropped off too. I sat there for a while, savoring those last moments of innocent, child-slumbering tranquility, then carefully extracted myself and went in search of Ria. When I found her, she was sitting in one of our chairs sipping from a glass of vodka and looking out at the trees. She put down the glass when I came in. "What are the girls doing?" she said.

"Sleeping."

"Good. Thanks."

"Ria, I..." I had no idea how to say what I wanted to say. I wanted to tell her how sorry I was, but somewhere in my mind I was angry with her for this, though I know it sounds cruel. Of all people she'd married Achilles, the killer of Casco, and brought him into our lives, and had made me love him too. I sat down in the other chair and lifted her glass.

"Look what I dug up," she said. She pointed to a rolled up piece of drawing paper on the floor beside her chair. I picked it up and unfurled it. It was the watercolor painting she'd done of Casco the day we spent together in the wigwam. I almost cried when I saw Casco's face the way it was that day. He looked content, proud, leaning there on one elbow, his braid of white hair rendered by Ria simply as a few swift lines to indicate shadow, the white of the paper stood for the rest. His shoulders were deep brown and muscular, the wampum belt circled a well-defined waist. I had forgotten how imposing he was. He was wearing the Peace Medal, which was clearly rendered in detail, even down to the feathering of the grass skirt on the Indian brave. The painting was signed, 'Ria Bang Aug. 20, '39'.

"Turn it over."

I looked at the back. There were the fragments of rubbings Ria had done of the Peace Medal, two of the border design, one of the brave holding the arrow and bow, and one of the wording on the back, with the scrape diagonally across it.

"I would like you to drive to Provincetown with me," she said calmly. "I want to show this to Achilles. And then I never want to see him again."

It was very clear, very damning evidence, and very clever of Ria to have remembered the painting from that day. But I could only imagine the grim task she had faced looking through her drawings for it. While I was reading about Bambi, she had been searching for proof that the husband she adored had killed, or had caused the killing of another person, a friend.

I stepped over to the chair, grabbed her hands, pulled her up, and took her into my arms. She put hers around me and laid her head against my chest. I kissed the top of her head as she began to cry again. We stood that way for a long time, swaying slightly. Every now and then, she lifted the hem of her skirt and blew her nose in it, wiping away tears that only refreshed immediately, then said finally, "Let's go, okay? Let's put the girls in the car before they wake up. You carry Ginny, I'll get Lottie's blanket." I knewwhich one it was: green with pink satin edging. She would never go anywhere without it. I let go of Ria reluctantly, not wanting to begin this trip. "Are you sure?" I said.

"Yes. Don't forget the catalog." Her face was ruined, but her look was determined, as bold and strong as she was when we were fourteen and she defied her camp counselors. Only this was an adult version, and it was formidable.

We drove the trip to Provincetown in near silence. Ria sat with Lottie in her lap staring at the road ahead. It was hellishly hot, but she insisted we put the top up. The wind whipped in through the open window, blowing her hair across her face, so I could only glimpse her expression. I pictured Achilles in his luxurious living room, dipping his fingers into a plate of black, wrinkled olives, pushing one through his lips as he contemplated some new acquisition sitting before him on the coffee table, a miniature marble statue or a jewel-encrusted brooch. I pictured us bursting through the door to stand in front of him, hands on hips, the catalog and incriminating painting defiantly thrown down in front of him by Ria, the girls hanging back, afraid. I don't remember what I was doing in that particular fantasy, but it wasn't at all the way it happened.

When we got to the house Cal greeted us at the door. "Come in. You should have told me you were coming up. I'll make us some lunch," he said smoothly. The girls ran out the porch door to the beach. "Damn," muttered Ria, and ran after them shouting, "Stay out of the water," then stopped abruptly and said, "Oh." I looked past her and there sat Achilles under a large striped umbrella. He was leaning on one elbow just like Casco in the painting, reading the paper.

"Darlings," he said as the girls threw themselves on top of him. "What a wonderful surprise." He looked over at us and waved. "Come on down. The water is perfect," he said.

"Can we go swimming, Daddy?" said Ginny.

"Of course," said her father. "Do you have a bathing suit on?"

Ria and I walked toward him as the girls stripped off their shorts and shirts and ran down to the water's edge in their underpants. Turning to us, Achilles chuckled, "Ah well, I suppose those garments are superfluous, aren't they?"

"Shall I...?" I didn't know if I ought to be there.

"Stay with me," Ria said under her breath.

We stood over him, our shadows running across his body and the blanket he was lying on. He twisted his head around, looking up into the sun, trying to shade his eyes so he could see us. "Sit down, will you? Cal will make us something. Did you see him?"

"Yes," said Ria, but that's not why we're here."

"Oh? Anything wrong at the house?"

"No." She looked over at the girls. Lottie stood at the edge of the sand letting little wavelets cover her feet. Ginny, on her stomach, kicked up a froth practicing the Dog Paddle in five inches of water. "I brought something I want you to look at. It's in the car." I made a move to go get it but she put her hand on me and said, "No, sit, Theo. I'll be right back."

Achilles folded the paper as I kneeled in the sand. "Is it a painting?" he said."Some new and exciting discovery?"

"It's a painting, yeah," I said after a bit.

We waited, watching Ria walk purposefully across the sand. I wondered if maybe this was the place to make the presentation. Perhaps I should have offered to stay with the kids while they went inside. But Ria was intent, concentrating on putting one foot ahead of the other. She cradled the rolled-up painting in her arms, the catalog in her hand.

Achilles sat up. "Oh, wonderful! I see you have a copy of the exhibit catalog. I was going to show it to you. I have a couple inside." He thought for a second and said, "But wherever did you get it?"

Ria didn't answer. She folded the pages back once again to the place and dropped it in the sand in front of Achilles.

"Yes, yes, isn't it marvelous? Fantastic reproduction of your diary, eh, Theo?" He picked it up to show me. "And did you see the item I lent to them?" He pointed to the photos of the Peace Medal, gazing down in wonder at them, gloating over his coup. As he said this, I watched Ria kneel down, unroll the painting and lay it on the blanket. Achilles stared at the image for several seconds while we waited. Then Ria said, "We have seen your item before, haven't we, Theo? Actually, I was the one who found it." Achilles looked at her sharply. "Yes, Achilles. We know it well. It was the summer Theo and I were at camp." I saw Ria's hands begin to shake as she held the picture open. "But I gave it to our friend Casco. It suited him, don't you think?"

We watched as Achilles laid his index finger on Ria's signature, slowly tracing the letters, the date. Abruptly, he smiled at us, smacked his palm against the top of his head and said, "I had no idea of your connection to this artifact. What a coincidence! I bought it from a guy I used to know. Come to think of it, he said he'd found it on the Cape."

Ria and I looked at each other. She nodded once.

"Yes," I said. "Walter told me all about your little visit to Casco's wigwam. I came along not long after and buried him."

Achilles' smile faded as he put it all together. Slowly, he shook his head and took a deep, raspy breath, letting it out in a long sigh. Ria let go of the painting and we watched the edges gradually curl into the center. After a few minutes Achilles got up, ducked under the umbrella and took a few steps. "It was Cal. I never wanted that," he said, turning. He waited for a response but we said nothing.

"I'm sorry my love," he added. Then he walked briskly into the house.

Ria sat down, crying silently, tears spilling down her cheeks. I put my arm around her. Down by the water the girls were giggling, rolling around in the wet sand. They stood up, completely covered, and called to us.

"Look! We're sand monsters." They danced crazily around and then plunged back into the water. Ria watched them for a few minutes, then said, "Theo, can you stay here with them for a while? I have to go talk to him."

"Sure," I said. I took off my shoes, rolled up my pants and went down to the water.

An hour later I had them dressed again, and we were making plans to go across the street for some taffy when Ria came out of the house. She scooped up Lottie in her arms and kissed her, saying, "Was that fun, or what?" She looked at me over Lottie's head. "Why don't you girls go inside," she said. "Daddy has something for you."

They ran off, and Ria said, "Let's take a walk."

We started off down the beach toward town. Ria tied a knot in the front of her skirt to keep it out of the water and waded in, walking along beside me.

"How is he?" I said.

"Pretty bad. Distraught." She looked at me. "Stammering. Begging."

"Oh."

"He has to leave. His reputation will be shot."

"Hm."

"I'm going with him, Theo."

"What?" I couldn't believe it.

"I have to. Try to understand. He's the father of my children. One of them isn't even born yet."

"I'll take care of you," I said quietly.

"I know." She took my hand. We didn't say anything more, just walked along, she in the water, I on land, holding hands. It had always been like that, I suppose, in some metaphorical way. And now it seemed we would walk in different worlds, our past the only connection between them.

The next day they were gone. I drove over to the house at lunchtime with Jack'sboys to say goodbye, but the place was locked, sheets covered the couch and beds, the porch furniture was stacked inside. I went into the studio, which had been stripped of most of the paintings, and sank into in my chair. Stunned, I sat staring out at the cedars swaying in the breeze. Finally the boys roused me and I drove them home.

And so it was that I became a loner. For the second time in my life, I felt abandoned by someone whom I had come to love, though in this case the feeling was one of deep bitterness. Unlike Casco, Ria was very much alive and had left of her own volition. My offer to take care of her, brushed aside for the implausible idea it was, tortured me for weeks. I went over that last conversation repeatedly, kicking myself each time I recalled her tactful sidestep of my proposal, my stupid, self-serving solution to her problems. I so loathed myself that I began to withdraw from all human company, gradually speaking less and less while at work, silently doing my job. All other hours of the day, I spent alone. At first I sat on the porch drinking beer until it was too dark to see, cooked a hasty pan of food and went to bed. The guys at the Ship Ahoy stopped expecting me to join them for our Saturday drinks. Nolan made a couple of visits out to the house, but they were so tense and silent I think he gave up. I wondered if Walter had become a regular again. I didn't offer an explanation about my own absence. Maybe they thought Walter was the cause. But I didn't bother to correct it. I stopped taking care of Jack and Laura's kids, and they stopped asking me to. I was miserable.

Then, one Sunday, I took the boat out. It was a beautiful day, the last bit of summer. The tourists were gone, and I had the place to myself, so I let the boat drift around for hours as I lay across the seat watching the clouds pass. I felt all right for the first time in weeks as I rocked gently in the current, going nowhere, thinking about nothing. A flock of geese passed overhead in V formation, practicing. Higher up, an osprey called, flapped its wings once, and dove toward the marsh. I heard the splash of a fish jumping. Something brushed against the side of the boat and I looked overboard. A juvenile sea turtle swam alongside making graceful sweeps with its wide forelegs. After circling the boat once, it took off in the direction of the ocean. The turtle reminded me of the day I met Casco, both of us peering at turtle eggs, but for different reasons. Thinking about that day, and who I was then, I decided to row over to the spot where it had happened, the inlet at Paw Wah, just for something to do. When I got there, I didn't walk around. There were too many ghosts lurking in the trees. I simply lay on my stomach, as I had done that day long ago, watching the tide flow out and slowly expose fiddler and hermit crabs, snails and mussels. Translucent sand shrimp appeared, backflipping in the sunshine. Tiny rivulets of fresh water trickled over the salty sand, small birds dropped out of the trees to tiptoe in for a sip. It made me smile, something I hadn't done in a long time. I felt I could have stayed there forever, letting the Bay's waters slip over me and keep me. I was back, back in the refuge of my true home after a disappointing foray into the world of people. For weeks, until it was too cold to do so, I began to row again, to row and look at the eelgrass, letting its long green undulating fingers lure me into reverie. The constancy of the tides, the faithful passing of seasons, the ubiquitous and everlasting forces of nature comforted me as they had when I was a boy. In those safe surroundings, I allowed myself to drift through my memory to the place I had so stubbornly refused to go: I thought about Ria.

By springtime, I had worked through my anger, and a new perspective emerged. I didn't expect to hear from her, and she didn't write, but I began to understand that Ria had made the only move she could have, given the circumstances. I'm sure the last thing she wanted was to leave her house and the Cape, but she had to stay with Achilles, even if she couldn't love him in the same way. I would never be more than a brother to her, and she was too young to live out life with me in platonic partnership.

Moreover, there was her art to consider. She needed the entree into Achilles' social sphere. What I could offer her was nothing but a peaceful existence devoid of the culture of the world she was born into. I understood, but the hurt has never really left me.

Meanwhile I monitored the town's events from the seat of the linotype. Another refuge from my troubles. Many changes took place on our little peninsula in the years following Ria and Achilles' departure. Tourism brought in more and more revenue, more motels, guest cottages, restaurants and related businesses. We are now a worldwide destination. The train discontinued its run up to Provincetown, replaced by a brand new three-lane highway and many, many more cars. In 1957 a drive-in movie theater went up in Wellfleet with a hundred-foot wide screen. Almost directly behind the screen are over three hundred acres of woodland and marsh running to Cape Cod Bay, which were purchased the following year from an amateur ornithologist and added to the Audubon Society's roster of nature sanctuaries. I spend a lot of time there.

Of course, the most important change happened only a few years ago. When JFK signed a bill to preserve almost forty miles of ocean beach including dunes, ponds, woods and bogs, the Cape Cod National Seashore was born. I'm sure this coast would be a duplicate of Miami Beach today if not for that bold action, and I for one am deeply grateful.

Much has changed here; much remains eternal. The tides, storms, gathering waters continue to scoop out the beach one year, fill it in the next, subtly reshaping the coastline. We still hear the summer sounds of children in sailboats on Pleasant Bay, though many of the camps have closed, and the whine of outboard engines has drowned out the flap! of luffing sails. Plenty of seafood is still harvested from its waters, sometimes even by me. I have rediscovered a fondness for scallops, even for shucking them, and, come November, I am among the first out on the water, culling table fixed to the rowboat's gunwales. I still sit on my porch in the evening, but not because I'm depressed. I like to watch the goings-on in the natural world, as usual. There is always something to see, cycles of life bringing freshness and regeneration, something larger than the folly of human beings.

I lean back in my chair, open my desk drawer, take out a folder. Inside is the meager collection of letters and clippings that are all I have of her. The letters are old, mostly from the time we spent apart while she was at school. There are a few newspaper articles, clipped by Phinneas from the New York Times, about Ria Bang Overton's remarkable rising star, reviews from galleries in Paris and London. I have only one photo of her standing with another painter in front of a huge abstract. She looks happy, but why shouldn't she? It's a photo of a celebrated artist. The article asks, 'When will Mrs Overton show in her own country?' I flip through the clippings, combing for factual information. I jot down a date, a famous name.

On my desk is a large manilla envelope, received just two days ago, addressed to me in a handwriting that has not changed in all these years, the same elegant script she learned as a girl. I carefully withdraw the contents. When I peel away the layers of tissue there lies the Peace Medal. And a short note.

"I now know that I found something far more valuable than this that day. If it belongs to anyone, it should be yours. And so should I. Can you forgive me, Theo?"

The image of Ria on the day she found the Medal replays in my mind, as it has hundreds of times. My beautiful friend running down the beach in her camp uniform, bangs swaying, eyes flashing, beckoning excitedly to me.

I'm tired now. It's been a long day. Sighing, I put my fingers back on the typer. I must write this obit or I'll never get any sleep. Nevertheless it is with a smile that I type:

OVERTON, Achilles Nikolaos...

Although Theo and Ria is a work of fiction, it is set in an actual town. Orleans is where I grew up, though years later than Theo and the gang. Many of the characters are based on people who lived in Orleans at the time. I interviewed many long-time residents who told fascinating stories about these and other characters.

I am grateful to Vera Johnson, Doris Taylor and Dana Eldridge for their remeniscences of life in Orleans in the 40s. Like Theo, Skip Norgeot used to row around looking at the bottom of the Bay. He showed me old Indian roads and told me about bass watching the moon for guidance. Sam Sherman's wonderful website of old photos provided a wealth of visual reference. He told me lots of funny stories about the old days, and corrected much of my wayward embellishment and grammar. Tom Cronin's video interviews provided additional color, and Dan Joy's descriptions of his grandfather, the painter Vernon Smith, on whom the character of Nolan is based, were invaluable.

I was fortunate enough to have access to back issues of The Cape Codder in bound form (thank you again, Dan), as well as the extensivearchive of The Provincetown Advocate, available from the Provincetown Library's website. The Orleans Library provided me with invaluable research material.

I am indebted to my wonderful family and friends, who patiently waded through earlier versions and offered suggestions, comments, and other feedback. And I thank my husband Bob for his eagle-eye editing and unwavering encouragement.

K N